HE STOLE THE LADY

JUDITH LYNNE

BOOKS BY JUDITH LYNNE

<u>Lords and Undefeated Ladies</u>

Not Like a Lady

The Countess Invention

What a Duchess Does

Crown of Hearts

He Stole the Lady

No Titled Lady

<u>Maids Done Waiting</u>

The Lord Trap

The Lady Escape (Forthcoming)

<u>Cloaks and Countesses</u>

The Caped Countess

The Clandestine Countess

The Castaway Countess (Forthcoming)

<u>Ladies' Own Bakery</u>

The Regency romance comedy serial

DISCLAIMER AND GENTLE WARNING

This is a work of fiction and as such its characters, events, words, and places are the product of the author's imagination.

This contains references to abusive medical practices and parents. There is character death and animal death. It is set on a farm that includes animals raised for food.

PREFACE

My dear readers,

Don't we always feel sorry for the gentle child who falls from nobility into the ashes of the fireplace? Especially when they so love their home that they cannot leave?

Even when they're a huge hulking man?

Geoffrey Eliot was a good friend to Miss Cullen in *The Countess Invention*. He deserves better. Can such a wise, gentle young man make his own luck?

You shall see.
Your obedient servant,
Judith Lynne

CHAPTER 1

*L*ord Geoffrey Augustus Townsend Eliot had come straight to the receiving hall from tending the sheep.

He carefully did not touch the drapes as he peered down the drive. The approaching carriage swayed on its springs, sun glinting off its gilt edges.

"My brother got a woman to marry him?"

It had been thirteen years and three hundred and sixty-two days since his mother last touched his hand and said *Look after them, Geoffrey. Your father, too.*

Others might measure Faircombe Hall by its soaring parapets and vast rolling grounds, but Geoffrey measured his home by the people in it, however difficult they may be.

Geoffrey had a foolish brother and a missing one, a sister who couldn't keep still, and his father, who had stood tearless at the news that his mother was dead.

And his mother's yellow drapes.

By his reckoning, he was succeeding.

His father, the Marquess, took another window. "Damn. The rest will be right behind her. Geoffrey, get out. Why must you look like the arse end of a wagon rut?" Then to the arriving butler, "Send for Lord Vere."

"The rest of what will be right behind her? And I've been tending your sheep. Your valuable sheep."

"Bollocks to the sheep."

"They could make you more than your horses ever did."

"Thank God after today I never need have this argument with you again," said the Marquess of Faircombe, shifting his bulk.

As large as he was, Geoffrey could still feel chills, and his father's words sent one down his spine. "I've tripled your flocks. I've explained time and again how the sheep have young so much faster than cattle, plus they give milk and wool."

"I'm not thanking you for it."

"I don't want thanks. I'm trying to *help*." For the millionth time, Geoffrey wondered if his father had really hated his mother. There seemed no other reason to ridicule the son that most reminded him of her.

For the millionth time, he didn't ask.

"I've let you do what you liked. And what do I have to show for it? Sheep in the gardens, sheep in the hunting grounds. Look at what I've spent building paddock fences, and for what?"

"To triple your sheep." Geoffrey well knew the Marquess' hunting style: to quietly surround an animal, then kill when it could not escape. Geoffrey wasn't sure what was happening here, but it felt eerily familiar.

"As I said, the argument's over. My plans are made. *Set*." His father glanced out through the damask drapes again with something like a smile. "Go on. I don't care *where* you go, as long as it's out of the house."

Vere slid in, *Lord* Vere, the heir to Faircombe, on shoe leather as shiny and smooth as his brushed-down hair. The caramel-colored hair so like their father's, and unlike Geoffrey's own white-blond shock. "She's here."

So Vere knew. And looked grimly pleased when the Marquess answered with, "Geoffrey's just leaving."

How this bride arriving and Geoffrey leaving were related, Geoffrey didn't know. But it all sounded final. Final, cold, and hard, like everything to do with his father.

Geoffrey looked over at Vere—and down. "You both know I'll go to the grave before I'll leave this house. Vere, have you even met this woman? I don't aim to offend, but I've known you all my life, and I've never seen any qualities in you that might attract a woman."

Vere tossed Geoffrey the glare he'd been using since his school days. "I have personal qualities."

No, Geoffrey thought to himself, *you don't.* "Playing cards and whoring seldom attracts a wife."

Lord Faircombe cut them off. "She's American. Haven't yet met. Geoffrey, this has nothing to do with you. Get out. I don't want her to see you here."

"She can hardly avoid it." Geoffrey didn't need to spread his arms to draw attention to his size. "So, Vere, you haven't met her. What if you don't like her?"

"One woman is pretty much like another," sniffed Vere, confirming Geoffrey's opinion about his lack of personal qualities.

"Shouldn't Charlotte be here to welcome her, as the lady of the house?" Geoffrey looked again out the soaring tall window; a gust of wind shivered its panes. "There are three carriages with her."

"Three! Girl travels like a duchess. Geoffrey... enough." Lord Faircombe didn't meet Geoffrey's eyes again. "Stop worrying about Charlotte, or this house, or the sheep. It's all to be Vere's and has nothing to do with you."

He was utterly serious.

Just like that, he'd shut Geoffrey out of Faircombe's future, and what remained of their family.

The endless roaring *why* that had swallowed Geoffrey's soul the day his mother died threatened to engulf him.

Geoffrey just tamped it down and folded his arms across his chest. He was the largest man at Faircombe, likely the largest in the county. If he did not wish to be moved, he wouldn't be moved.

"I WANT to see every inch of it." The raw, cold air from the open carriage window made Zelda ache, but she loved it. It was *new,* and that was *fun.*

Her mother, who wasn't fun, began gathering the little things scattered about the carriage during the journey: a silver box of caramels, a covered glass of posset, Zelda's silk and cashmere muff. Had the lap rugs fit, she'd have put them in the basket too. "You'd be more comfortable if you stayed inside."

Zelda didn't care if the smooth grass landscape was interrupted only by sheep and struggling flower buds. It was utterly unlike New York City, or the Hudson valley for that matter. And all Zelda wanted was something new.

Endless troops of ghoulish doctors had prescribed sulfur baths, bloodletting, and rest, rest, rest, rest, rest. Zelda had missed every dance.

But staying still hadn't helped. Zelda still ached all over, all the time, closed up for years in Bowling Green, staring across the circle at mansions that looked just the same. Zelda was dying for something *new.*

"You must let me at least try to do as other young ladies do. It won't take much. Just a touch of marriage and my future is secured."

Not the future you think. But that she didn't say.

"Why must you put things in the starkest terms, Griselda? Marriage is a bond with a great many subtleties to it. You make it sound like buying fish."

Zelda let herself smile. Years of plotting had finally got her out of New York. Now Faircombe Hall lay spread out before her, a castle she could eat like a cake.

Zelda gains title and dowry, prepares to see world. "Well, we're about to meet my fish."

"Don't refer to a British lord as a fish, Griselda. Do be restrained."

Zelda gripped her cane. "Of course, Mother."

But she was lying. To herself she thought, *I will never be restrained again.*

* * *

THE STAIRS WERE WORK. They took her attention. She hated pushing herself up each one. The motion felt both harsh and weak.

But she could see the Marquess waiting to greet her at the top, and she was determined to get there, one step at a time.

I must be pink, she thought at the top. She almost closed her eyes in relief. But she wanted to judge the gentleman's reaction. He'd just seen her obviously work hard to climb the stairs, and just as obviously saw that she wore a velvet pelisse and, instead of paste traveling jewelry, amethysts.

Zelda braced herself with her cane.

His eyes didn't meet hers, but caught on the huge Brazilian diamond on her hand.

So. He was that sort of man.

"Mrs. Lloyd Rawle, I presume. And Miss Rawle." He bowed a few inches. "I am the Marquess of Faircombe and delighted to welcome you."

She put as much feeling into her curtsey as he had put into his bow and promptly ignored him. She wanted to see inside.

She approached the door looking for a cave of wonders.

It was a house.

Her excitement collapsed.

There were the same Aubusson rugs they had at home. The same paintings of unlikely fat angels, the same carved walnut tables and crystal decanters.

Was it too early for a swallow of whiskey?

The disappointment threatened to flatten her like a sand castle. Fatigue flooded her. An ocean crossed, and nothing new at all.

Except—she stopped looking at the room and saw what was in it.

This room held a golden giant.

His arms were folded across his massive chest, straining the seams of rough linen and wool, and he stared right at her.

She had never seen a servant stare. *That* was new.

As imposing as the house, he looked far more original. He made everything else in the predictably opulent room look small and silly. He looked like a mountaintop piercing the clouds.

Touching gilt frames and porcelain vases as she went, Zelda circled slowly past all the furniture, pretending she wasn't watching the only interesting thing in the room.

Till she stopped just before him, and looked up.

His eyes were bluer than the cold gray sky outside, and frankly appraising.

He saw her cane, she knew he did, and her clothes. But his regard was different. Zelda felt he could see not just her stiff joints, but also how her body was shaped under her clothes, and perhaps even the secret wonderings she barely admitted to herself.

"Are you a little out of place?" Zelda murmured to the tower of a man.

He nodded, arms still folded across his chest, like a prince who never looked down. "I tend sheep."

Zelda didn't wish to stare as openly as he did, so she forced her eyes to slide away. There seemed so *many* ways he was out of place, she couldn't suppress all of her smile. "*Do you? Those sheep must not stand a chance.*" And she laughed.

* * *

Miss Rawle's laugh called to mind the kind of satisfaction that parsons frowned upon.

In London, Geoffrey had learned the laughs of young ladies who wanted to reassure men they were funny. Miss Rawle laughed for herself.

His first impression as she'd come in, framed in gold from the late light, was of her lush curve of hips and dark tilted head.

Now he could see her eyes, large and full of secrets, and they confirmed his impression. She was a Venus in velvet.

Those eyes had a sly gleam as they slid away while still looking at him. It was a trick that on another woman would have said *follow me*; but like her laugh, it seemed only something for herself.

This woman was an unlikely wife for the grand house at Faircombe. She wore bright jewels at mid-day and laughed when she liked. Was she loose-skirted as well? Was that why she wasn't already married?

Geoffrey had done his turn in London ballrooms, taking his sister on the social rounds, and he saw British aristocrats very clearly. One thing he saw was that they were all light in the pockets. Twenty years of war had left them looking for money.

His father had found it in this form. But would it really suit Vere to marry her?

Geoffrey watched warily as the woman approached his brother.

Perhaps his father had put him on edge. Marriage could be good for Vere, Geoffrey thought, watching his father move to Vere's side. When their mother had asked Geoffrey to take care of the family, she must have thought there would be children at Faircombe by now.

Vere, the daft rock, was waiting for his father to make the formal introductions. His father made them. "Miss Griselda Rawle, Mrs. Lloyd Rawle, may I present my son, the Earl of Vere and Baron Culwer."

As if Vere were his *only* son.

The young lady's low, husky voice managed to carry. "So many people in one!"

Perhaps the danger of her was that she saw things quite clearly, too. Vere was indeed everything to his father; Vere, and Charlotte, the horse-loving daughter who reminded him of himself.

The humiliation, the *loneliness*, threatened to burn Geoffrey down where he stood.

"Miss Rawle," said Vere, "I am so very delighted to meet you." He smiled the smile Geoffrey knew for a fact he practiced in front of a mirror, and touched her fingers to his lips in response to her slight curtsey.

So busy looking important that he'd barely looked at Miss Rawle. Still an idiot, even when faced with a Venus.

A Venus with luggage. Footmen kept coming, trunk after trunk stacked inside the door, and what appeared to be cases of wine.

"Bring Miss Rawle some warmed coverlets," Mrs. Rawle asked the butler as he stood, still holding the door while footmen trooped in and out and the temperature in the room dropped considerably. "And a glass of that whiskey, please."

Venus? No, Dionysus, apparently. Perhaps she'd be too busy drinking to discover Vere was an ass.

In fact, now that her smile had faded, Geoffrey could see the circles under her eyes. Glittering stones couldn't stop that fading. Geoffrey wondered if he'd have to carry her off to bed.

Like he'd do for a sheep. He hid his sigh.

"I am afraid I must retire," she said in that low voice that carried.

It was so in line with his own thoughts that Geoffrey almost missed his brother's answer. "Of course," Vere told her, "this house has been here for hundreds of years, and will await your pleasure even if you sleep hundreds more."

That produced an awkward silence.

"It won't be a hundred years. But I must sleep." Miss Rawle sank into the cushions piled on the sofa at her side. They'd been embroidered by Geoffrey's great-great-grandmother.

Geoffrey wondered if anyone else in the house remembered that.

Vere didn't notice how fast she was fading. "The finest apartment in the house awaits your pleasure, Miss Rawle. It overlooks the garden created for Queen Elizabeth's visit in 1594. Cheery enough for a young lady. And her mother," he belatedly remembered Mrs. Rawle.

Miss Rawle's brow knit. "My letter didn't reach you?"

Their father just shrugged. "Yes. You mean the first floor request? So it is."

"But it sounds as though it is up stairs?" Miss Rawle was clearly accustomed to her requests being met, and sounded puzzled that this one wasn't.

No more than Lord Faircombe was accustomed to being questioned. "Yes, quite."

"Miss Rawle requires rooms on the first floor, Lord Faircombe," her mother put in.

"Yes, as I said. Just above, and to the southwest." Lord Faircombe wasn't used to looking confused and gave it up after a second.

Miss Rawle and her mother were looking at each other and the older woman shrugged. "I cannot say it more simply. The first floor."

"Yes, it *is* the first floor." Lord Faircombe was getting a bit red in the face, and Vere's puffed chest had deflated.

This could go on all day, and Miss Rawle clearly wouldn't last that long.

Geoffrey cleared his throat.

The Rawles, and Vere, looked his way.

"It is clear the guests consider the first floor to be this one. If an American sheep wandered in, it would be on the first floor; if it went up the stairs, it would be the second, from their perspective. Is that right, Miss Rawle?"

As if silence could erase Geoffrey's existence, Vere didn't answer, but moved to block Miss Rawle from Geoffrey's view. It didn't work. He could see her.

"Yes, just so." Those slyly smiling eyes turned to him again, clearly laughing at the idea of sheep running up and down the stairs. "We wish to *avoid* stairs, in the manner of American animals. Following in their footsteps, I suppose. Or are they hoof steps? Do sheep have hooves?"

"Hooves like two thick toes," Geoffrey told her gravely.

"Ah." And it was the way she said *ah* that first convinced Geoffrey he had a problem.

That *ah* hit him below the belt. It wasn't just the sound, a half-sigh of amusement. It was everything about it. The way her chin went up and then dropped, the way those spectacular eyes widened a little and looked straight at him, the way her lips turned up at the corners with pure pleasure.

His blood was hot from one little *ah*.

He had a sister, cherished memories of his mother, and open eyes. He didn't blame women for men's lusts; he *was* a man, and a breeder of animals.

But he couldn't imagine that any man wouldn't react to that *ah*, and it only made him worry more for Vere, who didn't have sense enough to worry for himself.

"The sheep are waiting for you." Vere's disgusted glare ruined his shiny effect.

"My apologies, Lord Vere," said Geoffrey, forcing himself to bow the tiniest bit before he turned and left.

Pride made him pull the door closed behind him. Curiosity made him stop.

His hearing was good, and faintly he heard Miss Rawle say, "My mother will attend to the rooms. I'm afraid I must sleep."

"Of course, once a room is selected we will prepare—"

The colonial woman *interrupted* Vere. "I apologize; I must sleep *now*."

"Of course," Vere answered, as he did when he wanted to appear to have understood and didn't.

Geoffrey heard some rustling.

After a few moments, Mrs. Rawle said, "You may show me the apartments, Lord Vere."

Well. Geoffrey had heard Americans didn't defer to titles, and these didn't.

"But what of Miss Rawle?" Vere sounded genuinely confused.

"She will sleep."

* * *

THEY'D GONE the other way. Geoffrey cracked his door.

Miss Rawle, her embroidered velvet cascading over her curves, lay on the couch with a rug round her feet. Her head lay on those embroidered cushions. She was fast asleep.

Well, here she was, in his home. While *he'd* been told to get out.

With her magnetic eyes finally closed, he could see the delicate shape of her face and the point of her chin. Her hair was darker than any Eliot's, stark in her suddenly ashen face, and in sleep her lips flushed pink.

Her smile had faded away.

What kind of young lady joked with heirs and shepherds, dismissed a marquess and then just… fell asleep?

What kind of young lady said *ah* in just that way?

This woman was utterly wrong for Vere. Vere did nothing for himself, but when he tried, he emulated their father's blunt ways of bending people to his will. Geoffrey had an uncomfortable feeling that for all her slow movements, this woman wasn't likely to bend.

Something about her troubled face recalled Geoffrey's mother. The mother he'd showered in flowers as a child. Watching Miss Rawle sleep revived some long-buried impulse.

Near his elbow, early honeysuckle stems that had fought the cold and insisted on flowering were arranged in a blue-bellied porcelain vase.

Before he could think, Geoffrey pulled a branch from the vase, dabbed it dry on his vest, and laid it in the curve of her body.

Yes, that flower suited her, delicate in appearance but decadent in scent. And perhaps he imagined it, but he thought he saw her ease a little.

His head jerked up at the sound of rolling carriages.

Several more carriages, approaching along Faircombe's long drive.

The door was nearly blocked by Miss Rawle's luggage, which the footmen hadn't had the sense to unload elsewhere; and the room had grown cold from the open door. More visitors shouldn't come through here.

Besides, if they did, they would wake her.

When sad-faced Mr. Croft opened the door to greet the new carriages, Geoffrey just shook his head. "I'll send them round to the courtyard," he whispered, a finger to his lips to keep the man quiet. Slowly, the butler backed away. "Remember, Miss Rawle wants some warmed coverlets, as fast and quiet as you can. And a glass of whiskey, too."

Then he closed the door after the man, as silently as he could.

Even brazen temptresses come to trap his silly brother deserved sleep when they were ill.

* * *

"MY APOLOGIES FOR THE MISTAKE, SIR," Geoffrey called to the driver once he'd reached the bottom of the ridiculous front staircase, "but the side courtyard is best for receiving guests."

"Who the devil are you?" The driver gave Geoffrey and his workman's clothes a skeptical look.

Unable to claim himself as his father's son, Geoffrey felt hollow. When the driver looked about for someone important, the impossible happened: Geoffrey felt small.

The driver twisted in his seat till his coat buttons threatened to pop off. "Didn't see no road for a courtyard."

"Apologies. As I said, just go round in a circle and turn there. It's a large paved courtyard. You must have trunks to unload."

Geoffrey could see now that there were five, six carriages —no, seven. The second driver craned his head impatiently.

To the first driver he said, "Your passengers must not want this journey to last any longer than necessary. It's just round the bend."

Knowing Geoffrey was right, the fellow didn't argue further. Just raised his crop and urged the horses ahead one more time. The rest of the carriages behind him did indeed follow.

Geoffrey pulled snug his rough wool coat, suitable for the sheep pens. He'd walk around behind the carriages, ensure they didn't circle back this way.

And then he'd see his father.

* * *

ZELDA USUALLY DREAMED of majestic things waiting to be discovered: vast trees taller than bridges, an elephant she'd once seen, the white-capped waves of the ocean.

At Faircombe, she must have dreamed, but all she knew when she woke was that it had been something warm.

She *was* warm, surrounded by a mouthwatering scent of apricots drenched in honey.

Waiting for the pain to come as it always did, Zelda smiled and blinked her eyes open. The smell was real.

Her hand brushed something soft, almost crushed it.

A small branch of flowers lay in the crook of her body. She brought it to her nose. Yes, it was the source of the sweetness; its scent was heady and rich despite its delicate, slender petals. Lovely, but not majestic at all.

She let it drop to her chest. Fatigue had stolen important minutes, it always did; but it had brought her this mysterious little delight as well.

Lord Vere must have left it for her.

Gifts meant a great deal to Zelda. Her father had given her a little jeweled globe for her tenth birthday. "Take charge of it, Griselda," he'd said, off to do something else to make money.

In his absence, she had; even more when the pain began. He might have meant for her to take charge of the little silver toy, but Zelda intended to do far more.

As the first step in a much larger journey, Faircombe didn't impress her. Nothing else was as interesting as that shepherd, certainly not the ceiling. She stared at fat angels floating among clouds and floral garlands. *Famous art collection named Zelda after its benefactor?* Well, not here. These could stand some improvement.

Someone had covered her, too; she pushed off the heavy quilts. Someone had brought her beloved whiskey, too.

Well, she'd have a sip and explore more of her house.

She'd left New York at night on an Italian ship to cross a war-torn ocean; she wouldn't stop now. Even if she didn't intend to live here, this would be her house, her fat angels, *her* Aubusson rugs. Her *giant*.

A pallid parade of young men had offered to marry her, tin soldiers who watched her father for the answer and never thought to look at her. Money did that. They called her *frail* and meant *ignorable,* and they all wore smug satisfaction like hats.

The only words they understood were yes and no; Zelda always said no.

Lord Vere had some tin soldier features, too. But she'd had reasons to say *yes* before she'd ever met him, good reasons like a title, and money. Her plan to get both was in motion.

She was through being ignored, and she wouldn't be motionless—or silent—ever again.

The delicate flower, warm from her body, was easy to

tuck in her pocket. Its yellowy centers were surrounded by curving petal-ribbons; it never occurred to her it might cause a stain. Its surprisingly powerful scent followed her.

The very power of it made her uneasy. Lord Vere must have left it beside her, and she could not afford to develop a feeling toward Lord Vere.

If she were to crave a man, he'd be more like the golden giant. Tall, strong, and beautiful, like an alabaster column, if a column could move and make jokes about sheep. Just speaking to him in front of the Marquess had been something of a risk.

The tin soldiers of New York hadn't been that tempting. Zelda had dreams, and she was about to see them through.

But she'd just promised herself to be unrestrained. And ignoring that giant would take restraint.

CHAPTER 2

*A*nywhere else, Geoffrey would sit, careful not to oppress with his size.

In his father's study, he stayed standing.

The room was old, paneled with walnut and papered with ancient tobacco smoke. Everything in it, right down to the crystal liquor decanters, felt heavy and dangerous.

"Do you really expect me to ignore whatever cold-blooded deal you've arranged? And why *this* woman?" For Miss Rawle was no girl; she was definitely an adult. That sleepy smile in her eyes promised a selfish concern for plea-sure that… well, might be a match for Vere, but not in a good way. "Vere doesn't need your management; he needs to grow up."

And if she were willful, Vere would be in hell, caught between her and their father. For all Vere's card-playing and skirt-chasing, he was, in his own way, naive. He did what his friends did, or what his father told him to do.

Geoffrey had the feeling his brother would realize what he'd done just *after* the nick of time.

His father just rolled his red, rheumy eyes, wisps of

smoke disappearing around his face, and turned again to stare out the window. "You had the same high opinion of your own advice when you were four. I excused it in a child."

Geoffrey didn't recall him excusing anything.

The oak floorboards under his feet creaked; the sound was oddly reassuring. His father had never liked him, but Geoffrey was still an Eliot. The old bones of Faircombe Hall belonged to him in a way that went beyond a title.

They gave him the strength to speak of things his father ought to know. "Let Vere see what marriage entails. More time at Roseford Manor, perhaps. The Grantleys have a son, they're happy. Vere can see how it's done."

"How dare you mention Roseford?" The Marquess made a snorting sound of rage that reminded Geoffrey of a bad-tempered bull. "You've no idea. You should've seen the old baronet, that current chit's grandfather. What a nick-nobbled bastard *he* was."

How could he have come from a man so blind to his own faults? "You have a duty to care about Vere's whole life, not just the marriage. Vere's your *son*."

"Duty? *He* has a duty." The Marquess spread his arms wide. "Where is Vere's heir? Where is *his* son? I could die waiting for Vere to make a decision."

"Vere has an heir in Frederick." His middle brother hadn't been heard from in years. "And then in me." It would be too inflammatory for many reasons to insist that his father had enough sons. "Let Vere wait. My great-great-grandfather didn't have an heir of his blood until he was forty-eight."

"Yet your *great*-grandfather," the Marquess said with an odd mix of anger and desperation, "was dead before his twenty-third birthday. The title survives because he married when he was told, and had an heir. Vere is nearing thirty; high time he did his duty. That's what duty means. Duty to the *title*." Lord Faircombe pounded a fist on the arm of his chair.

"What of duty to *family*?" Geoffrey was no saint, and his father constantly tested his temper. "Your duty to your son, your *son*, not to lock him in a painful marriage for the rest of his life. You've already killed your wife that way. Must you do it to your son?"

"Don't... don't speak of your mother to me." The Marquess' face had turned red.

The howling wave of rage against inexplicable fate that haunted Geoffrey sometimes felt dark, almost visible; perhaps Geoffrey could see it, out of the corner of one eye. "I will speak of my mother wherever I choose. I don't wonder it shames you. I only wonder you dare try to stop me."

His father shoved aside his teacup and surged to his feet.

The teacup's clatter was the sort of sound the Marquess used to warn people against testing his ire. The cup was empty, so it no longer pleased him, and whatever didn't please Lord Faircombe was in fair danger of being shattered.

Geoffrey remembered how it used to frighten him as a boy—broken teacups, smashed crystal, guns thundering in everybody's ears. The Marquess liked his size and noise to keep people at bay.

Geoffrey had been small and timid, and preferred the quiet comfort of his mother's lap.

When she had died, Geoffrey had been frightened again. Then the house was quiet, but the quiet was terrifying.

But as time went on and his father returned to crashing and thundering, even though Geoffrey felt alone, something magical happened.

He grew.

There were broken bottles and the occasional cracked plaster wall, but for many years Geoffrey had faced his father with the calm that came from being a much bigger man.

That, and the unshakeable memory that his mother had loved him.

Memories his father tried to use as weapons. "Your mother babied you and you think like a woman. You think the world is soft and shapeless, like a field full of sheep. It isn't." The Marquess squared his shoulders. "The world is a forest full of hunters, and men must become wolves, not sheep. Vere must come out of your shadow. He's got to develop a fist."

"Marriage and fists. These go together in what passes for your mind?"

His father's small eyes narrowed further. "I never hurt your mother."

Geoffrey felt the tide of rage splashing upward and leaned closer. "Lie to me again."

The Marquess didn't step away, but his shoulders strained back, as if moving out of range. His father liked to hint at threats, but he ducked when they came back to roost.

"You're a useless puppy. Even now. Talking, talking, talking," his father sneered.

"You don't really want me to stop talking." Geoffrey's voice was quiet, but reached every corner of the room.

The Marquess scoffed, but didn't move closer. "Real men build things. *Make* things."

"Like my grandfather? Who earned the title of marquess for slaughtering Scots," Geoffrey added grimly.

"Which never would have bothered you if I hadn't let you spend all that time drinking your way across the northland, claiming to watch sheep."

"Learning to *raise* sheep. And tend their land."

"Bollocks. In any event, your grandfather also earned the coronet of Culwer. He built a *legacy*. Vere must guard that legacy. And you… are useless."

That hurt. His father knew it. Geoffrey knew not to show it.

Vere would be remembered by his titles and the history he handed down; Geoffrey wouldn't be remembered at all.

But it only made Geoffrey love the name of Faircombe more. It wasn't a title to him; it was family, and home.

His sister and brothers clearly didn't feel that. None of them had yet married, as if torn between the rotten example of their family and the terror of hope.

"Must Vere be a miserable bastard like you? Why not let him *try* to find happiness?"

A bark of laughter at that. "The one thing Vere isn't is a bastard. If happiness mattered to him, he'd have found it by now."

Geoffrey couldn't help recalling his mother, her white-blonde curls falling around her face. *Look after them, Geoffrey. Your father, too.* Not for the first time, he wished she hadn't said that. "He's your *son*. As am I. Why can't you be happy unless you're attempting to drive us in harness like horses?"

"Because this—" His waving hand seemed to indicate Geoffrey, the whole house, perhaps Britain, "this is all wrong. Vere should have been more like you. And you should have been a silent spare. Instead, Vere is always in your shadow, and that's got to stop. This marriage will put him in his grandfather's boots. He can finish the building plans. Finish Faircombe Hall."

"From this marriage." Geoffrey settled back. "So Miss Rawle must have quite a dowry."

His father's snort told him all he needed to know. "That doesn't concern you. Vere's chased enough birds of paradise, and you aren't needed." The Marquess waved a hand toward his pearl-inlaid *escritoire*. "There's two hundred guineas in that desk. Take it. Go to London. Go back to Scotland and cuddle sheep. Go *anywhere*. Just don't hover here, watching everyone like a sick owl. You make me bilious."

"If I am so superfluous, my lord, why did you *keep having sons?*"

The Marquess' eyes looked sunken in the flesh of his head, thought Geoffrey as he looked up, red-rimmed gaze thick and piggy. "I've done my duty to Faircombe, and Vere will do the same. It's time you left. Go to London. Take the money and go."

"This was my mother's house, too. Vere is my brother, as Charlotte is my sister. That matters to *me*."

The Marquess' waving hand flicked the comment away. Clearly the idea of caring for his fully grown family was absurd. "They're neither children nor sheep. I'll tell the steward to keep you out of the house."

Geoffrey'd be damned if he'd be threatened. "No man can keep me out of this house."

His father was turning red. "No?"

"No!" Geoffrey slowly unclenched his fist, then his jaw. But his voice was hard as bone. "What army do you have that could put me out of this house if I choose to stay?"

"That's the King's problem. I could disown you and let the magistrate deal with throwing you out. Without the two hundred guineas."

There it was. The last threat his father could make good.

The knowledge, the feeling that his father really would cut him out of the family, hit Geoffrey right between the eyes. He would have nowhere to live. It would hurt Charlotte. Vere might even notice. "I won't take your money," was all he could say.

"Says every well-born man who's never lived without it. As much as you love your damned sheep, you don't hate being Lord Geoffrey. Cross me on this and I cut you off for the rest of your life without one penny of mine."

Look after them, Geoffrey. Perhaps his mother had known that Geoffrey would have to choose, as he got older, between all-out war and trying to keep the peace, in order to keep his promise.

Geoffrey choked a little, but got out the words she'd want him to say. "For the sake of peace, I'll go as far as the sheep sheds, no farther."

"Fine." His father nodded toward Geoffrey's rough clothing. "You're dressed for your new life. Don't expect to dine with us. As far as I'm concerned, I have no other son."

"As anyone would expect you to say." Geoffrey turned and strode out.

* * *

WITHOUT A VALET, Geoffrey packed for himself; he'd done it for Scotland years ago, and to take Charlotte to London right before Christmas.

That didn't mean he was good at it.

It was quick to toss his few personal possessions on the bed: some family jewelry, items for shaving, a book he was reading. He added his mother's silver tobacco box; she'd never used it. Neither had he.

About to pile clothing on top, he looked at his riding boots, and stopped.

The boots he wore were sheep-chewed and dirty. Those boots on the floor were shiny, polished, and clean. The life he was about to claim matched one set of boots, but not the other.

He had friends in London: among others, a new countess and her husband. But he couldn't live on friendship. And he wouldn't leave his family.

Unable to stare at the room a moment longer, Geoffrey

swept up the coverlet by its corners, tossed it over one shoulder and stomped out.

As he descended the last stair, a swinging skirt just disappeared out of sight.

Had he seen a glimmer of velvet?

When he rounded the bottom of the stairs, yes, there was Miss Rawle, dark eyes wide, hand on a door-knob, caught in the act of escaping.

He felt raw, and she had startled him; he barked, "Why are you here?"

Her sly little smile spread wide with delight and she closed the door she'd been about to go through. "Are you *stealing* things?"

* * *

THE GIANT—*HER* giant—stood over her with a bright India-cotton bundle over one shoulder and an expression of massive affront. He looked far more interesting than any room Zelda had yet seen, and she'd poked her head into several.

"No," he finally said to her accusation of theft, despite evidence to the contrary. "My apologies, Miss Rawle, I meant to ask..." He couldn't seem to think of another way to put it. "What are you doing *here*? In the stairway?"

"Exploring," she simply said.

"Didn't a footman see you to your chambers?"

She stacked her hands on her cane to show the intimidating diamond. "Obviously not. Should they have done?" She glanced again at the cotton bundle on his back. "So I wouldn't see you stealing things?"

His shoulders sank. "Miss Rawle, I've never stolen anything."

Zelda didn't mind his side-stepping answers; she

preferred questions. "A shame. Theft does seem exciting." She contemplated whether she ought to take up stealing things. What might not be noticed? For later thought. "What *are* you doing, then?"

* * *

"LEAVING THE HOUSE." The weight on his shoulders wasn't from the bundle. The world simply felt heavy.

"Why?"

It would be humiliating to admit he was being put out, and humiliating to admit he was bending to a threat of disinheritance. He opened his mouth to say something meaningless, and instead said, "I don't want a war."

"Well!" This seemed to delight her almost as much as theft. "No sensible person would want to fight you, so that seems considerate."

He hadn't meant to say that, so he changed the topic.

Look after them, Geoffrey. If this were London, if Miss Rawle were some rich gentleman asking for Charlotte's hand, Geoffrey would have many sharp questions. Vere needed safeguarding even more; he was far less sensible.

"You're to marry Lord Vere?"

Those big, slow eyes blinked. "Yes."

"Why?"

"Why is a golden giant carrying away a sack of stolen candlesticks?" She tilted her head a little, smiled that sly smile. "See? As I said. Questions are so much more interesting than answers."

"You never said that."

"No? I thought it to myself. That's nearly the same thing."

"That is the entirely *opposite thing*, Miss Rawle."

If he wanted answers, he ought to interview this woman seriously, somewhere larger, and less… close.

Was that the smell of the honeysuckle clinging to her dress?

Or her skin?

"I'm afraid," he said, a little hoarsely, "that I must return to tending the sheep. Perhaps you'd like Lord Vere to show you the rest of the house?"

She tilted her head. "Do you think he'll be any good at it?"

He considered Vere, who had lived in this house his entire life. "No," he told her honestly, "I don't think he will."

"Why should *he* show me the house, then? Let's go together." She glanced toward the bundle on his back. "You should find lots more things to steal."

He was losing control of this conversation, as he was losing control of this house.

A footman opened the door behind him. "I have a message for you, L—"

Geoffrey whirled and cut off what would *not* be a felicitous introduction. "In a moment."

He expected the footman to show some surprise that Lord Geoffrey was closeted alone with Lord Vere's intended wife, but the footman said nothing, only bowed and withdrew.

When Geoffrey turned back, he saw why. Miss Rawle wasn't there.

* * *

Slipping away from the giant was less entertaining than going closer, but Zelda needed to practice doing as she pleased.

Practice involved opening doors, and each one revealed a new room, a different stage for a whole new set of adventures. One place dark and shuttered for secrets; another airy and bright, to take the sun even in winter. She hoped the house offered more company than Lord Vere and Lord Faircombe.

She wasn't given to fairy stories, but since she'd glimpsed a giant, she was ready for anything. And fairies would be nice.

The question of what she could steal rendered each newly revealed place more exciting. As something to do, it had never even occurred to her!

She wondered how an adventure novel would summarize that in the headline that ran along the top of the page. *Vice of the fallen heiress*, she thought. That sounded excellent.

Every room had something small enough to take. Chess pieces, in a gaming room that held a forest of little marble-topped tables. A tiny silver guillotine in a room haunted by cigar smoke. A cup carved from some glowing white jewel, standing alone on a deep, dark mantelpiece. All intriguing, but nothing she cared to have.

It was amusing to imagine her giant carrying things away; why, surely he could carry anything she saw. A carved oak footstool; an ethereal portrait of a young boy in blue; a *battle-axe* mounted on the wall—

Simultaneously attracted and repelled by the battle-axe—she hoped the stains weren't blood, but knew they were—she hurried through the next door.

And found herself in the room of her dreams.

No fairy story, no *horreur Gothique* could fascinate Zelda the way this room did. Medieval armor, full suits, were scattered against the walls; but they were mere decorations for the room's true jewels.

Maps.

Large maps and small ones, framed, drawn and painted, all mounted where a person could look at them closely. Well, a person slightly taller than Zelda.

Plus maps in vast open books on a room-filling table.

The shapes of continents she recognized instantly; but there were also shaded maps she couldn't decipher, in colors of earth and forests. Explorer's maps with rivers delicately traced in red and blue.

Zelda moved from map to map, sometimes laying her fingers on the suits of armor as well. She wondered why someone had paired the maps with armor; she found them antithetical. One was to close oneself in, protect oneself from possible attacks; the other was for setting oneself free.

She stopped in front of a collection of maps she'd never seen before, perhaps by the same cartographer. They traced archipelago after archipelago in the ocean past Asia, little spots of land dancing around to the other side of the world. New Holland just peeked up over the bottom edge of the map, insisting on showing itself.

And on a sideboard against the wall below them lay a compass. Its brass housing shone, as if someone had held it and contemplated it for many long hours. The compass rose inside trembled and glittered when she picked it up, and swiveled slightly, determined to point north.

It just fit in her palm, a little big for her pocket, but perhaps a perfect size to steal.

It was an obvious choice, too obvious, perhaps. But it was more than a tool for way-finding. It was sensuous; *loved*. Someone's fingers had worn away the patina on the brass. Someone's hands had cradled it through long journeys—days, or months. It had been someone's much-wanted companion.

Zelda had long ago given up being any such thing, but today, she wanted to understand it better.

Stealing was *exciting*, Zelda thought to herself as she just fit the thing in her pocket. It made her gown droop on one side, and, heart thumping fast, Zelda felt it must be notice-able. Perhaps she *should* find her rooms. Her betrothed would be at dinner, and she ought to dress… and find a hiding place for her new treasure.

Recalling how brazenly her giant had carried off a bundle over his shoulder, Zelda admired his boldness again.

* * *

BACK UNDER THE STAIRS, Zelda paused. No giants. It was far less interesting, being under the stairs without a giant.

If exploring the rooms alone had seemed a bit dull, that was simply Zelda failing to appreciate what she wanted once she got it. That map room hadn't been dull.

In the adventure books, the heroine traversed momentous obstacles alone. Not entirely alone, of course, as she had to have someone to witness her struggles and write the book.

Zelda had her mother, which made her wince; and she had Tansy, her maid. That was plenty.

She stood at the foot of the stairs, contemplating the climb. Each wooden riser was cleverly fit and beautifully carved into a corkscrew arrangement leading up and up.

Her body said *Not today*. So *perhaps later*, she decided, because her new plan of being unrestrained might well bear that kind of fruit.

When her eyes dropped, they caught on something blue.

She bent a little lower; down in the floorboards, it flashed again. It wasn't hard to find; it hadn't really fallen down into the cracks, just rested in a shadowed spot.

It was a man's ring, massive. She couldn't imagine a hand so large it would fit that ring. Perhaps her giant's, had he not been a shepherd; but surely even his hand wasn't that large?

It was not metal set with a stone, but rather one whole slab of transparent blue. One massive sapphire, she realized, with a woman's face carved in it. Its innermost circle was lined with gold. The woman's curls rested calmly on her shoulders, Zelda thought; on both sides of her, light scattered through the stone sides like rays of sunshine.

Why hadn't her giant tried to steal this?

Or had he?

* * *

THE IDEA of that woman alone in the house with Vere unnerved Geoffrey, but there was no genuine risk. She had her mother as a chaperone, and Vere might be foolish, but he wasn't stupid. He wouldn't anticipate the marriage bed, no matter how alluring his bride might be.

And if she stole things, she couldn't take them far.

He almost wished the house would tell him good-bye, but that was more fanciful than he had been in a long, long time.

At least there was one person here who would actually say it.

"Don't let the place burn down without me," he said as he entered the north drawing room. "I… will reside with the sheep."

Dainty Delina Farsworth, his sister's companion, was adding a mirror to an odd heap of objects on a table, preparing to draw the entire affair. "Are the sheep sick enough for that? What's happened?"

The last of his pride drove Geoffrey's chin upwards. "Did you know Vere is to be married?"

Delina paused, the mirror in her hands flashing light all around the room. "Is he? I suppose since Charlotte decided not to marry, your father has finally decided to pay attention to his heir." Then in the next second, "Does *Vere* know he's to be married?"

"He seems to have noticed."

"Well." The light flashed again as she put the mirror down. "These are the things that the nobility must do."

"The fault is in me. I can't think of Vere as a nobleman."

"Yet he is one, and we merely peasants." She shrugged a delicate shoulder. "Or rather, I am. You certainly are not, despite those clothes."

He was *not*. Yet with a few words, his father had tossed him out of his place in life as well as the house. "The new Lady Vere is here, and my father gave me the cut direct. In my own house. The lady thinks I'm a servant."

Delina's smile was wry. "And you looking so dashing. This costume is for a sheep?"

Geoffrey's shoulders drooped. Every conversation today was lowering. "I'm keeping a close watch on Guinevere."

"Guinevere must be the sheep." Delina and his sister were alike in their obsessions, Charlotte with horses rather than art. But Del was good enough to feign interest in sheep, though she did not remember their names.

"I'm afraid it's three lambs at once." There, he'd let his concern for Guinevere lead him down an inappropriate conversational road; no gentleman would discuss pregnant sheep in front of a lady. Even one he considered family, as he did Delina. "I know you'll watch over Charlotte, Del, you always do, but do… take care, I suppose I mean to say."

"Geoffrey. Look to *yourself*."

He smiled and raised his free arm. It was as big around as a small tree. "What could happen to me?"

"Many things," she said, her eyes sober. "Size doesn't keep you safe."

"Of course it does." Risks that stopped smaller men didn't faze him.

But her look told him she knew how he had been hurt. Could still be hurt.

"Perhaps it's time for a change, Geoffrey? Change always comes."

"Families don't change." *Look after them, Geoffrey.* His

brother would always be his brother, and his father, unfortunately, still his father. And Charlotte his sister, and therefore Delina part of the family; because Geoffrey knew they loved each other far too much to admit.

This was his family, ragged as it was. And if it fell apart, he hadn't done the job his mother asked him to do.

Delina seemed to read his every thought on his face. She glanced down at what she'd grouped together for drawing. A tangle of lace; honeysuckle in a vase; an early turkey feather. And lying face-down, the mirror.

"You haven't heard from Frederick in ages," she said, moving the turkey feather out of the vase's shadow. "Charlotte refuses to marry, but she needn't stay here." The pile of lace. "And now here you are, banished to the sheep sheds." She picked up and cradled the mirror. Her grouping now was just objects with no connection. "Not much of a family."

"What do you mean, Charlotte needn't stay here? Doesn't she *want* to stay here?" The idea shook him. He'd imagined Charlotte, and Delina of course, would always be here at Faircombe with him.

"She's reached an understanding with your father. He will no longer try to force her to marry; but they aren't exactly *comfortable* with one another."

"So I've failed." She was right. "Not much of a family. But as long as the shreds remain, I will fight to hold them together."

Even though it was one task where his enormous strength couldn't help.

A touch of pity crept into her voice. A delicate little person, pitying him. "Take the *real* risk, Geoffrey. What of a life of your own? What of *your* marriage?"

A marriage for *him*? "With lodging in the sheep sheds?"

He pictured someone like Miss Rawle—no, he pictured Miss Rawle herself, expecting to marry *him*. Preparing for a life in plain wool and sheepskins instead of velvet and amethysts. She would be just as sensual, just as intriguing. But would she ever smile?

No woman would.

"I have nothing to offer a woman. Especially now."

"That might depend on the woman. People get married for all sorts of reasons, Geoffrey. Why is this American woman marrying Vere?" She narrowed her eyes. "Is she horrid? Lord Faircombe might have kept the marriage secret because she's horrid."

"I don't know yet." Honesty compelled him to add, "She doesn't *look* horrid."

"Looks?" She waved at the table. "Looks are simply a matter of arrangement. She's likely horrid. And Vere can be horrid, too, so what is it to you if they marry?" She held the mirror up toward him. "I asked about *you*. You could make yourself a much better family than the one you have, you know. If you only looked to yourself."

The rough, stained wool and linen caught in the mirror's reflection. "I know. I look laughable."

She shook her head. Slowly and loudly, she said, "That is not what I meant."

She spent too much time dealing with Charlotte, who didn't hear things the first two or three times they were said, even though there was nothing wrong with Charlotte's ears.

But she went on. "Stop worrying about Vere. Worry for yourself. Let your father run Faircombe into the ground as he likes. Or truly challenge him, since you love this place. Why not?"

Because that would mean war. That's not taking care of him. And I made a promise.

"Who would that help?" he answered without answering. He wanted to kiss her cheek, but thought it best to avoid brushing the table she was arranging so carefully. The table was heavy, but it was old, his great-great-grandfather's, and Geoffrey had learned not to brush things.

He bowed slightly.

Delina said softly, "I'll miss you at dinner."

He knew she meant it. It was a comforting dose of sisterly affection; Charlotte, he knew, might not notice.

Although thinking of family meals at Faircombe reminded him of something.

"THE FIRE IS LIT." Mrs. Rawle laid the heavy quilted robe over a chair. The arrangement of things was important to her; she put fur-lined slippers by the fire, and the heavy, corked bottle of wintergreen oil on the dressing table, atop Zelda's rock-crystal tray.

Zelda's mother didn't fuss; she corrected. Just as she corrected the clothes for their late dinner by putting the red silk to the side and drawing a pale pink linen from the trunk.

The pink had a skirt that was embroidered with red all round, but tonight, Zelda wished to wear the silk. And she didn't wish to sit by the fire.

Arguing with her mother was like arguing with a painting; the picture didn't change.

Zelda would prefer to ignore that she had brought the biggest impediment to a new life of unrestraint with her. It was her mother, clutching a basket of little soothing things with secret teeth that could eat Zelda's life.

Next to the wintergreen oil, her mother put Zelda's little jeweled globe. Its surface was made of the world's truc shapes, carved of different rare stones, set together with tiny rivers of silver. It never tarnished; like the brass compass, it was loved.

She plucked it from its little walnut-wood stand and

rolled it in her hands, an eye on the gowns, then on her mother.

"I thought Lord Faircombe had a daughter? I wonder why she didn't greet us. Is she away? At a party?" She'd just reached Faircombe, but the idea of a party in the neighborhood lit Zelda's face. "We should explore the villages near here!"

"You have plenty of society in your new husband."

Zelda shrugged. "We haven't yet met any neighbors."

"Griselda!" Her mother nearly wobbled in place, she clutched her hands so hard. "It's when the wall looks finished that it's most fragile. Be respectful of your betrothed, or who knows what will happen? The contracts aren't signed. I know you're not serious. Surely you're looking forward to the wedding?"

Zelda put the globe back. The wedding gown in her trunk was a heavy pearl-colored satin, beaded with vines and oak leaves to flatter her new British husband. The thought of it left Zelda cold. "I think I need more sleep."

Her maid Tansy, starched and prim, had taken up both the pink linen and the red silk. Tansy had a politic air and tried to do as Zelda wanted without provoking her mother. Zelda loved that about her.

Her glance consulted Zelda about the dresses, and Zelda firmly nodded at the red one.

Then went to the window.

The room where she'd finally been settled, which required no stairs at all, did not look out over Queen Elizabeth's garden. But it was airy and bright and reflected the garden on every side. Each wall bore paintings of fanciful trees and flowers, and the damask curtains were sunshine yellow, just like the velvet ones in the receiving hall.

Zelda pulled the curtains aside to look out.

Delicate little columns edged her new private portico,

echoing the grand ones in front. And erected on poles was a silken tent, encasing a deep garden bench where one might lie and enjoy looking at the maze garden beyond.

Whose rooms had these been?

The fiery ache in her fingers warned her she'd been holding the curtain too long; she let her hand fall.

"Shall I rub your hands?" Her mother always noticed.

The wintergreen oil helped, but only so much. She'd had years to measure how much pain she must simply learn to live with, and how much might fade if her mother would just let her move. Something told Zelda that she *needed* to move.

It was also not much fun standing still.

Her giant could likely walk across England. France. The erstwhile Holy Roman Empire. Perhaps all the way to Russia.

Well, no one could walk for her but her.

Unrestrained, Zelda. Be unrestrained, she thought. She needed to occupy her mother somehow. "They've carried off all the whiskey. Hadn't we better keep it in here?"

"What, all of it?" Her mother was an unhappy observer of Zelda's whiskey consumption, forced to admit it helped when nothing else could.

"Well." Zelda pretended to consider. "Perhaps a couple of bottles."

It worked. The idea that anything with a medicinal function was more than an arm's reach away moved her mother out the door in search of the whiskey's resting place.

With the door closed behind her mother, it was only a few heartbeats before Tansy raised an eyebrow.

"Well? Have you changed your mind now that you have seen your intended?"

"Not at all. He's..." She should say *good-looking*. Or *polished*. "Boring."

A Bostonian of African descent, Tansy had joined the Rawles' employ just for this voyage; Zelda's previous maid had not wished to sail. Tansy was pretty and fresh-faced as ladies' maids were supposed to be, but she also had an appealing look of solid determination.

On the ship they'd had only each other and Mrs. Rawle for company, for long stretches of time. In private moments, they'd shared some confidences. Tansy had some of the same dreams, and she would keep Zelda's confidences, as Zelda would keep hers.

Tansy also had a clear view of reality, which Zelda admired. "Boring will be easier to leave."

True. It wouldn't feel hard to marry Lord Vere and then walk away.

Zelda had said no to *all* her suitors' offers, including stolen kisses and grappling behind parlor doors. Those suitors had been unappealing in every way, from their limp lips to their grasping hands.

She'd decided she was immune to men's charms. Then she'd decided, more sensibly, that they didn't have any.

Now the vision of her giant's broad shoulders came back to her every time she closed her eyes, and she wondered at herself. She didn't really wish to cultivate *vices*, but hadn't anticipated that some might become more tempting with time.

She'd sensibly closed a door when she thought nothing appealing lay behind it; but now there were hints that entire continents lay behind that door, waiting for her to explore, and this marriage would lock it shut.

She'd never really considered that her plan meant never exploring feelings that now beckoned. She didn't intend to *cheat* on Lord Vere. Just leave him behind.

* * *

"Oh, but Lord Geoffrey, you won't eat behind the needlework *screen?*"

Geoffrey didn't want pitched war with his father; perhaps this was… maintaining friendly borders. "My grandmother dined behind it."

As long as the cook didn't run to the housekeeper, who ran things just as Lord Faircombe wanted them, Geoffrey could claim this small territory in his own house without a conflict.

His grandmother had taken every meal behind the screen after his grandfather had died. No one ever said why. He faintly remembered knowing she was there, knowing he mustn't ask why, and knowing he had to finish his peas.

His grandmother had departed this earthly plane almost two decades ago. The screen remained.

As he contemplated it now, a grown man standing behind the same screen, Geoffrey suspected she might have eaten there because she hadn't had all her teeth.

He still had his, but the screen could serve him as it had for her: to be near the family without being seen.

Mrs. Davies kept touching the screen, the little table his grandmother had used, the screen again. "They'll hear your plate and fork, you know!"

She was right. One more thing lost: his plate of hot beef. "Can you bring some bread and cheese? And perhaps you'll be good enough to save something for me after the table is cleared."

"You? Eating kitchen scraps? What's happened?"

Geoffrey wasn't in the mood to discuss his father further. "I'll have the bread and cheese now, Mrs. Davies."

"This isn't right, you know. It's just not right."

She disappeared, muttering. Geoffrey sat in the chair, felt it creak, and wondered how long he could keep his elbows tight to his body. But at least he could see sliver-shaped bits of the room, and he could hear.

Had his grandmother dined here to be alone without abandoning the family, too?

He couldn't judge. His memories of her were so faint. And he couldn't remember his grandfather, the previous Marquess, at all.

* * *

"WHAT'S IT ABOUT, sir, sending us round to the side?"

"Perhaps you are not ready for our arrival?"

"It's a peevish way to begin a business relationship. My lord."

The handful of men seemed to fill the dining room with questions and complaints, a flock of annoyed crows in black coats attending Lord Faircombe.

At the sight of Zelda, voices all stopped. Apparently, they could not look and talk at the same time.

Zelda had expected raised eyebrows at her red gown, with its glittering crystals crossed between her breasts. It practically shouted that she was done being restrained.

The gown's sudden appearance actually on Zelda had driven her mother to despairing flaps of the hands. "It's an evening dress!"

"This is early evening." Zelda knew perfectly well that this was a late dinner in the country, not a ball; this dress shouldn't appear for several more hours. She didn't care.

"I must change to try to match you. When did you even acquire such a thing?"

"I'll ensure they wait for you, then." Zelda had no intention of explaining that Tansy was her co-conspirator.

And she'd had the pleasure of sailing off to the dining room alone.

Pleasure had always been a distant concept, since she'd had to forego the pleasures of dancing, sewing, and other such things. Zelda had long counted the days till she could have the pleasure of freedom.

She'd enjoy the way the silk swirled around her as she walked, and how pretty her skin looked against the rich color. *Why not?* That was her new motto. *Why not?*

No one actually spoke to her, so Zelda had time to look about. The room was vast as an ocean schooner, with a polished walnut floor, ranks of mullioned windows reflecting all the light, and a chandelier of a million crystals swaying above it all.

That chandelier looked made of knives, Zelda thought. Its points sparkled. Who built such a thing? Could she learn to do it? *Lady Vere, formerly of New York, known for her chandeliers*, she imagined reading in a headline. It would be one of those epistolary novels, sensational letters about a sensational woman. It was key to her daydream that someone else wrote them.

Lord Faircombe's thick chest boasted the dark coat demanded by fashion, topped with a cravat so fine it was almost transparent. A thumbnail ruby fixed its linen in place. He ignored her lack of a cane, just as he'd ignored its presence previously. He ignored things rather vehemently.

When Zelda tore her gaze from the menacing chandelier, and took in the little crowd of men in their serious coats and showy buttons, she faltered a little. What might all these men be planning for her?

But then she remembered what she was planning for them, and thought, *Why not?*

She nodded to a footman, and when he came closer, she said, "A glass of wine, please."

* * *

THROUGH THE SCREEN, Geoffrey saw his father ignore Miss Rawle, who looked even more like a goddess in silk that glittered and glowed against her skin.

Then her face went into a wine glass.

Geoffrey had been so focused over the winter on helping Charlotte find a husband, he'd never considered if Vere wished to marry, the great lump. Some part of him had thought Vere might fall in love.

Whatever made him think that, given a family like theirs, he couldn't imagine.

And now, when Vere faced this possible threat—possible joy? Definite risk—Geoffrey had been thrown out of Faircombe Hall.

The very thought of it made his muscles clench; the seams of his jacket creaked.

He forced himself to relax. A man as large as Geoffrey learned, as he reached adulthood, how to control thoughtless movements.

He truly needed to interview Miss Rawle. Might she be good for Vere? Persuade him to his better side?

Did Vere *have* a better side?

Or was she a hedonist who would push him the wrong way? She was already sipping her second glass of wine. Had she more potent mixtures in that luggage?

Had she *diseases*?

All Geoffrey knew was that his father's choice had been based on money. If Vere achieved Grandfather's plans for a gazebo but died insane, that wouldn't be a fair exchange.

Geoffrey hoped his father would agree.

He shifted, trying to ease his aching thighs while staying still. At his back was the corner door his grandmother had used. It came up to his chest. He wasn't squeezing through that.

He hadn't considered that, once here, he'd be stuck.

Ah, finally. There was Delina. And Charlotte.

"My daughter Lady Charlotte, and Miss Delina Farsworth." Lord Faircombe satisfied civility by waving between the two young ladies and Miss Rawle and then, introductions achieved, ignored all three.

He was absorbed with the unfamiliar men Geoffrey had sent round to the courtyard entrance. Geoffrey only recognized Mr. Wapping, the Faircombe solicitor. That gentleman looked like a long wet stick, with all the same personality.

Beside Wapping, three men stood talking together: a slovenly fellow whose speech screamed of the poorer parts of London, one obsessed with his watch, and one of African descent wearing an old-fashioned, richly-hued blue suit.

The three of them were united in ignoring a round little man like an apple, with a deeply aged companion whose fuschia waistcoat didn't draw the eye so much as yank it.

The worried one checked his watch. "Are your meals usually on time, sir?"

Lord Faircombe had no interest in the gentleman's time. "If I so choose, Mr. Wallinson."

"Is there some competing entertainment in the neighborhood that has delayed one of your guests?" Mr. Wallinson didn't let it drop.

Lord Faircombe dropped it by not answering.

He must be waiting for Mrs. Rawle, Geoffrey realized, but unwilling to admit it. A little politeness to a mere woman might read as weakness to this crowd.

Geoffrey rolled his eyes to himself and added one more thing to his life goals: lectures for his father on the company he kept.

"It is interesting," said the man in deep blue, "that you choose to mix our business with this family affair of your son."

As if Miss Rawle did not exist, grumbled Geoffrey

inwardly, forgetting that he still wasn't sure if Miss Rawle carried diseases.

It was more than odd that they were *all* here. Geoffrey couldn't recall any businessmen ever dining with Lord Faircombe. Nor even meeting him outside London.

The marquessate, as far as Lord Faircombe was concerned, marked a deep gulf between himself and men of mere money.

Even though he was now marrying off his son for it.

"Mr. Mendey," said the Marquess, acknowledging the man with a slight bend of his neck. And that was all.

That was apparently how far a marquess' neck would bend in search of money.

He bestowed a full sentence only on his own solicitor. "Mr. Wapping, how do you find your rooms? I acquired the leather panels last year."

Mr. Wapping had no care for decorations. "I would have preferred to be housed some farther distance from my neighbors." The way he peered down his nose at the apple-shaped man made it clear from whom he'd prefer some distance.

That fellow reddened. "I presume we and Mr. Highland are quartered together to keep men of the law contained."

Too true to be a joke, it fell flat.

Mr. Highland, in his fuschia waistcoat, tapped his cane soundlessly on the carpet. Out loud he said, "I hope there's tea."

This evening would be interminable.

* * *

MISS FARSWORTH WAS a little porcelain doll of a woman. "Shall we sit?"

That was kind, thought Zelda; Lady Charlotte was elegant and tall like Lord Vere, but kept looking about.

Her lack of attention was reassuring. No one would care if Zelda did as she liked. "I'd like to stand; a long evening provides plenty of time to sit. I assume your preferred evening entertainments also involve sitting?"

"Entertainments?" That caught Lady Charlotte's attention. Her green and brown eyes were intent, once focused on Zelda. "What sort of entertainments do *you* pursue of an evening, Miss Rawle?"

Wine. "Anything new," she answered.

Lady Charlotte only said, "Mm," with a piercing look.

Zelda wondered how the topic of entertainment had suddenly become a competition.

"Well." Miss Farsworth broke another silent pause. "How lucky, as anything we do must be new."

"Yes, exactly!"

"Do you play cards, Miss Rawle?" Lady Charlotte hadn't given up.

It was painful to hold thin cards in a specific position for long. "Not generally. And I am no player of harpsichords, either."

Remarkably, Lady Charlotte's response was to turn and leave the room.

Zelda closed her mouth. *That* was something new. "Well. I suppose I lost."

"Not at all." Miss Farsworth's expression looked faintly apologetic. "Lady Charlotte is an excellent musician. I can't be certain, but I would guess that she's just gone to see to the tuning of the pianoforte. It is a beautiful instrument, and she plays with great feeling, but the thing stays tuned for about five minutes."

"Ah." Zelda's sigh of relief was real. She had no wish to offend Lady Charlotte, and Miss Farsworth might be good company. Company would be nice. If there were one thing Zelda had gathered from watching her parents' marriage, it was that husbands weren't company. "Would *you* like to sit, Miss Farsworth?"

"I don't mind standing. Especially as Lord Faircombe has introduced none of the gentlemen taking dinner with us." Miss Farsworth was clearly a little wary of the bevy of guests.

"Ah." Zelda's slow smile returned. "That only makes them more interesting, doesn't it? And us more interesting to them." They rattled her a little, with their silence and stares, but how much more should she prepare for the peculiarities of men if she intended to marry one?

Miss Farsworth had a charming delicacy. "Surely you already interest them?"

Delicacy was one thing Zelda didn't have. "Because I am bringing Lord Faircombe a great deal of money?"

The young lady's eyes laughed. "How refreshingly clear."

Zelda tried to hide her smile behind her wineglass, but it didn't work. "It is *clear* they are here to do some business as soon as Lord Faircombe has possession of my father's money. All so eager; they've forgotten we are not married yet."

"But will be soon."

She surely would be. Yet something in her didn't want to say so out loud. "Of course, but—" She wasn't about to explain her plan to Miss Farsworth. Shrugging, she stopped herself.

"Finish what you were about to say?"

"I beg your pardon?"

Miss Farsworth's blue eyes seemed to see every detail of her, including her self-censorship. "Finish what you had been about to say. I'd like to hear it."

"Oh," Zelda shrugged with a careless, sly smile, "no, thank you."

At that, Miss Farsworth raised both eyebrows. "You enjoyed saying no!"

Zelda leaned conspiratorially close. "Does it show?"

"Quite."

"I did enjoy it. I intend to keep doing it."

Miss Farsworth tilted her head and studied Zelda intently. "A word of advice from someone else who isn't a Faircombe: keep that plan to yourself for the moment, would you? I think you'll find it's for the best."

* * *

BEHIND THE SCREEN Geoffrey thoughtfully chewed his bread and cheese, kept his elbows tucked close to his sides, and listened hard.

Surely he hadn't heard that right. To what, or to whom, did Miss Rawle wish to say no? Did she not want this marriage?

More importantly, Miss Rawle was about to be Lady Vere. She might enjoy being pigheaded, but she wouldn't enjoy how Vere would react to constantly hearing *no* from a new wife. To say nothing of Lord Faircombe.

The Marquess expected her agreement in many things, most notably to produce an heir for the line. Did she know that?

Miss Rawle's pleasure in clothes might be a match for Vere's. She knew exactly how that red gown clung to her curves, and how the crystals' sparkle drew attention to her *décolleté*. She was also already drinking her third glass of wine.

But she didn't seem to know one basic truth: as the wife of a peer, she would be expected to comport herself accordingly. Which meant doing as *he* wished.

Geoffrey was wondering how much Miss Rawle knew about the future that awaited her here.

He stared at the carvings on the screen that must have amused his grandmother through many a meal and took another bite of bread and cheese.

It bothered him, all of a sudden, that he didn't know if his grandmother had eaten years' worth of meals behind this screen because she had missed her husband terribly, or because she was shy about her teeth.

On the other side of the screen, Vere had finally decided to arrive. "Good evening, Miss Rawle. I am so glad you felt well enough to join us."

Her health? That was all Vere mentioned? *If you* want *to be married, you idiot, tell her she's beautiful. Tell her that gown is astonishing. Tell her you want to hear everything she wants to tell you.*

Then Geoffrey caught himself. He couldn't take the chance of helping this marriage along till he knew if he should hinder it. He wouldn't be protecting Vere if he let the woman give Vere the pox.

He wasn't stupid enough to think that she might be light with her favors just because she was beautiful. No, it was how little she cared for what others thought, and how focused she was on herself.

And it was the way she responded to his brother's luke-warm interest.

Her voice had that note in it, the same warm intensity that had hit Geoffrey so hard when she said *ah*.

"Lord Vere. Thank you for your patience. And your gift." Then she said something to him Geoffrey couldn't hear.

This space behind the screen was very cramped.

* * *

HE HAD RATHER A DASHING LOOK, Zelda's betrothed. London's sober fashions looked well on him, emphasizing his square shoulders and long legs. In defiance of those fashions, he wore a diamond on his right hand, winking in the candlelight; she liked that too.

But when he saw her, he visibly winced.

Well, he didn't seem to care for her clothes as much as she admired his.

Zelda had a wild desire to simply take her dress off, and see if he would still wince.

Where had that come from? She looked at her wineglass; it was empty. Ah.

After they'd exchanged formalities, Zelda leaned close to say quietly, "Your flower was a delightful gift; what was it?"

Lord Vere's eyes widened.

"There are flowers all over Faircombe, Miss Rawle," he said just as quietly. "I can have the gardener give you a tour tomorrow, if you wish."

Zelda smiled and nodded. Her eyes slid away. He wouldn't admit his gift? He'd changed his mind about her already? Had her gown given him that poor an impression?

It didn't matter, she thought, watching Lady Charlotte return. It would only be a complication if her husband liked her.

It would be best if she didn't like him.

She had dreams, and it was for them she made the sacrifice of getting married at all. She wasn't about to throw them away because her betrothed husband was relatively pleasant-looking and had given her a flower and wouldn't even speak of it.

She looked at him again. The regular cut of his features had nothing remarkable about it, except—yes—he had a very distinct chin. Distinct, with a small dimple. Chin dimples were appealing, weren't they?

She had never before considered that chin dimples might be appealing apart from the person or their personality. All these men-related questions were more difficult than she had thought.

Rawle heiress marries dimple would be terrible in print.

Her mother finally arrived, in dark purple with a frothing lace collar: overdressed, but providing Zelda visible support. She gave both Zelda and Lord Vere a brief nod.

Lord Faircombe had pretended not to be paying attention, in his vehement way of ignoring things, but immediately he moved to the table to sit. No honored positions for any of his guests, not even Mrs. Rawle; he waved Lord Vere to his right and Lady Charlotte to his left.

Mrs. Rawle let a footman help her settle in her chair before saying to their host, "You make a very regal figure for the head of the table, Lord Faircombe."

"Eh, thank you." Lord Faircombe seemed an inch taller from the compliment. "Though *regal* is best reserved for the Crown. As the Crown's humble servant, a man needs nothing more than a good son and a good daughter."

Lady Charlotte paid this no mind, but Lord Vere seemed startled.

* * *

A MAN NEEDS *nothing more than to have a good son? Just one, sir?* Geoffrey wanted to call out. That was rich, coming from his father. Even Vere looked like he might choke on that one.

And no wife, Lord Faircombe? Geoffrey thought with more bitterness than he thought he had in him.

It was one thing to be erased from the family in an afternoon. It was quite another for his father to erase Lady Faircombe as well.

His father had done quite a lot of work today, cutting

anyone out of existence who wanted their family to be a family rather than drooling devotion to the title.

* * *

Zelda had expected Faircombe to be more light-hearted than her father's money-focused New York table, but this affair was strained.

Strained affairs were no fun.

"I've never seen a chandelier that seemed so murderous," she remarked.

Her mother, seated opposite, just closed her eyes.

But Miss Farsworth gave her remark, and the glittering points of crystal, serious consideration. "It is stark and cold. Glass is like that. But does it have intention? It's so still. No, it isn't; I see that you're right. There are a few points trembling in some draft. They do seem menacing, don't they?"

"You're in no danger from our chandelier," Lord Vere reassured Zelda.

He didn't seem to grasp that she wasn't *frightened;* she was looking for *entertainment.*

"Your paper hangings," she tried again, "have texture to them."

"Yes." Miss Farsworth turned her perceptive eye to it. "The makers paint the pattern with a glue, and sprinkle it with the dust from weaving fabric."

"Really?"

"Do you not like it?" asked Lord Vere. There was a wish to please in his voice that said that if she didn't like it, the papers would be gone by midnight.

"I just wonder, who spends much time rubbing themselves against wall papers?" Zelda looked at the pattern too and took another swallow of her wine. It softened her joints. "Is that something people do here?"

* * *

GEOFFREY HEARD *THAT*.

He tried not to laugh, he did. But it escaped his control. He laughed, struggled to suppress the laugh, unavoidably coughed, and wound up choking on bread and cheese.

How long had it been since he'd laughed? Apparently, he'd forgotten how.

He felt it go down the wrong way. The coughs were horrendous. Even after the offending bite was cleared, the coughs just went on, as if in revenge. His burly frame shook until the teak screen shook too. Alarmed, he reached for it… but it just fell away, *splat*, landing on the carpet.

Everyone in the dining room turned to look at Geoffrey, rising like a volcano from behind his dead grandmother's screen.

So much for quietly maintained boundaries.

There was nothing else to do. Geoffrey simply drew himself up, bowed from the waist, and said, "I beg your pardon."

And left.

He must go out through the kitchen. It would be the fastest way.

His stomach rumbled as he passed a footman with the plate of sliced beef. It made him think the newest member of the family might be too busy drinking to eat. "See that Miss Rawle gets a nice piece, Matthew," he said as he passed, and the footman nodded.

CHAPTER 3

Zelda had expected her paper remark to get some reaction. She hadn't expected the collapse of a needlepoint wall, the explosion and subsequent emergence of her giant, and his very polite exit.

After the door closed behind him, Zelda burst out laughing.

The laugh came up from her toes and went all the way to her ears. She couldn't stop it. She almost snorted her wine, she laughed so hard. *American heiress drowns in wine. Helpless laughter blamed.*

"Excuse me," said Lord Vere stiffly, rising and leaving before she could stop laughing enough to acknowledge it. He followed the escaping giant out the same door.

As Zelda's laughter finally slowed, a hesitant footman offered her the platter he was about to place on the table. "Allow me, madam?" Zelda could only nod.

As she wiped her eyes with her fingertips, she noticed no one else was laughing. More, everyone was studiously avoiding watching *her* laugh.

Russia by summertime, Zelda thought firmly, taking up her

fork. Who were these people, planning to rub up against their own wall papers, to look at her oddly for laughing? They were the ones with menacing ornaments on the ceilings and enormous shepherds hiding in corners.

No, a mildly pleasant dimple and one flower wouldn't be enough to keep her here once she had her dowry and the safety of a married name.

* * *

VERE WOULDN'T LET Geoffrey escape. Geoffrey might be bigger, but Vere's legs were just as long.

He managed to grab his brother's elbow in the china room. "What are you trying to do?"

Geoffrey shrugged him off and kept walking. "Leave me alone, Vere." The tops of his ears were red; no doubt he'd heard Miss Rawle's laughter.

Vere had to put a stop to this quickly. "What did you intend? To embarrass me? If it was only for attention, I assure you I can keep the lady's attention on me."

At that, Geoffrey stopped and glared. "What does that mean?"

"Just what I said."

"Vere, you can't see ten feet in front of you with a candle. I am trying to look after you."

"You have always been a thorn in my side, and I don't underestimate the damage you can do. I'm through letting you take things from me."

"When have I ever taken anything from you, Vere? *What* have I taken?"

Vere snorted. "*My* bed in the nursery. *My* tin soldiers. And every fresh peach we ever had."

"You outgrew the bed! As well as the soldiers. And our nurse always split peaches evenly four ways. Always."

"Exactly! Why did you get a whole quarter of every peach? You were the littlest! Besides Charlotte."

"*Lord Vere,* you couldn't spare me part of a peach?"

Vere couldn't explain his conviction that, like the largest piece of the peach, Geoffrey could take Miss Rawle and everything she represented away from him. He must rid himself of the feeling, as his father said. He mustn't *let* Geoffrey take any of it away. "This mother-hen act of yours only makes you look foolish. And looking foolish makes you weak."

Geoffrey's eyes narrowed under his broad frowning brow. "You think avoiding a fight with you makes me *weak?*"

Just the words brought back that same sick confusion that Vere felt whenever he looked at Geoffrey. Everyone told Vere that *he* must be the lord of the manor; he was the heir, and had the title. But what did that *mean?* He hadn't been able to figure it out when he was little and his father first explained it, and it hadn't gotten clearer once two more little boys and a girl joined him in the nursery.

It made even less sense now. It couldn't mean that he had to be like Geoffrey, big, strong, and looking after everyone and everything, because *Geoffrey* was Geoffrey. But then what was Vere?

Just as when they were little, Geoffrey seemed comfortable as who he was; and since now he was one enormous fellow, Vere didn't like to go poking for the edges of his patience.

Which was currently strained. "You have it all, Vere. Congratulations. The title, the house, and now a wife. Courtesy of our father's *tender* regard for his sons."

Vere winced.

"Be careful. He wishes to cut out everything that doesn't suit his image of his family. What will he cut out tomorrow?

And what will be left?" Geoffrey didn't look the least angry now; he looked sad. "He once felt he needed more sons."

Vere wished there was a mirror on the wall.

Looking at Geoffrey made him feel small. In a mirror Vere could see *himself,* and he felt better. Clearer. He was tall, he was good-looking. His problem wasn't what he looked like. It was always having to compare himself to this particular younger brother.

His father's way of establishing order was always to repeat what must happen, and it did happen. Vere must learn to do the same.

"Geoffrey, you've no money. Charlotte has Mother's share and Frederick must have found some source of support, but you have nothing, do you? If his lordship set you aside right now, you'd have literally nothing. I'll give you five hundred pounds to leave Faircombe and find your own way, or we will have more trouble between us than you embarrassing me in front of Miss Rawle."

* * *

GEOFFREY *HAD* HEARD Miss Rawle's laughter behind him. And instead of making him feel small, it made him feel… *better.*

He'd turn back and laugh with her if he could. He'd been worrying about his family for every one of the thirteen years and three hundred and sixty-two days since his mother had gone. He'd just remembered he *liked* laughing.

It made even less sense now that she wasn't married. The men of the colonies couldn't *all* be that foolish. It made Geoffrey want to spend more time with her, and more suspicious of her, all at once.

Which was uncomfortable, but he might go through a great deal more discomfort to laugh again.

This offer of money to leave his own home, however, wasn't funny. It was humiliating. *He was of Faircombe, too.*

"Offer me money one more time and I'll swear not to leave this ground until I'm dead," Geoffrey said through his teeth without looking at Vere, and kept walking.

* * *

When Geoffrey returned to the sheep sheds, he knocked on the tilt-topped door set into the low building. He couldn't really stand tall inside, but he bent.

There was his India-cotton bundle, tied corner to corner, on Dandy's chair, where he'd left it.

Dandy, the old shepherd, clearly hadn't touched it. "Suppose you'll be explaining that," he said, thrusting his pipe toward the bundle.

"I… have no home, Dandy." Geoffrey felt the air leave him. "I'm out of the house." It was too painful to say *out of the family*. His father couldn't do that with an order; neither could Vere.

"Is that so?" Dandy gently whacked his pipe on the back of his boot. "If you're here to mope, let's do it into some ale."

* * *

The entire afternoon spilled out of Geoffrey along the wagon-rutted road towards the village.

"What the hell do *you* know about marriage?" Dandy sucked his teeth, then whistled for his collie to come heel. Chump left off snuffling into hillocks off the road and lolloped back.

Dandy's short-shorn hair under his hat was white, and he was always ready to listen. But he knew nothing of the life of the gentry. What he knew was sheep.

Though... what *did* Geoffrey know about marriage? "Nothing."

"Your brother's the heir. He's got to get married. You can do as you please. Why mope about *his* house when you could do what you please? Toss barmaids. Toss sheep."

"You're not following this at all. They'd be a terrible match, she's far too..." Delicate? Sensuous? Good-humored? He didn't know her well enough to be sure of all that, and if he were, he couldn't explain why that meant she shouldn't marry Vere. She *might* not be a lightskirt, but he couldn't just guess; this was too important. "And she has a laugh like... Vere can't marry a woman like that."

"Lord Vere is going to marry a woman like that, sounds like," Dandy said philosophically, scratching under his hat with a fingernail so rough Geoffrey could hear the sound.

"They wouldn't suit at all."

"Nasty bugger, is she?" Dandy nodded. "I've seen some nasty buggers in my day."

"You aren't even listening. She's not nasty. Kind of—" Geoffrey's hands started to describe her shape, then he remembered that he'd been talking of her personality, not her hips, which were memorable. "She likes wine and laughing and wonders about flocked walls and... and she thinks I steal things."

"Huh. Have you?"

Geoffrey wouldn't dignify that with an answer. "I worry that—"

"Stop worrying! You're a grown man! Worry is for old ladies!"

"Don't even try that. I've seen you stay awake all night—" *Over a sick lamb,* he was about to add, but was interrupted.

A village boy rushed out of the dark as fast as his two tiny legs could go.

"Quick!" the boy—it was Gary, Gary Potts—had barely

enough breath to speak. "Rusty fell through the ice into Frog Pond!"

Geoffrey knew Frog Pond, he knew the weather, and he knew the dangers of a little boy on thin ice. "Run to the inn, if you can, and get help," he called over his shoulder, already racing for the pond.

Long shadows from the moon might have confused his path, but Geoffrey knew it well from a lifetime of playing there. The blue light lay cool across dank green moss; but under the trees still lay frost. Had that fooled little Russ Wilson into trying to cross the ice?

In moments that seemed like years, Geoffrey was at the pond's edge. There was no sign of the child, just a black ragged hole in gray ice.

Geoffrey had no illusions that ice would bear his weight. He plunged in.

Already short of breath from running, the cold took all that was left of his air. Even only waist-deep in icy water, Geoffrey felt his muscles seize. He *could not* breathe.

But he couldn't let a child die, either.

The pond was tiny. As a child, Geoffrey had searched every inch of it, knew the shape of it under the water as well as he knew where to find robin's eggs. It was small, but far wider than the span of his arms.

Enough room for a little boy to drown.

Forcing his body forward, cutting through the ice, grateful for his sheepskin coat, Geoffrey reached the spot where it was clear the boy had gone through. He felt around in the water. He found nothing.

Russ was a tough little fellow; somehow, he'd swum. How far could he go? It must have been mere feet.

Trying to reach around under the ice, Geoffrey felt its sharp edge rip through the sleeve of his shirt and cut him.

This ice was between him and a little boy.

He didn't have to be restrained *here*.

He could let go.

Without another thought, Geoffrey clasped his hands together like a club, raised both arms, and brought them down on the ice.

It shattered in all directions, noise of the *crack* traveling out through the trees, ice bobbing in the waves he'd caused. Geoffrey gasped in as much air as he could, then ducked down, scrabbling under the water for any shape like that of a little boy. His legs were numb; the water burned against his neck and face and hands, it was so cold.

Nothing.

He surfaced, gasping, still fighting to breathe against muscles still locked.

Just yards away, in the shifting shards of ice, something soft came to the surface. It rolled, sickeningly similar to how a submerged log would roll. But it wasn't wood.

It was wool.

Sloshing heavily as a bear through the water, Geoffrey took two strides, three, swam a stroke or two as the pond reached its deepest point, and then he was there.

He pulled Russ into his arms and staggered toward shore.

The little boy wasn't moving. His lips were blue. It looked like when a lamb got tangled on the way to birth and ran out of air.

Had the boy breathed in any of the pond water? Lambs could do that too, on the way to being born.

Geoffrey held the little boy up by the ankles, easily, shaking him a little to see if any water came out. He put a finger in the boy's cold mouth to make sure it was clear. Empty.

He didn't know what else to do except, as he would with a lamb, to put the boy closer to his skin, and blow into his mouth to start his breath.

It was easier with a sturdy boy than a tiny lamb; Geoffrey wasn't so fearful of crushing him. He could fit his mouth over the lad's and blow. He heard air leaving the boy's nose, and pinched it shut—gently! He wanted the air to reach the lungs. He blew again.

The boy jerked in his arms, struggled, coughed, and breathed again.

Like a lamb, Geoffrey thought, and as he did with the lambs, all he could say was, "Shh, shh, we'll get you warm."

"*Rusty!*" The scream was Mrs. Wilson, the boy's mother. Geoffrey looked up to see her racing toward them, skirts flying, full-out between the trees. There were other people just behind, from the Stony Barrel by the look of them; the Potts boy had indeed fetched help.

Then it was a chaos of shouting, as the mother grabbed him from Geoffrey's arms, babbling her relief. The rest of the people started shouting orders, often conflicting.

That was when Geoffrey noticed he himself was shivering to the bone.

"Get that off." It was Dandy shoving at his jacket, and Geoffrey realized he wanted Geoffrey to take off his clothes. He stripped down to his trousers and someone wrapped a quilt around him. It burned like fire.

It must be because his skin was numb from the cold.

"Get marching, you hump-backed bull, march," Dandy was bawling in his ear, just like he did with recalcitrant cattle, and despite the burning cold, Geoffrey grinned.

"I'm not a cow, old man."

"*March*," but Dandy looked relieved as Geoffrey staggered toward the inn on his own two feet.

* * *

THE FIRE WAS WIDE and warm at the Stony Barrel. Geoffrey let the heat melt through him, clutching the edges of his quilt. If the sight of golden chest hair offended anyone, they did not mention it.

It was nice not to be judged for a moment on his clothes, or their lack.

All the way back to the inn, relieved men had pounded him on the back. Russ' mother had disappeared with her boy; once they reached the inn, and once the excited chatter died away, the thing was over.

He'd rescued a life, and oddly, he'd never felt more alone. But he'd also never felt more peaceful. It had been worth the risk.

He smiled to himself. He'd hidden behind a screen in his own dining room tonight, and rescued a little boy from drowning. And he was unharmed, just as he'd said to Delina. He was too big to hurt.

The barmaids gathered by the beer kegs, whispering among themselves and casting glances at Geoffrey. Well, he'd never bared his chest in an inn before.

He ignored his shredded dignity.

"Did you know there's a drawing, in the library, of my grandfather's goals for Faircombe? He built the Greek columns across the front, but he planned far more. White marble fencing around the grounds, a glasshouse alongside for fruits and flowers, a fountain in the front pond, a gazebo—"

"What the devil is a gazebo?"

Geoffrey thought how to explain. It wasn't easy, as several men nearby were gaming with dice, and someone was playing a tin flute. He raised his voice. "It's like a little house, with a half-round roof like an orange, and places to sit."

"What do you do there? Just sit?"

"Well… yes."

They were interrupted by the butcher. He stopped to squeeze Geoffrey's shoulder. "Well done, sir."

Geoffrey nodded. The courtesy was nice. And the friendly voice. "Wilson." The butcher nodded and went on.

"Faircombe don't need a gazebo," Dandy pronounced as if it were the final word.

"Well, it's got a new mistress who might give it a gazebo." It didn't seem the right way to describe Miss Rawle at all. He thought about her shape again, and felt his wet pants tighten. It was no help that parts of him thought of her as a woman, not a wallet.

"Doesn't sound as if she'll give a damn one way or the other." Dandy had scraped every speck of the stew from his bowl, but in case some spirit of the meat and gravy remained, he put it under his seat for Chump to lick.

Geoffrey had finished two bowls of the same stew, and a third was balanced on his knee. The innkeeper had waved away his coin, making Geoffrey wonder if he could earn his living by saving people from ponds. He hoped not. "It's odd. I don't know what she knows about the title she'll be getting. Or everything that's expected of her."

Dandy's eyes widened, the wrinkles in the corners pulling tight. "How much is there for her to do?" His eyes widened as the thought dawned. "You mean she don't know she's got to…" He made a gesture with his fingers that was all too easy to understand.

But it was a serious matter. "I don't think she does."

"I suppose fine ladies don't. What business of yours is that?" Dandy shrugged, his thick, scarred knuckles whitening as he tightened his hold on his ale cup.

Geoffrey didn't have an answer. He just worried about people. Including, now, Miss Rawle. At least a little.

* * *

LADY CHARLOTTE DID INDEED PLAY BEAUTIFULLY.

Full of food and wine, Zelda was draped over a stuffed armchair, far from menacing chandeliers. Her head lolled back and forth in time to the music. She should discover musicians, she decided. Perhaps for the public. *Miss Rawle's Guide to New Musicians.* Perhaps Tansy would transcribe.

Lady Charlotte, the pianoforte, and the soaring music all seemed carved from the same golden wood, studded with precious metals. It was like being inside a music box.

Zelda gasped. She suddenly couldn't take a deep breath. It *was* like being inside a music box. With the lid closed. She was shut up in it and would never get out.

Beside her, Lord Vere noticed her gulping air. He only glanced her way, silently, and the stiff way his profile was shaped made her think he didn't approve.

So many people around for her to be alone in this box.

She sat up, and her breathing eased. The warm, liquid feeling returned. She checked on her betrothed; his expression hadn't changed, not even down to his dimple. Why didn't he sway to the music as she did? Couldn't he feel the notes?

Lady Charlotte's quick fingers danced down the keys and finished the piece with a flourish. Standing, she accepted the little group's applause. There was only her family and the Rawles to enjoy it; the men of business had retired.

Her eyes flashed with pleasure and the tips of her ears reddened as Miss Farsworth applauded especially hard.

"So wonderful to be able to do that," Zelda murmured as she clapped.

Lord Vere looked surprised again. Was that to be his constant expression? It didn't look well on him. It gave him the air of an upset owl. "Is it? Young ladies in this country are expected to play."

Well, she couldn't. Odd how he had taken her pleasure and turned it back toward what she couldn't do.

People did that, the ones who pretended not to see the slight swelling in her knuckles.

Like her father.

She didn't want to believe it of him, but he'd stopped seeing her years after he'd given her the little globe with continents of jade and oceans of lapis lazuli. She wondered what he'd even said about her when those tin-soldier men had asked for her hand; none of them had repeated it. They simply appeared, one by one, in the parlor on Sundays, and told Zelda that her father had agreed, if she would accept.

She hadn't.

He hadn't come to the docks, as he hadn't wanted to be seen by a blockade-running Italian ship. He'd nodded his good-bye in their front hall. Only nodded. As if a voyage to Britain in wartime must be a small thing, because his wife and daughter were doing it.

Any life of Zelda's would be a small one, to him. A life to be spent inside small rooms. A physician could give her a word, *rheumatism*, but no explanation why it should plague a girl of fifteen when it usually plagued only old ladies. Those words made the world very small.

Zelda had hated stupid physicians and pity ever since. Their small plans could go to hell. She would not live a small life. She would live the biggest possible life. She would see every continent, every ocean on that small globe. No one understood what she could do. But she would do it.

So far, her plan had worked. She was in Britain, and her reward was to hear Lady Charlotte's exquisite music… next to her about-to-be-husband. Who didn't seem to understand a thing she said.

She hadn't pictured loneliness traveling with her.

"Don't you love it when your insides dance along to the

music outside?" she asked Lord Vere. "I wish medicine would explain *that*."

On his other side, Miss Farsworth's lips pressed together, and one side twitched; had that been a smile?

But Lord Vere himself wasn't smiling. "I think you'll feel less dizzy in the morning, Miss Rawle."

She wasn't dizzy. Didn't the way the pretty music jumped up and down and danced all through the air affect him at all? How could a fellow so dull have thought to leave her something like that lovely little flower?

"Lord Vere, how did you come to think of a gift like that lovely little flower?"

He looked confused again, and shrugged. "How does one think of gifts?"

Even his ear was boring. Basically attractive, but boring. Nothing about it invited further investigation. She couldn't imagine him making jokes about sheep. "I suppose that is what I am asking. How *do* you think of gifts?"

"Are there gifts you lack, Miss Rawle?" His face aflame with interest now. "What is it you want? It would please me to shower you with whatever gifts you like."

And that was lovely! It warmed her, not as much as the wine, but it did warm her, to see his enthusiasm for pleasing her. "I love *surprises*! Do you enjoy them too?"

With some fire in his eyes, she could see him, his true self. One not at all like she expected: a little cynical, but honest. "I don't think I care for surprises. How can I, when my life as I was born to it is so very much what anyone would want?"

Well, at least he wasn't unaware of his good fortune. "I adore surprises. I don't care what the surprise is. I love a day that starts out sunny and turns to rain. Although..."

"Yes?" He was so eager. "Do tell."

"We passed through London so quickly! I had hoped to meet more of its interesting people. Do you think we might have a party to celebrate our betrothal? Does one do that here?"

"I'm not sure how many people would leave London yet..."

On his other side, Miss Farsworth had clearly been listening. Her fan tapped Lord Vere's arm with obvious disapproval. "Lord Vere, don't discourage your intended! Though it is more difficult than you might think, Miss Rawle. The London season extends through the session of Parliament, and until it ends, few people of society venture outside the city."

"Quite." Lord Vere's brows knit in thought. "Would you care to return to London?"

"Oh no! The solicitors have all convened here and... no, we needn't." The notes of the music still bubbled inside her like sparkling wine. She *would* love a really good party. Full of interesting people. Like the shepherd.

Going backwards, though, seemed dangerous. She needed to keep pressing *forward*.

"If no one would attend a party at Faircombe, I must give up the idea." Then as it struck her, "I thought *marquess* was a very important title?"

She could see Miss Farsworth folding her lips together again as if attempting to keep something inside. Something funny, if Zelda was any judge of the look in her eyes.

Lord Vere just turned red. It was the most interesting thing his face had done yet. The tops of the ears especially were very red. Just like Lady Charlotte's. It must be marvelous to have a sister or a brother one could match in such surprising ways.

"Very much so, Miss Rawle," said Lord Vere.

About what? Oh. Marquesses being important. She had imbibed a great deal of wine. "I didn't mean to offend!"

"Not at all." It only seemed to confirm his redness. "We can certainly send invitations, if that is what you wish."

"A house party in spring!" Miss Farsworth looked surprised that Lord Vere had acquiesced. "There is a novelty for you, Miss Rawle."

Was it? "Lovely," Zelda said as warmly as she could, hoping to make up for any slight. It wouldn't be a surprise; she'd just asked for it. But it *did* sound lovely.

So lovely that she felt her eyes growing heavy again.

This whole marriage affair seemed more bothersome than anything, but a party would be so lovely. Perhaps they would be friends, she and Miss Farsworth. Perhaps she would even be friends with Lord Vere. The wine made her drowsy, made it hard to summon even a muddled image of her betrothed laughing and taking her hand.

She couldn't picture him laughing at all. In her mind, the image was of a man much bigger. And blonder.

Still trying to picture it, Zelda fell asleep.

* * *

THE BARMAID MADE a point of leaning against Geoffrey as she reached her pitcher toward his cup.

"Thanks, no more," he said gruffly, turning down both the ale and the softness against his back. He knew Joan; she seemed pleasant. But he wasn't in the mood for games tonight.

"So, no tossing barmaids," Dandy said, though quietly, as she left.

Geoffrey stretched out his legs, leaning back in his chair, and rolled his shoulders. He was cold and stiff. He'd had his fill of humiliation for the day, and if Dandy didn't already know his habits with women, Geoffrey wasn't about to enlighten him.

Darby watched her go. "You could go to London and get *other kinds* of women."

Geoffrey swerved his head to fix Dandy with one eye. "And what would I offer them? Pockets of sand?"

Didn't Dandy grasp that his home was *here*?

The old man shrugged his thin shoulders. "I can see steam rolling off that barmaid. You have something to offer women. Just not money."

Geoffrey snorted. "Are you going to tell me about my charms?"

"Nah, you know enough."

An endless supply of women didn't appeal. Geoffrey knew what he looked like; he hadn't turned down *every* barmaid. But when it came to women, he had strict requirements. She had to be unmarried, free, absolutely willing to tell him if she'd caught, and able to be sure it was his. Woman liked his attentions, but they tired quickly of the way he kept returning to hear if there was news.

He'd be the one Faircombe who didn't fill the world with children he didn't like.

Though perhaps his siblings all had the same idea.

"I'm not going to London." He was too old, and too large, to sulk.

"You can do just what you like, *Lord* Geoffrey." Dandy raised his cup to salute the title he never used. "As long as it don't require money."

On the other side of the fire, the noise of the dice game dimmed. One gamester stood. He was built thick, with a leather shield across his chest for protection while lifting things that were rough and heavy. His hair was too greasy to tell its proper color and his face was browned by the sun. "*Lord* Geoffrey! You ain't a lord of *Faircombe,* are ya?"

Geoffrey just rolled his eyes and buried his face in one hand.

The man left the others rolling dice and came to loom over Geoffrey. Who wished he hadn't. He smelled.

"We been haulin' stone up there for weeks, haven't seen *you*. You hide in those big rooms all day, boy? One of the Marquess' milk-fed brats?" He plucked at the quilt still wrapped around Geoffrey's shoulders. "Wrapped in a baby quilt?"

"I have no quarrel with you," Geoffrey said, keeping his eyes on his ale. He'd had plenty of scuffles with men deep in their cups who wanted to feel big. It was a losing fight however he played it, and he was in no mood tonight.

"You're just a bowl of jelly with no jacket, aren't ya?" The unwanted visitor flexed his arm. "Want to see what muscles it takes to do real work?" He reached out with a clutch like a snakebite, took hold of the quilt. "Want to see a real man?"

Sighing, Geoffrey stood up. And up. He let the quilt fall. And turned to face the man, whose eyes were measuring Geoffrey in every direction and not liking the answers.

Geoffrey said, "So you like rolling the dice?"

Whatever the fellow had thought was underneath that quilt, he hadn't expected Geoffrey's wide, muscle-ribbed, golden-haired torso. "Nah," was all he said, retiring back to his game.

The dice-rollers by the fire filled in all the jeering anyone could have wanted. Geoffrey waited a beat or two to see if the man wanted to renew their engagement, if the jeering egged him on, but apparently he'd had enough.

Geoffrey wrapped his quilt back around him and sat. "Where's my coat? Isn't it dry?"

Dandy looked apologetic. "Sorry. Don't know what made me bugle your title that way, tonight of all nights."

Geoffrey just shook his head. "I am going…" But where? Where was there to go?

Dandy saw him pause. He didn't like deep introspective

moments; he didn't look straight at Geoffrey when he said, "Bernie's shed, y'know, it's empty till he gets back from fawning over his mother." He watched the gamesters from the corner of one eye.

"He's not fawning over his mother; she's ill." But Geoffrey took the hint. There was a bed there, at least for a little while.

"Eh. I hope he gets back before too many more lambs come. We need that little hand of his."

"I just hope Guinevere waits."

Assuming that satisfied Dandy's need to say things without saying them, in a manly way, Geoffrey pushed out of the chair. Where *had* they put his coat?

Unable to see it anywhere, Geoffrey clutched his quilt and his pride around him and dashed across the yard to the inn's kitchen hut.

* * *

JOAN WAS IN THERE, flapping his coat toward the flames of the cooking fire, and the sight melted his irritation. His shirt lay across the back of a chair. "They're not dry," she blurted as he reached for it.

Silently, he put out his hand.

"Don't," she protested, but gave him the shirt.

When he dropped the quilt and slid the shirt over his head, his breath sucked in like he'd been stabbed. Geoffrey gritted his teeth until the clammy linen warmed a little from his skin.

"You'll freeze." Her eyes kept tracing the edges of his shoulders, even though they were now hidden under the linen. The fine soft edges of her face glowed with firelight. She came closer when he didn't move any nearer.

"The coat is sheepskin," he said, "the vest is wool." They'd keep him warm, even soaked. Didn't make it pleasant.

"Don't go," said Joan, brushing a tendril of golden hair behind her ear. She looked up at him, half in wonder, her lips parting a little as she drew even closer.

She was warm, willing, and liked the look of him, and all she wanted was a romp. She'd be done with him in a few hours, and tired of him in a few days, when he kept visiting to ask if there was news.

He had one bit of luck: she wouldn't grab him while he was covered with icy clothes.

He could make this short. "Do you know when you last had your courses?"

"What?" She pulled back. Her eyes weren't so full of wonder now.

"I'm cold. I'm tired. You're making a generous offer, so I'm asking. Do you know when you last had your courses?"

"Yes." Backing away, she looked at him with suspicion. As if she hadn't been about to latch on to him.

"So tell me."

"I'm not telling you!"

He just nodded. "I don't lie with women who won't tell me. And I'd require you not entertain other men until your courses come again. Is that a bargain that interests you?"

He hoped not. This was simply the quickest way he knew to end the conversation. It had ended it with several more persistent women in London, and quite a few others, too.

He'd learned not to mind attention from lasses who wanted to topple the biggest man they could find; but he hated the scare afterward from ones who refused to tell him anything. He'd do without before he took that risk again.

Her arms were crossed now, and she tossed her head. "I never!"

"Fine with me," murmured Geoffrey and, giving her a slight bow of the head, slid on his vest and coat, still heavy with water.

They'd warm. His feet were cold, but he'd manage.

Back in the inn, several people murmured greetings to him as he made for the door. It wasn't like being at home; but there was warmth to it. They liked him, he thought, even when they didn't care for Faircombe.

The blacksmith, sooty shoulders almost as wide as Geoffrey's, rested against the wall. He nodded as Geoffrey passed his bench. "All right there, Lord Geoffrey?"

"All right, Augie," Geoffrey reassured him, and the blacksmith accepted this as an entire conversation and leaned back against the wall.

At least people in the village—all kinds of people—knew his name. There were good and bad aspects to staying his whole life in the Faircombe village, thought Geoffrey as he set off into the raw, chilly night.

* * *

"You said she was crippled. You didn't say she was stupid."

"Vapid, perhaps. Not stupid. The girl has a brain."

Vere hadn't reached this level of frustration in years. Why wasn't his father listening to him? "The *girl* has a bottle and a half of wine in her, not to mention that shot of whiskey after dinner."

Lord Faircombe scratched his chin. "She does like that vile colonial stuff."

"Her only conversation is of presents and parties. And the paper hangings on the wall. What was that about?" Vere was pacing the width of the hallway. He was so agitated he'd pulled at his hair; one lock was out of place. "And now she's asleep again."

"You'd be asleep too with that much wine in you."

"She can't stay awake an hour. I can't marry a woman like this!"

"You *can*, and you most certainly will. You think every match is an easy one? She's not ugly. And she's bringing you money. The Faircombe name, future generations, depend on accomplishing what my father planned for this estate."

"Future generations depend on her being able to bear a child. How can she do that if she's constantly drunk off her feet?"

Lord Faircombe shrugged. "I'm sure it's been done. It's likely just a bit of fun before she's wed. You'd begrudge the girl a bottle of wine? You've drunk more at a sitting."

"That may be. But this is my future *wife*. Do you expect me to look away while my wife behaves this way? For the rest of my life?"

"No, I expect you to take the reins." Lord Faircombe's frown was all disapproval, except for a dash of confusion about why his son found this so difficult. "Get control of her. You think a woman always does as you say without direction? Get a backbone. You ought to do it now before she gets the best of you."

An unusual flicker of distaste ruffled Vere's otherwise smooth features. "Is that how you managed your marriage, sir?"

Lord Faircombe's thick chest heaved as if at a fast-drawn breath, but his face stayed impassive. "Don't question me."

Well, he ought to have expected that.

"Lord Faircombe. I assure you." Vere's face, so much leaner and narrower than his father's, looked young in the light of the candles and wore a look of desperation. "This cannot be the right match for me. You cannot want me to spend my days despising my wife."

"Happens all the time." Lord Faircombe turned as if he had nothing more to say on the subject.

The sight of his father turning away snapped something

in Vere. "You would not give me at least a chance at some kind of love?"

His father's broad shoulders slowly turned. His face looked as beaten as a used battering ram. Unwittingly, perhaps, he called his son by his childhood name, the name they shared. "You're just a boy, Grant. You have no idea what love means."

And with that he went, leaving Lord Vere standing in a pool of light from a silver candelabra, with a drunken fiancée asleep in a chair in the next room.

* * *

DELINA, just inside the music room door, waited a few moments before fully opening it, so she could pretend she hadn't heard every word.

She found Vere pacing. "Mrs. Rawle thinks Miss Rawle will sleep for some time. Why don't I have the footmen carry the whole chair to her chamber? Her mother and maid can manage from there."

"Just leave her there."

Vere was an ass, but he wasn't cruel. No, that's not so, Delina reminded herself: he wasn't cruel to her or Charlotte. Miss Rawle might be categorized along with his brothers as a person to disdain. "She will sleep so much more comfortably—"

"Her comfort is her own affair! If she wanted to sleep in a bed, she wouldn't have drunk herself stupid over dinner."

"Really, Lord Vere, there are plenty of footmen who can—"

There was a footman standing in the hall, in fact. Vere whirled on him. "No one moves Miss Rawle. That's my order. She can walk on her own two feet or bloody well stay where she is. Understood?"

The footman, stiff-backed, nodded.

Vere stalked off into the shadows.

Delina looked after him for a moment.

The footman, clearly glad his master had gone, bent his head, unsure if he should obey. "Miss?"

"Never mind, Albert. Miss Rawle seems comfortable enough. Her mother will likely stay with her; you might move in a larger settee so that Mrs. Rawle can sleep as well."

Welcome to Faircombe, thought Delina.

"Yes, Miss Farsworth."

CHAPTER 4

Zelda's eyes fluttered open and her mind, still largely asleep, reveled in that moment of being not-yet-awake when she felt fine.

Then she took the chance of moving.

Her hips, back, knees, and elbows all screamed at once. How long had she been sitting in this chair?

For a moment, she let her head loll and closed her eyes again. She could never decide whether it was better to have that moment and lose it, or be woken by pain. The nights she woke from pain dragged her spirits so low they caught on every pebble in her path.

Then she opened her eyes again. Was that her mother, still dressed, sleeping on a settee?

Zelda looked around. The dark polished wooden floor stretched in every direction; moonlight shone faintly at the windows. No candles? Where had everyone gone? What hour of the night was it?

Her tangled mind wondered if she should have brought her purloined compass.

This was a wine problem. She suppressed a groan. It

warmed her and helped her sleep; but then it cooled again and left her aching and stiff and awake in the middle of the night.

Yet it hadn't left her completely. She was still full of wine.

Not even a footman lurked about. She ought to wake her mother and get both of them to their chambers; it couldn't be too far away. Until her fingers loosened, she couldn't undo the hooks and buttons of her own clothing, much less her mother's.

Tansy and Delphine, who waited on her mother, might have gone to servants' quarters many floors away. Where even the cloven-hooved sheep seldom go, she thought a little wildly. So much farther away than at her father's house.

She'd have to find *some*one.

Zelda pushed herself to her feet as quietly as she could, including stifling any noise she might make at the sensation of straightening all her limbs. Fortunately, the floorboards were solid and quiet. Nothing creaked as Zelda slowly crossed the empty space to the door. Why was *every* room so *big*?

Zelda had no idea which way to go.

To her right was the dining room she already disliked. She'd go left.

The corridor ended in a vast parlor with deep blue paper —not for rubbing, it appeared—and a great many statues. With a door on its far side.

Zelda kept going.

Each room connected to another, but as Zelda progressed, they got smaller. Almost human-sized. The paper became less grand; Zelda even recognized some of the coral-flowered prints. The doors grew smaller.

Her joints had loosened and she was a little more awake, but curiosity kept her exploring. Would she wind up in a tiny cavern of sprites? Would they feed her? What kind of paper hangings did sprites like, she wondered?

Zelda establishes first sprite embassy, she thought.

When she found a room full of china, porcelain platters stacked all around and tureens big enough to bathe babies, she felt that some sort of reality must be close.

And there, through the next door, she found it. A kitchen. Full of low tables, three-legged stools, shelves full of cooking things built up the walls, a huge dish bin and a deep, wide fireplace.

And her giant at the hearth, lifting down a huge black kettle.

Zelda didn't mean to spy, but his back was to her, and she was transfixed watching his big hands moving delicately among the chains and hooks. His shoulders bunched under his clothes as he lifted down the massive iron cauldron, and she could see the muscles in his arms flex. Those weren't delicate at all.

If he turned, he'd see her, and she didn't wish him to drop all that metal on his toe.

"I beg your pardon," she said quietly, trying not to startle him.

The cauldron almost dropped anyway as he twisted to look, a living artwork of strength.

He was nearly too much to look at straight-on. Zelda's experience of men had never included someone with that kind of square, strong... *everything*. He made her want to be careful. But she also wanted her curiosity indulged. "What are you doing?"

* * *

THE CAULDRON CLANGED QUIETLY against the flagstones.

Geoffrey almost bowed before he recalled how he was

dressed. Odd for her to ask that question; he hadn't stopped thinking about it since Dandy had asked the same thing. Perhaps it didn't matter who he was, only what he was doing.

"Taking down the kettles for scouring, madam." As familiar as the sheep sheds were, coming up to them in the dark had seemed too cold and quiet. He'd known the kitchen hearth would be banked. Who could object if he came in to dry his clothes? Especially if no one saw him.

Once the heat started to leach into his clothes, his skin, and mercifully, his toes, he decided to pay rent on his spot by the hearth by lifting down the kettles for scouring. He had no idea how they usually did it, but he'd heard Mrs. Davies say it had to be done.

Was working a mistake? Ought he never to have gone to Scotland to study ways to make the sheep herds pay? Ought he have stayed in linens and silks and answered only to Lord Geoffrey?

Ought he never to have come home?

Miss Rawle didn't seem to mind that he hadn't bowed. Her slow eyes traveled everywhere, but their touch felt like curiosity, not like the barmaid's hungry stare.

He stood, transfixed, as she glided closer. He'd gone from utterly alone to a world filled with her walking toward him, all in an instant; it was shocking, how quickly the world changed.

The way the fabric clung to her shape was temptation itself. Tempted to stare, tempted to watch. He could watch the silk's little undulating movements all night. He had to shake himself. No, he could *not*.

She shouldn't be alone in the kitchen with a servant. Or rather, a man. Or rather, him.

She reached the kitchen table, and he realized she likely just wanted to sit. Hurriedly, he pulled out a rough stool for her, as a footman would.

She sat as if it were a gilt chair. Standing behind her, Geoffrey could see a small dark freckle on the slope of her breast just before it disappeared under the silk.

She didn't turn round. "Don't you ever get to rest?"

"I've rested too much in my life till now, perhaps."

She sighed. "I've rested too much in my life until lately as well."

Like the *ah* that had hit him before, he felt her sigh go through him. For some reason, it made him think of her stretched out on a riverbank, languid in the sun.

He swallowed. He should move away. "Perhaps that's why we're both awake in the middle of the night."

It might be his imagination, but he thought he could still smell that faint aura of honeysuckle, and it made him want to rub his nose against the dark twist of her hair.

He had to back up a step.

But she looked just as appealing from farther away, all curves wrapped in sparkle and glow.

He went back to stand by the dying coals. They gave off less heat.

She looked up and up to meet his eyes, and he thought he saw her cheeks color a little. There wasn't much light, only the banked hearth's orange glow, but it was enough to see her dark eyelashes, and Geoffrey had an inexplicable urge to touch them.

"I'm awake in the middle of the night because I slept a great deal earlier," she told him. "Also, I'm drunk."

That made Geoffrey laugh.

"Are you laughing at me?" She had a funny way of asking the question. She wasn't annoyed; she had a smile playing in the corners of her mouth.

Had he ever looked at a woman this closely before? Of all the women in the world to consider touching, it couldn't be this one. "I hope you meant that to be funny."

"I don't *think* I did. I *am* drunk. Not terribly drunk, but I know when I'm drunk, and I'm drunk."

"I see. You're an extremely articulate drunk, madam."

"Thank you!" She seemed very pleased, and leaned back to see him better. She started to tip backwards and Geoffrey jerked forward to catch her, but she recovered herself. He believed her now. She was drunk. "That is a compliment."

"Are you drunk for any particular reason, or do you just like it?"

"Eh." This question made her settle herself down into the seat as if for something serious. "It helps me fall asleep, it loosens my joints. But I do find that I don't stay asleep through the night."

"Perhaps take a little less?"

"I think…" She frowned; she'd clearly forgotten what she meant to say. Then she remembered it. "I think I should have had more whiskey."

Geoffrey laughed again because he couldn't help it, but he said, "The whiskey's better?"

"Oh, the whiskey is *marvelous*. It makes a thick warm feeling go all down my arms and legs and even up my neck." The diamond on her gloved hand flashed as she ran her palm up the back of her neck.

Just the idea of anything traveling down her arms and legs, much less up her neck, made his blood throb, but he decided to ignore it. "So it helps your limbs, but does it help you sleep?"

"Sometimes." The shrug of her shoulder was quite loose and careless. "If I sleep too deeply, it hurts to wake up. Something always stays too long in a wrong position. But if I don't sleep at all, everything will hurt. The wine and whiskey seem to help, but then I can wake up with quite a head."

She was going to wake up with *quite a head* tomorrow, if Geoffrey had his guess. He could reach out and pull the ribbon out of her hair right now, and run his fingers through from the nape of her neck to the top of her scalp. That might help any pain in her head. He was willing to try.

He backed away again. His reaction to her was excessive. As an interrogation of his supposed new sister-in-law, this wasn't going well.

He was less and less able to imagine her married to his brother the more they spoke.

"In fact, this stool is not comfortable," she announced suddenly, and stood, right under his nose.

She looked so soft. He *could* imagine pulling her into his arms. It was sufficiently difficult to dispel the image that it made his voice a little rougher. "Why are you here? Did you need something?"

Her lips parted. "*Do* I need something?" No, she wasn't being seductive; she was genuinely confused.

"What brought you to the kitchen?"

"Fairies, I think." She waved a hand around all the kitchen with its blackened beams and flagstone floor. "I kept walking, and the rooms became smaller and smaller till I wound up here. Is it meant to be an illusion?"

Geoffrey didn't think Vere, Charlotte, or even Delina had ever visited the kitchen. Was that what had brought her all the way to Britain to marry? She liked a large house? "The older the room, the smaller. Generations of Faircombe lords have built larger additions as the years have gone by."

"Ah." She turned in a circle. "How old is this kitchen?"

He must stop looking at her. He must look somewhere else. He looked around at the kitchen as if he had never seen it before. "Not old. It was rebuilt here… oh, sometime after the Restoration. Not a hundred and fifty years old. But more than a hundred. The last one burned."

"Oh my." She *must* stop making such noises. "We have nothing in New York that is a hundred and fifty years old!

Nothing English or Dutch, anyway." He saw a thought hit her. "Do you suppose native people had such things, and we tore them down?" Her lower lip trembled. "That's so *sad*."

It was sad, but he suspected her emotion was due to wine more than any sudden realizations about what colonists had done. She was capricious drunk as well as sober.

Then she added, "There's an obbul - an obellel - there's a pillar in Constantinople that was ancient before it was even put there. It was thousands of years old before it was even *put* there."

"And when was it put there?"

"Thousands of years ago! Did you know that?"

"I didn't, no." Worried she might trip if she stepped back, he leaned around her to push her stool under the kitchen table.

"No, thank you," she said.

"Excuse me?" Geoffrey straightened.

"No, thank you. Oh, I thought you were going to pick me up and carry me off to bed."

At that, the blood thundered in his ears as if he'd been running. "*What?*"

"I thought you were going to just pick me up and take me away. No thank you, please. I don't mind being carried *or* pushed about in the chair, when I need it. But people think if you don't mind it once you never mind it, and sometimes I mind it." Her face contorted as if she'd sucked a lemon. "At home, my father built a very clever box in the house, so the servants can pull on ropes and haul me up to the next story. It hauls me quite as I imagine stones must have been hauled by the builders of great monuments in Egypt." She shook her head. "It doesn't make me feel particularly human."

"I'm sorry to hear that." He was. It sounded as though her difficulty with movement wasn't new and wasn't temporary.

"Up *four* flights of stairs. Why do they say flights of stairs? I'd *like* to see stairs take flight, but I don't think it happens."

"I don't think so either."

"Louis the Fifteenth had a chamber like that to move his mistress up to his apartments secretly, you know." She tilted her head back to look him in the eye and shook her head slowly from side to side, very deliberately. "I think that's rude."

Geoffrey wanted to ask if she thought it was rude of Louis to have a mistress, or to have her hauled in a box up to his rooms.

She was better company drunk than anyone in his family sober. He decided questions about drugs could wait.

"Miss Rawle," he murmured, "did you require something?"

"I was exploring, as I said. Though now I've found the kitchen, I am hungry. I don't suppose you have any food?" She yawned, covering her mouth with one hand by reflex. "I think I am hungry."

Well. Even a hedonist needed food, and the idea of feeding her appealed. Geoffrey knew the kitchen well, from childhood raids as well as treating sheep. Growing up, he had eaten a *lot*. He'd never prepared food, but how hard could it be?

As it happened, there was quite a bit of food, but he wasn't sure what to take. There was a pea porridge burbling on the side of the coals, but he doubted Miss Rawle's ability to manage a spoon at the moment. There were apples, but only a few; perhaps Mrs. Davies had counted them out of the limited spring stores for some reason?

It was more difficult than it looked, being a servant.

Finally, Geoffrey found a crust of leftover manchet bread, soft and white, wrapped in linen. If it was intended for toast in the morning, someone would have to do without. He located a bowl of butter, too, applied one to the other, and handed it to her, feeling rather accomplished.

Her dark eyes grew wide. "Mmm!" she said, stuffing a huge bite in her mouth all at once.

Then she put it down to toy with the knife he'd used and put down on the table.

"Here, now." It was unsettling to watch her spinning the thing on its side, apparently bewitched by its glitter. He couldn't shake the feeling that she was about to sink it into her own finger, or perhaps her chest.

"It's quite all right, I know how to do this," she said, even more unsettling. And, in between bites of bread and butter, spun the knife again. She leaned forward to peer at it while it spun, heedless of the amount of soft skin that showed when she did.

Fortunately, he'd have a cold walk back to the sheep pens.

Watching her devour the bread, bite by bite, was both oddly satisfying and hunger-making. When it was gone, she spent long moments licking crumbs from her fingertips.

"Shall I fetch your maid?" Ice couldn't hurt him, but there was something dangerous about this Miss Rawle.

"No," she said in the same matter-of-fact tone and stood. "I'm going to take this," she said, grasping the handle of the knife as she started for the door. Was she wobbling? No, she seemed steady enough.

She wasn't his family, not yet. And she was the lady of the house, or nearly. If she wanted to steal kitchen knives, she could.

Yet Geoffrey found his worry for Vere and all of them still left room somewhere inside him to worry a little for the house's drunken new lady.

Then she stopped just inside the door, still on the flagstones, and looked back over her shoulder. Had she been looking for fairies? She looked like one herself. "Good-bye."

"Good night," Geoffrey said softly.

* * *

HE FOLLOWED HER, of course. She made an unerring path through several dark, cavernous chambers to the music room, where she disappeared inside. He waited till she re-emerged with her mother.

"Why do you have a knife?" Geoffrey could just barely hear the elder Mrs. Rawle as they moved slowly arm in arm down the hall.

"They're so handy for toast," Geoffrey faintly heard Miss Rawle say.

"I do hate waking in the middle of the night," grumbled her mother.

"So do I," said the daughter as they disappeared.

Yes, a long, cold walk would do him just fine. His clothes were far more dry. He couldn't spend any more time staring at Guinevere. He'd make the sheep anxious.

No, he was calmer after Miss Rawle's kitchen visit. Listening to her, feeding her, had been soothing, in some odd way.

But he'd take a turn outside before trying to sleep.

CHAPTER 5

"*G*ood morning!"

Jerked awake, deep inside a pile of pillows, linens, and coverlets, Zelda thrust her arms out into space. She pawed at the air to make the noise stop.

Someone yanked open the heavy curtains. Sunbeams slammed across Zelda's eyes.

Her nightdress was not sufficient protection. The fluffy pillows might be, if she dug her head under them. She ought to try that. But who was causing this thundering pandemonium?

She slit open one eye.

"I'm so glad to meet you finally, Miss Rawle," said the curtain-snatcher. "I do apologize that we did not speak yesterday. Lord Faircombe thought you would want a day to recover from your journey."

It was a woman, some woman Zelda had never met, dressed in snowy linen and unnecessary smiles. Zelda's fingers wiggled feebly in the air in front of her face, hoping the vision would go away.

It didn't; it drew nearer to the bed. The woman had her hands folded together at her waist. "I am Mrs. Truett, the housekeeper. We have a very full list of items to attend to today."

"May I… have… you… not here?" Zelda was finally able to string together the words she wanted. Yes, those seemed the right words.

"Ah ha ha ha!" Mrs. Truett's laugh stabbed, too, both eyes and ears. It made Zelda's *brain* throb. Why was her laugh so eye-stabby? "You are so droll, Miss Rawle. Yes, it's a pleasure to finally meet you. I took the liberty of arranging for you to review the staff, as I know you'll want to meet everyone, and then to visit the larder. I have suggestions for dinner and supper, but I do not wish to presume. Of course, now that you are here, you will want to decide such things. I'm fully prepared to explain Lord Faircombe's tastes to you."

Zelda did not want Lord Faircombe's tastes explained to her. She wanted nothing from this woman but silence. She wanted to be alone, and she wanted to find a very deep, dark hole to crawl inside and stay inside until the pounding in her head subsided. That would likely take years.

"Thank you. I don't wish any of that. Tansy?"

Mrs. Truett had a long face, accented by the razory type of nose that gave noses a bad name. Having finished her hearty false laughter, she was having a hard time arranging her face in an acceptable formation for the greeting she was getting.

"Of course, Miss Rawle." The housekeeper's eyes rested pointedly on the floor beside the bed. Zelda had a dim memory of dropping her stays there.

If Mrs. Truett thought Zelda would be swayed by disapproval, she had an educational morning in store.

"Tansy?" Zelda called again.

When Tansy appeared, starched and ready—good, Zelda hated waking her—Zelda waved a hand between her and Mrs. Truett. When even that motion rocked her head, she reduced it to just wiggles of her fingers. "Tansy, Mrs. Truett was just leaving. I am so sorry I won't be able to keep our appointment this morning." Politely, she did not mention that she had not known of any appointment. "You'll show her out with my apologies, won't you?"

As Mrs. Truett was standing right there, this barely qualified as a reasonable dismissal. The razory nose quivered.

But she bore up bravely under what must have been a sore disappointment about how she was going to spend her morning. "Of course, Miss Rawle," she said again, and Zelda could imagine her repeating it *ad infinitum* until the words lost all meaning. She pictured it in print: *Of course Miss Rawle, Of course Miss Rawle, Of course Miss Rawle...* "At your convenience, of course. I can see that you must be... indisposed. Let us pursue the topic of housekeeping at a later time."

"Thank you so much. You are so gracious." Zelda waited until Mrs. Truett had crossed the vast floor and Tansy had shut the door after her.

"Thank you, Tansy. I would like to die quietly now, so please don't admit anyone else."

"I won't, Miss Rawle." Tansy truly did look apologetic. "I'm so sorry I did not lock this door. Should I lock it now?"

Zelda sighed assent as she pulled the coverlets over her head and stuck out just one hand to wave it magnanimously. "No apology necessary, truly," she said from the depths of the bed.

Then wonderful quiet settled, in wonderful dark, and Zelda had time and space to contemplate the previous night's decisions. Though she did not believe in looking backward, when one woke feeling like this, it was prudent.

Had she talked to a giant in a fairy kitchen last night?

They'd been inches apart. She had been *alone with him;* she remembered quite well. Nothing untoward had happened.

Well, of course not, some functioning part of her mind snapped, *what sort of untoward thing would you have* wanted *to happen?*

That was an interesting question.

She'd never spent much time imagining untoward things, as she hadn't planned to indulge in them; but this morning it seemed practically urgent.

"Tansy," she said again from deep inside the pillows.

"Yes?"

Zelda had to somehow shake the feeling of being out of place. She intended to be out of place for the rest of her life; she couldn't afford to start disliking it now. "Would you be kind enough to ask downstairs for a large bouquet of flowers to be sent to Lord Vere's apartments with my compliments?"

Tansy was truly prim and proper. Zelda listened to her silence.

"It's a—" Zelda wanted to explain it was a gift in return for the flower she'd gotten last night, but that would take too long, and besides no one knew about that but her and her intended. She enjoyed having a secret with him, even if she wasn't going to keep him. It made her feel more loyal. "All the flowers, Tansy, all the flowers you can get."

"Of course, Miss Rawle."

From Tansy, it wasn't as distressing.

"Good. Thank you." Zelda sank back into the pillows. "I'm going to stay here and quietly die."

* * *

"What the devil are you doing?"

Someone was kicking Geoffrey's boot and asking him yet again what he was doing. As if he knew.

He was busy not being a lord, in a borrowed shepherd boy's bed. Couldn't they tell?

Then a dog licked Geoffrey's face. A familiar dog. "Chump. Stop."

Dandy tried again. "Hey. What the hell are you doing sleeping?"

"What, I can't sleep now? You can't fool me. Servants do sleep." Geoffrey squinted. Dandy stood at the foot of the bed and squinted right back.

The sun was high. That was only to be expected, he supposed, when he'd spent much of the night moping at the alehouse with Dandy, then snuck into his own kitchen, only to have a most extraordinary conversation with the new mistress of the house.

No one could have called it a successful night.

Except for the boy Russ. That memory came back; and it felt good. Geoffrey was glad he'd been there to help. What a tough little lad, rallying like that.

His bad mood was ebbing when Dandy kicked his boot again. It came back.

The reward of defying his father was palpable. He liked the sheep pens when he left them and went back to his warm room. His warm *tub*.

Now the earthy animal smell had crawled all through him; it probably clung to his *hair*. His floor was packed earth instead of ancient oak, his ceiling was thatch with sparrows nesting in it, and outside sheep bawled and men shouted.

It was uncomfortable enough to be cut from the family. All the rest of these discomforts were just piled-on insults.

Geoffrey scowled. "You *suggested* I sleep here. And I can check on Guinevere here."

Which sheep then shoved her way past Dandy to stare at him suspiciously, square muzzle slowly chewing hay.

"It's not *my* fault," he told the glaring sheep. At least she was eating.

Dandy judged the ewe's chewing. "She's definitely got three lambs in her."

Geoffrey restrained an oath. "I don't want to lose her because she's got three." With a groan, he pushed himself upright. He ached all over—was that from the cold of the pond last night, the exertion, or simply sleeping in a shepherd boy's bed?

He hadn't thought the bed would hold him, or that if it did, the thing would still stand in the morning. But the bed was heavy and well joined, with a large straw tick that must have been fairly recently refreshed. "That boy doesn't need a bed this big. He doesn't need a third of it. Unless he's been up to things I don't know about."

"If you've got girls on the mind, get out of Bernie's bed. He's too young for impure thoughts."

"He's sixteen, Dandy. He has impure thoughts."

Geoffrey stretched anyway and swung his feet to the ground. His mouth tasted of dust; he needed a shave. And he wanted breakfast. And coffee.

He'd slept in his *boots*.

Dandy watched. "Going to the house to fix things with your father?"

"Fix what? That he's an ass?" Geoffrey scratched his chin; it itched. The world did look better with his feet on the ground.

If he couldn't wash, shave, or break his fast, at least he was still at Faircombe.

"I still don't see why Lord Faircombe doesn't want me here."

Dandy sucked on his teeth. "Same reason a carriage can't

have two lead horses. You can have two on the front, sure, but one's gotta follow the other."

"I'm not the lead horse. I've never been a lead horse."

The shed was built into the hillside; Dandy had left its simple panel door open to let in light. Now the bright sunlight was blocked by a woman's figure.

"What the hell are you doing?" asked Charlotte.

Why did people keep asking him that? Geoffrey spread his arms. "You can see me, can't you?"

He could barely see her with the sun was behind her; he squinted. Charlotte obliged him by coming in. She had to take off her riding bonnet to do it.

She picked her way through the tufts of hay on the floor and gave him a questioning eyebrow.

He tried a more informative answer. "I'm watching the sheep."

"Going a bit too far, I think," she observed, looking about the spartan place and noticing Guinevere watching *him*.

That was typical of Charlotte, not realizing that she insulted Bernie's quarters, and by extension, Dandy's across the yard.

Delina was usually sympathetic, but Charlotte was chancy. Geoffrey decided not to explain his night last night. Firstly, he couldn't. But second, if there was genuine trouble ahead for him with his brother, he didn't want Charlotte to catch any share of it.

"You can't *want* to look this common," said Charlotte, cementing his determination not to confide in her.

"Charlotte, do you recall the conversation we had last winter about not being so obviously haughty?"

"You're sleeping in straw."

Geoffrey patted the straw tick. "It was comfortable. We ought to adopt them in the house. The straw cradles one very accommodatingly."

"I'm not sleeping in goat food and that's the end of that." Charlotte's profile tilted a little higher. In her fine riding costume and boots, Geoffrey couldn't imagine her sleeping in a shed, that was true.

But then he couldn't normally imagine it of himself either. It had only been weeks since he'd squired Charlotte around London in search of a husband. It was astonishing how quickly one's life could change.

"You sleep in the clippings of sheep coats," he said absently, his heart not in it.

"What *are* you doing? Del said Father put you out of the house? I'm surprised you didn't go to London." Charlotte peered out at the rolling green that swept away from the chewed earth of the sheep pens and met the sky. "One can barely see the hall from here."

"What would you do if I went to London?"

Charlotte peered at him with the same sort of blank confusion she had just used on the lawns. "The same thing I'll do even though you're here. I have Lord Pillit's horse to take trotting, and then Mr. Caprica's gelding to take round the jumping range. He is learning not to balk at a fence, finally, though I doubt he'll ever be a hunter."

"What do you care? You hate fox hunting anyway."

"Yes," his sister said more gently, "I do." She watched him shove himself to his feet; he bent his neck to keep his head below the thatched roof. "Geoffrey, you know me so well. But I'm quite a grown woman. We settled that in London, and I'm happy with my life. We're not in the nursery, and you needn't look after me. Is that the only reason you're here?"

"You might need me." Geoffrey felt like he couldn't make a good case with his neck bent over so he didn't scrape along the thatching. "Or Frederick might come home."

"You really think that?"

"And I'm not at all sure about this American woman for Vere. What if she traps him into a terrible life?"

"Do you think Vere is having a wonderful life now?" As always, there was Charlotte, blunt to the point of unpleasantness. "Are *you?*"

"He's awright. He's going to clean sheep's feet," put in Dandy.

"I beg your pardon?" Geoffrey craned around to look at the old man.

"You're going to clean sheep's feet. Can't shear them while it's this cold and they're lambing. Still plenty to do. We're going to move all the good ones to the new paddock. Feed the orphans and clean the sheep's feet." Dandy looked quite calm as he said it. "And one cow has an udder gone bad. Though before you do any of that, there's a goose with a bad eye."

Charlotte stared at Dandy, then at Geoffrey. "You can't stay here."

"Charlotte, do you have the least idea what I do most days? They need help," he said, spreading his arms to indicate all the creatures bleating outside this shed and all the ones wandering the property, cropping the grass.

Though usually he would only have tended to the sick creatures. Dandy was piling it on a bit.

Charlotte looked appalled. "Is that *always* how you choose how to spend your time? Who needs help?"

"Isn't that the best way to choose?" Still half-bent, he made for the door.

Dandy was right. He needed to keep busy. While he looked round for the ailing goose, he'd contemplate the homeless life of a marquess' son who slept in borrowed straw.

And he absolutely would not return to the house to check

on Miss Rawle just because she *might* need some help. She'd be fine.

* * *

ZELDA HAD MADE her way slowly down the hall, not because her joints hurt, though of course they did, but because she was afraid her head might roll under one of the larger pieces of furniture and be quite difficult to get out.

She ought to have had a tray and eaten in bed, she told herself for the dozenth time. But if she developed the habit of simply staying in bed when she felt unwell, she'd die there. The world was too large for that.

She might have lost bits and pieces of the conversation with her giant, but on the whole, she remembered it quite well. It had come back to her when she'd found a kitchen knife on her dressing table next to slightly butter-stained gloves.

She put both in the dressing-table drawer with the compass and the blue-stone ring.

He'd given her bread and butter. Pulled out a chair for her —well, a stool. And he'd given her something of the history of the house.

This room must be quite new, then, as it was so large. At least new by Britain's standards. She'd meant what she told him; she knew the signs of old Lenape life in Manhattan quite well. Her father was one of the Buttonwood men, and she'd visited Wall Street many times. The actual wall was long gone; only wooden butts from the trees that had formed it remained, tamped between the cobblestones.

She'd seen a print of Lenape houses, long low buildings supposedly once covering the shores of Manhattan; but when she'd gone north on the post road for a convalescent summer on the Hudson, she'd seen no houses like that, though Lenape people still lived all along the route.

Now why had she never thought about that in New York?

Constantinople had a pillar that had been ancient when it arrived, but New York loved tearing down its history. She wasn't sure how she felt about that. She wasn't sure how she felt about a house that simply kept adding layers like the shell of a snail, either.

Then she wanted to laugh at herself. She wasn't satisfied when the Faircombe receiving hall was so much like her father's at home; then she wasn't best pleased when she couldn't find similarities between the old British home and the ones Manhattan used to feature, if indeed that were true. They were all foolish fancies, like flocked wall papers, that others wouldn't understand. She'd keep those to herself.

She was still crossing one of the meadow-like carpets when she met Lord Vere coming the other way.

He'd received her present of flowers. He must have. That would explain the pleased little smile he gave her.

As she drew closer, she saw him surveying her demure pink walking gown, and realized he was pleased over that. Had her dress yesterday offended him *so* much? So much that it occupied more of his mind than her gift?

"Miss Rawle." He pulled himself up smartly. He was really quite tall, not giant-sized, but for a mortal fellow, tall enough.

Zelda had never thought about it before, but she was beginning to discover her attraction to a man with some height.

She gripped the head of her cane and fought the urge to twist her hands together the way she had as a little girl. It was only the set of his head that rattled her, she decided. It had unassailed confidence, did Lord Vere's head. "My lord."

"I see you have unpacked some more suitable costumes. You must be so much more comfortable."

Comfortable again. Zelda looked down at her gown. She wore coral beads, too, at her neck and wrist, and liked those better than the dress. "It's adequate."

"I'm sorry I had to take such stern measures last night, but presumably the point has been made and we need speak no more about it."

"What point?"

"Erm, eh…" And his confidence just… crumbled away. The dashingly tall Lord Vere turned into a hand-twisting schoolboy himself.

It did make Zelda more comfortable, seeing him give in to the urge she'd just had. "If you've made a point, surely you can repeat the point?"

"No, I don't think so," he surprised her by saying, "suffice it to say that it was made."

"Surely."

"Thank you." He nodded.

"It's been made."

"Yes."

"Though not to me, because I haven't any idea what it was."

"Yes… yes?" This thoroughly bent his shoulders. "Ah hah."

Surely she could rescue her intended from a little social discomfort? Now that he was a person, and not merely words on paper, Zelda felt a twinge at the idea of marrying him and sailing off just after. They ought to be friends at least, Zelda thought. And there was something sweet there that thought of giving her flowers in the first place.

They needed to spend some time alone. They had many things to resolve.

Well, in the beginning of a negotiation, her father was open and quick. Zelda would adopt his model; she had no other. "Lord Vere, do you think we might spend some time together later today? If you are not otherwise engaged, of course."

"Miss Rawle, I assure you that you are the only person to whom I am engaged."

The way Lord Vere said it made Zelda immediately suspect that he had attachments elsewhere. "How do you amuse yourself during the day, if I may ask?"

"Oh, the usual ways! Usually in town, I must say, where I generally play cards…" His words trailed away as he changed his mind about what to share about his interests. "But here I go riding, as all Eliots do."

"So fortunate for me that I was not born an Eliot, then, as I don't think the activity would suit me."

"But you will be as much an Eliot as anyone once the contracts are signed, banns read, and ceremony performed."

"You believe so? That's kind of you. I suspect those born to the name will still have slightly more claim to it than I might gain through a ceremony."

"Less, actually," muttered Lord Vere, and looked out one of the distant windows.

"So, shall we say we have an engagement? I mean, this afternoon. Later. I am in no way ready, but later this afternoon?"

When they looked into each other's eyes, she found herself smiling. And he smiled back.

"Yes, why not? Why not indeed?" said the Earl of Vere and Baron Culwer. He was a stiff sort of fellow, but not so bad. And he echoed her new motto. *Why not?*

* * *

SHE HELD on to that feeling all the way to the small breakfasting room, after first going to the dining room. A footman there told her that wood paneling and murderous crystal weren't fit for late-morning meals.

"Ah, Miss Farsworth," she said as she finally stepped into the sunny little room filled with the scents of sausages, boiled eggs, and toast.

She thought of feeling the walls, but didn't.

"Miss Rawle." That was all. The little woman went back to violently buttering her toast. The flash of the knife brought back Zelda's headache.

"Your morning has already gone awry?" Because that was clear enough. Whatever ailed her had nothing to do with Zelda; Zelda had just got here.

"Every flower in the place has gone missing. The staff know to have bouquets in my drawing room, the receiving room, and the yellow parlor at the very least. None today, none. I would say there's a flower thief, but who would do such a thing?"

"Oh dear." Zelda had the very specific disorienting sensation one has when one has done something unforgivably empty-headed, followed by the sick and sorrowful knowledge that she wasn't going to admit to it at all. "Why does it concern you so?"

"I use them to draw, Miss Rawle. A flower makes a very interesting and agreeable subject; it has a great many different surfaces and shadows, it doesn't move, and it doesn't talk."

"Ah." Zelda wanted to remark that whoever had done it must surely not have known about that, because otherwise they would never have done it. But likely everyone in the house did know.

Including the staff she'd asked to send all the flowers to Lord Vere's room.

Clearly, they hadn't explained to Miss Farsworth.

Now Zelda grasped the power, and the danger, of her

position; the staff would clearly happily inconvenience a woman who'd lived here for years at the behest of the heir's new wife.

Which made some sense as she'd intended to please him, but they weren't yet married, and the effort had been a waste. Perhaps he was just shy?

"Might I offer you some other amusement, as a—" Drat, if she said *apology* that would incriminate her as well. "As a solace?"

"What other amusement?" Miss Farsworth paused in her violent buttering and blinked at the newcomer.

"Ah… I've no idea. I've just engaged to spend the afternoon with Lord Vere. He seems to wish to do something with horses."

"Horses." The way Miss Farsworth gave her toast a last scrape was truly vindictive. "Every Eliot is mad for horses. And they're useless. They won't stand still for five minutes and they're far too big."

"The Eliots?"

Miss Farsworth glared. "*Horses* are useless. Though now you mention it, the Eliots can be quite similar to them. Not every Eliot is devoted to horses, but too many for comfort."

"Really? What Eliots aren't devoted to horses?" Zelda thought she remembered hearing that Lady Charlotte adored them, and both Lord Vere and Lord Faircombe were obviously of the same stripe.

Miss Farsworth paused in crunching her toast. She looked around, as if the paper hangings were as distracting to her as they were to Zelda.

"I don't believe Lady Faircombe was that fond," she said quickly, and cracked her egg with her knife.

Zelda thought. What else might have flowing surfaces and interesting shadows that Miss Farsworth could draw? As she was clearly out of sorts from losing her daily flowers.

"Why don't you draw the laundry?"

"Pardon me?"

Zelda waved a hand in a way that suggested a fluttering sheet. "Shadows, surfaces, and they neither move nor talk."

"Hmm."

The way Miss Farsworth visibly brightened made Zelda's headache recede almost completely. "I look forward to your laundry-themed art, Miss Farsworth, I expect it to be quite interesting."

* * *

"Did you find that goose?"

"No." Geoffrey hadn't expected to feel so awkward, being among the servants. After all, he'd worked alongside them before. But now it had changed, they all knew it, and it felt stamped on his face.

It was different when he had nowhere else to go.

He'd settled the cow, but he hadn't yet brought himself to venture across the grounds in his current state. Gritty and discouraged, he wanted a wash, but had skipped it when he saw the men behind the stable breaking ice atop a communal tub.

It was one thing to work with the sheep; it was another not to be able to do anything else.

"That goose won't heal itself. Bernie sees to the geese, and you're using his bed, so..." Dandy made little walking motions with his fingers.

"I'm starving."

Dandy eyed Geoffrey's bulk. "Not so's you'd notice. G'wan, get after it, and I'll get you a share of the bread and soup."

Geoffrey didn't want bread and soup. He wanted sausage and coffee. He left before he said so.

Once he got his stride going, it wasn't so bad.

One thing that surprised him was how the constant wave of anger lapping at his feet was just... gone. That must be why he spent so little time in the house even before he'd been tossed out, he mused as he walked. There was no chance out here he'd encounter his father.

The walk was calming, the sun clear, and nearly every blade of grass held a memory. He'd been a little boy with his siblings, running over this grass so many years ago. He had no claim to the house or the grounds, but the memories were his.

He did find the geese marching self-importantly across the Faircombe lawns. The one that thrust its head at Geoffrey like a knife, that was the one; it tried to frighten Geoffrey off with flapping wings and angry hisses.

It was a handsome bird, a gander, and it would have looked regal at rest, with its shining gray head and striped neck feathers. But it wasn't at rest, and looked like it wouldn't be any time soon.

"Shut it," Geoffrey muttered as he grabbed the goose finally, sweeping its body up in his arms. Tucking it close to his ribs, he grabbed the beak with the other hand so it wouldn't peck at him.

Yes, the eye was swollen closed. He headed for the pond in front of the hall. The water was cleaner there than in the troughs, he thought.

"It won't be any huge thing to mend." He found himself explaining things to the goose while he walked. Well, it listened as well as his father. Or Vere.

He paused for a moment, kneeling at the pond's edge, careful not to take out his frustrations about everything he couldn't control on a bird he could. When he dunked its head in the cold water, he was careful not to submerge the beak.

"Wnggh!" squalled the goose, trying to whack him in the head with its wings, but Geoffrey did not let go.

"I know, nasty business," he murmured with some sympathy now, but just submerged the head again, careful to swish it slightly in the chilly water.

When the goose came up again, the eye was red, but open.

"Well. Whatever you got in there, we'll have to pay attention."

Who was we? There was no one but him.

When he let the goose go, it flapped its wide striped wings, honked its irritation, and walked off, shaking its head.

Just more disapproval, he thought, but with a smile.

Reluctant to eat the rough breakfast despite the growling of his stomach, as it would mean he'd given up hope of anything better, Geoffrey followed the goose. It waddled past the older wing, and he looked toward the breakfast room. Was Miss Rawle in there cracking an egg with those delicate little hands? Or would Vere do that for her?

Perhaps she *couldn't* crack an egg. She hadn't seemed that weak last night. He must find out what plagued her.

He walked a wide circle, passing the mews where the hunting birds lived, the kitchen gardens, and of course the stables. Where was his father?

It was oddly good to think *nowhere close,* even as the house beckoned.

There was Charlotte at her task, riding a horse out of the pens, just as she'd said. Working, just like him; but she'd eventually return to the house. Their *home*. His good mood faded a little.

Well, he might be better off out here.

When he looked toward the stonemasons building yet another wing on the hall, he noticed a fluffy white shape. It had ventured closer to the stacked cut stone, where there should be no fluffy white shape.

Geoffrey strode after the fluffy white shape.

By the time he reached it, a mason was threatening the sheep with a hammer. Apparently too stupid to know that the sheep was even more stupid, and wouldn't care.

Geoffrey couldn't identify every sheep on sight, but he thought he knew this one. A placid, vacant ewe with a yen to wander. Her lamb was at her tail. She'd lambed three weeks ago, he thought, and her baby's size confirmed it.

"Come on, lass, come on," he said as he approached. Most of the Faircombe sheep knew his voice well enough to at least notice him when he called.

If this one did, she couldn't be bothered.

The mason swung the hammer again, this time more viciously.

Geoffrey was close enough with a lunge to stop it with his hand.

The mason looked up. It was the same man who'd taunted him at the inn.

"It's a sheep," Geoffrey said, one huge hand wrapped around the hammer head that might have given the sheep a fearful blow.

"I can see it's a sheep!" The man recognized Geoffrey, too, by the red in his face.

"It's not your sheep," Geoffrey went on, as if perhaps the man didn't know that.

"I suppose it's *yours*."

Strictly speaking, Geoffrey didn't have a sheep to his name. But he'd be damned before he'd let someone hurt it, no matter whose sheep it was.

"I wouldn't damage a Faircombe sheep if I were you." Geoffrey only let the hammer go, and his words were mild. Still, the mason took them as the threat they absolutely were. Sometimes Geoffrey's size worked for him.

"It's in the way."

Geoffrey looked at the animal, placidly chewing grass and, yes, watching the mason with a blank sheepy stare. "She likes you," he said before he thought.

That made the man's face even redder. The implied affection of a sheep was too much for him. He swung the hammer back.

Geoffrey just calmly stepped between him and the sheep. "Can't imagine why she likes you," he said, and gave the man a second to think about what he was about to do.

CHAPTER 6

*W*as that her giant outside those French windows?

Men were working out there, fitting stones together in a way that seemed mysterious to Zelda, but those men were just blobs of clothing and tools. It was the blond giant that caught her eye, out there speaking to a stonemason.

A voice sounded behind her. "Ah, Miss Rawle. I must consult you about dinner."

"Must you?"

Mrs. Truett had the knack of most appalling people, turning up at just the wrong moment to ask things Zelda couldn't answer. And her demand for attention prevented Zelda from craning her neck around to see what the giant was doing.

"Yes. Lord Faircombe has very specific tastes in—"

Whirled around by inspiration, Zelda said in a rush, "Mrs. Truett, what is the most entertaining dish you've ever had?"

Mrs. Truett's chin withdrew almost into her neck. "I beg your pardon?"

"Something that made you sit at the table and say, *ah*, this is something. I will never forget this."

Mrs. Truett appeared to have to think for a long, long moment. "I saw an aspic tower in London once," she finally said, slowly, "clear gelatine, a foot and a half high, with pink scallops of fish and red tomatoes embedded in it. It was very pretty."

"My!" Zelda turned to give her a look of surprised approval. She hadn't expected such a satisfying answer. "There you are, Mrs. Truett. Build a table around that. Such a dish cannot fail to entertain his lordship, can it?"

The idea of *entertaining* anyone seemed never to have occurred to Mrs. Truett. She turned it over in her mind now. She thought, and thought some more, and then finally she said, "I'll speak to the cook, madam."

"Good. Please do. I'm in such a hurry. Thank you, Mrs. Truett!"

And Zelda sailed out the French windows before the housekeeper could ask anything else about menus.

* * *

"The stone is beautiful."

Miss Rawle, arrayed in bonnet, gloves, and a long quilted walking coat closed with golden clasps, leaned over the edge of the portico. She smiled at the mason too, but smiled longer at Geoffrey.

Instantly, he felt on alert. "You oughtn't be out here, Miss Rawle."

"Oh, I shall be warm enough for a moment!" she assured him, airily waving a gloved hand, as if the chill were her only concern in the world. The huge diamond she wore over her glove winked in the sun as she turned to the mason. "The stone-building is beautiful work. Do you think it will last a thousand years?"

In the face of such a specific question, the mason reluctantly lowered his hammer. He didn't so much as bob his head to the lady, and Geoffrey wanted to bristle. But the man did say, "It's Portland stone. It'll outlast us all."

The young lady only nodded, the feathers on her bonnet bobbing as she looked up and up the pillars. "No competition for Egyptian obelisks, but very pretty."

This confused the mason into silence.

She went on, "I hope that sheep isn't giving you any trouble?"

Geoffrey looked from the placid ewe back up to Miss Rawle, leaning over the low stone balustrade. Leaning quite far. He was both glad and sad that her coat buttoned up to her neck. "The sheep's cooperative enough."

Miss Rawle pointed at the lamb. "I thought animals with babies became quite fierce."

Geoffrey hid his smile by bending over and picking up the lamb. In two steps, he reached over the balustrade himself, as it stood barely above his waist, and placed the little creature at Miss Rawle's feet.

The fuzzy fellow took a moment to adjust to the new location, and then, apparently taking Miss Rawle's coat for another lamb, head-butted her right in the shins.

Seized with worry, Geoffrey gripped the stone balustrade as if to vault it.

But Miss Rawle only laughed.

She bent down and rubbed the little lamb right at the top of its head. Blissful, it rubbed back, then leaped straight into the air on all four feet. Landing, it darted away across the marble portico.

Miss Rawle glanced briefly to be certain that the ewe was not enraged, then followed the lamb.

Slack-faced, the stonemason gaped at Geoffrey as if to say *What are you doing?*

Tired of that question, Geoffrey followed the lamb, too.

* * *

"OH NO!"

Zelda could hear the giant approach, but had her hands full. The garden bench was deep as a bed, but also a perfect height for the lamb to run under. The little creature raced in happy circles under there, heedless of its sharp tiny feet ripping the curtain's edges.

She scrambled to pull the curtains up on the bench itself. *Heiress ruins curtains, sheep* was all she could think.

Her face must have shown her concern, because the giant took the problem literally out of her hands. He scooped his enormous arms around the entire mass of fabric, lifted it, and dropped it on the wooden seat. "It's fine," was all he said.

"Oh, *thank* you," said Zelda, lowering herself down with both hands on the bench's edge. The pain in her knees nearly stopped her, but she kept going. She'd never seen a lamb so close.

There it was, a black spot on the hind leg, dashing back and forth under the bench as if discovering the world's best game.

"Is it a boy or a girl?" She must sound more sane, and sober, today.

"Entirely hypothetical."

Well, that was an odd answer. Zelda's eyes followed the lamb; but it wasn't telling.

It saw her staring and stopped. All four feet planted. Its little loaf-shaped head turned her way. "Beaahhh," it bleated, its tiny tongue stuck straight out.

Zelda couldn't help it. She laughed so hard she fell over.

"Miss Rawle?" The giant seemed concerned, but Zelda just rocked on her back, her hat's feathers brushing the marble as she shook with helpless laughter. That little *face*. That amazing *noise*.

The lamb seemed as surprised by her helpless laughter as the giant, and darted out from under the bench to butt her again, this time in the thigh.

"Here now," the shepherd said, scooping it up in one massive hand.

Just then, a lumbering sheep, wide as a table, came up the marble stairs. Her belly swayed like a ship on the sea. And upon seeing the lamb, she said "Beaahh!" too, but with a deep voice like an angry sailor.

Zelda fell about laughing again.

The shepherd bent over her. "...shall I help you up?"

"In a moment." The stone was cold, her slippers not thick enough. But Zelda wanted to stay in the memory a moment longer. She'd be laughing for days, every time those memories crossed her mind. "Beaahhhh!" she called at the mama sheep, who said "Beaahhh!" right back.

She pointed with a mittened hand. "Help the mama, would you? She is worried, even if she does sound like an old sailor. Do let the baby go."

"It didn't hurt you?"

"Not at all."

The giant bent way, way down to put the lamb on the ground again, and after a little skidding on the stone, the lamb scampered to its mother.

Then the shepherd turned to her.

"I'm perfectly willing to simply place you on the bench." He had a warm, gentle voice as plush as his sheepskin vest. "But I recall that sometimes you want help, and sometimes you don't."

"Yes, it's fine," Zelda said carelessly, still catching her

breath from laughing so hard, expecting him to offer her a hand. The chill of the stone was leaching through her clothes.

Instead of a hand, a whole arm came round her shoulders, as solid as an oak beam. Another slid under her knees.

And all in a rush, he swept Zelda up off the chilly stone and up into his arms.

Time stopped. Her body was suspended, then pressed against his. Warmth washed over her, and she wasn't sure if it emanated from his massive body against her shoulder, her hip, her thigh, or if something had been ignited in her as well.

He smelled of leather and wool, cool water and smoky fires, all at the same time. Zelda wanted to relax into his scent, his arms. *He* felt strong enough to outlast an Egyptian obelisk.

She didn't imagine it; he held her, longer than needed to simply move her off the ground. He *held* her, and it was the opposite of alarming.

Slowly, he leaned over the garden bench and set her down. Even her feet were no longer touching the cold stone. But the bench wasn't warm the way he had been warm.

Zelda fought the urge to ask him to pick her up again.

* * *

"THANK YOU," and she sounded a little breathless. No doubt from laughing so hard.

Sheep needed their feet checked from time to time to make sure no stones got wedged between their toes. Their ears, their skin, their wool had to be inspected, and the insides of the mouth.

He'd learned that habit, that was all; that was why Geoffrey didn't want to put down his armful of soft, wriggling woman, and why he had this urge to start at her toes and inspect her all the way up till he was lost in all that long, dark hair.

"You are welcome."

"I will remember all this." She sat with her feet tucked together on the dark wood, wrapped her arms around her knees.

"I've only showed you a lamb."

She looked up and her eyes met his and Geoffrey knew it wasn't only the lamb. "You must tell me your name."

He was christened Lord Geoffrey Augustus Townsend Eliot, third son of the most honorable Marquess of Faircombe and Lady Faircombe, granddaughter of a duke.

"It's Geoffrey," was all he said.

"Geoffrey." She laid her knees to one side and turned to look at him, a Cleopatra in linen today. "I won't forget."

How did she spin so quickly from unbridled glee to wistful innocence to sly siren? They all drew him closer, and that was exactly what he didn't need.

He'd already been tossed from his home because of her. It wasn't fair to blame her; still he felt wary.

Why didn't *she*?

It wasn't looking good for the Faircombe family that Miss Rawle had no sense of proper restraint at all.

Tearing his eyes away from the depths of hers, Geoffrey noticed for the first time that the stonemason had gone. He frowned at the stoneworks creeping within yards of this portico. "You should be wary of the workmen, Miss Rawle."

"Should I?" She looked out over the stoneworks, the lawns, the maze garden, with the untroubled gaze of someone who had known worry but never real danger. "He seemed harmless."

"He's not."

That slow, sly smile again. "You mean he may distract me

with a baby animal and then, when I am off my guard, sweep me off my feet?"

"That's not—That isn't what—"

"That is precisely what happened."

"*Not* intended as such, I assure you."

Her smile wavered a little as she looked down at her hands. "Oh," he heard her say faintly, as if it were a pity.

Yes, quite dangerous for the Eliots, and dangerous for her as well. He needed to sit down with this young woman and have a long, long talk. Better yet, her mother should do it. Where was Mrs. Rawle's sense of responsibility? Miss Rawle had no more self-preservation than the lamb.

"Miss Rawle, you must have a care for yourself."

She nodded, still without looking up. "I would like to have a care for myself. Yes, that is what I *would* like." Without putting out her hand for help, Miss Rawle slid to the edge of the bench and carefully rose. Geoffrey looked about for her cane, but it was nowhere to be seen.

She saw him looking; she must have guessed what he sought.

"I'd like to *suit* myself." She drew herself up. "I *am* capable."

"Undoubtedly." Money had not made her that way, or at least not money alone. Geoffrey would bet that Miss Griselda Rawle had come into the world able to decide about herself for herself.

Her secret eyes slid his way, and a sliver of the smile returned. "I stole a compass, you know."

There was no reason at all for that to make him want to laugh, and scold, and haul her up into his arms again. But it did.

Why was such a bewitching woman betrothed to his brother? There she stood, all soft dark hair and ruffled collar, announcing proudly that she'd stolen a compass.

"Why?" Against his better judgment, he really wanted to know.

The breeze played with a lock of her hair, brushing its dark swirl against her cheek. "I can tell you, surely? Because you won't repeat it, and you aren't likely to converse with Lord Vere anyway, are you?"

She thought he was a servant. She really did. All that had made him a gentleman was to be in the house.

Geoffrey just nodded, unable to summon words.

Miss Rawle had all the words. "Because I am going all around the world, Geoffrey. Have you ever looked at a globe?"

He could only nod again.

"I am going northeast from here, to Amsterdam, or I will go by the southern route if I must, and around the last of the Empire to Russia. I am going south to see Anatolia and Greece, then go through Constantinople before I sail down the coast of Africa to Mozambique and Madagascar. I will take the trade wind ships to India, then up to China before going east to New Holland and the islands scattered so far from one another that it beggars the imagination that ships can sail among them. I am going to see Cape Horn, then sail up by Chile and Peru and cross Amazonia to see Brazil. I am going to lie on sunny sand in Mexico, sail along its coast, and when the United States are in sight again..." Her gaze returned from far away and she smiled, this time a simple, sunny smile that he'd never seen on her before. "Why, I shall just keep going."

Stunned, Geoffrey could only stare at her, dark hair curling against one soft cheek.

The latch turned on one of the French windows. Without thinking, Geoffrey flattened himself against the wall behind it.

Mrs. Rawle came out and did not see him. She frowned at

the raw spring breeze, and the young lady with arms wrapped around herself despite her quilted armor. "You must come in, Griselda; the sun is lovely, but it is much too cold."

"Yes," said Miss Rawle, but didn't do it.

Her mother simply disappeared inside, leaving the door open.

Satisfied that she had chosen her own moment, Miss Rawle looked out over the garden one more time. The ewe and lamb had wandered toward its hedges; they bleated to one another, one squeaky high, the other a bass note, and Miss Rawle smiled again.

Then she turned. She gave Geoffrey one clear, long look, letting him know she knew he was there, that he had just hidden from her mother, and that she was choosing this moment to leave him, too.

Then she went inside and latched the door.

He had to chase that ewe back toward the lawns and away from the garden. That was what he had to do.

He forced his feet down the steps, shooed the ewe in front of him around the extending stonework and away across the bright spring grass.

He had to look like a shepherd.

But his mind was whirling round and round one simple thought.

He had wholly underestimated the extent to which Miss Rawle had no idea what was happening to her.

"The picnic is ready."

The courtyard flagstones made a dull gray mosaic underfoot; two wings of Faircombe Hall marched down either side of it, forcing even the wind to go around.

Lord Vere stood at the bottom of the courtyard steps, dressed to hat and gloves and already looking impatient. Zelda wanted to turn right around and go back to her rooms.

She wanted to go right back to her giant.

The sensation of his arms closing around her should have been terrifying. Instead, she'd felt not just safe, but peaceful.

Her giant—Geoffrey, rather—was beginning to be a real problem.

Why had she blurted out her whole dream to a shepherd? He wouldn't tell, but that didn't feel like the only reason she'd done it. She had wanted to open up to him, tell him things, give him things. She'd never had *any* of these urges with a man before.

"Miss Rawle?" Lord Vere addressed her again.

Zelda looked about. Several servants carried baskets. Lord Vere carried nothing. His thighs in those trousers might have been vaguely intriguing, had she not been in Geoffrey's arms a short while ago.

It was becoming difficult to remember why funding her travel through marriage had seemed like a good idea.

Still, it was the plan she had. And she'd asked for this outing. She must get to know this man if she was to marry him. "Where shall we go?"

Lord Vere looked pleased with himself. "We will visit the edge of the woods; there's a good view there over the ponds."

"Will we?" Zelda couldn't see what trees he meant. Just rolling grass, dotted with sheep.

"That way," said Lord Vere, hand flicking carelessly toward nothing.

Setting off over the green toward nothing? She'd rather meet the sheep. Perhaps they all sounded like cigar-smoking sailors.

Explaining her reluctance didn't appeal. But she had to

say something. "Lord Vere, you surely realize I don't walk that far."

"Yes, of course, it isn't far at all."

Wasn't far? She couldn't see it. That was farther than Zelda usually walked in a day, though she'd wandered the halls of this house and suffered no ill effects.

Zelda could close her eyes and see again all those maps in the map room. The whole world would just be brown lines and blue ones unless she could prove everyone wrong and live as big a life as she could see in her dreams.

Determination pulled her upright.

She'd walked out of that Bowling Green house. Out of New York and their expectations about poor Miss Rawle.

"Yes, of course," she said, trying to make it sound careless, and set off across the flagstones.

CHAPTER 7

The sun had warmed the grass, and Zelda could feel
its springiness under the soles of her shoes. She
would have paused to enjoy it, but Lord Vere kept pressing
on.

"Are you quite well?" he asked every fourth step, and
Zelda knew he'd have marched away had he not been waiting
for her.

She considered explaining the nature of an illness that
never left her, but she didn't have the breath.

"Yes," was all she said to him, because she refused to say
no and his demeanor allowed for no subtlety.

The servants followed along behind, mincing their steps
to keep pace with her too, and awareness of that bore down
on her. Inside, she was still the Zelda that surfaced so easily
in front of giants or after wine; but outside, she turned into a
struggling thing.

World explorer stopped after fifty feet. No, she wouldn't be.
She kept at it, and after some yards, she thought her limbs
swung a little more easily. She loosened her grip on her cane;

the ache in her hand warned her she'd been holding it too tightly.

The give to the ground spoke of rain, or thawed snow; but her walking shoes held up stoutly, and her quilted coat kept her quite warm.

A carriage rolled onto the drive; she enjoyed the distraction. "Not your father?" she asked with a minimum of breath.

"One of those merchants." Lord Vere clearly didn't have the same thrill at the idea of someone leaving or arriving.

"Money affairs don't interest you?"

"Money affairs never interest a gentleman. Our sort doesn't stoop to such things."

"Except now you have."

Lord Vere looked disbelievingly over his shoulder. Zelda wasn't sure if he had a hard time believing the truth, or that she had said it. "My father necessarily must make plans." And a little more quietly, "I'm not sure why he has to make them at the house."

So. Merchants and solicitors were at the house because Zelda was at the house. Her intended preferred not to notice that their marriage was based on the exchange of money.

That seemed foolish. Her plan for her dowry was *her* only way to make money, and this marriage must make her *father* some money too, she realized, or he wouldn't have proposed it.

Their relationship did lack charm.

Though the lawns had looked smooth, now that they were walking, Zelda found they had little ups and downs to them. It was harder to go up than down, even tiny inclines.

Lady Vere circumnavigates the globe, she pictured in her mind, and kept walking.

Though that would make *his* name famous, and that didn't appeal at the moment.

A fat sheep ambled by, and even as she labored to keep up

with her betrothed, Zelda noticed it was followed by a leaping little lamb. The sheep stopped every step or two to eat a mouthful of grass. Zelda was jealous. She'd like to stop.

Then she noticed that the lamb had one black spot upon its leg.

* * *

THE DAMN GOOSE was following him.

Geoffrey tried to wave it off, assuming it wanted vengeance.

But it refused to fly away. It seemed to know that Geoffrey couldn't escape it inside the big stone manse. After Geoffrey attempted a few times to discourage it, when it just flapped its wings and settled right back down on the ground, Geoffrey ignored it, and it waddled along after him.

"You're an idiot," he told it. Politeness, and the habits of a lifetime, might prevent him from bluntness with fellow human beings; but a stubborn goose was fair game.

It didn't seem to care. Whether hoping for food, or biding its time to repay him for an icy dunking, it stuck to Geoffrey like the baby lambs did to their mother.

"Fine." Geoffrey would ignore it.

Dirt had worn into his heavy trousers and the woolen socks in his boots. His fingernails had grown dark all around the edges. It was as though he were slowly transforming into a different type of person.

If he had the chance to touch Miss Rawle again, she'd shy away from hands like these.

He had to check the feet of the sheep still penned. The adventurous ewe with Miss Rawle's lamb, as he thought of it now, still roamed the grounds; he ought to bring her in, too.

There she was, ambling and cropping grass with the black-spotted lamb beside her, and he felt a surge of satisfaction that they were on the side of the great house far from the mason-work.

Then, past the sheep, he spotted people. Walking out across the grounds. They weren't stonemasons. That was Vere. And Miss Rawle.

Behind them trailed servants with baskets, as if they were going to a picnic.

Anger, that wave of anger he shoved aside before he even admitted it was there; yes, Vere had the same effect on him as his father. Geoffrey was disappointed in himself. Was it just the sight of the older brother who would inherit all this, even the sheep whose feet Geoffrey cleaned? Or was it because he'd set off across the green with Miss Rawle *walking*, and likely had no care if she could manage it or not?

Geoffrey knew exactly the spot Vere would go; though Vere didn't act like it now, they had been children together. They both knew the woods and ponds between Faircombe and the village, and they both remembered how their mother had liked the little hill where the sun shone and one could look down into the mysterious trees spread below.

She'd liked to tell stories about the trees, too. Geoffrey wondered if Vere remembered that.

But that spot was a good mile and a half from Faircombe Hall, and Geoffrey also wondered if his mother had dropped Vere on his head as a child. Because there was no way Miss Rawle could walk that distance.

Though she'd begun it. He could see her. But her head was down and her feet moved slowly.

The grass was damp, the ground soaking wet. Every animal on the estate had hooves full of mud; they were tracking it everywhere. In Guinevere's case, right into the shed where he now slept.

Miss Rawle's toes wouldn't fill with mud, but he worried

about her balance. She might fall. That cane was there for a reason.

He changed course.

* * *

"There's… the shepherd." Zelda had been about to say *your shepherd*, but changed her mind. He wasn't Lord Vere's shepherd; he was hers.

"So it is," and even walking behind him, she could see Lord Vere's shoulders tighten.

In moments, Geoffrey was with them. How could such a big man walk so fast? But then Zelda could see he had long legs, just like Lord Vere, only far more muscled. "Lord Vere," he said, surprisingly familiarly for a servant.

Well, they had likely grown up on this estate together.

"Geoffrey," his lordship's clipped tone confirmed her guess. "The sheep went that way."

Were they *angry* with one another? The tension between them made even the air unpleasant. But Zelda had exhausted her ability to wonder about men for the day; she ignored them.

"Quite." Rather than taking the broad hint, Geoffrey fell into step with Lord Vere.

Awkward, Zelda thought, but bold. She liked it.

Not that she had time to pay attention. Her feet had grown heavy, so heavy. Oddly, her joints did not ache. Zelda felt every pulse of her blood in her body, and it was warm and soft, not unlike the effect of wine. But it was harder and harder to take each step.

Perhaps she ought not to have gone to the breakfast room herself this morning. Perhaps she *should* have had a tray. But she hadn't even known then that she would have a picnic with Lord Vere. Had she? She didn't think so. Her memories of just this morning were growing muzzy.

"Is it very much longer?" She hated having to ask, but had to know.

"Yes," said Geoffrey, just as Lord Vere said, "No."

The two of them glared at each other, and Zelda was no wiser than before.

Was she holding back the servants? She wanted to walk fast enough to get there in good time. Those baskets seemed heavy.

Though no heavier than her. Raising and lowering her foot with each step took a monumental act of will. There was the embarrassment of being ill before her betrothed, and before the servants, and now before Geoffrey; she did not want to seem ill in front of her giant. But there was also the insistent voice inside her that said if she couldn't do this, she couldn't do anything.

And her dreams were all she really had.

Slowly, something shifted. Zelda realized not merely that she was working hard, but that something was wrong. Her heart pounded and the world looked slightly red.

She had no choice; she had to stop.

"I believe…"

Geoffrey stopped and looked back.

Lord Vere did not. "Look," said his lordship, "the edge of the trees is just coming into view. There is a hill there that should be quite dry."

"I believe," Zelda said again, and it felt like it was too quiet inside her head; there were no headlines in there now. "I believe I will not join you today."

"It's just there," Lord Vere said again, pointing, but Geoffrey had moved to stand by her. "Miss Rawle?"

"Don't address my betrothed," snapped the young lord, and though Geoffrey turned to retort, Zelda lost interest.

She discovered that standing was no longer possible. She could sit or fall, so she sat.

The grass *was* as springy as it looked, one part of her mind mused as she felt it against her palm. But it meant no more to her than the moon; sitting upright took all her attention.

*   *   *

GEOFFREY'S WORRY ballooned into something like fright.

Blame for his brother jostled with blame for himself, but he had little attention to spare for either. He didn't know the nature of Miss Rawle's infirmity, but even a lowly shepherd should not have allowed her to put herself in danger. He'd spent too much time wondering how to protect Vere from a stranger and not enough time thinking about how to protect her from Vere.

He had vivid memories of his mother's illness, and how one day she had just been gone. Here was another lovely woman Faircombe could destroy if no one stopped it.

But now he was full-grown. *He* could stop it.

"May I return you to the house, Miss Rawle?" he asked as calmly as he could with the blood roaring through his ears.

"Yes, all right," she said in a vague way that was unlike her.

Just as he had on the stone portico, Geoffrey reached down and scooped Miss Rawle into his arms.

She wasn't tiny, but she was no burden for someone like him.

"Put her down," said Vere behind him, but Geoffrey just walked toward Faircombe Hall.

"You aren't going to carry me all the way back to the hall?" she said, though still with little feeling.

"Yes," he simply said, and "All right," was all she said back.

"Put her down," Vere insisted again. "Fred has an oilcloth. She can sit on the oilcloth."

Geoffrey was no physician, but he trusted his instinct. "I think Miss Rawle has had enough exercise for the day."

"Yes," she said again, so dully that Geoffrey's insides clenched again with that fear.

Had it been hiding inside him all these years, that fear? It was so familiar, so ready. And he had never even imagined it was there, right behind the anger he so ruthlessly tamped down.

If he didn't give Vere some answer, his brother would only continue to fight. "Regardless," he told him, "Miss Rawle's coat is now damp, and she should change."

He could feel the clammy linen against his arm. This was no ground for sitting on, barely out of frost as it was, oilcloth or no oilcloth.

The waiting anger shoved its way to the front for a second. If he could have struck Vere in that moment, he would have.

Not that Vere could see that. Behind Geoffrey, he just said, "I see."

So Vere wouldn't accept the reality of how far Miss Rawle could walk, but he would accept the reality of a damp dress.

He really was an ass.

Geoffrey also bet he was the sort of lordling who would not trail after a servant. Even one who was actually his brother.

And sure enough, a few seconds later, as Geoffrey's legs ate up the ground and he paid no mind to anything else, he heard Vere's voice again. "No sense wasting the picnic, then, as you'll see her to her mother. Fred can accompany you."

Geoffrey spared a glance behind him, where Fred, a slender youth, clearly couldn't work out how to both follow

Geoffrey and carry the oilcloth and things for the picnic. "No need, Fred."

"Fred, go with him."

Geoffrey turned, and slowed, enough to give Fred a direct look. "No."

He was sorry for making the boy openly decide whom he should obey. No one would win in a war between himself and Vere, including anyone caught nearby.

But Fred was cleverer than Geoffrey realized and gave Vere a plausible excuse. "The basket is very heavy, my lord, and you are unaccustomed to carrying it. I had better come with you."

"Yes, I see," and Geoffrey knew Vere was still trying to decide how to send along a chaperone as Geoffrey hastened his pace and left them behind.

* * *

ZELDA DIDN'T HAVE the same thrill in Geoffrey's arms that she felt earlier. Instead, it was something infinitely better: she felt as though someone else could handle this, when she could not.

It had not occurred to her that it was possible for her to walk so far she couldn't walk back; now, she realized that was just what she'd done.

She laid her head against Geoffrey's solid chest. It was warm, and hard, and soft, all at once, and so improbably comfortable.

"You must carry a lot of ladies." She could imagine him striding over the countryside, rescuing sheep and ladies wherever he went.

He only snorted.

"Is it too far?" If it was too far, that was fine. They could both sit down.

"No," but she could tell he was working. That big solid chest rose and fell in regular rhythm, and she could see the heat gathering in his face.

"I'm too heavy."

"I assure you, you're not."

"I can't do it." Her head fell against him more limply, and she felt tears gathering in the corner of her eyes. "I won't be able to do any of it."

Geoffrey would know she meant traveling the world, not walking to a picnic. She'd blurted out all her secrets this morning; she remembered it like a fever dream, it felt so long ago.

"Miss Rawle, I gather you've been ill?"

"I will never not be ill." The sigh was heavy, but it was so much easier to say it. She wasn't frail, and she wasn't a poor thing. But she would always struggle. Why couldn't people see that without her having to explain?

She expected him to say silly, wrong-headed things, like not to lose hope, or that miracles happened.

Instead he said, "Racing horses aren't just sent out to race. They're trained, and they condition their muscles. Do you often try to walk?"

"I'm not to condition muscles. I'm to sit still and never move. Never go anywhere, never do anything. But I'll tell you, I'd rather die."

Now why had she said that? It was as if she were full of wine.

She expected him to ignore that, but again he surprised her. "Dying would be foolish, since then you lose all your chances."

"At what?"

"At anything that might happen."

"Hmm." What an annoyingly right giant. She'd come to the same conclusion years ago.

She might have dozed, rocking along in his arms as steady and strong as an oak chair, because the courtyard for Faircombe Hall was very near.

"I'm sorry to go in and part from you," she said. It sounded less appropriate once she'd said it, but it had only been simple truth.

Had she felt his heart thump particularly hard? Surely not.

"You are not a racehorse, and I know nothing of your illness, and little of you. But once you rest, if you wish to travel on your own two feet, we will find a way."

What a lovely sentence. It was as warm as his arms, and even more comforting. It had a *we* in it, too. "Will we?" she said, alert enough to marvel at the way he carried her up the courtyard steps with no apparent effort.

"It's up to you," he said, before telling the footman at the door, "Warn Mrs. Rawle or the maids we are coming, and have some whiskey and warm coverlets sent to Miss Rawle's chamber, please."

As they moved through one of the corridors that led from the courtyard, his legs never tiring, Geoffrey's voice dropped a little so only she could hear it. "Dreams don't come true in a day. How much did you give up to get this far?"

This. She'd given up this, and never known it. She'd never been held in a man's arms, hearing his heartbeat under her ear, and feeling like she wasn't alone.

But she hadn't known her giant before. No other man's arms would have felt like this.

Geoffrey went on as he turned a corner. "Sometimes a cow becomes ill and refuses to get up. Those are the cows we lose. I'm sorry to compare you to a cow, Miss Rawle, but do you see what I mean? Cows can't imagine the future. We do. Don't stop now."

She liked his version of her. He took the version of her

that she had pictured for herself so long ago and made it seem much more real. His faith in her was a rebuilding experience.

"I won't stop. But I don't know what I'm doing."

* * *

DIDN'T SHE? Well, neither did he. They were two of a kind that way. That was why he wanted to help her achieve her dreams; that, and that she still *had* dreams, while his were slipping away.

Till he worked out Miss Rawle's goals for his family and Faircombe, he ought to keep *some* distance.

Offering to help was not keeping his distance.

He had no idea how to help a person move better, and if he sought her out to try, it would not look innocent; it would not *be* innocent. Even if he didn't give in to any urges to hold her differently and kiss the color back into her face.

Not that the idea had crossed his mind.

If he helped her, they would spend time together, and he would touch her. That was the part he left out of his stories about race-horses and cows. He'd need to touch her even if he didn't want to. And he did.

Geoffrey wanted to be a good brother, he always had, even before his mother had charged him with looking after all of them. Vere seemed to have been born with some sort of jealousy of Geoffrey, and perhaps Geoffrey couldn't fix that.

But he could no more leave Miss Rawle to the mercy of his brother than he could leave an injured animal collapsed in an icy brook. She could freeze to death amid the Faircombe family.

"I will help you, Miss Rawle."

She didn't answer. She'd fallen asleep in his arms.

The door to her chamber was open. Geoffrey knew

exactly where it was, from the moment he'd seen her on the little portico.

Because these had been his mother's rooms.

The sensation he had, carrying her into that bedchamber, was indescribable. It felt like he was living his childhood over again; panic, hope, horror, and something he refused to name.

Her maid turned down the coverlets. But Geoffrey didn't lay her down.

"I don't wish to wake Miss Rawle, but her clothes are damp; she must change before she sleeps," he said as softly as he could.

"I'm awake," Miss Rawle said, perhaps from sheer stubbornness. "I can do it. I can stand."

The calm of her words didn't match her expression, which was still pale, and her eyes were closed.

But when he tried setting her on her feet, her eyes opened, and she nodded at him.

"I'll see to it, sir," said the maid, and Geoffrey took her at her word. He turned and left as swiftly as he could so she could prepare Miss Rawle to lie down comfortably.

He'd have to talk to the lady again before he could be sure of what she wanted. She'd allowed him to carry her into her chambers right now, but there was no decision to it. It was simply the only possible course.

She planned to marry his brother and abandon him. That was hardly keeping Vere safe. But Geoffrey had to do *something* to help her. He could never walk away from anyone or anything that needed help, and her life was about to topple.

CHAPTER 8

"I don't want to go to supper, but I'm going."

Mrs. Rawle just clucked at this, tucking the bedding around Zelda as she did so. The way she had when Zelda was little. "Far too taxing a day. I'll have them bring you a tray. You must be hungry."

Zelda *was* hungry. She'd also slept the afternoon away, and woken far less stiff than she expected to be. Only tired. She knew the difference between this level of tired and the sea of exhaustion that had swallowed her before. She could get up, and she would.

"Tansy, I'll have the blue evening gown."

"Griselda." Her mother looked shocked as Zelda pushed herself out of the bed despite being tucked in a moment before. Her feet were bare, and Mrs. Rawle rushed to put slippers on them.

"I'm quite warm, Mother; there's a roaring fire."

"You must stay in bed."

Zelda crooked her finger, beckoning her mother to look her in the eye.

And when her mother did, Zelda said distinctly, "I. Will.

Not."

"*Griselda!* You're always so sensible. What's come over you? I apologize I was not here this afternoon to dissuade you from the picnic idea. I thought you were old enough to know your limitations. You ought to have let them push you in the chair, or not at all."

"Mother, it had nothing to do with you."

Mrs. Rawle drew back as if someone had offered to strike her.

"What a bad temper you've woken in. That's not like you."

The number of things her mother knew about what she was actually like were so small that Zelda didn't know where to begin.

It had been so easy to blurt out to Geoffrey her intent to see the world. Perhaps because he had no idea what it was like to have such big dreams and no money to carry them out. She needed her dowry money to do it.

Her father had refused, year after year, to simply settle the money on her. But he would give it in the form of a dowry. And she still needed her mother's help to complete the marriage contracts.

She wiggled her toes. She also needed the ability to walk more than a few yards by herself.

The truth lay before her. Unless she wished to be pushed across the world in a wheeled chair, she needed to prepare not just her money, but herself.

So many doubts. She doubted her physical abilities more than she ever had before the more she tried to use them. She doubted she would get her dowry money unhindered. And unless she found a way to establish some bond with Lord Vere, she'd never feel a man's arms wrapped around her in passion. She still didn't know what that entailed, but for the first time in her life, she desperately wanted to know.

She doubted she could do without it forever, but on the

other hand, doubted she would find what she sought in Lord Vere's arms.

"Mother." She should be honest, but not too honest. "Faircombe is quite safe. I intend to move about more. It makes me feel better, not worse."

"Better? To collapse in the dirt?" Her mother didn't gesture toward her stained coat; she didn't have to. It lay crumpled on a chair.

"I didn't have the strength to go so far. But I like the feeling of trying. I like *moving*. I will do more of it and see if I can't get a little stronger."

"Griselda, I don't understand. You've told me for years you wanted to leave the States. You wanted a marriage abroad. Now we're here, Faircombe is *absolutely* lovely, and you want to endanger your health by pushing yourself too far. Just when you are on the verge of being wed."

Zelda wasn't so sure Faircombe was absolutely lovely. But she kept to her point. "And I thank you, Mother, for bringing me all this way. You've indulged my whims all this way, and I am asking you to trust that I haven't lost my mind."

"Well, of course you haven't," said Mrs. Rawle in her brisk way.

It heartened Zelda. "Then trust me. Trust me more than those grim doctors. You always have. I must move more, I'm sure of it. Let me listen to my own body instead of other people's rules."

"Griselda…" Mrs. Rawle clasped her hands together tight. Zelda wondered if she didn't want to speak in front of Tansy, who remained quietly by her dressing table ready to brush her hair. But no, it seemed she just needed a moment. "You have no idea what it is like to watch your child struggle and hurt."

Surprised, Zelda slid farther, till her feet touched the floor. They hurt, and it was an effort, but she stood.

And as she watched her mother's face, she saw it cost her mother something to watch.

Mrs. Rawle went on. "You are more than precious to me, my little girl. You are everything. Since the moment I laid eyes on you, I felt that the whole world revolved around only you, and I've never changed my mind."

"Mother." Zelda held out a hand, and her mother took it. Her mother had aged. The palms were dry, and the knuckles a little heavier too. Did they pain her as Zelda's did? Why hadn't she known?

Now her secrets felt a little guilty.

Would nothing ever be easy?

No. Everything had been easy till now. Now her dreams called for real determination. Either Zelda had it, or she didn't.

"I know you love me. I love you too. How lucky I am."

"How lucky we both are." Her mother squeezed her hand, gently.

Then Mrs. Rawle bustled about, arranging for the wheeled chair to be brought—which Zelda did not refuse; she really did not feel up to walking to that ship of a dining room—while Zelda considered how odd it was that she sometimes didn't know what she thought before she said it. She *was* lucky to have a mother who loved her.

And her mother felt lucky too? To have a daughter who couldn't walk a mile or brush her own hair?

Zelda hadn't known that.

* * *

GEOFFREY WOULD CRAWL sideways through that tiny door of his grandmother's if it meant being in the dining room tonight.

But his father had forestalled it.

"His lordship had the screen put away," Mrs. Davies told him apologetically, with the half-moment of attention she could spare him.

The urgency he felt to be in that room seemed reflected all around him. He wasn't often in the kitchen before supper, but the place struck him as unusually hurried. There were tubs of ice on the floor and several of the kitchen maids had their heads together, making sounds of disagreement. "Is there anything wrong?"

"An odd menu," was all Mrs. Davies said, with a peculiar half-sad, half-determined look. "I do the best I can, you know."

"Of course, I know." No one could find fault with Mrs. Davies' cooking.

"I wish I could do more for you, Lord Geoffrey, I do, but…" Her attention was grasped by the *tsk*-ing kitchen maids. Geoffrey couldn't ask her for more.

He had to trust that for tonight, Vere *and* Miss Rawle could take care of themselves.

* * *

GEOFFREY COULD HAVE PICKED up a trencher of the servants' porridge and waited by the hearth for news of how the dinner progressed.

He couldn't sit still that long.

Fortunately, before he was even out the kitchen door, he nearly tripped over the steward, Bill Rike.

"Lord Geoffrey. I've been looking for you." Bill bobbed his head as if Geoffrey weren't dressed just like him and grimy as hell. "Dandy thought I should have a word."

"What word?"

"I've got a lame cow could use a heavy hand, if you know what I mean."

Geoffrey frowned down. "I don't."

Bill scrubbed the back of a callused hand against his stubbled chin. He didn't seem to want to elaborate. "She's mean, this cow, and she's got to have a hoof trimmed to let the bad out, and I could use all the hands I can get. Dandy said you'd help."

Thanks, Dandy. "Yes, I'll come. Where is she?" It would keep him occupied.

"Right now?" This took Bill aback.

"Is the cow lame now? Let's do it now." It was perfect timing, in fact. Geoffrey was just in the mood to wrestle an angry cow.

Which mood did not improve when he found himself outside the kitchen facing, not an angry cow, but Lord Faircombe.

His father said nothing. His clothes were raked and stained from thrashing greenery; he must have been riding. Geoffrey had a moment's thought for the horse; he hoped the animal wasn't as abused as his lordship's clothing.

Bill Rike clearly wished he had taken another door, eyes darting back and forth between father and son as if seeking an exit in a fire.

"Go on, Mr. Rike," said Geoffrey, and then as the man departed with all speed, "As you see, I am outside the house."

His father didn't bother to glance at the kitchen door a yard behind his shoulder. "My staff do as I have asked. As does Lord Vere."

"In what way am I failing you, then? As a servant, or as a son?"

Lord Faircombe didn't answer, just tapped his gloves against his thigh, staring measuringly at Geoffrey.

The whole world could bend to his will and it would never be enough.

"Then let me ask it differently," said Geoffrey, free of his father's miasma of anger, but more puzzled than ever. "How are you failing me, as a master or as a father?"

Those words seemed to hit his father somewhere in the chest. But Lord Faircombe said nothing, his eyes simply warning Geoffrey that his orders had better be obeyed.

Before he could move, Geoffrey felt one last question ripped from him by the silence. "If you only ever needed one son, *why* did you keep having *so many more?*"

His father could have said something about the vicissitudes of life, or childhood illness. Anything that would have made sense. Instead he only said, "It's better this way," and walked away into the dropping dark.

* * *

"Do you want your cane?" Mrs. Rawle had to put down the basket in her hands to fetch it.

"Yes."

"Shall we go?"

"Yes."

One word was all Zelda could manage at a time. She'd slept for hours, but she wasn't refreshed. She'd ride in her chair; but she wanted that cane. And she was dispirited. *World traveler... wasn't.*

As a footman rolled Zelda toward the dining room, they slowly passed other doors, and Zelda didn't even wonder what was behind them. Not tonight.

When she reached the dining room, no one paid her any attention. Lord Faircombe was in some sort of glaring match with Lady Charlotte, of all people. And as she drew near, Zelda could hear them.

Lord Faircombe wore a scowl. "I can't waste time listening to complaints from Mrs. Truett. Miss Farsworth can't annoy the maids while they are doing laundry, and that's the end of it."

Zelda once again had that sick flash of insight, this time coupled with the realization that she could not pretend tonight that she didn't know something was her fault.

She considered going back to bed.

"Shall I take you to the table, madam?" the footman half-whispered behind her.

"No, I will walk from here."

Lady Charlotte's eyebrows were climbing as the footman retreated. "Miss Farsworth is *my* friend and not subject to your domineering."

"Miss Farsworth lives under my roof, and only as long as she doesn't disturb the household." His lordship's head had settled between his shoulders.

"Household? It's just a pile of stone with some things in it," Lady Charlotte tossed her head. "If she must leave to get civility, you know I will go with her."

"She's a damn companion. Like a governess for adults. She'll do as she's told."

"How many times will you say that till you realize there's no one left to say it to?" And with that, Lady Charlotte sailed out.

Well, apparently Lady Charlotte and Miss Farsworth wouldn't be joining them for supper.

Zelda did not want to address Lord Faircombe. She did not want to be at Faircombe Hall. In truth, she did not want to be in England.

"Lord Faircombe," she said in a rasping whisper. "Has something gone amiss?"

"Enh, just maids complaining." The Marquess brushed off the complaints the way he'd brushed off his daughter's words a moment before. "Miss Farsworth has been down in the laundry drawing all day, and the maids don't like to be stared at."

"Was she drawing them?"

"Says not. Says she was drawing the laundry. Bollocks." Lord Faircombe didn't notice Zelda's startlement, nor did he seem to realize that people did not say *bollocks* to her. "Wapping. You done with those contracts?"

"There are details still to negotiate," said the stick-like solicitor, taking Lord Faircombe's greeting in stride, along with a glass of gin from the butler's tray.

The butler brought the tray of glasses closer and glanced at Zelda to see if he should offer. She just shook her head a tiny bit. This was no time to relax.

Lord Faircombe went on. "Get it done over supper. How far apart can you all be?"

"Some distance," was all Mr. Wapping said, which made no sense to Zelda; hadn't they all come for some mutual goal? No one came to her father's house in Bowling Green unless they intended to proffer a deal.

"Ahhh… *ahh-KFEWWWH!*" This explosive sneeze preceded Lord Vere into the room.

Which was for the best, as otherwise Zelda would have been alarmed by the sight of him.

His clothes were faultless as always, but his eyes were red and his nose looked swollen. Zelda wondered if someone had hit him.

For a moment, she hoped someone had.

"My chambers," he said, and his voice was clogged as well. "Someone has filled my chambers with flowers. I thought I had a slightly runny nose from the cold. Sat there all afternoon waiting for it to improve." He did not add *while my betrothed slept,* but Zelda heard him think it. "And now look at me."

Zelda couldn't stop looking at him. A huge handkerchief

flapped in his hand; he needed it. "Ahh... ahh... *ahh-CHEOUGHH!*" he said again.

It would not have surprised her had his head popped off.

"Does the springtime always affect you this way?" she asked him, as politely as she could.

"No," was all he said.

The merchants trailed in one after the other, and Zelda had the impression that they, too, had been holed up together for the bulk of the afternoon. Likely not with Lord Vere, as his sneezes openly alarmed them.

"I say, take supper in your rooms," said Mr. Wallinson the clock-watcher, as a sneeze tore his attention away from the time.

"Feel free to dine alone," said Lord Vere shortly. Zelda hoped his irritation was not about this afternoon. Then she changed her mind. His irritation had *better not* be about this afternoon.

Mr. Mendey trailed in last and looked about. "Lady Charlotte has not arrived? Nor Mrs. Rawle?"

Startled, Zelda realized her mother hadn't yet followed. "My mother was just with me, sir. She will be here shortly, I'm sure."

Lord Faircombe gave her an odd look, but said nothing. Was *speaking* unacceptable now too?

"Why isn't there tea?" Mr. Highland wobbled a little on his cane, and Zelda worried he might actually expire if not provided with tea.

"Why isn't supper laid on?" asked Mr. Lyndon, the fellow whose clothes and manner reflected the less exclusive parts of London. The table was full of food, laid out in its usual square pattern, but there was an empty space in the middle, and Mr. Lyndon's stomach wanted to know why.

At that, the little cook darted in from the china room.

"We're just waiting for you to sit, my lord, and the last course will be served."

"Get on with it," said Lord Faircombe with his usual lack of graciousness, and settled his square bulk at the head of the table.

CHAPTER 9

$\mathcal{O}$nce his guests were seated—with chairs left vacant for Lady Charlotte, Miss Farsworth, and Mrs. Rawle—Mrs. Truett's head appeared around the edge of the door, as if surveying a battle front.

"Truett," and Lord Faircombe's tone was truly threatening. No further waiting for supper would be tolerated.

Her head disappeared, and a whole phalanx of footmen staggered into the dining room bearing the most incredible platter Zelda had ever seen.

World stunned, thought Zelda, but then couldn't think of the rest of the headline.

"Mrs. Truett." His lordship pronounced her name slowly and thoroughly. "Tell me what this is."

"A gelatine tower, your lordship," she said, with a bobbing of her knees.

"A what?"

It was clear to all that the question was formed from malice, not genuine desire to know.

"A gelatine tower, sir," said Mrs. Truett, with fading confidence.

Zelda regarded it with interest. It was an evil shade of pale yellow, and boiled bits of beet were stuck in it here and there. They should have looked like jewels but instead looked like raw chunks of something—or someone—who'd had an untimely end.

Strips of carrot were also featured, in what might have been patterns but had clearly slid.

There were other nameless blobs of this and that, but Zelda decided they should be ignored, like a rude gesture.

"Mrs. Truett." The way Lord Faircombe's face worked, it showed his inner struggles, and Zelda waited with interest to see which way the struggle would turn.

She was concerned for Mrs. Truett, and for herself, because this was more than she could cheerfully lie about. But it was impossibly dramatic, wondering what Lord Faircombe would say. Would he deign to ask a question, such as *why* this was at his table? Would he let his temper burst? Rail at Mrs. Truett? Eat the gelatine?

The suspense was incredible.

"Take it away."

Zelda felt simultaneous relief and disappointment. The responsibility to eat the thing was gone. She decided to tilt toward relief.

Mrs. Truett, however, as Zelda had experienced, did not give up without a fight. "Every kitchen maid has worked on this all day." She did not describe the horrific process of obtaining the gelatine, which Zelda did not want to hear. They clearly did not cook the stuff often, as this version was far from clear. The work, mess, and expense must also have been tremendous.

"I don't care if they died for it; get it off my table." Lord Faircombe looked around. All the merchants, all the solicitors, were stunned by the gory apparition on the table, standing several hands high. Well, a few, Zelda revised, as she watched the top sink in on itself.

It seemed too bad that everyone had worked so hard for it, only to get this reception from the lord of the manor. On the other hand, Zelda didn't want to try it herself.

No, wait, *yes she did*. This was likely the first time Mrs. Truett had ever done anything that she didn't already know his lordship wanted. Perhaps it was the first time she had ever done anything simply because she wanted to do it.

Wanted to do it so badly that she had chivvied all the kitchen staff through an entire day of making this thing purely from her description. For if any cook had ever seen the like, they could never have made anything that looked like this.

Lord Faircombe's annoyance wasn't Zelda's first concern. Entertainment was. Not only hers, but others' as well. Even Mrs. Truett's.

"Mrs. Truett, this is an amazing thing to see. You were quite right. That is a sight I never will forget."

The housekeeper's shoulders slumped with relief, and her nose looked less pinched. But Lord Faircombe just turned his attention to her. "Miss Rawle? This has something to do with you?"

Lord Vere shifted uncomfortably in his chair. Zelda assumed he would soon sneeze.

"Yes, Mrs. Truett consulted me about the menu. I asked her to make a surprise for us." They were all surprised, that was undeniable. Unfortunately, half-truths tended to pull one another along; she might as well spill them all. "I also asked her to fill Lord Vere's chambers with flowers, and then when I realized how I'd inconvenienced Miss Farsworth, suggested she draw the laundry."

"You. Suggested she draw the laundry." The very idea of

something new happening in his house appeared to stun him.

"Yes." Zelda didn't know what he was going to do next, but that was entertaining too. She felt the corner of her mouth turn up. "I haven't seen the resulting artwork. Is it good?"

"*You* did." Lord Faircombe didn't rail. He said nothing. Just stared at her.

"Yes." It did feel good to admit it all, though Miss Farsworth wasn't here and Zelda would have to apologize. Also to the laundry maids, apparently. She turned to Lord Vere. "I do apologize. It was only because of—"

"Miss Rawle, I don't know where your mother is, but please retire to your chambers. I'll have a tray sent in."

"Oh, but—"

"I will have a tray sent."

The chill that settled over the room was gruesome, and so were all the eyes locked on her now. It was a long table full of men, and every one of them was staring at her. Waiting for her to acquiesce to the Marquess' orders.

Woman shunned, thought Zelda, as a footman pulled out her chair for her and provided her cane. *Wedding canceled due to gelatine.*

She smiled a little smile at Mrs. Truett. "Be sure to send me a piece," she said, knowing it wasn't necessary to say of what.

And slowly she made her way back to her chair, where the same footman leapt out to roll her toward the door, feeling all their eyes upon her the whole way. Even the eyes of the young man she was soon supposed to marry.

She wasn't in control of any of this.

* * *

As soon as the door was closed behind the retreating figure of Miss Rawle, Lord Faircombe waved to the footmen. They relieved the table of the gelatine tower without a further word.

"I'm surprised at you, Mrs. Truett," he said, not even looking at her as Mr. Lydon passed him a plate of tiny roast birds, and he helped himself.

Mrs. Truett curtseyed and left, and only a few at the table thought they heard her reply faintly, "So am I."

"Well, you were right, Vere. She's feeble. I don't like to admit it, but there it is. The contracts had better specify where her dowry goes once she's committed."

Vere blinked his red eyes. His father hadn't said *if* she was committed. "Her mother may not agree."

"Her mother doesn't enter into it." His lordship's jowls trembled as he looked down the table at his own solicitor, then at Mr. Highland. "No sense in hiding the truth we're all staring at, is there?"

"Not at all," said Mr. Highland in the same perpetually cheerful, slightly dazed tone he used for everything. "Bring me another cup of tea," he told the footman behind him, who bowed his head and leaped toward the kitchen.

Mr. Mendey only surveyed his colleagues; Mr. Lyndon reached for a dish, and Mr. Wallinson said nothing.

"You see why I wanted to be so careful with the contracts," put in Mr. Wapping from the far side of the table. His knife cut into a tiny bird, so small that a quarter of it was an entire bite; he put the whole bite into his mouth and chewed, bones and all. The entire table could hear the crunch.

Vere's head felt stuffed full of wet rags. He couldn't think. He certainly couldn't think what to say. He felt dreadfully ill, the staff had been inconvenienced any number of ways, and no one would eat that gelatine tower. But the idea of sending his bride to an asylum didn't appeal.

He had no stomach to raise the question at the table of what he was supposed to do for an heir, or even feminine companionship, if his wife were in an asylum. He suspected he knew the answer, and it was unpalatable.

Not as unpalatable as that gelatine tower, he thought. But unpalatable. He pictured himself visiting a cold, drafty building far in the country, trying to conceive an heir with a woman who did not want to be there.

Duty.

* * *

THE COW WASN'T that mean once Geoffrey was supporting all her weight.

Geoffrey hadn't known how the animals, and the servants, had previously awaited his pleasure. He'd come and helped when he wished, did the work he liked, and left the rest alone.

Now he was dirty all over, wishing he'd stolen some food from the kitchen before he'd left, and holding up a cow.

For the dozenth time, he elbowed her flank. He had her foot between his knees, and the foot clearly pained her; it felt hot, and she could lose the hoof.

But he had not intended to comfort the cow by letting her rest her weight on him while he tried to shave away horn to find where the wound began.

The cow, however, didn't care what he intended. This large person had gotten her foot off the ground and was very comfortable to lean on besides. Things were looking up.

"I'd feel foolish cursing a cow," Geoffrey told her under his breath, elbowing her for the thirteenth time. "But I may start."

The cow happily urinated, the yellow fountain spattering the ground.

"She's got an evil hard hoof, that's the truth," said the herdsman. He and Bill Pike were hanging off the cow's horns as if she might gore Geoffrey. Perhaps pretending that she was mean made them feel better about having no way of handling her without Geoffrey.

Geoffrey glared at them, too. They could have had six men take turns trimming the horn; or they could have Geoffrey, strong enough to trim away sliver after sliver of horn chasing the dark spot that showed where a wound had started under the hoof and had to be drained. They'd brought him to the cow and left him to it.

He felt sweat bloom under his shirt.

Well, they probably didn't know they were grinding into him what it meant to be something besides Lord Geoffrey. Dandy, Bill Pike, the herdsman in front of him, even this cow. They all wanted to grind him down till he was only what he could *do*.

Well, he didn't know how to be a servant in his own home. But he by God did know how to heal a cow.

With a final mighty twist that nearly snapped the steel, the last bit of hoof sliced away and the resulting trickle of fluid showed that he'd finally drained the wound. He trimmed more, then still more, to get to the living flesh below and give it a clean, clear opening.

It took even longer than draining the wound had.

When he dropped the hoof and straightened, he felt he'd aged about twenty years.

This called for less lordly behavior. He looked Bill Pike right in the eye. "You bastard."

"Sorry," the man said immediately. "Dandy said you could do it."

"Dandy says a lot of things."

"But you *did* do it."

Damnable man was right. The cow would keep her hoof; the accomplishment felt good. Geoffrey let out a breath. "I'm going to walk her through the beck."

"You don't have to." The herdsman, too, seemed apologetic. He knew who Geoffrey was; yet he wanted the cow's hoof fixed more than he wanted to treat Geoffrey in lordly fashion.

Well, Geoffrey wanted that too. He felt his ire ebb.

"I'm going to walk her through the beck till the wound is clean and cool," said Geoffrey, in tones of certainty harder than the hoof had been. "And you are going to find me some clean clothes. Because I'm also going to bathe."

"Not in the beck!" Bill Pike was appalled. There would likely still be chunks of ice.

"In the beck." Geoffrey or Lord Geoffrey, he had to bathe somewhere. He'd had enough.

* * *

THE FRENCH WINDOWS went all the way down to the floor, and the moon was full.

Tansy had dressed Zelda in a nightrail with a thickly quilted wrapper and gone to the rooms where the maids were housed. Zelda's return alone from a supper that had barely begun had shocked Mrs. Rawle.

"No, of course not," was all she said when Zelda suggested her mother join his lordship to eat, and they ate companionably together from the tray the kitchen sent.

They poked together at the gelatine.

"It's extraordinary," said Mrs. Rawle, and Zelda wanted to explain how true that was. It had nothing to do with culinary success and everything to do with discovering there was something Mrs. Truett actually wanted to enjoy.

But she was not in the habit of telling her mother what she was thinking. "It *is* astonishing," was all she said.

There was plenty of food, though Zelda didn't want the little roast fowl on its tiny porcelain plate; her mother just picked at it. They had slices of beef, too.

Zelda wondered if she could ever bring herself to eat that tiny lamb with the black spot on its leg.

"Shall I read to you?" Mrs. Rawle asked her, drawing a book from her basket, but Zelda shook her head.

"I'm going to sleep, Mother." Zelda smiled. "Will you be able to amuse yourself?"

"I think I will." Mrs. Rawle clasped the little volume to her chest. "It has been a long time since I have had the chance to read myself to sleep. Without being knocked about in a pitching ship."

"Do it," Zelda urged. "Enjoy yourself."

And Mrs. Rawle, like Mrs. Truett, and Miss Farsworth, took her suggestion. Zelda could only hope it would go better for her. "I will."

Once her mother had gone, Zelda sat in the chair by the fire for a long, long time, her little jeweled globe cupped in one hand, and looked out over the garden in the moonlight.

The world was far larger than the globe showed. Every person on it had their own universe of dreams. Hers seemed so petty, even small.

She'd come this far only to find even small dreams were hard to hold on to by oneself.

And she wasn't sure how much further she could go.

* * *

THE FOOTMAN BROUGHT the tray back to the kitchen. "They did eat."

"Very well, Albert." Mrs Truett didn't look up. "I've nothing more for you here."

The kitchen maids bustled about, none of them going near the tray. Did they think it bad business, or bad luck?

Mrs. Truett, perfectly starched black and white linen clothes standing stiffly away without once daring to hug her body, looked at the china plate, ruined vestiges of gelatine shining on its rim.

She'd had a dream for a few hours that day, and dreams change a person, when they're truly and deeply felt.

* * *

To Pike's credit, he got a thing done once he set out to do it. At the side of the beck, he handed Geoffrey a bundle of clothes.

The borrowed linen shirt might have been a woman's shift, it billowed so. But it was large enough. Without a collar, its ties would show at the throat. Without small-clothes, the wool of the trousers would rub. Geoffrey wouldn't complain. The coat and trousers looked like they'd fit. They were worn a bit raw at the elbows and cuffs, and the coat-tails had ragged edges; the trousers were for hunting, stained at the bottom, but they'd be hidden by his boots.

They must be clothes of his father's, Geoffrey realized. No one else was so large and had cast-offs like this.

"I'll return them," he told Bill Pike, feeling as he never had before that even such clothes as this could be precious.

"When you like," the graying steward said, with a little embarrassment. Perhaps he felt bad about subjecting Geoffrey to this; perhaps he just wasn't sure what to do with a son of the marquess living among the livestock. "Brought you this," he said, offering a scrap of rough cloth, "crush it up, it'll scrub." Then he climbed the bank and joined the herdsman.

Geoffrey put the clothes aside where the cow wouldn't step on them, then led the animal into the water.

"She's going fine," said the herdsman, and the cow did look happier. Still, the fellow stood on the bank and let Geoffrey do the work.

Geoffrey felt the last of his pride trickle away as he marched through a running stream in his boots, pushing a cow's bony behind when she wouldn't follow. His most desperate hope at the moment was that the wound wouldn't grow worse, so he wouldn't have to cut that hoof again.

Simple life my arse, Geoffrey thought as he watched the cow amble up the bank towards the herdsman. She was eager to get out of the water; the men were eager for somewhere warm. Pike waved as they all disappeared over the hill.

What would be simple would be to go up to the house, have a hot bath in buckets of water carried by servants, shave, dress in his own clothes, take the money from his father's desk, ride off to London and never return.

Instead, Geoffrey stripped naked, right there on the grass. His feet were already chilled in wet boots, but nothing like how they burned once they were bare. Then the burn eased; perhaps his dunking under the ice yesterday had hardened him.

Perhaps not, as he bent his knees and the cold water made him shrink so fast he yelped.

It didn't matter. No one was here.

The clean, burbling water made even his skin clench as he waded deeper. He wouldn't be able to stand this for long, but he could get some kind of clean.

Belatedly, he remembered the scrap of wool crushed in his fist. Well, Pike had said to crush it. He wet it in the water, then started rubbing it along one leg, hoping to remove at least the worst memories of cow.

To his surprise, the wool bubbled.

Only slightly, but it did. Investigating it quickly, he found it was a sort of half-sack made of soft wool, filled with torn ivy leaves. Further rubbing drove the bubbles to froth and foam.

He wet it again and started to rub it all over his body, his motion sending droplets flying; he felt like they'd turn to tiny crystals of ice before they hit the ground, though it wasn't that cold. But he'd do almost anything to be clean again.

He wouldn't be a lord when he went to see the mysterious Miss Rawle, but he wanted to be clean.

Bracing himself, he ducked again to wet his hair, his gasp echoing in the trees.

CHAPTER 10

The walk to the great hall warmed him.

The walk, and, unfortunately, the memory of Miss Rawle in his arms that morning.

Ungallantly, he peeked in the window, just to see if she were sleeping. She must be, after such a day.

She wasn't.

No, she reclined in the armchair by the fire as if it were a throne. Her head was not bowed in sleep; she looked up, and out, at the whole world.

At him.

It did not surprise him that she rose and came with a graceful glide to the French door.

She mustn't come outside with frost forming on the ground. He slipped in.

"You must sleep," was the first thing he thought of to say.

"I must think," she told him with one of those sly smiles, but it faded fast.

"Are you recovered from this afternoon?"

"No," she raised a slender shoulder, "but I will be. It is the least of my concerns."

Collapsing on the wet ground was the least of her concerns? "Miss Rawle, I question your priorities."

"So do I." She gestured. "Will you sit?"

As if he wore a silk collar, instead of no collar at all.

"I'm not fit for a lady's parlor," said he, a little grimly, but he did take a step in. And told himself it wasn't to get closer to her.

"I may not be either." She reclaimed her armchair, and her arms folded around herself as if she were cold. He immediately thought he ought to warm her, even though he'd been standing in icy water half an hour hence and she was closer to the fire.

Ignoring the urge, he took the chair opposite.

There was a rueful edge to her voice, and Geoffrey wondered what he had missed. "Were you injured at all?"

"Not at all." One slender shoulder shrugged. "Perhaps my mind needed the shake."

Geoffrey forced himself not to go touch her, ensure she was not hurt. "Should someone fetch a physician?" His mind raced. The nearest physician was likely no closer than London.

"*Please*, no. My body is as well as it ever is." Another dismissive shrug. "I've arrived at a new understanding."

He still sat immobile, willing his heart to slow down. "Which is? If you'll tell a lowly shepherd."

"Who would I tell if not you?" She clasped her hands together and stared at them; loosened them after just a moment. "In fact, that is my situation. I find myself friend-less, with a dream I feel I will lose."

"Yes?" She looked whole. She'd felt whole in his arms. He had only to close his eyes to imagine her there again. He didn't close his eyes. "From your illness?"

"Not illness, Geoffrey. Foolishness." She gave him that slow, sleepy-eyed smile, and it told him the joke this time was on herself. "I cannot travel the world by myself; I cannot visit a *pond* by myself. My intended… will not help me." Here she looked toward the fire. "No one will help me; I feel quite alone. And I think… not quite safe."

His blood roared from his feet to his face. *Look after them, Geoffrey,* but his siblings were grown, and his father didn't want him.

This woman needed him, and he needed that.

"Miss Rawle, I can assure you that you will be safe."

"Can you?" That sidelong look of hers, and this time he realized she had no idea how alluring it looked. "You have work to do, not that it would be proper to have you by my side day and night."

That thought lay between them uncomfortably. She shifted a little.

And went on, "This world of scheming money-hungry men… you are not part of it."

She didn't know who he was. Or at least who he had been. "I've been part of Faircombe my whole life. All Lord Faircombe wants is to ensure his line. His legacy." He stopped short of explaining how far his father had gone to do it.

"Geoffrey, I've been around such men *my* whole life. Men claim many reasons to want money. But the desire for it is obvious. Lord Faircombe wants money. I assure you, that is the only reason I am here."

He struggled inside with the need to justify his father. She was right. Why did he feel an urge to justify his father?

Unknowing, Miss Rawle went on. "And I thought I could turn their purposes to my purposes. But I'm finding this water very deep." Her smile lurked in the corner of her mouth. "And do you know, I cannot swim?"

He envisioned lifting her, dripping, bare, from the water, and holding her to his chest.

That was it. Perhaps it was only his body's betrayal—she would see it if he stood—but he had never felt such a rush of pure longing in his life.

Dandy was right. He needed a woman. And Delina was right. He needed something for himself.

And if there was nothing more he could do for his long-gone mother, there was something he could do for the lush, live woman in front of him.

"I think you can do whatever you please." She wouldn't realize how much work it was to keep the roughness out of his voice, or how difficult it was to actually plan to foil his father and cross his brother. But he did. He did all those things. "And I will help you."

ALL UNKNOWING of the bridge he had just crossed, Miss Rawle only shook her head. "You can't imagine what it feels like, Geoffrey, to want nothing more than to escape the home you grew up in, to *do* it, just to find you've walked into the same cage again."

"No," he admitted. "I can't." He couldn't imagine wanting to escape this home; all he wanted was to be *in* it.

Though right now, among much larger new thoughts, he could admit to himself that he missed being warm, and clean, and well-fed, more than he missed being in this house. Here especially, in his mother's rooms, he felt how much time had passed. Perhaps it was his childhood he missed more than this house.

Really, it was just his mother. Someone who had cared about him and let him care back.

Miss Rawle went on. "I imagined things would be… a little easier. That the people would be a little easier." For once, she met his gaze squarely. It made her slow, sleepy eyes look serious. "Everyone's life has plenty of pain. Why not seek out more pleasure?"

The heat that flashed through him at her words shocked him. She'd said nothing salacious, and she wasn't talking of him. Still, his body didn't believe that. It was at her beck and call.

"Why not indeed?" he asked, his voice, too, pitched so low no one would hear.

"I wanted people to enjoy themselves today. I wanted to give Lord Vere a gift in return for the one he'd given me, and to distract Mrs. Truett with something pleasant. And to amuse Miss Farsworth."

"All noble goals." What gift had Vere given her?

"Instead, everyone ended the day unhappy. Including Lord Faircombe."

Geoffrey found he didn't care about the happiness of Lord Faircombe. Not at all. *Look after them, your father too*, his mother had said. But she hadn't asked Geoffrey to make him happy; because it wasn't possible to make him happy.

"Miss Rawle," he heard himself speak even before he had decided to do it, "what would make *you* happy?"

That drew her attention. She looked at him, stared at him by the light of the fire. He saw her breathing grow quicker, and her lips flushed, parted, as if they had already been kissed. "Are these the kinds of things you learn as a shepherd, to ask people such personal questions?"

"Yes," he said, leaning even closer to her, and wishing he'd moved his chair closer before he sat. "In between bouts of sheep-tossing. Yes. You didn't answer. What would make you happy?"

It pleased him desperately that she wouldn't tell him. She might be saucy, but she wasn't wanton. And if she wouldn't tell him what she wanted, he strongly suspected it had something to do with him.

And he desperately wanted it to have something to do with him.

"Oh, don't ask that," she answered with a little groan that went straight through him. She broke their gaze and looked into the fire instead. "I have learned too many things today about who I am and been disappointed by all of them. I can't disappoint myself again tonight."

* * *

HE OUGHT TO LOOK RIDICULOUS, in his shabby coat and worn trousers, with no collar, the skin of his throat peeking through at the closure of his shirt.

He didn't.

He looked majestic, and he glowed like the hottest part of the fire. His white-gold hair caught the light, and the edges of his face where the sun had touched him made mysterious shadows. Even the stubble on his chin only invited touch.

And he was asking what would make her happy.

Zelda had a new policy of giving in to temptation. But surely this was more temptation than she ought to take.

"Perhaps to return to New York," she said, experimenting with the sort of lightness in her tone that other people found easy to believe.

But he just shook his head, gravely. "I don't think so."

"No," she said, calculating that he would believe a swift turn-about, "to sail on. I ought to engage a boat for Amsterdam right away. I don't think the southern route will be open, do you?"

"I don't think you want that either. Not right now." He jerked his chin up, as if to look down his nose at her. "The problem with being a liar, Miss Rawle, is that it becomes a habit. The kind of habit that can prove your downfall at the most inopportune time."

That straightened her back. "I'm not a liar!"

"You steal things. And you plan to promise to love, honor, and keep your husband till death do you part, and then sail away."

"Hmm." That made her shift in her seat. She sank back into its cushions and watched him try not to smile and show how he knew he'd won. "I've got to be married to be respectable." She didn't mention her dowry. "I had planned to keep him. Just from a distance."

That clearly bothered him.

But he only said, "There's a good deal more to marriage than respectability and money. You must be sure of what you are doing."

She smoothed down her hair, though it didn't need it. She was beginning to be very *unsure* of what she was doing.

She ought to ask. *Do* you *know what I'm doing?*

What if he didn't?

What if he did?

"No matter where you go or... whom you marry," her giant went on, without meeting her eyes, "you ought to be strong enough to do as you choose."

"So you meant all that business about race horses?"

He nodded most seriously. His blue eyes looked dark in the firelight. Or had something happened to him from looking at her? "Entirely. You must build up your strength, Miss Rawle. If you have time. For it will take time."

"I will make the time." She would. She could be her father's daughter in her own way and foul up deals that would otherwise be smooth. *Daughter missteps, Rawle fortune takes tumble.* If she had to, Zelda thought grimly. She just needed enough money to see her around the world, after all. The goals of all these money men might have to take second place. Everyone's might have to take second place.

Except Tansy. She'd promised to take Tansy to see Europe, and she would.

It turned out that *why not?* was a very complicated question. It tested what one truly wanted, and what one believed.

She had been put to several tests tonight, and to sit here alone with this breathtaking man was but another one. A test she wanted to fail.

Because the real and final truth was that Zelda just wanted to go to him, put herself in his arms, and let him do whatever he wished until *he* was well and truly stolen.

He would be hers, all hers, then. She didn't even know how she knew, but she knew. He wouldn't fit in her pocket, but she would have stolen him nonetheless.

"So what must I do for you?" she said, half-realizing that it sounded scandalous as she said it, and utterly thrilled with herself.

* * *

SLEEPING among the sheep had changed Geoffrey. Cutting cow's hooves. Washing in ice water.

He wasn't Lord Geoffrey now. Everything he'd ever had before was out of reach. She was not.

Remembering why he shouldn't have her was becoming more difficult every second.

"First of all, never ask a man what you can do for him."

"I never have before."

He should be stern. He didn't want to be stern. He wanted to put her on his lap and bury his face there, at the base of her neck where the curls hid the softest spots.

No, those wouldn't be the softest spots.

That sleepy, suggestive look in her eyes wasn't intended. She surely didn't know what her own body could do, let alone his.

He cleared his throat. "The question is what you can do for yourself. With yourself. Your body will tell you, but you must listen."

She blinked. And blinked again. Even the flutter of her dark eyelashes made him want to touch her. And when she bit her lip, he had to swallow. "I've had something of the same idea. But I am not in the habit of talking to my body. It is *me*."

How could he have this conversation and remain a gentleman?

For God's sake. Did he have control of himself or not?

Before he could stop himself, he stood and went to stand behind her chair. "You're tired, aren't you?"

She didn't flinch at his nearness. No, she trusted him. Her head fell forward. He could just see where the curve of her shoulder met that long, slender neck. "I am so tired."

He was going to do this.

All in one motion, he cupped one hand around the back of her neck. The fragile tendons and bones and soft skin moved at his touch, so alive. She didn't jump; she only leaned into his hand, trusting him to hold her.

His voice would give away how affected he was, but he must speak. "I can feel the tension in the way you hold your head. Can't you feel it, too?"

"I suppose." She let out a soft sigh. "I ignore those little signals; they never tell me anything good."

Geoffrey was glad she couldn't see his half-smile. He'd discovered the lying thief in himself. "Listen now," he said as he bent slightly to have better access.

Both his hands fell upon her shoulders, and she made a ragged little moan.

"Don't make noises," he chuckled, so softly no one else could possibly have heard. "Listen."

* * *

He wanted her to listen? She couldn't hear anything over the noise of her pounding heart.

Perhaps she usually tried to ignore her body, but her body never felt like this. His hands on her shoulders were hot, heavy, huge. She could feel them through the quilting; they practically burned.

Then he squeezed.

"Your legs will carry you," he said in a voice of quiet confidence that made nothing else so real. "Perhaps not at first, not as far as you'd like. But they will. We ought to exercise your muscles nearly every day."

Zelda did not care why he said *nearly*. "Mmm," she said.

After a pause, the delicious pressure of his hands worked along her shoulders to stroke the base of her neck. "This is worry. Not strength."

Zelda had plenty of worries. Or she had until he'd touched her. *Woman melts away*, she thought, wondering what would be printed underneath.

"I, ah…" Had she wanted to say something? She was wrong.

Because his hands had moved down to knead the flesh of her upper arms, just lightly, and slide to her elbows.

"Does this hurt?"

She hadn't realized that he would have to bend so close to touch her this way. That his voice would be inches from her ear.

"No, n-no, there is a little soreness in the joint but no, that does not hurt."

Hurt? It felt glorious. The gentle pressure he exerted released the tension she hadn't realized kept her stiff. And the warmth of his touch softened her better than whiskey.

When he moved even lower down to take one of her

hands in his and gently manipulate the flesh of her hands, the soft part below the thumb, and so over to her smallest finger, Zelda obeyed an impulse deeper than thought and let her head fall backwards to be cushioned against the shoulder she knew was there.

So solid. So strong.

She felt his breath huff suddenly, as if he'd been punched; but his voice was as calm as ever. "Sometimes the horses grow calmer if we rub their forelegs, too."

She had to laugh. "And cows and sheep?"

He stilled. How she longed for him to simply pick her up in his arms. She knew he could do it. What could she say that would make him do it again? Could she get away with it?

He only chuckled again. "We don't usually rub cows and sheep. In fact, a cow nearly crushed me tonight."

"What?" Tension came back to her limbs as she started to move. Why, she wasn't sure; he was whole and unhurt, right next to her. She simply had the urge to inspect him to be sure.

"Never fear, madam. The cow lost."

His arms tightened around her as if to keep her in place.

She relented, but turned her head.

There was his face, bent over her shoulder, so close she could see every whorl of his ear, every golden bristle on his chin.

"Geoffrey," she said, and used one hand to turn his face toward hers.

She hadn't been sure he would know what she wanted when she didn't know herself.

But he did.

* * *

THE FIRST SIP of her was sweeter than wine and twice as intoxicating.

Her lips parted for his and he couldn't remember why he had wanted to hold back. She was luscious, delicious, coffee and chocolate and every indulgence all rolled into one, and the kiss fit them together so perfectly that his eyes closed as he became lost in her.

His body instantly screamed for *more, more, more*, but he brushed aside the urgency. She tasted like coming home. He could live here. He could want to do this for a long, long time.

Her hand stroked his cheek, heedless of the bristles, and the sweetness of it called to something inside him that had never seen the light of day. *She could have you*, it whispered to him. *You could have her. You could have each other.*

"No," he felt himself say into her lips, breaking them apart.

"No?" Zelda's heart sank. She knew it was her heart; it had been beating, then it stopped. "Should I apologize?" Was this how low she could sink? Taking advantage of a man who couldn't refuse?

"No, that is—Not what I meant, Miss Rawle. I only meant —" He stood, so quickly it felt like a cold breeze, and Zelda felt the chill of his loss. "I should not have done that when you are promised to another. That is—I shouldn't have done that to a lady."

"No?" She ought to say something more intelligent, she should. One of the servants had just kissed her—no, she'd kissed one of the servants, and she was indeed betrothed to Lord Vere. "I should not have done that to a shepherd. I *do* apologize."

"Well," he said, still behind her though he no longer touched her, "you've admitted your character flaws already."

That stung a little, though Zelda wasn't sure why; she had. "What are your character flaws, Geoffrey?"

"Still being discovered," he muttered, pacing before the fire back and forth like a restless animal.

When he stopped, he did not look directly at her face. "I will help you, Miss Rawle. Can you find a way to visit the north pasture in the afternoon? It is a long walk, but I ought not to accompany you. Can you find someone you can trust?"

"I will," she said, looking up. A muscle twitched in his jaw, but that only made her want to touch it more. "And Geoffrey."

She startled him into meeting her eyes. He was only feet away from her.

"Would it be too scandalous for you to call me Zelda, since we are to do this together?"

"Yes, it would," he said in the same rushed way, but then he gave her an extravagant bow and swooped down over her hand, capturing it and bringing it to his lips. They just touched her, lightly, softly, only reminding her by contrast of his big, hard body. "Very scandalous."

Then his eyes actually twinkled at her, and before she could stop him, he'd escaped back out the way he came.

CHAPTER 11

"*I* need paper. And ink."

Dandy just scratched his chin. "I need a palace and a whole roast cow but that ain't happenin' either."

Geoffrey paced. The shed was too small. Three strides and he had to turn to cross it again. "Just get them for me."

"Oh, back to givin' orders, are we? Need another lame cow to bring you down a bit?"

Geoffrey stopped pacing long enough to peer closely at Dandy with his boots up against Geoffrey's wall. His borrowed wall. "What are you implying?"

"Just wondering what kind of man you'll turn out to be."

"Aren't we all?" He went back to pacing. He might chastise Miss Rawle for stealing things, but found some sympathy for the impulse in his own desperation. "I can't get them from the house, but if you'll ask one of the maids…"

* * *

"THIS BONNET MAKES me look dreadful. Yellow isn't my color. Oh, Tansy, why did we ever bring it?"

Tansy's eyes widened. Zelda loved yellow. "I'll get the blue bonnet. What ails you?"

She was off to see her giant! Zelda had woken zinging with excitement. So excited that she forgot to wait for her pain. It was there; she was just too busy to pay it heed. "Yesterday was such a disaster. I must impress Lord Faircombe more favorably today."

"Blue bonnet, blue walking dress, and the blue wool cape," said Tansy in her decisive way, and Zelda had to refrain from asking her to hurry.

What was her giant doing now? Capturing sheep?

* * *

Dear Lady Rawleigh,

I hope my address does not offend you, as I think the title correct based only on hearsay.

I write because of your husband, whom I recall counts some older ladies among his patients. I am familiar only with the ailments of sheep and the like; I can claim no knowledge of a physician's science.

Perhaps you would ask him for advice on rheumatism, especially in a lady who is young and yet sorely afflicted.

Her past physicians wanted her to rest, and it does her no good.

I hope you have passed the cold winter safely and well, and look forward to any word you care to send.

Yours most sincerely,

His own signature gave him pause. He would normally sign himself at least Lord Geoffrey Eliot, if not his full name. He did not feel like that person today.

Geoffrey Eliot

His name looked so plain that way. And yet it was just who he was. Just like Lady Rawleigh (whom he thought of as

Miss Cullen, but who might prefer Mrs. Burke), it mattered less what people called him than how he thought of himself. The title didn't make him a different man.

* * *

"No, Mother, no need for you to come. Tansy and I are only going out for a small constitutional walk."

"What?" Mrs. Rawle reached for her basket, even though it was nowhere nearby. "You had a terrible day yesterday, and it is early!"

All the better to catch Geoffrey before he became engrossed in sheep, thought Zelda. Then she glimpsed how high the sun was. Drat. It was likely too late.

"You needn't come," she said again. "We're only planning to see a corner of the estate you won't like."

"Won't like? Why?"

Her mother's question dragged Zelda back to the present moment. This was what came of not paying attention while she talked. "Bees." She said the first thing that came to her. "Far too many bees."

"Bees!" Mrs. Rawle marched off in search of the basket, as if there were bee remedies inside it. "I am definitely not letting you stroll into clouds of bees by yourself!"

"Bees?" Tansy asked with the same dry lack of appreciation she'd had regarding the perfect bonnet.

"There could be bees," Zelda tossed back.

There were no bees and both of them knew it.

"Have you decided not to marry?" Tansy, as determined to reach the far side of Europe as Zelda in her own way, demanded answers if the plan was to change.

"I will marry." *Probably*, she thought. "There is no harm in talking to people."

"Talking? No, not much harm in that."

"So when we see him, be sure to distract my mother, would you? Otherwise, we'll have no privacy at all."

"For talking. Certainly. You just tell me when the bees are in sight."

"Is sarcasm a feature of our growing familiarity, Tansy?"

"Yes," said her maid, before leaving to fetch herself some stout walking shoes.

* * *

GEOFFREY HADN'T EXPECTED to see Miss Rawle walking over the lawns toward the cow pens. He hadn't expected how it lifted his morning out of the cow muck and up into the sky.

Had it really been that long since he had simply enjoyed something?

He *definitely* hadn't expected to see her with her maid and her mother as well.

She wasn't much for following directions; this was late morning and far from afternoon. The quiet glamor of the firelight last night was long gone. She was real, she was *here*… and every man jack on the estate was watching.

"What an interesting cow!" she said, waving one hand as the three of them approached.

Geoffrey looked at the beast, its jaw slowly working in a circle. It drooled. It was not interesting.

The herdsmen bent their heads. Geoffrey couldn't hear everything they said, but he heard a few words like *load of mischief* and *hopper-arsed*. One man whistled, low.

He bit out over his shoulder, "Respect for the lady. And guard your mouth." Maybe they thought he didn't know those words. Miss Rawle was neither a loose woman nor too wide in the hips. They didn't need to look at her hips and they definitely didn't need to comment.

"Oh aye," said a fellow taking a break from shoveling out

the barn to watch the show. "We'll try not to scratch our sacks while the lady is watching."

Geoffrey just looked down his nose. He might not be a lord of the manor anymore, but he would not let them subject a lady to sack-scratching either.

He ambled the cow toward the ladies. Behind him he heard a cough muffling a muttered "Schoolteacher!"

"Miss Rawle. I'm glad to see you looking more well today." There, what could be safer than talking about her health?

Damn it all. Hadn't he mocked Vere for doing just that?

She didn't seem to mind. "Thank you. And how are you?"

He looked from side to side. The livestock men all watched their every move.

This was more awkward than conversation in a drawing room full of grandmothers.

He couldn't touch Miss Rawle—Zelda, as he had begun to think of her; and they could hardly continue their conversation from last night. He did not want to think about what her mother would say if he tried to examine the tone of her muscles.

Morning or afternoon, he hadn't thought this through.

How stupid was his smile right now? It felt like it stretched from ear to ear. He tried to shake his face loose.

He bobbed his head toward the elder woman. "Does Mrs. Rawle wish to visit the dairy house?" Perhaps he should pretend she did.

"No," said Mrs. Rawle, her broad-brimmed hat tilting back a little so she could fix him with eyes even darker than her daughter's. "I am here in case of bees."

"I see."

He didn't, and looked toward Miss Rawle for some sort of explanation. None was forthcoming.

They all waited for an awkward couple of heartbeats for something to happen.

"Oh look, there are peacocks over there," Miss Rawle's maid finally said. "Have you seen them, Mrs. Rawle?"

"Why, no."

Luckily, at that moment, one of the male peacocks, sensing he was the topic of conversation, spread his tail and displayed all its magnificent color.

Once Mrs. Rawle exclaimed her surprise, it was easy for the maid to draw the older woman over for a closer look, leaving Miss Rawle to stay by Geoffrey.

He should scold her, tell her she was embarrassing him.

He couldn't, because she didn't. Seeing her was pure pleasure.

"You look better this morning," he said low enough it would not carry. He ought to sound more like the cattlemen, he realized, and tried to imagine what they'd say, and say it. "No barrel fever today?"

"Barrel fe—Oh! No." Her smile today was different. Wide and sparkling. Apparently, she'd rested and wasn't whiskey-bitten. It would be nice if some of that smile were due to him.

"Did you walk all this way?"

She looked back over her shoulder toward the square shapes of Faircombe Hall. "I did!" she said with pardonable pride. "And it wasn't that hard," she added, clearly surprising herself.

"Very good." The way she beamed made the praise worthwhile. "Now you must turn around and go back."

"Go back!" Miss Rawle raised a hand toward his arm across the cow's neck, then noticed the watching farm men. She moved to lay her hand on the cow instead. Then she thought better of her gloves and just gave up. "I've only just arrived," she said, just as softly.

"And what did you think would happen?" She was taunting him, surely, thinking there was anything they could do or say with her mother yards away. She deserved a little teasing in return.

"Just… something. Because you are here. And so am I," she clarified, shooting a sideways glance at the men who were clearly trying to hear.

She knew damn well their touches by the fire last night had not been entirely innocent. She knew damn well she couldn't have them here.

"Aha." The woman was a daredevil. "And what exactly would you and I do, Miss Rawle, with your mother just there and about to tire of peacocks?"

"I—" She settled in on her heels. Thwarted. Geoffrey felt unaccountably pleased. "Something," she muttered, as displeased with the world all in a second as she had been pleased with it the moment before.

He stifled a laugh.

She was just as eager in her own way as Joan, the barmaid. But she gave him the impression that she actually liked him. She was eager, but she didn't know for what, and that was disconcertingly attractive.

There was no man so big he couldn't feel taller when a woman looked at him that way.

And she'd walked a long way. "You've done very well for your first morning. You mustn't overextend yourself. Go back, break your fast, rest. Perhaps sleep."

"I don't want sleep." Her fingers twitched as if still searching for a way to touch him.

"Go on," he said, "and I'll visit again tonight." He didn't ask, just promised. Softly, so no one else would hear.

He saw her think it over for a moment. "Very well," she said with one of those sudden reversals of mood, and she smiled again. "But Geoffrey. After last night, I think you can call me Zelda. Don't you?"

"No," he said, but she wasn't listening.

She sailed away, her hems brushing the damp grass as she joined her mother. "My, isn't he stunning?" she observed loud enough for anyone to hear.

Geoffrey didn't think she was that impressed by the peacock.

This would lead nowhere good. She simply couldn't visit him here in the paddocks day in and day out.

But she'd looked the way he felt when they'd drawn closer to one another. And when he even talked to animals while he treated them, how could he avoid talking to her? For he was still determined to help her.

* * *

WITH EVERY STEP back to the great house, Zelda's thoughts snarled more and more. She'd been *so* excited to see him, and he had been merely pleasant. Had she walked all that way for him to be only pleasant?

Yes, there was the problem presented by her mother's company, and Tansy's, but he hadn't even given her any kind of sign. They should have set up a sign. Perhaps a code. Something with blinking.

The Zelda Code blinks sentences in moments, she pictured the headline. But what did she wish he'd said?

Wasn't that something *he* should know?

The walk back was so much quicker; the distance from the courtyard to her room was growing smaller. Was she growing stronger just wandering Faircombe's halls? Her giant had been right about that.

Geoffrey, she reminded herself to think the name.

"Go ahead to break your fast, Mother," Zelda waved as

175

she bent to slip off her now-damp shoes. She needed time to think.

"Of course I will wait for you."

"It is only that I feel a little awkward after last night." Zelda really had to make up a store of lies, if getting some distance from her mother was going to be a regular need. At least this was better than bees. "Do go first, would you? And when I come, I shall sit beside you."

Casting a look towards her daughter as if she wondered more for her mind than her joints, Mrs. Rawle nonetheless slowly departed through the connecting door to the chamber she occupied on the far side.

"Awkwardness, and bees." Tansy was not convinced. "Was that all so you could stand beside a cow and talk over it to that heap of a man?"

"He's not a heap."

"He's not your betrothed, either. Miss Rawle." Tansy had her feet planted, and she clasped her hands in front of her as if to lecture. "We have a bargain, you and I. We both wish to see the world. If you stay here, I will not get where I wish to go. If you go home, I will not get where I wish to go. You see my concern."

"Tansy, I've forgotten nothing. I just need more time. A little more time before the wedding."

Her betrothed wasn't that satisfactory; neither was her giant. Bouncing from man to man would avail her little; she didn't know that many, and she didn't have the time.

Zelda's stocking feet kicked and dangled off the edge of the bed. The contracts. They controlled all of this. "Tansy. It's the contracts. The gentlemen who control those, control everything. We must find the everlasting contracts they are arguing over and find out what is truly at stake."

Tansy's eyes narrowed. "You've never had the least interest in those contracts."

"Well, I have now. And if you want to get to Europe with me, so do you."

* * *

THE REST of the men milled around, taking up tasks, not meeting Geoffrey's eyes. But one stayed put.

"She's a fine-looking piece of flesh."

Geoffrey felt himself swell as he looked down at the man. "You had better mean the cow."

The man snorted, shrugging with his hands in his pockets. "I'm bein' friendly. Are you one of us, or aren't ya? If ya live here now, ya might want to know." He looked over his shoulder where Miss Rawle had gone. "I'm not sayin' it's for that particular lady, mind. But there's a cottage."

"What?"

"There's a cottage. In the woods out north."

"Lord Geoffrey's not interested in that." Augie, the village blacksmith, was just leaving the barns. His box of tools was carelessly slung over one thick shoulder. He had not come out to see the fuss when the ladies arrived.

"He's a man, ain't he?"

The soot-smudged cheekbones of the blacksmith stood out in stark shapes. "He's a better kind of man."

The herdsman snorted.

It hadn't felt like a compliment.

It was awkward to hear, especially in this company. "No, I'm really not," Geoffrey told them both, wondering if he believed it. "But there's no cottage out there." Geoffrey lifted his head and looked that way.

There were farmlands to the west and south, and as a child he'd always played to the east, in the little woods and the pond. The sheep paddocks went there now, as the little group of ponds watered the sheep when they were moved from field to field. His mother's hill, where Zelda had tried to go yesterday, overlooked all of that—sheep paddocks, woods, ponds, all stretching towards the village.

That was what surrounded Faircombe's estate. No cottage.

The man just nodded. "You *are* titled, aren't ya? Know-all."

"What are you on about?"

The fellow lost interest in the conversation. "Just telling ya. There's a cottage out there if you had a lady you wanted peace and quiet with. But never mind." He swatted a hand back toward them as he walked away, as if ridding himself of both of them.

"There is a cottage out there, you know," said Augie with his calm certainty.

There was no cottage to the north of Faircombe Hall that Geoffrey didn't know about. And Augie did not know more about Faircombe than Geoffrey did.

But he'd been startled a lot lately.

"Look," he said, "will you show me?"

* * *

Zelda craned her head around the door. The room was empty. She slid in through the wide-paneled door, Tansy right behind her, and silently closed it.

"The chambermaids say the solicitors are in here all day. Mr. Wapping doesn't like Mr. Paltz," Tansy added.

"Oh, believe me, I know that."

As soon as she said it, she remembered the dinner last night. All the businessmen had been there, and the solicitors… but not Mr. Paltz.

And not her mother.

Before her were stacks of neat paper on a low table surrounded by chairs.

Eagerly, Zelda plopped down before them. "We mustn't confuse them."

With more presence of mind, Tansy locked the door, leaving the key in the lock. "What are you going to do with them?"

"Read them!" Undismayed by the thickness of the stack, Zelda lifted the top sheet, as evenly cut as any piece of paper she had ever seen. It reminded her of Mr. Wapping's straight lines.

She took it to the desk behind her, so she could rest the paper on something while she read. "We can read, and these are words. Sit there, and you start on that pile while I start on this one. How hard can it be?"

ZELDA'S FOREHEAD rested on the desk blotter. She rocked her head back and forth, no longer caring if her face left an imprint on its thick cotton paper. "Well, now we know how hard it can be."

Tansy too sprawled in her chair in the least ladylike pose Zelda had ever seen her make. "It's like I've forgotten how to read. The words are there, but they don't make sense."

Zelda thumped her head once. The paper almost touched her nose. "What does *indemnification* mean? Is this our defeat?"

Tansy just gave her a look. "Steady," she said, as if they were back on the ship. "You have the right idea. We may need help."

Help. Her giant offered help. It was a new concept to Zelda, but worthwhile. Though she suspected that while her giant could do many things, reading the dense writing and even denser language of contracts surely wasn't among his talents.

"All right. Yes. Let me think." She sat up and glared at the papers. "I can't follow everything, but it's clear there's a great deal of money in play. Not just between my father and Lord Faircombe, but all the gentlemen here. I do see plans for a great deal of profit. What I *don't* see is my dowry."

"I told you," Tansy lifted a sheet of paper she was still carefully keeping to its right spot in the pile. "This mentions your dowry."

"But it remains with Lord Vere. That cannot be right."

Tansy laid the papers back down, then let her hands fall to her knees. "Who would possibly be willing to help us?"

"Let me think." She had one idea. It was a great risk. But *why not?*

* * *

"It's a ruin."

"Not really." Augie had left his toolbox behind and strode easily through the woods straight for the place. He walked around the pile of rubble along one end and pushed aside a little stand of trees fighting for the light.

The stones on the ground were blackened, and burnt beams thrust up from the ruin, their edges softened with rain and time. The saplings had grown from the scars.

Geoffrey followed him through the little stand of trees, trying not to snap the saplings in two. He winced when they creaked.

On the other side, the cottage was intact, overgrown, with two windows left. They weren't filled with glass in the modern way, but with wooden shutters.

"It must be full of animals," Geoffrey said wonderingly as they approached a small door almost hidden in the side, clearly an original door that led to the cellar.

"It gets that way, but people clear 'em out when they

wanta—uh—" Augie looked sheepish. "Don't get angry, but you know. For ladies and such."

No lady would come out here to get tumbled in a burnt-down shack.

But it had once been a fine cottage, and Geoffrey hadn't even known it was here. "What was it?"

"House," said Augie with the simplicity of a person who didn't worry much about the past.

"Whose house, man?"

"Don't know." With a shrug, he lifted the latch, then stepped back so Geoffrey could open the door.

There was no sign of small animals nesting in here from the winter. The walls looked sound, and the little door, which Geoffrey could barely squeeze through, led to a wide kitchen. The hearth was still there, the chimney looked fine; something must block the flue because the hearth wasn't full of birds' nests.

While it was chilly outside, inside it was even chillier. But this part of the house was whole.

"I'm not bringing any ladies here." Geoffrey would not chance more gossip about Miss Rawle than he could help, much less about Miss Rawle and himself. "But this amazes me. Why didn't I know it was here?"

Augie shrugged again. "You haven't needed a place to take a woman for a tumble."

"How many people—never mind. Don't tell me."

Geoffrey didn't want to know how many locals used the place for *rendezvous*. But he did want to know what the house was doing here. He'd not only never seen it before, he'd never heard it mentioned. "Do all the servants know about the place? Does everyone in the *village*?"

"Ya know, I don't think so," mused Augie. "Your men in the barns told me about it. Villagers don't come here." He rubbed his chin, extending the black soot smudges around the edges of his jaw. "I've never heard anyone talk about it in the village. Someone must, though. Maybe old Mrs. Hull."

"How did I not know it was here?"

Augie's eyes were kind. "Yer not a bad sort, sir, but you have that lord problem of thinking you know all there is to know."

Geoffrey rolled his head around to look at Augie, whom he'd known most of his life. "Of all people, you don't have to say *sir* to me. You never did."

As Geoffrey turned around in the center of the room, barely discerning in the speck of light that made it through the shutters that there were no gaps in the stone walls, nor holes in the roof, he realized that Augie also knew something about him he didn't. He *was* looking for a place.

And while this wasn't it, it shook him. He'd always felt Faircombe to be as big and solid as himself. But if Faircombe had secrets hidden away in its hollows, what did that say about him?

* * *

"Lord Vere!" Zelda had napped for much of the afternoon, recovering what energy she could. Tansy had just managed to dress her for dinner. "Where is everyone?"

"Lord Faircombe and the businessmen have gone riding, and the solicitors are at work."

Zelda hoped they wouldn't notice any difference in the way their piles of papers lay.

She wanted to ask after Lady Charlotte and Miss Farsworth, but it was more important she have a few minutes alone to talk with him before her mother arrived. "I have a favor to ask you, sir."

CHAPTER 12

"You don't mind if we sit?" She led him to an alcove with chairs that looked out over the expansive Faircombe views. "Is there a place in this house that doesn't look out over lawns and sheep?"

"The new wing will look over the glasshouse. How can I serve you, Miss Rawle?"

Zelda preferred businesslike men, but what she was about to ask needed to be prefaced. Preferably with some sweetness. She needed him to think well of her right now.

"Lord Vere, I realized today our relationship has been hampered from the start; not by its attachment to business, but by its attachment to *secret* business."

He bit his lip; she'd struck a nerve. "What secret business?"

It wasn't hard to look hopeless. "You see, I'm not sure. There are our lawyers and your solicitors, locked up all day, fighting over something with those merchants your father summoned; but I don't have your ability to ignore it all."

"I don't concern myself with it, Miss Rawle, and you

mustn't either." His nerves settled, and he gave her a calm smile of supreme confidence. "That's all being taken care of."

A dead end.

If she couldn't make the great lump curious, could she make him chivalrous? Surely he had something of that in him; he had a title.

"I wish I could!" She could cry when needed, but not quickly enough; forget tears. She frowned as hard as she could and combined it with what she hoped was a terribly fearful look. "I have so many worries about the wedding, and being married…" She looked down. What would she say if this were Geoffrey? "It's a bit nerve-wracking, you know, preparing to… submit to someone I barely know."

"Miss Rawle!" Chivalry wasn't stirring in him. He looked appalled. One of his smooth locks of hair nearly fell over one eye, he was so shocked. "Let us not speak of such things!"

If they couldn't speak of it, doing it would be difficult, Zelda thought, moving her betrothed farther and farther down the list of interesting men. "Nonetheless, you do see what I mean. I cannot feel calm, not knowing if I will be entirely *safe* in this marriage."

"Why wouldn't you be safe?" said the heir of Faircombe without meeting her eyes, and Zelda suspected him of a very specific idea of why she shouldn't feel safe. It was a skill of hers to spot bad liars, as she could be one herself.

But she had a true reason for possible trepidation. "I had a friend in New York who married a man her father had arranged. Impeccable references, from Maryland, supposedly a cousin of one of her father's friends. Then—you'll never guess."

To his credit, he leaned in a little. "I won't?"

"You never will. There she was, six months later, her dowry gone, along with her supposed husband! And after that, a *baby*! So I heard. She never came to a party again."

"I should hope not." Perfectly comfortable banning a young woman from good society if she fell for such a ploy, Lord Vere's look changed to one of disgruntlement. "You cannot mean to imply any such thing will befall you."

"No, no! For one thing, you really do seem to own this house. At least, the man you call your father does."

Lord Vere opened his mouth, but Zelda went on.

"But that's just it, I don't know! If the contracts contained extensive agreements about how you leased this entire estate in order to raise peacocks and sheep, and are only its caretaker until its real owner returned, I wouldn't know."

"Why do you mention peacocks and sheep, specifically?"

"Lord Vere." One more try. Zelda half-whispered, leaned close, and laid a confiding hand on his arm. "I appeal to you as a man of honor. Can you not find a solicitor in London who would assist me in understanding my legal fate?"

Legal fate just made him nervous again. She thought he might start twisting his fingers together.

She decided to push. "You can go under guise of inviting people for my—our engagement party! Won't that be fun?"

"Quite possibly." He turned his Roman-emperor profile her way and stared out over the greens. "I do believe I can do something of use to you in London." When he looked back at her, he was somber. "I do wish you well, you know."

"That seems a sound basis for marriage!" *Ugh*. Zelda must change the topic; even she didn't believe herself on that one. "I do appreciate your consideration. You are kind."

"I hope so," he said the same way, half to himself.

* * *

THE SUN WAS WELL on its way towards the horizon when Geoffrey saw Vere round the corner of the kitchen wing and head straight toward him at the hen-house.

Well. Geoffrey wasn't hard to find. He dropped the chicken he'd been holding and just nodded.

Vere looked pointedly at the chicken, strolling away unconcerned, looking for grubs. "You've moved up to chickens?"

"They can get mites." Geoffrey was in no mood for sniping. The half-burned cottage to the north weighed on him, and he wanted to know if Vere had known of it. But Vere was hardly cooperative.

"Is there anything you won't physic?"

Geoffrey could have said *you* as he would have when they were little boys throwing insults at each other. He might have even meant it.

Faircombe was the bedrock of Geoffrey's life. The house, the grounds, his family. His family was unraveling, and to learn that the grounds weren't what he thought either shook him.

Fortunately, Vere wasn't waiting for an answer. "As it happens, your incessant need to be a mother hen is why I'm here."

"Really? *You* have mites?" Geoffrey looked at his brother warily.

"My intended."

Geoffrey's spine straightened. He said nothing.

"I must travel to London, and you should make sure nothing happens to her while I'm gone."

Geoffrey looked away so his brother wouldn't see the turmoil in his face.

He realized he was looking toward the mysterious cottage, and dropped his eyes. "Why go to London now?" Geoffrey realized he knew nothing of his father's planned timetable. "Won't you be married soon?"

"Miss Rawle suggested I go." Vere never worried about anything; he looked worried now. And somber, and a bit sad.

"She asked me in confidence, and I need her to begin our marriage, at least, with ongoing confidence that I will help her in any way she needs."

"*Begin* your marriage? Only begin?"

Vere ignored that. "You know I would not ask you to watch over her were it not serious. I worry for her a little. So frail in body and mind."

Geoffrey didn't think frailty was Miss Rawle's most obvious characteristic. "I won't let any harm come to her."

"Don't let her harm herself." Vere tugged at his gloves. "Do you know, she has a peculiar sort of sweetness to her. Less than an hour ago, she laid her hand on my arm as if it weren't quite improper. I could have scolded her, but it's hard to do. She's like a child."

Geoffrey felt his bones grow cold at the mention of Zelda laying her hand on Vere's arm.

Just as she'd tried to put her hand on *Geoffrey's* arm that morning, in full public view.

Had he been blinded by his body's reaction to her? Hell's snowflakes, of course he had. He'd touched her last night, he'd *kissed* her, forgetting that he still didn't know why she was so desperate to leave New York. And sail around the world, at that.

Hadn't Geoffrey begun by wondering what was wrong with her, that she had to come all this way for a marriage? Dandy had speculated that she was simply appalling, and so had Delina. And without finding out more about her, the closer he'd gotten, the more Geoffrey had simply seen her eyes, and her figure, and her appealing laugh, and treated her like a gently born lady, albeit one who stole things and drank prodigiously.

He still didn't know if she smoked opium or seduced men, in addition to taking all that whiskey. He'd thought she was shy about what was in his pants. Maybe she knew *very* well.

Maybe she'd decided to play one brother against the other for her own reasons.

"She won't harm herself, nor will anyone else. I'll see to it that she behaves as the next lady of the house should behave."

"Thank you." Orders delivered, Vere turned.

"But."

Vere stopped.

"If Lord Faircombe sees me near the house, he'll cut me out farther."

"Don't be seen." This unsympathetic advice was all Vere offered before turning to go again.

"Is that all? If I keep watch on your treasure woman, what can you do for me?"

Vere just cut him a glare. "What would you have me do?"

Geoffrey couldn't recall Vere ever saying that before. This meant more to him than some random woman. This was his brother. Perhaps his moment to make a difference to his brother. "Stop playing his game. You are your own man. If you must threaten me, do it in your own voice."

Vere straightened his spine, much as Geoffrey had moments before. "I am his heir. I am inheriting a family legacy you can't imagine, either in importance or in weight."

"I can imagine it. I am your heir, you know. Or at least Frederick's."

"You will never inherit this title. You haven't the least idea how heavy that responsibility is."

When Geoffrey looked at Vere, he still saw the boy who had been his bigger, more handsome brother. "Then show me by how you wear the responsibility now. Will this title belong to you? Or do you belong to it?"

Vere slapped a glove against his thigh, displaying his

impatience. "Of the two of us, I am not the one who fails to know his place."

* * *

LATE THAT NIGHT, when Geoffrey stole up the marble steps to the lady's French windows, his blood was considerably cooler than it had been the night before.

This Miss Rawle might need help. But that was all he knew for sure about her.

He must not let his habit of ministering to every hurt creature in his path lead him by the nose. He had some experience of women; he had to remember what he knew. If he could turn a cool back on a fiery barmaid like Joan, he could keep his distance from Miss Zelda Rawle.

Through the glass he saw her reclining on the bed, rolling something back and forth along the coverlet. The slow lazing motions didn't suit Faircombe life. Charlotte never sat still, and Delina always had a pencil in her hand. Though a pencil would be too painful for Miss Rawle to grasp.

At least, he thought so. How much of what she said was the truth?

There certainly were no bees.

He'd come with no idea what to say. Refusing to acknowledge that a part of him wanted to be in that room, by that roaring fire, with his hands gliding down her neck, her arms, her back as he pulled her against him—

He'd come at the behest of something other than his sensible mind.

It was too quiet in there, too private, and much too warm. He'd speak with her tomorrow about training her muscles. And he'd find out more about her vices as well as her charms.

There should be rules around their encounters. No more than twenty minutes at a time, perhaps. They ought to be chaperoned, but Geoffrey knew that wouldn't suit the American woman's goals.

Whatever those were.

* * *

WHEN she so often needed to sleep and couldn't climb stairs, Zelda carefully guarded what remained of her pride.

He'd rebuffed her across the back of a *cow*.

Still, when she caught sight of movement out of the corner of her eye, she kicked the rug off her feet and darted toward it.

She had the French windows open before she remembered how she was dressed. The cold breeze clutched at her chest.

But she was glad she'd hurried; there he was, just about to walk away.

"Geoffrey?"

His look was cool and wary. That was odd. He'd looked friendly over the back of a cow.

"Good evening, Miss Rawle." And he started down the portico steps!

She was by his side in an instant. "Aren't you going to come in?"

"Miss Rawle. You mustn't be out here."

For all her difficulties, Zelda seldom caught cold. "But *aren't* you coming in?"

Instead of answering, he turned and bundled her back into the room like a child, not stopping except to close the windows until she was seated in the armchair by the fire.

An armchair which he lifted, Zelda and all, and moved closer to the flames.

His display of strength was over far too soon. There

Zelda was, planted back on the carpet, wondering how she could get him to do something so thrilling again.

"Weren't you going to speak to me at all?"

"No," was all his gruff answer, and he stalked to the other side of the fireplace.

Away from her.

This was fine behavior from a man who had been more welcoming when they had a cow between them.

Thinking back, Zelda recalled that they had actually exchanged few words, and almost all of it at his behest.

It seemed that no matter their station, men liked control.

She might not have a title, but she did not have to be British aristocracy to be someone. She didn't have to put up with gray moods from a shepherd.

She loved new things, and this new thing was important to know. Men could be interesting, and alluring, and still be heartless two-faced louses.

Even as her heart fell, she raised her head. "I see. Very well. You may go."

But he didn't go. He stood there, his eyes darkened by shadows and fixed on her. "Since you insist on conversation, privacy is best. I do have questions, and you may find them unpalatable."

Unpalatable questions? How did he know how questions tasted?

But she didn't ask, because he clearly wouldn't answer.

* * *

GEOFFREY SAW her realize she couldn't manipulate him with a sad face. Her shoulders dropped, and he saw in her again the regal poise that had made him think of Venus and Cleopatra. Dismissively, she said, "I am not as interested in your questions as I thought I would be."

What had he done to give her the impression that *he* could be dismissed like that? It reminded him of the burning sting when his father had ordered him out of the house. Which solidified his determination to stay right where he was.

"Is that what drives you, miss? The thrill of the new?"

CHAPTER 13

"Actually, yes."

Well, she was blunt. And the flush in her face seemed to show she had some shame left.

Though perhaps it was just the heat from the fire.

He faced her. "And that is why you are here? A hedonist's urge for some new pleasure?"

"Quite," and she relaxed back into her chair, though her eyes were wary.

"Then why the Faircombe family?" He stumbled a little over the words, about to say *my brother*. "Why not marry in New York?"

"If I had married in New York, I would have had to stay in New York."

"But you don't intend to stay here? You intend to marry here, and then sail on around the world."

She said nothing, just watched him with those slow, secret eyes.

"Is it your thought that Lord Vere will sail with you?"

"No." That answer was quick.

"Then why?"

Miss Rawle looked back over her shoulder to where she had lain on the bed. Geoffrey refused to follow her eyes. She might be very practiced in the art of leading a man's thoughts; indeed, it seemed she was.

She finally said, "I don't believe you would understand."

Her words only piled on to the weight of dismissal, the pain of being cut from his family and home and everything he had ever cared for. No one thought Geoffrey capable of understanding; not his father, not his brother, and apparently not Miss Rawle.

But Geoffrey thought he understood all too well.

"Try me." Acid fairly dripped from his words.

Tossing her head, Miss Rawle stood. She was not a small woman, but she barely came up to his shoulder; nonetheless, she advanced on him with the fearlessness of a queen.

"Apparently, men cannot imagine themselves as anything but essential." He had not heard that cynical note in her voice before; he was seeing the hidden Miss Rawle now. "My father would have handed me over to a husband and expected him to keep me the same way I had been kept: in four walls."

"But that's not enough for you." How many men had been prospects for her marriage in New York? How many had she sampled and not found exciting enough?

"No, it isn't." She didn't look the least ashamed; well, he admired that. Women who wanted him in their bed sometimes got him; confidence had a definite appeal. It was the consequences that galled him, when they left him twisting in the wind about the results; and he could see now she was the sort who made a habit of secrets.

Now that she was talking, he couldn't let her stop. "You might as well tell me. What couldn't you find in their arms that drove you across a whole sea?"

She blinked, and some of the sleepiness fell away. He saw

the pulse jumping at the base of her throat. She was being honest now. "A dream of my own. Something for myself."

"Have you ever had an unselfish impulse?"

The words escaped him before he thought them. They hung there, spoken, hard.

She blinked, and just like that, her thoughts were shuttered again. "Perhaps not," she said, as if she didn't care.

For some reason, he felt guilty. But he couldn't waver. No one was seeing to Vere's safety if he didn't do it himself. "What do you indulge in besides wine and whiskey? Opium?"

"What is opium?" She was always ready to hear about some new salacious thing, Geoffrey thought sourly as her interest showed.

"A drug that dulls the mind. Lulling. Dreaming."

"I have been prescribed laudanum. I hated it."

Of course, opium would not be exciting enough for her. "You no longer take it?"

"I could have slept my whole life away." Agitated now, she rubbed her own arms, just where he had rubbed her the night before. The memory of her, soft and warm under his hands, tautened his belly.

But he would not be distracted any more than he would be moved. "There was nothing else unique to America that you found sufficiently stimulating?"

"Stimulating?" That caught her attention, too. "Coffee. And chocolate. You have both here, you know. New York is different, but not that different."

"So New York's charms paled for you, and you decided to go abroad?"

"No," she said, walking away from the fireplace, walking away from him. "I think it was the other way around."

He had a glimpse of the graceful base of her neck, as her hair, still tied up in ribbons, left the skin there bare. It caused the tightness in him to grow into a roar. "Surely not, Miss

Rawle. You never found the charms of New York men sufficiently exciting to hold your attention, and you decided to go to Europe. Amsterdam, perhaps. Russia. And you want to keep going, hoping something, some man, would hold your attention. Yet their thrill always fades."

The look she tossed him over her shoulder was disdainful. "Men are not thrilling."

Lies. Pure lies. Because this same woman had thrilled to *his* touch the night before.

A lie he could disprove.

In two steps, he was behind her. "No?" he said, bent just so the air from his lips as he said the word would strike that bare skin that was distracting him till he could see nothing else.

She might spin stories to control his brother, but Geoffrey wouldn't be so easily moved.

THE TINY SENSATION was more powerful than any device for moving her whole body.

Zelda's eyes closed. The waft of warm breath, the nearness of his mouth, seized all of her. Muscles clenched in places she never thought about, and the tingling shiver in her arms made her draw in a breath. She grew hot and heavy inside without moving at all.

She'd mistaken her giant. He didn't like her. He even seemed angry, for some reason. But his power over her body was undeniable. No wonder he wanted her to listen to it.

"I can see your shoulders draw tight," he said, as if he was not inches from her bare skin. "I can see the flush of heat moving upwards."

It felt like a moment of decision. Zelda felt more alarm at his nearness, at the knowing words, than she had climbing into a ship and crossing an ocean. It felt as momentous. It challenged her commitment to asking *why not?*

Well, why not? She had never wanted anything more.

"How many men did you enjoy in New York?"

Zelda was done being restrained.

She turned, and the way he'd been bent down to breathe against her, her arms fit perfectly around his neck.

"Like this? None," she said, and kissed him.

His arms surrounded her, bent her against him, and she willingly softened to fit. She'd meant the kiss to be an answer; instead, she forgot all his questions. Their relative sizes ceased to matter as they became one figure with intertwined limbs, mouths one, bodies one.

This wasn't teasing or tentative. This was all-encompassing. He had her, in his arms, full against him, drinking her in. She ought to feel crushed; instead, she felt like she was flying.

When she tightened her arms around his neck, his little growl surprised her; even more when he straightened, lifting her off the ground, burying his face in the crook of her neck.

When he bit her there, she groaned. "Don't stop."

She knew he heard her; his arms tightened more.

"You know perfectly well how to drive a man mad," he muttered into her throat, and Zelda loved that idea. Imagine, something she hadn't known she knew until right this moment.

"You know how to thrill a woman, I'll give you that," she gasped as he pulled her tight against him again, and kissed her.

How could she want him to devour her so? His mouth was soft and hard and demanding and giving all at the same time.

"You are a show-off," she murmured when he let her breathe again. It was galling; he controlled when she could *breathe.* But she wanted him to do it again.

"That's not showing off." As close as they were, he was still somehow distant. As long as his breath felt that good against her ear, she didn't care.

He lifted her a little higher, and in three steps, backed her into the bed. When he gently dropped her, she fell back on to her elbows. He knelt.

"This is showing off," he growled, and tossed up her skirts.

Zelda thought herself imaginative. She was wrong. She could never have imagined this mountain of a man spreading her bare thighs with his hands and looking at her like that.

One of his thumbs brushed her curls, just barely, and there was a challenge in his eyes as they met hers. "Would you like to be thrilled, Miss Rawle?"

A challenge, and a twinkle she recognized. He was oddly angry with her and distant still; but he found this *fun*.

She did love a person who knew what entertained them. She felt herself smile. "Will it make you call me Zelda?"

"It might."

And then he bent and kissed her again. In a very different way.

It was everything, all at once, and it overwhelmed her. Surprising, shocking, embarrassing, all while it was also shiveringly, lusciously *good*. A river of heat flowed through her, no, an ocean, towards his mouth and away from it at the same time, radiating all through her till she felt she must melt.

She collapsed.

Her hated limbs, that so poorly obeyed her, now strained towards his mouth and the beautiful things he was doing with it. She felt soft and strong at the same time, clenching and undulating towards him with motions she didn't know she knew.

When his tongue flicked hard against her, she let out a small cry. Nothing could feel this good. It wasn't possible.

She put her hand over her own mouth in case he did that again.

Indeed, he seemed to take that as a goad. Deeper he dove into places that were hers alone and made them his. The slick heat built and built till Zelda could not help but writhe; he put his big hands on her thighs and held them still.

He was right. He was thrilling her.

He knew he was right, too. When he lifted his head, the look he gave her was smug, and superior, and full of a power she didn't know and couldn't recognize.

Still, Zelda liked to be fair. "You're right. This *is* showing off. Don't stop."

That *don't stop* hit him somehow; his smug smile faded, and he looked hungry. "So what do you say, Zelda? Is this thrill sufficiently new?"

How could she lie when they were this close? "I've never imagined anything like it."

Confusion snarled his forehead a little, but she didn't want to go back to conversation. Her belly felt tight and the heat between her legs throbbed.

"It can't *stay* like this," she panted. Surely not. She lifted her head to search his face. "Can it?"

"As long as you can stand it," he said, and Zelda had no time to imagine what that meant before he lowered his face to her again and most brazenly dove into her with his lips, his tongue, everything he had.

No, not everything; one of those enormous hands slid in along her thigh and Zelda barely had time to feel embarrassed by that—it was too incredibly intimate—before she felt his touch tease her apart then amazingly, astonishingly, slide inside.

"Oh my *God*," she cried around the hand clasped over her

mouth and bucked against him, unwittingly pushing him deeper before she realized that was *good*, she *wanted* him deeper. It was invasion, but it was welcome.

"Tell me," and he might kneel like a shepherd, but he ordered her like a king.

She wanted to tell him. She loved everything new, and this was the most new she had ever felt. "That feels so huge. It's a little stretching, a little… invasive. But I like it!" she rushed to add as she felt him start to slide away. Then when he pushed back in, "Oh. I like that *more*."

"How can that be a stretch? That is but one of my fingers."

That wasn't possible; it felt huge. "That's not possible," she said, letting the hand over her mouth fall; it had started to ache.

"It's very possible," and when he pushed back in again, it was a vastly larger, stretchier sensation. "For instance, this is how two fingers feels."

She couldn't cry out again, she couldn't breathe. Her knees and hips ached a little, but it was as nothing to the huge swirling hot tension he was pulling tighter and tighter in her core. She wondered what would happen when it reached its tightest.

The suspense was indeed incredible.

He kept her wondering for so long she forgot to wonder, just breathing in and out, raggedly, at the mercy of his fingers and his mouth and anything he wanted to do to her, anything at all.

Then she squeezed, an experiment with a muscle she'd never used before, never noticed before. Squeezed the fingers that felt so incredibly good.

And it set off something, something explosive like fire-works, deep inside her. Another new wonder.

"I think," she said with her last ragged breath, and then she exploded too.

The pulling, twisting waves of pleasure grabbed him tighter inside, and she felt their ripples detonate away from his touch and bounce back at the edges of her. She couldn't contain it all; she *did* contain it all. Every hot shivering sensation was inside *her*. *She* was afloat in an ocean of pleasure.

She had to breathe. She had to.

When her heart slowed a little and she could raise her head, she could see her giant's shoulders moving in the firelight.

"What are you doing?" Because the hand that still touched her deep inside was motionless.

WHAT HE WAS DOING WAS TRYING to finish himself off left-handed, because he didn't want to let her go. He wanted his mouth on her again. His hands, his everything. He wanted to dive into her arms and *live* there.

Her hair had come loose from its ribbons and spilled in dark waves over the snowy sheets. She was spread out before him like a feast, more wanton and willing than any woman he'd ever seen.

Her thighs trembled with the effort of staying open for him.

And he didn't want to let her go. He wanted this. He wanted her. Still.

The soft waves of her pleasure had rolled against his fingers, against his mouth, and forced him to unbutton his trousers with painful urgency. Awkwardly, his left hand had grabbed his hardness. He'd already been about to spend just looking at her, feeling her, tasting her; a few strokes would send him over the edge.

"I'm enjoying this," he said gruffly, the hoarse words inadequate to everything he felt.

"Doing what?" And against his will, since he hadn't used both hands to keep her still, she wriggled around on the bed to see what he was doing, all unheeding of the way it forced him out of her.

"Just what you did," he managed to say. He couldn't keep her still, but she wasn't leaving; just twisted around till she could hang her head over the edge of the bed to see where he gripped himself.

"Oh my," she said softly, her hair sliding off the sheets to puddle against his thigh.

That was it. He couldn't hold back.

The pleasure seized and shook him, then finally let him go; he caught his breath. He'd gone mad. This wasn't him.

His gasp was as quiet as he could make it. Christ, her mother's rooms weren't far away.

But there was Zelda looking over the edge of the bed, evidence of his pleasure escaping his grasped fingers, and he had a feeling that came out of nowhere that this wasn't her, either.

"I suppose you've had the like before." He couldn't quite catch his breath. She'd taken him out of himself. God, at least he hadn't buried himself inside her as he'd wanted to do.

She looked up at him with eyes that were wide open for once. "Has anyone ever had anything like that before? Why don't they speak of it all the time? That was *astonishing.*"

And then she looked back to where he was growing soft. "Are you quite all right?"

Was *he* all right? Who *was* this woman? He had a suspicion now that she wasn't at all the wanton he had thought.

In which case, he'd just completely debauched the woman his brother was set to marry.

CHAPTER 14

"*Y*ou've *never* enjoyed anything like that before?"

"No!" Zelda was very confused. People couldn't possibly do things like that and not talk about it *all* the time.

Then it hit her that this, *this* was what chaperones were supposed to prevent.

But this wasn't what happened in dark corners at parties. Surely… surely not.

"Oh my *God.*" She'd said that before, in the grips of heart-wrenching pleasure, but now it was from realization. "That was… did you *compromise* me?"

Geoffrey just sat on his knees, catching his breath, that massive chest heaving. He must be short of air. But then he had been working very hard. And the look on his face… he looked shocked.

By her? She hadn't done anything.

Well, nothing except what he *caused.*

The whirlwind of feelings inside her caught up a whole new host of questions and tossed them around. "Why did you *do* that? Will I have a baby now? Oh God." Thinking of the whispers about her friend who had been banished from society, she covered her mouth with both hands. "I can never go to a party again!"

"No, no. That's not true." Scrambling, Geoffrey buttoned up his trousers and stood. He was *so tall*. She had to look up and up to see his face.

Why did *he* look so stricken? He'd *done* that!

Though—Zelda *did* like to be fair—she had participated.

"Why did you do that?" she asked again. Astonishment was rolling up through her and pushing away all the other emotions. "I can't have a baby. If I have a baby, I'll have to marry you, and I can't marry you!"

"I did not ask you to," but he still looked shocked, and pained, and flushed all at the same time. He was so fair; the tops of his ears were like apples.

Something clicked back into place, some unfamiliar reserve of shame.

She pushed her skirts down over her knees and slid off the bed to stand. "I can't believe I let you in here! Why did you *do* that?"

"Stop asking me that!" His hand shot out and grabbed her by the arm.

Was he going to *hurt* her?

The thought flashed through her mind at the same moment that she realized she had asked him in. She had asked him to sit. She had entertained him, a very large man, in her room. *In her room.*

She had pushed away every money-seeking young man in New York and practically invited this one to her bed.

He let go of her at the same moment she pulled away.

She knew nothing about him, she'd just engaged in an astonishing intimacy with him, and Zelda felt in that moment that life was a trap.

* * *

HE COULDN'T CALL himself out in a duel.

He thought about telling her so, but he didn't think she'd understand.

"Miss Rawle—"

"Don't you dare. Don't you *dare*."

He couldn't think why that enraged her so, till he remembered her request that he call her Zelda.

It was a peculiar name, but these were appalling circumstances and right at this moment she had the right to request anything of him.

"Zelda." She calmed a little but still watched him through her eyelashes, arms wrapped around herself.

She looked hurt.

And he knew it was partly his pride, but he couldn't leave this room with her looking like that.

"That was my fault. All my fault."

"I *know*." She rubbed her hands against her arms. "What *was* that?"

He couldn't just herd her into the chair next to the fire now. He couldn't touch her again. He'd been so vastly, so earth-shatteringly wrong, and he knew no way to make it right.

"That was me accidentally taking advantage of your innocence."

She narrowed her eyes.

He didn't know what his face told her, but his sincerity at least must have shown.

She pulled a little farther away, just behind the bedpost, and Geoffrey felt even lower. She was nervous of him now.

She might be nervous of men forever, and it was all his fault, because he was a massive thickheaded tree and he had no idea how to fix this.

He couldn't explain that he ought to have known better, because as far as she was concerned, he was just a rough shepherd.

Which, since his life had taken this turn, was true.

"Miss—Zelda." The name was growing easier to say. "I thought you were—Christ. I thought you were the kind of woman who toys with men… that way."

"Who toys with men that way?" Zelda gestured toward the bed, then looked away as if she couldn't even bear to see it. "No, but I mean, *who*?"

Oh, God. He might as well cut his guts out and leave them on the floor. He had just treated a chaste woman like a street tramp.

In fact, he'd *never* treated a street tramp like that.

What was *wrong* with him?

"Zelda." He had to sit on the edge of the bed. He couldn't stand to loom over her any longer. "I'm sorry. I mistook some of your words for—an invitation."

"Which words?"

His heart was pounding. He actually thought he might faint. This was so much worse than the first time he'd seen a cow slaughtered, and he'd fainted for that one.

Not that anyone had told his father, but Geoffrey knew. And the livestock men knew.

This gave him the same sick feeling.

No. He had to breathe. He hadn't been inside her. Well— he *had*, but not in any truly dangerous way.

Not unless Vere threw her out for being faithless if she didn't bleed on her wedding night.

Christ.

He ought to run far away from her, when he wanted to soothe her worries away and keep her warm.

When she'd just insisted that she couldn't marry him.

Which was true; where would they sleep? He was using a borrowed bed.

"Zelda." He stood again. "You did nothing wrong. I'm a terrible man, but you're not hurt. Even if you bleed a little, you're not truly hurt. Do you understand?"

She looked suspicious, but also her knees shifted inside her gown. She must be—no, he would not think about what she was under that gown.

"You thought I was a whore."

He winced.

But she wasn't watching. She was thinking. "That's what a whore does? That's what you meant, isn't it? A woman who enjoys lots of men?"

He wasn't about to explain the ins and outs of prostitution. "Not quite a whore. But a woman of loose morals."

"Well." She looked back at the bed, and at least she didn't look alarmed any more. "If that is what comes of loose morals, I can see the appeal."

Geoffrey was even more unnerved by her growing calm.

"And *will* I have a baby?" She seemed resigned to the concept.

"No." He could be emphatic about that. "That is not what comes of what we did."

"No? What sort of thing results in a baby, then?" Her curiosity was getting the better of her. He could see it in her eyes. The excitement, the pure joy. All from something new.

Like stealing a compass. Or being ravished in her bed.

He closed his eyes. He hated himself.

"I cannot explain that right now."

His reticence made her a little more thoughtful. Well, if it conveyed to her the serious situation they were now in, good. She *had* been compromised.

"Then," she asked, "what does come of what we did?"

Burning shame, some guilt, horror at himself, and a lingering desire to do it again.

"Pleasure," he said as abruptly as he could.

"Well."

The whole series of thoughts he saw traveling behind her eyes were worrisome in the extreme.

"Miss R—Zelda. Don't take it lightly. It's dangerous."

And that she did hear.

"I can *tell* it's dangerous. Geoffrey. I am going to be married. I respect a little deviousness. I like you, with your alluring lambs and your fireside kisses and…" she looked again at the bed, "*that*. But there are things going on in this house that you can't possibly understand. There are people's lives at stake, people's dreams. And money," she added almost as an afterthought, "but lives and dreams are difficult without money. I won't be seduced by you again."

"You won't be… seduced… by me…" He couldn't finish it. Had he gone mad? Were his ears working properly?

"Though I would appreciate a little more information about what sort of thing results in a baby."

She stood there, blinking those big dark eyes at him, the deep shining dark of her hair tumbled all around her shoulders, still flushed from his lovemaking. *His*.

And she scolded him for seducing her. And accused him of not understanding what was going on in a great, important place like Faircombe Hall.

It was all too much.

"You need to get out of the house." It was the only lucid thought in his head.

"Yes, I know. You told me to go for walks, and—"

"No, I don't mean down to the cow sheds to tease me."

"I never!"

His head was swimming. He had never had this thought

before, but he needed to go dunk it in some ice-water. There was plenty outside.

"Last night you said you didn't feel quite safe." He didn't want to know what she'd told Vere. He didn't want to know what she lied about and what she didn't. He didn't want to be alone in trying to understand Miss Rawle. "You should have an ally outside this house. Someone of… your station. If you feel a shepherd can't help you."

"The village?" She perked up. As if she hadn't just followed a dizzyingly fast ravishing with scolding him about things he didn't understand. "In the village? I saw it from a distance but have not been closer!"

Christ no, not the village. Zelda Rawle, running amok amongst the villagers, was the last thing Faircombe needed. "No, the nearest society family is Sir Michael, the baronet of Roseford. He and Lady Grantley would likely welcome the company."

Perhaps he could keep her under his watchful eye, and out of trouble, and *not* being seduced, for two whole hours. Maybe three.

"And take your mother. And your maid," he warned her, just before unlatching the French windows. She should take a damn brigade of soldiers.

He stopped before he opened the glass-paned door. She looked so soft and lovely there, leaning against the bedpost. And her eyes… they were different. Looking at him.

He hadn't done one thing right since coming into the room.

He felt he had to do this.

In a few short steps, he had his arms around her. "I'm not seducing you," he murmured into her forehead, kissing her there.

And then, though he'd promised himself he wouldn't, he stole a quick kiss from her lips, too.

"Sleep well," he whispered, and then he was gone, too fast for the icy breezes to creep in.

* * *

"WELL," Zelda murmured to herself, wondering what actual seduction would look like.

She loved surprises, and that had been the biggest surprise she thought she'd had in her life. She felt like she'd been swept up over the earth in a balloon, able to see all the earth from above for the first time.

She'd forgone *that* for all these years?

No. She hadn't. She knew with unshakeable certainty that none of the young men who had offered for her hand before would have given her *that*. Not that kind of sweeping possession, desire, and certainly not pleasure.

This was definitely a problem.

Tansy had put the wash water ewer and bowl right by the fire, so they wouldn't get too cold. A stack of clean pressed linens sat right next to the bowl, along with a glass-stoppered vial of rosewater.

Zelda poured some water, and washed herself, feeling rather new in many places. She loved new things. The sensations were odd, but lovely.

That shepherd knew far more about her body than she did. It should have been unsettling, but it wasn't. He had the right word: it was thrilling.

Yes, definitely a problem.

She could send for Tansy and change for bed at any time.

She didn't want Tansy to see her. Zelda wasn't ashamed at all, but she wasn't ready to share the new feeling, either.

She found that there were shoulder buttons for this dress that she could reach; they let down the little apron that came over her breasts, and there were ties holding up the rest of the gown that tied below them.

She loosened the whole thing, shimmying out of it and laying it across a chair with her chemise. There was another heavy, warm night rail warming by the fire; she wiggled into it but found it too hot.

He'd left her very warm indeed. Warmer than whiskey.

* * *

"I THOUGHT I would visit Roseford Manor today," Zelda ventured as she buttered her toast.

Miss Farsworth and Lady Charlotte sat opposite. Miss Farsworth didn't look like someone recovering from Lord Faircombe's ill-temper; she seemed fine. Rosy-cheeked and cheerful.

Lady Charlotte, on the other hand, suddenly looked as if she'd tasted a lemon.

Perhaps it was something Zelda had said. "I'm sorry. You don't care for the Roseford family?"

"No." To Miss Farsworth, Lady Charlotte said, "You'll fare well, Delina? Shall I stay with you today?"

For some reason, Miss Farsworth's cheeks, already pink, brightened even more. But she just shook her head. "No, I expect to do some fine work today."

"Very well. Miss Rawle." And that was all Zelda got from Charlotte as she made her exit.

"Is she only abrupt with me, or is it everyone?"

Miss Farsworth smiled. "She does tend to sound that way. And the Grantleys are not friends of hers."

"Nor yours, either?"

"No. Business rivals who have made life more difficult for Lord Faircombe."

Zelda was quite delighted to hear about someone making

life more difficult for Lord Faircombe. "Lord Grantley doesn't care for Lord Faircombe, then?"

"He is addressed as Sir Michael; he's a baronet. And no, I don't think Sir Michael cares for Lord Faircombe at all. But the horse-training interest isn't his. It's his wife's. Lady Grantley."

"Well." Even if she had been inclined not to trust anything Geoffrey said now that the sun was up and she was free of his overwhelming presence, Zelda couldn't pass up meeting a lady whose business affairs annoyed a marquess. "That *will* be new."

CHAPTER 15

Geoffrey still didn't know what to say to Zelda in the morning. It plagued him until he saw a figure walking towards the stables, and he forgot to be embarrassed in his rush to see if it was her. Guinevere the slow-moving, nearly-bursting ewe got one last pat, and he was gone.

Even his new goose companion could barely keep up. Whether it plotted vengeance or had fallen in love, it barely gave Geoffrey a moment to himself. Geoffrey ought to name it.

But the figure walking over the lawns wasn't a woman. It was Fred the footman, in livery. "The new lady wants a carriage," he said, standing just inside the stable door, looking nervous of the horses and trying to keep his boots clean.

Apparently, Miss Rawle had taken his suggestion. "I can drive the Rawles to Roseford," he said, puffing a little. The goose, who had followed him, flapped its wings.

The stablemaster gave the goose a hard eye. "Fred's already in livery."

Geoffrey had a lot of faith in Fred when it came to carrying baskets, but not when it came to driving all the way to Roseford with a cargo as precious as Miss Rawle. "Better send someone heftier," he advised the stablemaster. "There's no one else to spare, and Lord Vere's intended deserves safety."

Will, the stablemaster, wasn't particularly tall, but he had a stare that worked on stallions, and he turned it on Geoffrey now. "I've already heard rumors, Lord Geoffrey. It'd be worth my job to let you do anything that might cause more. Plus, you're like another carriage tacked on back, as far as weight for the horses to pull."

Geoffrey screwed an unaccustomed frown into place. There were four horses. His weight wouldn't be *that* big a problem. "William, it's worth your job if something happens to the next Lady Faircombe. Maybe your life. And my brother asked me personally to make sure Miss Rawle was safe."

That was the pure and honest truth, which presumably the stablemaster could see in his face.

"Awright, but just… be the driver. That's all. Right?"

"Right," said Geoffrey, swinging himself up.

* * *

ZELDA'S EYES widened as they came down the stairs in the courtyard to the waiting carriage. That driver looked large. Very large. And he wasn't in Faircombe livery. He also had a thick shock of white-blond hair that shone even on a cloudy day.

If she just kept her mother chattering, perhaps she wouldn't notice.

"I can't imagine what you like about being in a carriage,"

her mother was complaining and fussing with the basket of essentials.

Zelda felt herself breathe a little easier once the carriage was rolling. She shouldn't trust that man; he'd believed shocking things about her, and he'd *done* even more shocking things. She *didn't* trust him.

But she was glad to know he was only a few feet away.

"I love everything about being in a carriage," she said airily, watching her mother root around in the basket, then out the little glazed window. "You can see new things from the windows and breathe new air. And at the end of the ride, you're someplace new, where entirely new things might happen."

"Griselda, what *is* this passion for novelty? I didn't raise you that way."

Zelda stomped on the internal cry of *No, you didn't*. Then wondered why she had. At some point, she would have to share those internal cries with her mother, or accept that they had nothing between them but the faint ties of blood.

"No, you didn't." She settled her hands in her huge woolen muff, which her mother had already warmed with a porcelain box full of coals. "It was extremely tiring, always indoors, often lying down, wishing I could go shopping with the maid or even walk down the street."

"You could hardly expect me to read to you *all* day." Mrs. Rawle shifted uncomfortably in her seat across the carriage. "We read all of *Pamela*, you know."

"I didn't expect that. I'm not talking about anything you did or didn't do. I'm talking about myself, Mother. *I* was terribly bored. For *years*."

"Well." Mrs. Rawle clearly wanted to explain herself further, but didn't want to be corrected again. "Of course you were. You were *ill*."

"And I will *always* be ill. But I need not be bored." With a flash of memory, Zelda recalled suddenly the exact pattern of wood knots in the beams over her bed. *Exact.*

She would not go back to that. She *could* not.

"This is a very expensive way to be amused, Griselda, carriages here, ships there."

"You're quite right, Mother." It was. And Zelda intended to find a way to keep it going.

* * *

"You're joking."

Letty, whom the Eliots called Lady Grantley, put her hands to her temples in horror. Her frizzy blonde curls flew out of her cap every which way; she had yet to make it to the stables this morning; and her tiny son had spewed upon her skirts.

"I assure you I am not joking, madame." The butler looked, if anything, apologetic.

"Callers? Unannounced? At Roseford?" The manor was too far from London and its turnpikes. They never had unannounced callers.

Except here they were. "A Mrs. Lloyd Rawle and Miss Griselda Rawle, from New York, Lady Grantley. I put them in the front room."

"I hope you closed the door!" The room was just inside Roseford's broad hallway, where any minute Sir Michael could go zooming past on the wheeled cart that supported his leg. Likely without a coat. Or even waistcoat.

Letty had some trouble keeping Michael fully dressed.

At that moment, a tiny baby's cry sounded in the hall.

Letty hurried to their bedchamber, arriving at its door just as Michael emerged from the library.

He rolled over at speed, as he liked to do on the bare wooden floors. "Why so worried-looking, my love? John Mary is just awake."

It had been a difficult few months, and Letty, who had never spent time around children, was only just getting used to the rhythms of the baby, who seemed to sleep a few hours at a time around the clock.

But this wasn't even the baby. "Guests. Unannounced guests. Michael. I can't."

"They don't want to see *me*." He followed her into their chambers and shut the door. "Let me see what John Mary wants. Perhaps he will settle for my company."

"As long as he's not hungry."

She didn't want to arm-wrestle her husband over the chance to pick up their baby, but it was always a race. Michael wanted John Mary with him all day. Letty adored it.

And since, to be honest, John Mary seemed to prefer his father's company as often as not, Letty worried a bit, but let them be.

The baby wasn't hungry. "Just lonely, you darling thing?" murmured Letty, nosing the fine hair at the top of his forehead.

"Disgraceful. The Captain can't be lonely." Michael's fake brusque tone was at odds with the tender way he touched his son's hand.

"Well, he's still too little for Carolina or Tommy to amuse him. Give him a little more time."

Sir Michael had waited long enough; he scooped the baby up in one arm, and Letty watched her son cuddle contentedly in that strong, warm space. Well, that was reasonable; she liked it too.

So then on to the second problem. "I can't receive visitors! I look disastrous!"

"Nevertheless, they are here," said Michael with the perfect calm of one born to be a baronet and not the least interested what others thought. "You always look delightful. Here, let me unbutton that gown, slip on a clean one, and pin back a few of your curls. Or let them loose, I never can judge."

As much as Letty enjoyed letting her husband play lady's maid, there wasn't time to enjoy it now. Quickly she shimmied out of the dress and into a fresh one, and smoothed her hands over her hair. "That will have to do."

Michael, baby still in his arms, pushed himself to the door. "Perhaps send for Mrs. Castle. Or Miss Hastings? They might wish to help you entertain guests."

Before she could praise him for the thought, she realized what he was about to do. She jumped for the door, but not fast enough to stop him.

He'd already gone, flying down the hall on his wheeled cart at top speed. The baby *loved* that.

But the cart's wheels weren't silent. Michael *didn't* have a coat on. And the door to the receiving parlor, despite her worry to Griggs, was *not* closed.

A beautiful woman in clothes that had never seen baby stains leaned out the door and braced herself with a cane. She looked after where Michael had disappeared down the hallway.

She looked back at Letty with wide, dark-fringed eyes. A few curls undulated and shone over one shoulder, catching light like the trembling jet beads on her bonnet and sleeves. She looked elegant, and sultry, and she turned to Letty with frank astonishment.

She pointed after where Michael had disappeared, rolling on his cart.

"Can I try that?"

* * *

Two women her mother's age arrived and captured Mrs. Rawle, asking if she'd like to see the gallery. Zelda's mother seemed glad to meet some peers, and she disappeared without a single fuss over Zelda. Perhaps the conversation in the carriage had done her good.

Zelda wished she didn't feel so awkward about it.

Lady Grantley wasn't what Zelda had expected at all. She looked ruffled, and busy as a housemaid. Zelda envied her and wondered about her at the same time.

"I wasn't expecting any visitors," the young lady said, patting at her hair as if it would make the curls lay down. "Certainly not from Faircombe."

Zelda had a sudden urge to tell Lady Grantley everything. She might be flustered, but while they spoke, her hostess also cleared away some knitting, brushed the ashes back into the hearth pan, and rung a bell to call for someone. She liked putting things to rights.

She was also an active little thing. Zelda felt a wave of tiredness wash over her, and she'd spent her morning riding in a carriage.

Lady Grantley couldn't sit. "Bring us some tea, Mrs. Childs, would you please?" she told the woman in a dark dress who stopped at the door. Her hands fluttered a little as she turned back to Zelda, as if not sure what to do unless they were busy.

Zelda reassured her, "We can share a lack of affection for Faircombe today. I'm quite glad to be free of it for a few hours."

"Oh?" Lady Grantley drew nearer. "You're not enjoying your visit?"

"It isn't a visit; I'm to marry Lord Vere."

"Really!" That made Lady Grantley pause. "Oh, I can see that. I haven't met him, but I hear he's very… shiny."

Zelda smiled. "Am I shiny, too?"

The little woman cocked her head. "A bit." Her eyes drank in the details of Zelda's gown. "You're very beautiful, so you must make a good pair."

Busy and sweet. More compliments already than she'd had from her intended. Or the shepherd.

Though she'd never once missed Lord Vere, and she was already wondering where the shepherd had gone.

"I suppose it must." Zelda knew she should sound more excited. Free from the need to appear the way her mother expected, she just wasn't. "I can tell you honestly, Lady Grantley, the whole affair feels a bit more uncomfortable than I'd like."

Why was she even worrying about it? She didn't plan to stay. It would be a marriage in the eyes of the law only.

But the law, as she'd learned by staring at it for long hours, was a tough and impenetrable thing. Not that different from iron bars. The law didn't care if she and her husband agreed on the nature of their marriage; and that seemed less and less likely.

Even if she didn't divulge what had happened with Geoffrey.

Zelda shook herself. "So you've not visited Faircombe? You know nothing of its people?" If this lady couldn't tell her any more about the family she was set to join, who could?

"I'm afraid my work competes with that of the Marquess, so we are not on the friendliest terms. But I've *met* Lord Fair-combe, and Lady Charlotte—" here she winced a little, "and Miss Farsworth. I haven't met any of his sons, though others here have."

"Sons?" Zelda frowned. Lady Grantley really would be no help at all. "Lord Faircombe has one son. Lord Vere."

"Oh yes?" Lady Grantley didn't seem to notice that she'd made a mistake, just twitched at the window curtains as if about to open them, then changing her mind. The sun was watery, but aimed their way. "And he didn't accompany you?"

Still tired, Zelda felt again the urge to defend him. Why should Lord Vere dance attendance on her? She'd disappointed him, yet he'd gone to London for a solicitor to help her. If there was anyone who deserved to be despised, it wasn't Lord Vere.

And no shepherd who thought she was free with *those* kinds of favors would make her feel guilty about her wedding plans.

But here was Lady Grantley, wondering why Lord Vere hadn't come with her. "There was no need, I assure you. There's a great brute of a shepherd at the Faircombe estate, and he seems to turn footman when needed. He drove us here."

"Indeed." Lady Grantley twitched the curtains open. "Does he look like that?"

There out the windows of the parlor stood Geoffrey in his sheepskin coat, stomping up and down in the raw cold air and casting the occasional eye toward the house.

"Yes."

There was another new problem: the way her heart leaped when she saw him.

But if she didn't tell him, he wouldn't know. Why was he there instead of inside the nice, warm stables? Was he watching for her? Just to take her to the carriage or... because he worried for her?

It made Zelda feel stronger just to know he was there.

"It's odd he's outside the door," she said as casually as she could. "I would have thought him in the stable with the horses. He's always got some animal following him."

"Mm hmm." Lady Grantley took the tray of tea and cakes that arrived at the door.

* * *

"Mrs. Childs," said Letty, leaning close and speaking in the housekeeper's ear, "do send someone quickly down to the cottage, and ask my brother to come find out why the youngest Faircombe son is standing outside pretending to be a shepherd."

Letty had a finely honed instinct for when something was awry. She didn't know Geoffrey Eliot, but she had heard exactly what he looked like, and there couldn't be two men in the county that size.

Well, Anthony would get to the bottom of it and tell her everything.

A thin baby cry sounded in the distance, and Letty, who had been sitting all of four seconds, jumped up again. Torn between the baby and her guest, she paused.

"Oh please, if the baby needs you, do go! I only wanted a little amusement and fresh company, and you've already been that. And tea!" The elegant lady sipped from a cup and put it down slowly and silently.

"Shall I bring him here?"

Miss Rawle looked a little unsure at that. "I would like to meet him; I doubt I'll be able to hold him for long, but I'll try."

"Oh, I didn't mean you had to labor over the baby!"

Letty darted out to call down the hall. "Do come in, Sir Michael, and bring John Mary. *Please* put on a coat."

Which was why Sir Michael looked slightly aggrieved when he arrived, shrugging on a plain coat over the shoulder that wasn't supporting his son.

But their guest was all smiles. "I shall make the requisite fuss over your little lord and master, but I admit I'd rather try that rolling thing of yours, sir!"

"Yes? We know a person who will build you one if you'd like, Miss… Rawle, is it?"

"Bother. I should have introduced you, shouldn't I?" Two years ago Letty would have been seized with worry over social failures, but it barely touched her now. She rocked her son in her arms and settled with him near their guest. She was Lady Grantley, and no one could take that away.

That particular confidence must show on her face. Miss Rawle seemed to notice it.

"Such a grand thing," she said softly but with real feeling, "all this yours!"

"Roseford is a beautiful old place," Letty agreed with pride.

The lady's face bent over the baby and hid her expression. "I didn't mean the house."

Feeling a little concerned for their guest—or perhaps just sympathetic—Letty laid John Mary into her arms.

The baby had reddish hair like his father's, but a much more cheerful disposition. Whatever had caused him to cry out a moment ago clearly had ceased to bother him; he waved his chubby, stubby little hands in the air in a way that looked random, but his wide eyes clearly caught the glitter of the dangling beads around Miss Rawle's face.

"Tell us about your visit, Miss Rawle," said Sir Michael, swinging himself into an armchair opposite.

She had a sly little smile and a sparkle to her eyes as she said, "Insight regarding your competition?"

Sir Michael, older by some years and rarely surprised by the world, regarded her thoughtfully. "If you like," he said in an easy way, "but I just meant to meet you."

"You must not meet many people from the colonies?" The young lady was enraptured by every tiny, jerky movement of John Mary's clenched hands. "Perhaps you'd like some news about crossing the ocean despite blockades by our own ships?"

"Miss Rawle," said Sir Michael so that she would look up, "I asked about *you.*"

That startled their visitor, and Letty subsided, knowing Sir Michael saw what she saw. Something was amiss with this young woman.

"There's very little to tell. But," said the guest, with a flash of something wicked in her eyes, "I would gladly tell you everything I know for a chance to roll around in your cart."

* * *

GEOFFREY HAD no reason to stand by the door of the house; he just wanted to be nearby if Zelda called him.

It was cold, but he'd grown accustomed to the thin wind, and his sheepskins kept him fairly warm. He ought to have brought the hat as well. He had a cap with him, but it kept blowing off.

The third time he picked it up, when he straightened, Anthony Hastings was standing right in front of him.

"Anthony! You can startle a man."

The man bowed slightly, from the waist, his dark eyes taking in the sheepskins and everything else. "Surely you wish to come in, Lord Geoffrey, and meet Sir Michael and Lady Grantley? I have often spoken of you to them."

"No no. No no no. I'm not—" How to explain that he was a servant now in his own house?

Or, far more difficult, that he wasn't here for the Grantleys, but to look after Zelda Rawle?

"Very well." Anthony accepted smoothly and quickly, in the way of one who allowed others to keep their secrets, if only for that moment.

He started across the drive and down the hill toward the stables. "I'm glad of your visit. We've a sow that just farrowed, and she's swollen, without milk. Don't I recall hearing that you have a good hand with sick stock?"

Did he recall that? Geoffrey looked back at the house again. But there was no sign of Zelda, and Anthony, he well knew, missed nothing. If he didn't go with Anthony to the pigpens, he'd have to have a reason.

This sow better be interesting.

* * *

THE BABY MADE the most fascinating expressions. It was as if every moment he discovered something new to do with his face.

Her father's house in Bowling Green, Zelda mused, had been boringly free of children. They ought to have had one in every room. They were enchanting.

No wonder Lord Faircombe had arranged a marriage for his heir. Faircombe *ought* to have children in it by now, at least a few, given Lord Vere's age. And Lady Charlotte's.

But then, Zelda was the same age herself.

Giving up the vehement urge to try rolling down the hallway on that cart, Zelda didn't ask again. Sir Michael didn't offer, and she realized, now that the urge had faded, how rude it had been. The abrupt ending of his trouser leg just below the knee made it clear that he needed the cart; it was not for amusement. At least not hers.

He'd loaned her his baby, after all; that must do.

Zelda hadn't been able to hold him for long, but Lady

Grantley was happy to take him into her arm and hold him so that Zelda could continue to watch his fascinating little face. "I had no idea Lord Vere had decided to look for a wife abroad."

Zelda blinked. "Do you know, I've no idea how Lord Faircombe and my father came to have correspondence on the matter. I suppose that's odd?"

"Is it? I know nothing of society." Her hostess looked to her husband.

He only shrugged. "A bit odd. Most families who arrange marriages between them have knowledge of each other. Hereditary ties, or money affairs."

"My father hasn't entertained an Englishman since the start of the war."

"Well. Lord Faircombe and Mr. Rawle must have known of each other somehow."

Zelda thought again of the feeling of walking out of the dining room, with all those men's eyes upon her. She had not had the feeling they wished her well. What did they know? And was it about her?

Sir Michael saw something in her face. "And you trust your father?"

Zelda's head snapped up. It made the beads round her bonnet shake; the baby cooed at them.

Did she trust her father? She'd seen so little of him over the years that she tended to picture him as he'd been when she was little. The man who'd given her a jeweled globe. *Take charge of it, Griselda.*

But he was also the man who had refused to settle money on her personally except in the form of a dowry.

The sinking sensation that came from moving forward without knowing where one was going, and finding oneself stuck with no way out, was different from all other sinking sensations, she decided. *Our heroine discovers she has not been wise.*

But here she was, having committed herself by sailing across the ocean. What would she do now? Go back?

Lady Grantley had clearly had a lifelong interest in training horses. Zelda had no interests by which to support herself, should she decide to stay. And neither did her mother.

This problem was *very* new.

Zelda was tired of how they kept piling up.

* * *

"WE JUST BUILT THE PENS." Anthony bent over the low wood-beam fence toward a fat sow grunting in the straw. "I worried that she might have eaten something? A nail?"

He truly didn't mind being shown to the pig pen instead of the parlor, Geoffrey mused as he stepped over the fence to join the sow in question.

She looked uncomfortable, and her litter looked desperate. The tiny pink piglets were nosing at her teats, but getting nothing. The mother was a good-natured thing, with a pleading look in her beady little eyes.

"It's not a nail. Have you got another mother you can put them on?"

"No." Poised, self-possessed Anthony looked genuinely worried about the tiny squirming piglets.

"Damn." Faircombe's village was two hours away. But it was worth a try. "There's a cobbler near us with a sow about to wean her shoats; we could take the pigs there. See if he'll take one in exchange for letting her feed these little ones. For the mother, you need to rub her, get the bad milk out. You can use goose grease."

"Very well."

Geoffrey looked at Anthony just standing there. "Now."

"What, *right* now?"

"Yes. How long has she been this way? She won't last, and the piglets won't either."

A little man, shorter than Zelda, came out the stable door. "I knew you'd be here," he said to Anthony, pressing a shoulder into Anthony's.

Anthony's face, voice, and body were all morose. "We've got to milk the pig."

"Well, you don't want to lose her." The newcomer had a golden, otherworldly look to him, but he climbed into the pen without hesitation and patted the sow's ear. "And I suppose you don't want to wait on these piglets either."

"No…" Geoffrey was sorry for the sow and piglets both. It wasn't *only* that he'd like to cut the visit short and see Zelda again. "Perhaps someone should ask Miss Rawle if she's willing to leave soon? I can take the piglets to the village, if the ladies agree. It would save you the trip, and I'd like to see them settled."

"Yes." Still watching the sow, Anthony turned to go.

"Anthony…" When the fellow paused, Geoffrey said almost shyly, "Just Geoffrey, please. As long as we're here."

"Interesting," said Anthony, but he didn't pause to investigate all the whys and wherefores, for which Geoffrey was grateful.

* * *

GEOFFREY WAS SO busy helping the little man, who introduced himself as David, treat the sow that he didn't pay the least bit of attention to anything happening around him.

Till he heard a shuffling, snorting commotion and looked up to see a stallion in a pen across the stable-yard, snuffling at a ready and receptive little mare.

It made him glance toward the house, even though Miss Rawle was safely inside. As if he just needed to know where she was at this delicate moment.

And no, she wasn't in the house. There she was, coming slowly down the hill, cane in hand, with her mother behind her.

CHAPTER 16

"No! Miss Rawle!" he shouted, but no one seemed to understand why he showed such loud concern. Not David beside him, or the stable hands, who went right on with the mating.

Only the lady's mother, who stopped dead in her tracks in horror.

Miss Rawle herself kept walking down, only directed to look that way by his frantic attempt to distract her from the sight.

She wasn't that far away; he saw her eyes widen as the stallion, suddenly long and eager at the exact wrong moment, climbed his forelegs up the back of his waiting mate and thrust inside.

Mrs. Rawle saw it too and pressed both hands to her chest. "Oh! *No!* Griselda! Turn away!" Geoffrey could faintly hear her cry. She waved both hands vehemently, but was far behind her daughter; she couldn't block Zelda's view.

Geoffrey hoped she did not suffer a heart attack. He worried a little that Zelda might be alarmed by the stallion's size or suddenness; but her mother looked apoplectic.

Indeed, she may have lost the ability to breathe because she slumped backwards. Anthony, just behind her, caught her and helped her sit; David vaulted out of the pen to join him. Heads close together, words were exchanged, and then David raced off. Anthony awkwardly patted the lady's arm.

Mrs. Rawle's continued life, and consciousness, were proven by her faint pleas to Zelda to come back this minute and stay away from the nasty beasts, accompanied by waving of the hands.

All of which Zelda ignored to simply stand on the grass and watch as the stallion, exhausted, slumped over the back of the mare. He clung, actually drooping his forelegs over her haunches, till he managed to gather himself enough to slide away from her. In fact, he only managed more of a controlled fall.

Zelda's mouth was open a little with surprise. "What on earth is the—Oh." She bent down a little, holding her cane out of the way, to look underneath the horses. She clearly grasped the mechanics of what had just occurred, despite how the stallion's very visible excitement had now disappeared. "*Oh.*"

"No. Don't look. Oh my God above, *Griselda.*" No, Mrs. Rawle hadn't lost consciousness.

Her mother's distress didn't seem to impact Zelda at all. Her mind was clearly rolling over all the details she'd just accidentally seen, and her mother's upset only served to explain what she'd seen, and why she was not supposed to see it.

"Don't look!" Mrs. Rawle waved feebly toward her daughter.

Zelda's eyes turned to Geoffrey, though he would rather she not look at *him* right now either.

How was he supposed to reassure her now? Especially after last night? He was the last person who could talk about this with her; and he felt that he *should*. Because her mother clearly hadn't explained anything to her about-to-be-married daughter.

That stallion had just provided an excellent explanation of what Geoffrey couldn't bring himself to say the night before. But how was exposure to *this* going to strike a sly-eyed virgin?

Zelda didn't look alarmed; Geoffrey assumed she was too sensible to think men and horses comparable in any alarming way. She did look thoughtful. And a little troubled.

Geoffrey stepped closer. Their quiet conversation whipped back and forth, both vitally aware that they had only moments of privacy. "Are you well?"

"Quite. I'm not as fragile as my mother thinks." That puzzled frown was for Geoffrey, not the horses. She didn't look round to check that her mother hadn't moved. "That isn't—you weren't going to do that to me?"

His mouth went dry. Last night, he'd lost track of his senses; he might very well have ravished her more completely, had he not stopped to think. Only slightly too late. "Not without your agreement, no."

"I don't quite understand."

He changed his mind about explaining everything. "I think it would be best if we didn't discuss this."

A curious head-tilt. "Best for whom?"

Words couldn't explain his urge to make sure she understood what marriage entailed, and his desperation not to talk to her about it. Not rationally. Probably not at all.

The worst was that she seemed to take his conflicted silence as judgment.

When Geoffrey didn't answer, her eyes moved back toward the pen, where the stallion now nosed at the mare's flank. The mare was a steady thing who simply accepted his attention as her due.

"It doesn't look pleasant. But Madame Horse doesn't look hurt." Zelda contemplated the mare, who looked bored, if anything. "It is for his benefit, it appears."

"Was last night?" Those words escaped him before he could stop them.

She had a knack for standing in public and discussing the most astonishing things. Apparently, it was catching.

And he wanted to know.

The change between them crackled in the air. Was she breathing faster? She didn't meet his eyes. Nor did she answer directly. A bit of a smile curled one side of her mouth. "I suppose there are… significant differences. Certainly in the size of the appendage in question."

In a better world, he'd be able to sit right down next to her on the grass and laugh and laugh, and perhaps he could hold her hand to reassure her. And her mother would be somewhere else. Anywhere else.

He wanted that so much it ached.

But since he couldn't do that, he did say what he thought she must know. "The differences should be primarily in the time it takes. And the delight of the lady."

That widened her eyes. Then her smile faded. She looked down at her hands stacked on her cane. "I think… I had better not listen to you anymore."

Then she turned and walked, slowly but deliberately, up the hillside to join her sighing mother.

Mrs. Rawle still reclined on the grass, hands clasped over her face. An older woman with a crown of golden hair knelt by her head, murmuring to her.

"Geoffrey," Anthony murmured at his elbow, startling Geoffrey into tearing his eyes away from Zelda's back. "Mrs. Rawle ought to get home."

He didn't say anything about the young Miss Rawle, as it was clear that the moment had most damaged the mother.

When Geoffrey turned to face him, Anthony thrust into his hands a crate stuffed with straw and starving piglets.

"This will seem funny tomorrow," Anthony said.

* * *

"Why won't you just explain?"

It was a measure of Mrs. Rawle's discombobulation that she barely commented on the crate full of wriggling piglets at their feet.

"It's not the most pleasant prospect!" Mrs. Rawle had applied the wintergreen oil, so good for Zelda's joints, to her own wrists when they'd reached the carriage. It did seem to brace her, but only enough to lock her jaw shut.

"Does he have to climb up her back to—"

"*No!*"

Zelda pressed her lips together, tight. She had seldom been so frustrated with her mother. Now they were stuck in this carriage together for more than an hour's ride home, and she *would* understand why her mother was so close-mouthed about this before that carriage door opened again.

She leaned back.

"I would imagine if it's anything similar, women must be far larger inside than I ever suspected."

"Oh, merciful heavens." Mrs. Rawle looked as if she would be ill.

Zelda would call to Geoffrey to pull this carriage over if need be, but she would not stop her questions.

"So the reason this is all secret from young ladies is that otherwise, they would never get married and subject themselves to such a thing."

"Not at *all!*" Color washed back into Mrs. Rawle's cheeks. "I can barely stand to think of my little girl being subjected to such things, but I wouldn't want to *trap* you!"

As far as Zelda could see, a great deal of trapping of young women went on, on both sides of the ocean.

"But it does hurt," she pressed.

"No. I mean… it needn't." Mrs. Rawle had composed herself a little, but still looked anywhere but at Zelda. "It can be pleasant enough. It shouldn't hurt."

"But it can."

Mrs. Rawle said nothing.

"I don't suppose it is ever the lady's request."

When Zelda thought of how Geoffrey had swept her up in his arms, the liquid fire he had set loose in her veins, she could imagine how *that* would be by a lady's request. But not what she'd just witnessed.

But Mrs. Rawle wasn't in agreement there either. "I suppose it could be. From some ladies." She wouldn't look at Zelda, far more interested in the window.

Hmm. Meaning it must sometimes be more pleasant than it had looked, or that the sort of ladies who requested it were idiots.

Zelda found herself humming over the whole problem in her brain. Her first reaction to something new was to try it. She'd always been that way, even as a tiny child faced with some new dish at supper. But she didn't have any urge to try *that*.

The mare hadn't shown any excitement. Not like the stallion. She'd stood, head down, and waited through it.

Zelda supposed if that were necessary to make a fascinating little fellow like the Grantleys' John Mary, it would be reasonable.

But she didn't understand why no one would discuss it, or why she wasn't supposed to know about it.

"This makes no sense. *You* make no sense."

"Griselda, I'm doing the best I can." Opposite, her mother slumped a little, and still wouldn't meet her eyes. "Mrs.

Castle was terribly kind. She said it's hard for a mother to know what to do, and I wish my own mother had lived long enough to tell me that! But she also said unmarried young ladies should probably know more than we tell them, and I can't agree. More knowledge doesn't seem to help anyone."

"Knowledge never hurts."

"You've heard speeches on the evils of too much knowledge all your life."

That was true. "I don't think I ever believed them," Zelda said slowly, thinking of all the maps she had pored over hour after hour. It was part of loving new things. She loved knowledge.

"Better that young people were not curious about things they are too young to understand."

"Understand? Or do? Young men have made offers for me for six years."

"And had you accepted any of them, it would have been pertinent."

"Mother. I've accepted one *now*." When had her mother expected to explain any of this?

"We're nowhere close to a wedding. Once the contracts are concluded, it's still two weeks of banns, and who knows what other nonsense."

Her mother wasn't as cheerful about the prospect of this marriage as Zelda had thought.

Looking back, her mother hadn't *ever* been.

"Mother, what is wrong with the contracts?"

Perhaps it was only the relief of talking about something she found far less uncomfortable, but for once, Mrs. Rawle actually answered. "I can't make sense of it myself. Your father and Lord Faircombe are entering into a business deal with a third party and it might be any of those merchantmen, or all three, I can't tell. Mr. Paltz is kind enough, but Mr. Highland won't say anything but to ask for tea, and it is lowering to talk to shopkeepers about your father's affairs."

Mr. Mendey, at least, had clothes the equal of any man with a title, but her mother lumped them all in together. "I had no idea you looked down on tradesmen so."

"Of course I don't," her mother snapped. "I'm married to one, aren't I?"

Zelda leaned back into the plush upholstery of the large Faircombe carriage and watched the piglets crawl over each other and squeal.

For the first time, she thought she had been so cavalier about marriage because her parents' example might not have been the best one.

Marriage and the horse's mating and what had happened last night; Zelda could see that they related, they were all related. But her mother wouldn't talk about the first two, and Zelda would keep her questions about the third to herself.

Men couldn't possibly compare to that horse, though she bet some of them claimed they did. So then what was the harm? A baby, if unwanted, could be catastrophic; but a baby wasn't inevitable? No, she suspected there was no controlling whether or not a baby resulted, except not to engage in the first place.

She was more confused, not less.

That lamb-carrying shepherd had swept her off her feet and *done* things to her that were so beautifully addictive that she couldn't stop thinking of them even now. He had secrets to pleasure she had never even heard whispered about. But those things weren't *that* thing.

Perhaps he'd been telling the truth that he hadn't endangered her with an unexpected child.

But she couldn't trust his honest-looking face.

He'd hidden terribly dark thoughts about her. And he was hiding something else. Had she imagined that people at

Roseford seemed to know who he was? That dark-haired fellow had looked as if he might bow.

Was it only gratitude for helping their pig?

Zelda couldn't stay slumped in the cushions for long; she had to shift. At her feet, the piglets squeaked, and she felt the same. Sulky and hungry and rather feeling the absence of a mother's reassurance.

The feeling stayed with her all the way back to Faircombe.

* * *

AT THE CARRIAGE block in Faircombe's courtyard, she let the footman hand her mother out first.

"What a day! I must rest. It's been shocking. In fact, we didn't dine. Griselda, are you hungry?"

Zelda looked at the piglets. All they needed from a mother right now was milk. She needed so much more.

She could see Geoffrey through the carriage window; he stood by its door. Worry looked quite comfortable on Geoffrey's face. It somehow fit the broad cheekbones, the heavy brows, the wide jaw. And the piercing blue eyes.

She should be wary, but he was the person most likely to give her the answers she needed.

She leaned out the open carriage door, letting in an icy breeze, and addressed him directly. "You're to see if the fellow in the village will take these piglets, aren't you? I shall deliver them on behalf of the Grantleys."

That wasn't necessary, and everyone knew it.

"Griselda! You cannot take to your heels all over the countryside—"

"If only I could. In fact, I *should* walk. But right now I'll deliver these pigs. Driver."

It felt wrong not to use Geoffrey's name, but she didn't want to give her mother yet another reason to fret.

"It isn't safe! You must have a chaperone! Let me at least get your maid! Griselda—"

"I've never liked that name, Mrs. Rawle," said Zelda, feeling as cold as the breeze, and waved again to Geoffrey. "I *will* deliver these pigs."

"I'll see the young lady safe home," she heard him murmur to her mother, before swinging his big body back up into the driver's seat, making the whole carriage rock.

It was a great deal to think about: how big he was, how small she was, and how much she did and did not trust him.

And how much she did or did not wish to marry Lord Vere.

CHAPTER 17

"Wasn't that the Faircombe carriage?"

Lord Geoffrey hadn't darkened the doors of the Stony Barrel in days, and Joan worried that she'd missed her chance.

Now there went the Faircombe carriage, and even in the distance, the size of the driver hinted at only one person.

"Three sisters and still no one tells me anything important!"

In truth, Beth was the only one in the yard, her skirts tucked up, occupied with the rise and fall of the ax. She was chopping wood.

"Everyone in the village will tell stories all night and all morning about it," said Beth with supreme boredom. "You'll know more than me when you leave the inn tonight."

"I'm not after *gossip*, Beth," and Joan had to dance not to trip on split logs as she ran back inside. She was in the middle of making a pie, and was covered with flour. This was luck, but at the worst possible time.

* * *

THE PIG SITUATION must have been urgent. Zelda half-hoped that Geoffrey might drive them somewhere quiet where she could sort this out with him. She wasn't even sure what *this* was.

He didn't.

Zelda tried to enjoy the views of forest, and the glimpse of water through the trees. She wanted to like the cottages with their neat tiled roofs, the packed-earth road widening, and the poles left on the town green from the last market day. The village had a bakery that smelled like heaven, and even luxurious little shops; a bookseller, a haberdasher, and even an apothecary.

The carriage did not stop, and Zelda tried to enjoy herself anyway.

When it finally rolled to a stop by a sign in the shape of a shoe, Zelda hoped Geoffrey would simply forget she was there.

Unlikely though that was, since there was a box of pigs at her feet.

Then the door opened.

"I'm not getting out."

He filled the whole door. "Don't. I must get these fellows out of the cold."

Zelda peeked into the straw. Was she imagining it, or had the pink piglets become less frantic? Was that good or bad? "They look well enough."

"They will likely die soon."

"Oh no!" Zelda was seized with a sense of loss. She ought to have cuddled them during the long, cold trip. Why hadn't she seized the chance? "I didn't know it was so dire!"

"They're cold and hungry. Nothing can live that way for long. Stay there."

Zelda was both cold and hungry. But she was tougher

than a piglet. "I *am* getting out. You take the piglets and I'll climb down."

Geoffrey's shoulders hunched, and his mumble sounded like *killing me*. "Stay here while I talk to the cobbler, then I'll hand you out."

He scooped up the entire crate of piglets and disappeared.

She didn't wish to wait.

Zelda was pleased to find climbing down fairly easy. She left her muff behind, and her mittens nearly slipped on the edge of the door; but she managed it.

When she finally emerged, Geoffrey was already at the cottage door, saying something with great emphasis to the husband and wife who had met him there.

She'd simply follow.

She made it to the door just as the couple came outside. Geoffrey, far more proper than Lady Grantley had been, said, "Mr. Heaton, Mrs. Heaton. This is Miss Rawle."

The matching little pair of round people, with cheeks like they often laughed, couldn't stop looking back and forth between each other, the piglets, Geoffrey, and Zelda.

"You will take the piglets?" Now that she'd made herself a part of the pig problem, Zelda would see it through to the end.

"Oh, aye." Mr. Heaton brushed a hand over his leather apron. "I don't mind earning another pig by keeping the mother in milk. Do ye think the Grantley sow will freshen, L —, uh… Geoffrey?"

"She might. If not, I'm sure Sir Michael will repay your effort."

"He's very good with animals." Somehow Zelda felt Mr. Heaton would be calmer if she attested to Geoffrey's skills.

"Yes indeed, my lady, we do know. Everyone knows how… Geoffrey is good with the beasts."

Wonderful, Zelda thought a little sourly. *I wonder if that includes me. New York heiress trained to beg.*

Though she wasn't sure what had brought that to mind.

"I'm just Miss Rawle," she told them, while smiling and bobbing her head to Mrs. Heaton. "You are the mistress of the house, of course?"

"Of course!" The little woman was too flustered to be angry at the insinuation.

"Of course! So then you outrank me, surely."

"She's from the colonies," Geoffrey said when the Heatons couldn't puzzle this out.

Both the Heatons made sounds of dawning understanding, which made no sense to Zelda. Frowning, she tapped the crate with the top of her cane. "Let's sort the piglets."

"A pigpen's no place for the likes of a lady!" Mr. Heaton gasped like her mother.

The prospect of something new in the way of a pigpen cheered Zelda. "Nonsense. Lead on, please."

Geoffrey just shrugged, leaving the Heatons to whisper. Zelda followed them around the little cottage to the pens in back, Geoffrey and piglets bringing up the rear.

There was clean straw, packed hay, a tight dry shed, and a pump-fed trough in the little cottage yard. It all housed various chickens, as well a sow, and six much larger, much fatter piglets.

"She's good-tempered, likely won't mind a bit. The shoats'll let me pen them up with a bit of grain. They're almost off the milk. Begging your pardon, my lady."

Zelda let the *my lady* pass. "They're so plump!" The shoats were indeed roll-y and pink, squealing their disapproval as Mr. Heaton used a board to shoo them into a corner of the pen. They silenced when he scattered grain in the trough.

He scooped one up and carried it back to the mother,

nosing her own trough, trying to make food appear. "He'll keep her calm. He's her favorite," he explained.

Indeed, the sow was so busy making little *nk, nk* noises with her baby that she barely noticed the cobbler pushing her over on her side. She was a massive mound of coarse-haired animal, but passive as a hillock when the cobbler brought the sad little piglets out of their packed-in crate and nestled them next to her belly.

"They're a bit old," he said dubiously, watching the piglets squeal and tumble over each other, fighting their way to the nourishment.

"She's kind. That's why I thought of her." Geoffrey leaned over to scratch the sow's hairy side.

He knew the sows in the village, and he knew which ones had babies ready to leave them. And which ones were kind.

This was an odd fellow, Zelda decided, watching him lean over the fence to nudge a wandering piglet back to its target, but it was hard to imagine him being devious or mean.

Even given evidence to the contrary. As he certainly had done things that, while very pleasant in the moment, seemed less than kind in retrospect.

Mrs. Heaton didn't seem to know what to do with herself while her husband and Geoffrey were absorbed in the pig. "Are you hungry?" she asked Zelda. "Have you been driving long?"

"I am, actually. I've had nothing all day but some tea." She was famished.

"Not at all," Geoffrey had appeared at her elbow and smiled at Mrs. Heaton. "Miss Rawle will dine at Faircombe. No need, Mrs. Heaton."

Zelda turned and glared at the side of Geoffrey's head. She didn't care if the sight of it made her want to rub her cheek against it; she wanted to eat. "I am hungry."

"You're not."

"I—"

A nudge from Geoffrey was like a nudge from a wall. Zelda stopped.

"That's right, I forgot; I'm not hungry, Mrs. Heaton."

"Oh no. Won't you have some tea?"

Zelda shot Geoffrey a look out of the corner of her eye. "Apparently, I haven't time."

"I must return Miss Rawle to Faircombe. She only wanted to make sure the piglets would survive."

That hadn't been what Zelda wanted at all, but now she felt petty, small, *and* worried about the piglets. "They will, won't they?"

Geoffrey surveyed them somberly. "They look well enough."

And that seemed to be that. He put his hand on her elbow and steered her back toward the carriage.

It was just a hand on her elbow. But it made all Zelda's jumble of thoughts return. Along with a sweet sort of ache inside, low and warm.

It was new to find her insides didn't agree with her head, but not entertaining at all.

When they rounded the cottage corner, a woman came flying off the street and straight at Geoffrey. Zelda readied herself to duck.

She was so taken aback she wasn't sure what was happening till she realized the woman hadn't attacked Geoffrey; she was clinging to his coat and kissing his shirt. And crying.

As new things went, it was disconcerting.

She had no time to ask what was happening before Geoffrey gently disengaged the woman. "Are you all right then, Mrs. Wilson? How is Russ?"

Zelda thought Russ might also be a pig, or a sheep, but

Mrs. Wilson said, "Tucked warm in my own bed at home and doing fine."

Hopefully, Russ *wasn't* a pig or a sheep.

"You haven't fetched a doctor?"

Mrs. Wilson made a face. She wiped away her tears, but couldn't wipe away the broad smile she wore, beaming up at Geoffrey. "None much closer than London, and what would he do? Old Mrs. Hull gave him willow bark tea, and he's eating like a pig."

Which meant a great deal more to Zelda now. "Willow bark? Did he have a fever?" At Geoffrey's surprised look, she added, "I've often had willow bark tea. It helps the pain."

"Are you feeling well now?" So overcome with emotion that unchecked tears trembled on her cheeks, the weather-worn woman laid a friendly hand on Zelda's arm.

It was more concern than anyone at Faircombe had shown for her since she'd arrived. And it made something snap together inside her.

Or perhaps apart.

"I'm fine, thank you," she told the woman gently, with a reassuring pat of her own.

Mrs. Wilson nodded before turning back to Geoffrey. "I saw you going round Heaton's cottage and I've been meaning to call on you! Look what I've hitched to your carriage."

Geoffrey and Zelda both stepped round to look.

There was a cow there, a pretty little cow, Zelda thought, with big black patches spread along her back and sides and a very pink nose.

Geoffrey didn't seem to think her so pretty. "Mrs. Wilson, now. You're not giving me a heifer."

"Yes I am, and don't argue. Mr. Wilson and I, we heard about your troubles, and there's no repaying the good turn you've done us. We've only one son, and but for you, we'd have lost him."

Zelda gasped.

Geoffrey wasn't having it. His thick blond brows bushed together and he seemed to be looking for words. "Mrs. Wilson. Truly. I didn't do it for payment."

"I know! But a man can't eat pride, can he? You look after everyone's stock, never mind that horrible Lord Faircombe. Time for you to get something back for your work, and why not? But this isn't that." She put up a hand to shush him. "This is thanks because we want to thank you. Joanie is a good little heifer, good-tempered, and she'll be a good milker. Her mother is."

"Mrs. Wilson. I can't take her."

"Can and will." From beaming tears, the woman had become fixed as a boulder, and giving Geoffrey a steady eye.

"Eh."

It was amusing to watch big Geoffrey stymied by a little mother he clearly didn't wish to offend. Zelda couldn't imagine what he was going to say.

The suspense tickled her.

"Mrs. Wilson. Here's what we will do. You take Joanie home, as I don't want to walk her behind the carriage. I must go fast enough to get Miss Rawle home quickly, and the wheels will throw up rocks. They could hit Joanie when there's no need."

Mrs. Wilson didn't even look at Miss Rawle, but made a face of grudging agreement.

"You take her home, and I'll come by soon to see Russ and we'll discuss it. All right?"

"All right. But I'll tell you now, Mr. Wilson and I have already discussed it. And when we discuss something, it stays discussed."

Zelda admired her unshakeability.

"Oh! And I almost forgot. There's a crate for you at the inn. Fellow tried to deliver it at Faircombe Hall, but the housekeeper sent it to the inn. Great big thing it is. Of course they kept it for you."

"A crate?" Geoffrey looked puzzled by this, and down at Zelda. "I really must get Miss Rawle back."

"Nonsense!" cried Zelda. Famished was one thing; crates were another. "It's a surprise, Geoffrey. I can't resist a surprise. We must go and find out what it is!"

The bushy brows again. "I'm not taking you to the Stony Barrel. Miss Rawle." He lowered his voice. "You should not even be here. Not without a chaperone."

The very word *chaperone* gave her the same feeling as that vision of her old ceiling. Trapped; unwanted; hopeless. "I prefer to make my mistakes in full view of the public," said Zelda, head held high. She made a large show of looking around for the inn while Mrs. Wilson untied the cow. "Stony Barrel, what an exciting name. Is it far?"

Was that a grunt or a growl that had come from somewhere deep inside that mountain of man? "Get in the carriage," he said ungraciously.

* * *

At this early hour, the inn was mostly empty. The sun was still up, after all.

The rich scent of stew greeted them both. "Mmm." Zelda couldn't stop the little moan. "I don't suppose they would feed us?"

"Aye, I would." A plug-shaped innkeeper appeared, wiping his hands on his apron. "How goes it, sir?"

"Well enough." Geoffrey pulled the man aside to say under his breath, "No *lord* today, Rob." Presumably after the last encounter at the inn with someone who'd heard his title, the innkeeper wouldn't ask why.

He kept one eye on Zelda as she picked her way round the tables to a low wooden chair by the fire.

She must be cold as well as hungry. She might love thrills, but she didn't complain when they resulted in discomforts. Her sigh as the fire warmed her said that Geoffrey hadn't taken sufficient care with her.

"Warm enough?" He lowered himself into the chair opposite. He knew these chairs; knocked together from saplings, they looked rough, but could hold his weight.

"Much better. And truly famished. Why didn't you let Mrs. Heaton feed me?"

"Mrs. Heaton has a hard enough time feeding them both. Rob here can spare some stew."

"Oh." He saw her chagrin. "I must appear very selfish. I am, I suppose."

"No, I don't think that of you."

"You said last night I never thought of anyone but myself!"

Geoffrey wanted to scrub his hands across his face. "Can we not agree that I was wrong about you in many ways?"

"I don't know; can we?" Her words were rubbed with dry sarcasm.

Geoffrey tried to look as primly disapproving as a big, young man could be. "Is there a way to ask your forgiveness so we can be friends?"

That turned her look thoughtful. "Will we be?"

"Why do you keep asking *me* questions?"

"I'm not sure, Geoffrey. Perhaps because you claim to know all the answers."

"I surrender." He wished Rob would bring the food. She must be starving. She had been thoughtless, not cruel. "I suspect you have not met many different types of people before."

"My father's house had quite a few people in it, when I

could attend meals, but I think now they were all quite similar. I'm glad to meet new people; I've neglected people as a source of entertainment till now." She shifted her feet closer to the fire. "And the Wilsons, are they poor? Is that why you wouldn't take the cow?"

Geoffrey scratched his nose and hoped she couldn't see his chagrin. "No, the Wilsons have a large herd and sell butter and cheese for miles. They can spare a heifer."

"You simply don't want it?"

Geoffrey's shoulders bunched up around his ears, then dropped. "I'm not sure what to do with it, that's all."

Zelda pulled off her silk mittens and rubbed her hands together by the fire. "You seem to know all the answers about other people and none about yourself."

"I do seem to." He nodded towards her hands. "Your hands ache?"

She bunched her shoulders up the same way, then let them drop. A smaller shrug; clearly dismissive. "More than I'd like at the moment. For all my mother is constantly fussing with the wintergreen oil, I wish I had it now."

"What does it do? I know nothing about it." Geoffrey's frown this time was thoughtful, and he leaned forward to take her hands in his. He turned them over to examine first the soft palms, and then the backs, with the knuckles.

That was a mistake. He'd reached for her like he was anyone or anything that might need his help. Her hands felt small in his, but more alive. Restless, like a bird.

He let them go before he caressed them.

She curled them protectively into one another. "Our American plant is very helpful. It makes an oil that soothes the pain; we brought quarts, so I would not go without. It smells a bit like mint."

"Yes." He nodded. "I noticed that."

That surprised her. "You noticed it?"

Now why had he said that?

He couldn't seem to control his impulses around Zelda, and after last night, he should keep his distance.

But after last night, he felt he owed her things; honesty, perhaps, and more care.

"Oh, of course you noticed it." She sank back. "You doctor all sorts of animals."

"I try." That wasn't why he had noticed the scent of wintergreen, not at all.

But he was in a terrible position. He'd essentially despoiled a virgin last night, without her knowing. Worse, it was the virgin intended to marry his brother.

That was the truth. But when he looked at her, he forgot Vere existed. He only saw Zelda. Inescapably lovely, surprisingly passionate, and ready to do anything for a new pleasure. He could spend weeks exhausting all the possibilities between them.

Months. *Years*.

But she couldn't be his.

And he was beginning to realize he *did* want something for himself. Not London or barmaids or society balls, but not sleeping in a sheep shed either. He wanted something; he wasn't sure what. And he was afraid that what he wanted most of all was Zelda Rawle.

"Zelda," he said quietly, drawing back her startled eyes. "I recall your scent when you're not near."

CHAPTER 18

He went on. "I ought not admit that. I ought not be here. As far as society is concerned, what we are doing now is far worse because it can be seen."

"It can't possibly be worse!" Was that a flush of color? Last night had been startlingly intimate for both of them. She nearly hissed, "We are fully clothed. No one is touching. And we are not hiding."

"Not hiding makes it worse."

"Why should that matter to me?"

She *must* have been sheltered, if gossip meant nothing to her. "It will matter to Lord Vere. And to Lord Faircombe."

She looked not at him, but into the fire. "Geoffrey, I think my mother loves me. She does. But I spent the last ten years lying abed, staring at the ceiling while all my friends grew up, married, and forgot about me. There is nothing more boring than living in one room, except living in one room while in pain." One hand rubbed the knuckles of the other. "I am not going back. I cannot go forward, not without money; and I will have no dowry unless I marry. I have some questions about marriage I should have been sensible enough to ask before; but I'm sensible enough to raise them now, frankly, because of you." The distrustful look she gave him almost sent him to his knees. "I don't know if I can believe you, but sadly, because you've opened my eyes, so to speak, you are the only one I can ask."

So she didn't just want this marriage; she *needed* it. He was a cad. A horrible rake, the kind who despoiled innocents unknowing.

So much pride he'd taken in not leaving children around the countryside. Only to do this.

Well, he'd worried from the start that she had no idea what she was getting into. Here they were.

The innkeeper appeared, balancing two big bowls of stew on one arm and a trencher full of bread and slabs of butter in the other. "Food."

"Can you lift that?" Geoffrey felt that the big wooden bowl would be too heavy for Zelda.

She took the thick vessel in both hands, balanced it on her knee. "I'll manage. Mmm, it'll be empty in a moment."

As Geoffrey relieved the innkeeper of the rest of it, he said quietly, "A few minutes alone, will that do, Rob?"

"Aye," and if he'd winked, Geoffrey would have had to do something. Instead, he just nodded as if people came in and asked to have the inn to themselves all the time.

"My thanks." When, out of habit, Geoffrey felt for his purse, he remembered it was holding his last coins under the borrowed mattress where he slept. He felt his face grow warm.

But Rob just waved a hand. "Your money's no good here, lad. I had a little brother fell through the ice too. He drowned." The plug-shaped man's eyes grew wet. "He was the best of us."

Zelda's gasp this time was all shock. "You rescued Russ Wilson from drowning under the *ice?* You *deserve* a cow!"

Geoffrey's face went warmer, and he knew it was red. It was the curse of being so fair.

Rob, the traitor, just agreed. "At least. The very least. So if you need something, sir, you just say so."

When he left them alone, he went out through the door to the kitchen and shut the door.

Still, Zelda seemed to want to keep her voice down, and found it difficult with this new information. "Drowning under the *ice*? You could have died!"

"I'm very large."

"Large people can drown!" Still wide-eyed, she settled back into the chair, and between delicate bites of the stew, shook her head at him. "Neither one of us has any sense, do we?"

No, he likely didn't have much sense. Because the heiress intended for his brother made him smile. "Apparently not."

She smiled back.

Zelda's gaze dropped to her bowl and she took another bite; when she'd swallowed, she said, still without looking, "And all at once, we talk like friends."

That tugged at his chest. He'd thought her a libertine, the female version of a rake. She was just the lonely daughter of a rich man.

He said, "I'm more your friend than enemy."

"How can I be sure?"

"I don't know. If I were a good friend, I would have left you at the hall with your mother. I suppose I am the sort of friend who drives you to the village when he shouldn't."

She considered that, nodded. "So will you let me ask questions?"

"Yes." He was truly going to have this conversation. So much worse than discussing pregnant ewes. Well, if he hadn't lost his claim to being a gentleman the night before, he'd lose it now.

The solution came to him. "You've seen me around sheep, and geese, and pigs, and *horses*," he said with special emphasis, "so why don't you ask me about those?"

"Because horses don't need dowries," she said in a burst of cynicism. "And *horses* didn't do anything that *we* regret."

Geoffrey took up his stew. He knew his face was a bit red. "I can apologize again," he said, reasonably, "or you can ask questions."

She rolled her eyes and huffed, and he preferred her that way.

"I assume the *horses* were paired off to create another horse."

She was good at games, and she'd be good at this one, he could tell.

He had to keep his face serious as he answered. "A foal, yes."

"But without that… *thing*… inside *her*, there would be no foal."

"Yes."

"So just assuming that *someone* did *something* that wasn't putting such a thing in such a place, no foal would occur. Am I correct?"

"Absolutely, Miss Rawle." He stuffed a chunk of buttered bread in his mouth, all amiable carelessness. She was moved to kick him in the shin.

"Ow," she said with some surprise. "You're like iron. Very well. Are all such activities other than that one harmless? Because I heard from an unreliable source that they can be dangerous."

What unreliable source? Oh yes: him.

"There are diseases that can travel from person to person that way."

"Oh. Oh, dear."

"Quite. Diseases that can leave one raving mad and finally

dead." He ought to explain. "If someone—some mare, rather —gave such a disease to a prize stallion, I would be sad to see it. That wouldn't seem fair."

He saw her puzzling out his meaning. "Aha! You mean— Yes. I can see that." Reaching past him to take a piece of the bread, she muttered, "You *are* protective of everyone."

Well, better she think that than the truth.

When she'd swallowed her bite of bread she went on, thoughtfully, "It rather makes a person want to lock themselves up in a room and never leave, except I've already done that and won't do it again."

He felt something tug inside. "Were you locked in?"

"Have you never experienced the delights of medical care? One physician thought me hysterical; he said locking the door would give me a feeling of comfort." She took another bite of bread. "It did not."

"And your parents allowed this?"

"My father left it to my mother, as he considered that her affair; his is making money. My mother thought it best to listen to learned men until the day she decided to stop."

"What made her decide?"

Zelda waved her arm. "My sleeves won't permit me to show you, so take my word that there are plenty of marks where I was bled. They put a little stick there with a blade, you see, and then whack it with another stick to cut the vein."

The sensations her words gave Geoffrey were indescribable. A crawling, cringing feeling in the skin of his arms as he imagined what she must have endured. A terror he felt everywhere. And a cold rage, unlike any sensation he'd felt before, that pulled his bones tight.

"I've seen them bleed horses," he said through his teeth, trying not to show it.

"Yes, aren't we discussing horses?" One of her sly side

looks. "In any event, the day came when you could practically see through my skin. A new physician came and suggested ice baths to calm me, and wanted to bleed me again."

"*Ice* baths?"

"He was not my favorite. I barely remember him, because my mother took one look at me and had him thrown out."

Well. Mrs. Rawle had some sense in extreme moments. Her performance earlier today had said otherwise; but then, today Zelda had been in no real danger.

"So, regarding horses." She'd shifted the bowl from one hand to the other; he took it from her. "Oh, thank you. I'll take it back in a moment. So at Roseford, the lady horse, the mare, didn't seem all that excited."

"Did she not?" His mind was still back in the room of horrors she'd escaped.

"Whereas when *other* horses did those *other* things, the mare was very excited."

She couldn't meet his eyes when she said that. He forgot his food. "Yes?"

She soldiered on. "So does *that* particular activity with *that* thing not produce the same sort of excitement?"

"In well-matched horses, yes, it does. Yes. Zelda, don't—" For some reason, in that moment, Zelda giving in to one more thing she didn't want seemed the worst possible fate. "No mare should settle for less."

"What, never?"

"*Never.*"

"Hmm." She shook out her hands and took back the bowl. Her hands must pain her, but all she did was look through her eyelashes at him. "It's hard to trust broad statements like that from the mouths of untrustworthy horses who do *quite important* things without much warning, but I'll take it under advisement."

Christ. "We should change the subject now."

"Now? When we've almost finished eating?"

"Definitely now." So he would have some time before he had to stand up again. "Did you forget Rob has a crate for me?"

* * *

"We shouldn't unpack this here. I must get you home."

The huge crate had been left on the sheltered side of one of Rob's stables. Its raw wood squashed the tender grass trying to grow beneath it despite the still-frequent frost.

Zelda walked from one side to the other, surveying it. She smiled her knowledgeable smile that captured attention and didn't let it go. "I believe you've met me. Do you honestly think that I'll leave without knowing the contents of your crate?"

Her stubborn determination to consort with him in public began to alarm him. If her reputation were destroyed, and Vere decided not to marry her, what would become of her?

She certainly couldn't sleep in a borrowed sheep shed.

Why did he keep thinking about that?

"This is an inn. People may see you. There's nothing I can do to protect you from the damage to your reputation."

She shrugged again; she had a knack for it. "I spent years locked in the same house and came all this way just to marry Lord Vere. My reputation is spotless. One spot won't hurt it." She sent him a sharp look and said under her breath, "The only things that have happened to me my whole life that could truly damage my reputation happened behind closed doors, and no one else knows of them."

Then she slid straight from making him feel guilty to making him think her reputation deserved more spots.

"Is this something you stole in London? An accomplice has sent it to you? Oh!" He was beginning to be familiar with that look of wide-eyed delight that the idea sparked in her. Familiar with it and captivated by it. "You stole it from the King, and if discovered, you'll hang!"

"Try not to sound so pleased by the idea."

She looked the crate up and down. "It would seem too large for me to put in my pocket. But I'm willing to try."

Half-afraid it was a mummy—he knew of the craze for Egyptian things, desperately hoped no one he knew would send him a mummy—Geoffrey used the inn's crowbar to pry off the top.

Zelda's head was inside before the crate wall hit the dirt.

"What on earth is it? It's like half a cart." She poked at the wooden thing packed tight in straw. "Sir Michael's cart had four wheels. But this reminds me of that somehow."

She was right. The contraption was confounding. It had two large wheels, one in front and one in back. A frame connected them and supported a narrow platform seat. A rod at the front, like a rudder, seemed intended to steer by turning the front wheel.

"I've never seen anything like it," said Zelda.

"Because it's extremely peculiar," said Geoffrey.

"This looks like something fun."

"Fun how?"

While Zelda poked and prodded at the thing, Geoffrey noticed a letter tied to it with string. He pulled the knot and took the packet, for it was indeed a full packet of papers.

The first said:

Dear Lord Geoffrey:

I am delighted by your letter and a chance to return the favor you did me at Morland. Can that be over a year ago now?

I have been corresponding with a German baron who hopes

this *laufmaschine* will let people convey themselves across the landscape. Napoleon's bureau denied his patent; I had not heard from him for months. But mail can go back and forth to the continent now, and after it began, I received this case.

It could be for serious uses, but ought to be good exercise, and good fun, too. My customers have no need of the thing, and I can think of no better trial for it than the young lady you describe. See if it suits her. The baron will no doubt wish to hear your assessment.

Most sincerely,

your friend Cullen

Below this was a note in a different hand which must be Dr. Burke's.

Sir.

I'm sorry to hear this young lady suffers so badly.

In my experience with rheumatism, exercise benefits the patient and I heartily endorse sending you the enclosed for your use—rather, for hers, as I suspect you are too heavy for the thing.

I can only recommend what I have seen help; it's nothing clever. Gentle exercise is a good plan. The medieval idea of humors is surely false, yet I do find that foods that excite the blood, like sugar and wine, provoke more pain. Some of my patients now avoid meat (the new fashion), yet are still in pain after drink or too much pastry.

If I find any interesting papers on the topic, I will endeavor to procure you a copy. One is enclosed.

Of your patients, I notice you don't mention horses. If they interest you at all, you might visit the Veterinary College. It's more than twenty years old now and may soon be bursting with students, if the wars end as I think they will. Why not consider study? I've sent a related volume.

Regards,

Burke

Yes, there was a wide object wrapped in paper at the base of the crate that must be the book. And along with the letter, there was a folded broadsheet, a research note about rheumatism. Geoffrey tucked the papers in his pocket before anyone around him could see their contents.

He understood Dr. Burke's implication. There were treatments, but no cures.

It was hard to contemplate that Zelda might never be free of her pain, but Geoffrey had grasped long ago that health was a temporary state for all living things, and that life could not wait for it.

* * *

ZELDA SAW him slip the papers into his coat. Had they truly been friends, he would have shared them with her; at least the gist of them. They weren't; he didn't.

But it was impossible to mope about wishes while faced with such a fascinating object.

"I think one sits on this seat," she said, "and one could roll like Sir Michael. But without four wheels, one would topple over!"

Geoffrey's big hands easily lifted the thing from its box. She wanted to tell him to put it back in and do it again. He couldn't possibly understand the thrill of watching his massive, effortless strength. Zelda didn't think she found it so knee-weakening just because of her illness; she suspected he had the same effect on women in general.

Did he go around astonishing them all the way he'd astonished her when he thought her a libertine?

He balanced the thing on its two wheels by holding the bar in front. "You mustn't try it here."

"What?" Her hearing must have failed her. He didn't seriously think she could wait.

He frowned and shook his head. "You've already started gossip, likely throughout the county, by going to the village and delivering a box of piglets. I'm sure you wish to try this thing, but not out here where anyone could see."

"*Try* it?" Zelda clasped her mittened hands together with zest. "I'm going to ride it!"

"Later."

"When? And where?" Zelda tried to pull the thing from his hand. She'd prefer now.

"I think the difference between us is that I do *try* to be sensible, and you clearly don't."

"I think you mean *boring*."

"Someone will *see*." There was a shout from the pasture beyond the stables, and Geoffrey stifled a groan. "Just like that."

"We are *outside*." Zelda had a much better grasp now of the things ladies weren't supposed to know, and wondered why anyone bothered with chaperones in public. Indoors was the dangerous place to be.

But then she imagined Geoffrey doing what he'd done last night somewhere outdoors, and her knees weakened further.

A crowd of little boys came running into the yard, shouting and crowding one another. Geoffrey let her have the machine.

"We thought that was you, sir!"

"So glad you're not sick!"

"You got a dunking!"

That last was from the littlest of the bunch, a tiny person whose fat fists latched onto the tail of Geoffrey's coat.

The child's obvious worry disappeared the second Geoffrey swung him up off the ground to look him in the eyes. "I did, and it hurt," Geoffrey told the tiny fellow.

The idea of Geoffrey hurt was a whole new sick sensation in Zelda's stomach.

He just went on with his tiny student. "So don't walk on ice unless someone bigger says that you may."

"But Gary says I may!"

Zelda didn't know Gary but guessed who he was from the mortified way the boy pulled his head into his shoulders. His whole face was red, but not the tips of the ears the way Geoffrey's did—

Shock straightened her back.

The way Geoffrey's did when embarrassed. Like Lady Charlotte's at the pianoforte. And Lord Vere's.

"Gary isn't what I mean by big." Geoffrey's conversation with the child went on, heedless of Zelda's shock. "Big like me."

"No one's big like you!" the tiny fellow quite rightly pointed out.

No, but Lord Faircombe was close, Zelda thought.

Why had she not noticed that they shared the same square jaw, the same heavy brows?

Because Lord Faircombe's brows were always bunched up in frowns, and his jowls flowed past his jaw.

But still.

The familiar way the shepherd had addressed Lord Vere came back to her. They must indeed have known each other all their lives.

Poor Geoffrey, to have such a rich family within view and be relegated to sleeping with the sheep!

It explained his streak of suspicion. No wonder he wanted to despise her: yet another rich person come to flaunt wealth at Faircombe. Yet his fear had been for Lord Vere, that she might give him some sort of disease.

In the next instant, the whole picture crumbled again. If he had been born a bastard and only tended sheep, why had Mrs. Wilson mentioned his "recent troubles"? And where was his mother?

And why had someone sent him a crate with the most extraordinary device she had ever seen?

No, she didn't know all his mystery, but she was sure she had a part of it.

Hopefully Lord Vere would return soon with a solicitor she could trust, and she would understand the legal mire deepening at Faircombe Hall. That must be first.

But it was impossible to entirely keep her distance from the unfolding story of her giant.

When she again paid attention, the tiny boy in Geoffrey's outstretched hands was nodding. "Big like a mamma or dad. I'll remember, sir."

"Good." And Geoffrey swung the little boy up on his shoulder as carelessly as another man would pick up a salt cellar. The boy clung to his head, thrilled at his new height. His little hands pulled at Geoffrey's thick hair; Geoffrey patiently moved the boy's grip.

She had mountains and chasms and oceans to cross, but it was impossible to ignore the melting pull of watching a very big man hold such a small child.

Had she seen Geoffrey holding the Grantleys' baby, Zelda mused, her resolve might have been well and truly shaken.

The little boys not clinging to Geoffrey's coat watched with rapt attention as Zelda hiked up her skirts on one side and tried to fling a leg over the device's seat.

"Z—Miss Rawle!" Geoffrey lunged for her but couldn't decide whether to grab the machine or her first.

She put her foot back on the ground with a little wobble. "How else am I to ride it?"

"You need… a more voluminous skirt."

True. She had a riding habit, even though she didn't ride; it was one of the things her mother had insisted be in her *trousseau*. "But I'd like to try it *now*."

Geoffrey's bushy blond eyebrows bunched together and Zelda wondered how she had ever missed the resemblance to Lord Faircombe. "Some restraint?"

"Why?"

"Because little geese are watching."

"There are no—" The way he jerked his chin toward the gaggle of tiny people clustering round his legs made her pause. "So?"

"So they do what they see. As good a reason as any for you to practice some restraint."

Well, she'd try a little; but there was no need to stand about doing nothing.

"I won't ride; I just want to see how to mount the thing." It wavered as she balanced on one foot; Geoffrey steadied it.

Pleased, Zelda tried bunching her skirts up around her legs and poking one leg over the seat. The breeze on her stockings was cold; it even crept above her garter. "One ought to have a mounting block."

"One ought to have a traveling tent. Thank… everything these boys aren't older."

"What do you mean?" She could get her leg through, but her skirts bunched around her knees no matter how she wiggled. The riding habit might do. "You aren't leaving this here? Till you come back to the village to get your cow?"

"Joanie doesn't need urgent attention. And this is going back into its crate."

Zelda and the children all chorused a sad sound.

Geoffrey didn't relent. "Back in its crate, and you can try it another day."

"Tomorrow?"

"Another day. Gary, get Augie from the blacksmith's. He'll help me put this on the carriage."

The children's disapproving noises went on, and Zelda agreed. But she could try to have some restraint. Perhaps Geoffrey was right that she had gone too far running away from the immobile isolation of the last few years.

But she wouldn't wait long to try riding that machine. She wanted more of it. She even wanted more of those disapproving eyebrows.

* * *

Joan slipped around the side of the inn; she'd have to go in the front instead of straight to the kitchen house. Even free of flour, she wasn't about to appear next to a woman dressed like that.

She'd never seen a fine lady waving her leg around in public, showing her stockings to the world. It had to be the heiress here to marry Lord Vere, it just had to be. No one else was traveling this way.

Lord Geoffrey seemed to know her, even though rumors were that he'd been banished to the stables.

How had this free-footed heiress attached herself to that anxious young bull of an Eliot? Wasn't she supposed to marry his brother?

Joan had to think it an intimate connection if he was reassuring the woman, in front of half the village children, that Joan would have to wait.

Incensed, Joan gave the big pot of stew bubbling a punishing stir. The lady must be grasping as well as free with her favors, and Lord Geoffrey deserved better. Why, if Joan hadn't been so startled by his demands the last time they met, he might well be sleeping comfortably in her bed!

It could be that Lord Geoffrey was simply cut from the

same cloth as his father. But Joan didn't think so. She believed he'd fallen from family favor, and Joan wasn't stupid. She had a great deal to offer a man: she kept a clean house, cooked good food, and made a very warm bed. And she was pretty.

Prettier than that lady, Joan thought with a sniff, unless one only liked the darker type.

She'd fumbled her first offer, but she wasn't done yet.

* * *

WHEN THE STONEMASONS' working day was through, they got themselves to the pub through stubbornness and insults.

"Pick up yer feet, Harry, my cup's dry."

"Maybe you can wait for supper, ya fat ramper, but I can't."

"I'll eat yer arm if you keep me from my supper, Coop, so help me God I will."

"We ain't gettin' paid to sit here and look pretty. Pick up yer feet."

That last one hit raw, because the pay did not come regular from the Faircombe lord. Sometimes his steward came by with a few coins at the end of a week; most often he did not.

He wasn't a rum one, the steward, only doing what he was told. But they were all getting tired of missing their money.

"Maybe next we see if we can get Faircombe's fat arse in the stewpot, Harry."

Harry Rowe's lip curled. "That'd make us more sick than starving." He'd asked half this crew to come to this puff-gut's job, and he'd like ten minutes alone with the bastard to sort him out. The Portland stone was heavy, and they were tired;

it was only a matter of time before someone lost toes, or worse. And they weren't getting paid.

The insults and friendly challenges got them all down the road together, heading for the inn that was their nightly warmth, and ale, and food. His lordship paid for their dinner, but not supper; and on quarter-pay, they had to live as rough as they could.

The snow and ice this winter had made it all harder. Jim Dennys had gone home with croup after Christmas, and hadn't come back. If Harry had been able to read or write, he'd have known his fate. As it was, it was better not to know.

When the masons reached the inn yard, they heard children screaming and laughing.

"What's so funny?" said one.

"Who cares? Stew. Stew, stew, stew."

Harry didn't blame their priorities, but he'd always been a bit more curious; he stuck his head round the corner to see what was going on.

And damn his eyes, if that wasn't the bitch-prodding son of Faircombe himself, the one who'd been scuttling after its animals. Watching some tart wave her leg in the air and mount her crotch on a machine Harry couldn't have begun to describe.

An eyeful for the kids, but then that's what happened around gentry.

They didn't look cold, or hungry, flaunting the woman's body right out under the trees like she was a much cheaper toss-pot than her clothes seemed to say. Whatever game she was pulling on the Faircombe lot, Harry wished her luck with it; they were tight-fisted enough with their men, he doubted they'd be tossing much money at her.

But that whapper of a son, he must be playing with her, or she wouldn't be out here in the cold anyway. She'd flashed her eyes at him up by the house; perhaps she was hoping for a better ride than she might get from the old man. Harry couldn't imagine what other reason she had for hanging about.

No, it was that son who made Harry see red: fed, and clothed, and getting himself all the petticoat flags in the county. It only burned Harry more that everyone in the village loved to fawn all over the great lout. If they hated the father, couldn't they see the son had his part in it too?

And had never yet come back to square accounts with Harry. It was a piss-poor excuse for a man, he felt, who let others insult him in public and did nothing about it.

For tonight, he'd join his mates in their inn; he wanted supper same as them. But he hadn't forgot about that *Lord* Geoffrey, and he wouldn't.

A heavy hand clapped on his shoulder. "Yer mates are inside."

Harry turned to face that soot-covered blacksmith. "Just watching the show."

The blacksmith—what had the lordling called him? Augie?—looked over Harry's shoulder; easy enough for him. "Lord Geoffrey's got nothing to hide, but he likely don't want to be gawked at, either."

"It's no matter to me. Just here for Rob's stew." And Harry left him and went inside, steaming.

Why was everyone so nice to that son of a boil-bottomed fat rat?

* * *

THE CRATE BANGED in the rear-mounted seat of the carriage every time a wheel crossed a rut.

Zelda had few minutes to picture what to say to her mother, but she was using the time to imagine herself flying over the ground on that rolling machine like Sir Michael had flown down the hallway. *Fastest woman on earth*, she could imagine the headline, but was still wondering how the novel below would read.

When they turned into the drive for Faircombe Hall, they rolled to one side and stopped. Zelda pushed back her curtain.

It was growing dark, but she could see the fine painting on the passing carriage and, as its curtain drew back too, she could see the grooved face of Mr. Mendey.

"Mr. Mendey!"

"Miss Rawle, good evening to you, and good-bye." The somber man raised his stovepipe hat a few inches and dropped it. "I doubt we'll meet again."

"Oh, ah… is your business concluded with Lord Faircombe, then?"

"I will not be conducting business with Lord Faircombe." The merchant studied Zelda for a moment. "Have a care, Miss Rawle. I have no idea if you share the goals of your father and Lord Faircombe. But since I suspect that you don't: have a care."

"A care for what? I know nothing about my father's business affairs, or Lord Faircombe's." He half-frightened her. Strange men gathering to do business was familiar; men declining it for secret reasons was not.

"For yourself. Be well." And with that, he reached up with his own cane and tapped the carriage's roof; his driver waved the reins and the horses, and the carriage, lurched forward.

By the time they reached the courtyard, Zelda still could think nothing but that she ought to ask Geoffrey what he meant.

And Geoffrey, she found, had the same thoughts. Because as he handed her out, in the few seconds they had before the Faircombe footmen arrived to escort her inside, along with her mother who must have been waiting by the door, the shepherd said, "I've no idea what he meant either. Don't let it alarm you."

But it had.

Zelda found herself, oddly, reassuring the big man in return. "I'm quite calm, and I'm sure everything is fine. Don't forget me tomorrow."

"I won't." He wore an oddly gentle look as he said it.

"I will find a way to venture out; I am going to ride that machine."

CHAPTER 19

Zelda dreamed of flying over the ground, grass disappearing behind her like the water on the ocean.

But when she woke, she was so, so heavy.

Even the memory of trying to cast a leg over the rolling machine seemed impossible. She knew this feeling. Sometimes, she simply couldn't get out of bed.

But she'd never before had such hopes to look forward to, and had them dashed.

Was this what her mother wanted to keep from her, all those years inside? From dashed hopes? Because they were painful.

But she doubted they'd ever have been as painful before she met Geoffrey. She wanted to fly over the ground *with him*. Since that could only happen in dreams, perhaps it was best to lie abed.

Muzzily, she lay and looked out the French windows at the wide world. The skies were gray today, clouds carelessly piled atop one another.

The farther horizons—Amsterdam, Italy, Russia—seemed farther away than ever.

Was that why she had set her heart on them? Because they gave tomorrow a colorful possibility that she'd desperately needed when her todays had been nothing but the same?

Did dreams need a why?

Tansy seemed far ahead of her the moment she came in. "I'll bring you a tray," she said, giving the coverlets a brisk pat. "Just rest."

"In a moment." Zelda's head even felt heavy as she turned sorrowful eyes toward her maid. "I had plans to go out, Tansy. You cannot imagine the device someone sent the shepherd. It's a machine that you *ride*."

"Do you indeed? That sounds inappropriate."

"Quite." Zelda managed a smile.

With a sigh, Tansy slid one of the heavy chairs to the bedside and plopped down in it. "What are you doing, if I may ask?"

"In this bed?"

"With that shepherd."

"Nothing of note."

"And your betrothed, the Earl of Vere and Baron Culwer, wasn't it? Would he think it nothing of note?"

"Here's the heart of it." Zelda pulled the thoughts together as she said them. "When you've never done anything —*anything*, it's hard to divide the world into what you may do and what you may not."

"Hard?" Tansy's hands folded themselves together. "Or just requiring effort?"

Why was everyone so determined she should behave? There had been advantages, she realized now, to being just the frail Rawle daughter, never seen and never heard.

Not many, she decided, but some.

"Never mind it." Tansy pulled a thick tome from beside her in the chair. "Guess what I have found to pass the time?"

Zelda didn't have the strength to guess. "A book."

"A *law dictionary*." Tansy lay the book on her knee, began turning pages. "I read a few pages. Did you know that to *abdicate* means to renounce or refuse anything?"

"I've abdicated plenty in my life already, Tansy." Crankiness aside, this was exciting. Zelda was still Zelda, and some spark of her interest remained, even if she had no fire. "Did you find *indemnification?*"

Tansy turned pages. "It isn't here."

"What? How are we to make progress if the most difficult words are not even in the dictionary?"

"I have no idea." Tansy settled herself against the cushions. "Shall I read? Or will you have your tray first?"

Zelda sighed. "Please read."

Tansy's finger slid down the open page. "*Indemnification* ought to have been right here. I'll read *indemnity.*"

The page was something about bishops that Zelda couldn't follow at all. Her eyes unfocused. She stared upwards. This bed had a canopy and curtains, pulled back to let the air flow freely. At least they weren't the old pattern of tree knots.

She let Tansy's voice lull her out of the anger she wanted to feel that she sometimes *had* to be restrained. So why not let her do things when she could?

* * *

"You're distracted."

The ballet dancer, who had been entrancingly lovely on the stage earlier, now couldn't keep Vere's attention.

This didn't bother her; she simply smiled and moved on. The club was full of young aristocrats that evening; she didn't need to catch Vere's eye.

The comment had been from his unknown drinking partner, who shook his head. "You're ill when you miss out on a juicy peach like that one."

Perhaps it was the word *peach* that reminded Vere, unpleasantly, that he had come to London on an errand, not to carouse.

It was a funny time to remember it, now that he was here, coat missing. A ruby-faced wench in long trousers and naught else had offered to "unrig" him "like a pirate"; she'd taken his coat and unbuttoned his waistcoat. The coat was likely gone for good.

He couldn't decide if he'd rather have had the ballet dancer or the pirate wench, and that was a good sign he'd had enough ale.

Still, an odd moment for conscience.

"Got the pox? Or just too much barrel?" The man sitting opposite obviously didn't care a fig which answer it was. He was just sitting there companionably enough, watching the women and enjoying the spectacle.

"I do need to find someone."

"What? Are you going to toss your accounts?" The man opposite looked ready to leap up, wary now Vere might spew on him.

Well, he might, but that wasn't his point. "No, looking for a man for my wife."

"You're in a funny place to find a man for your wife." The fellow relaxed back in his chair.

Reclining on the room's long walnut table, a woman with skirts tucked up in her waistband sang while playing a lute. She was quite admirable for doing two things at once; three, if one counted having jugged cherries nibbled off her thighs.

This club was Vere's favorite for a good show of an

evening, but he couldn't concentrate. He'd been in London... how many days now?

That fragile little waif he was supposed to marry needed help. He couldn't stay in here forever.

Well, he could, but eventually his father would come and demand he be married, so he might as well get on with it. "I think I have some business to attend to."

"Yes, you look it," said the man across the way.

* * *

"I DON'T SUPPOSE it would entertain you to be drawn?"

"No," Zelda said on a sigh, but smiling. "Kind of you to offer. Oh! But I would like to see your drawings of laundry!"

"Ah." Delina settled herself in the chair Tansy had vacated. Clearly word had spread that Miss Rawle wasn't well, and Miss Farsworth had come to keep her company for a while.

The visitor ruffled among sketches in a huge leather *port folio* by her side. "Some of these were quite interesting, I thought."

Zelda surveyed the large paper sheet. "If it is interesting, you must tell me why."

Delina laughed. "If I must explain it, how interesting can it be?"

"Interesting to you, of course. The artist. Tell me what interested you in making it. How else can I know?"

That question gripped Delina, and she bent over her own sketch. "How can you know? The subject, I suppose. What I've chosen to put inside the frame." She spread her little hands at the corners. "If there were a frame. You can imagine the frame."

Zelda's laugh was quiet. She had slept for hours since Tansy had gone, and had some soup; but she was still worn and felt far too heavy. It was hard to remember, when she felt like this, that she had ever been cheery.

"You are very kind to entertain me. This must be detracting from valuable drawing time."

"I don't mind a little rest. I'll soon have all the time I like."

"What do you mean?" It was a simple declaration, but felt chilling.

Delina shrugged, her china-doll face rather impassive, but her eyes were sparkling. "We are moving to a *cottage*, Miss Rawle. Isn't that exciting?"

It didn't sound it, but Delina was so animated. "Please, call me Zelda. Is it exciting? And who is we?"

"Oh. Lady Charlotte and I, you know." Delina dipped her face away, smoothing out the drawing, but then looked at Zelda again. "I think we will be much happier out in the country."

"This is out in the country, surely!"

Delina laughed. "Only a day from London! And we are both through with that."

"But you… don't you ever intend to marry?"

"No," Delina said with soft seriousness, "we don't."

She grew animated again as she shifted one sketch below another. Zelda could only imagine this house without them in it. They had not grown close, but soon the house would hold only Lord Faircombe, Lord Vere… and her.

And somewhere outside in the sheds, a sturdy, scolding, seductive shepherd.

That sounded incredibly lonely, and somehow wrong.

She wondered if the solicitors would stay on.

"Miss Farsworth. Delina. Won't Lady Charlotte miss her home?"

Delina looked around the room with its yellow jacquard curtains and fanciful trees. "She misses the home she had."

Zelda struggled upward. "You don't mean these chambers were hers? Have I displaced her? Never say so!"

"No, no, of course not! These rooms were her mother's. The late Lady Faircombe." Delina patted one of her hands. "It is completely right you should have them."

"Oh. I should have known." Zelda sank back. "But the rooms are so fresh and clean. His lordship must miss his wife very much, to keep these rooms so well made."

Delina wouldn't meet her eyes again. Zelda wished she played cards; she might win quite a lot wagering with the other young woman. "I don't think his lordship cares very much."

It must be Lord Vere who asked the maids to wipe the paintings and keep the chimney clear; even the hangings round the bed showed not one speck of dust or cobwebs.

Zelda let Delina keep talking about shadows and the cost of paint. She wished she hadn't learned that these rooms belonged to Lady Faircombe. That just thrust forward that she herself was soon to be Lady Vere, and eventually Lady Faircombe, and it was becoming harder and harder to imagine any adventures committed by such a person. *Lady Faircombe sails around India. Lady Faircombe's rare porcelain collection revealed. Lady Faircombe fails to produce heir.*

Because she knew now what she was supposed to do. She wasn't just to stand in a church and make vows to Lord Vere that she might or might not keep. She was to lie with him and produce an heir for the title; and if she didn't, there was no way to hide that.

She could imagine anything but that.

"Delina," she said, interrupting some treatise on shadows. "I'm sorry," she immediately said, but her visitor waved it away.

"Please. You had a question?"

"It isn't about the art. Which is lovely! I want to hear about this cottage you intend to buy."

"Ah." Delina subsided in the chair. "I have a small share of money I inherited from an aunt; my father is going to use it to purchase the cottage for us."

"Why your father?"

"Well, he will give us the use of it, of course. But women cannot own property."

"What? Of course they can." Didn't Zelda have a faint memory of a widow in the Hudson Valley purchasing an estate of her own? She was sure she'd heard her mother speak of it.

"Not in Britain, Zelda. Not often."

"What?" She had already felt too heavy to rise; now she felt she must sink through the mattresses and down to the center of the earth. "What did you say?"

"I assumed you knew. Though, why should it matter to you? You will be married to Lord Vere, and a husband takes care of all money for a wife."

"And my dowry?" Her dowry, which she had carefully planned to stretch all the way around the world.

"That becomes his as well, of course."

"But what if something happens to him?" He was young, hale, and hearty; she'd seen him days ago. But now it seemed as though everything and everyone could disappear at any time.

"You get the widow's portion. And I suspect he would be generous with you. Especially if you provide him with an heir."

If she did. *If* she did. She'd listened to so many business dealings among men. All men.

Her father had laid a trap for her.

He had done this deliberately.

He hadn't just ignored her; he'd doomed her.

As Zelda lay in the late Lady Faircombe's bed, all the years of her life slotted together in very new ways. She saw that she had never been as important to her father as money.

Neither, she suspected, was her mother.

"Are you well?" Delina sounded worried. What must she look like, sinking into pillows and realizing for the first time the depths of how unwanted she really was?

"Well enough." Her spirit could match her body, she found, weaker than she had ever suspected.

* * *

"WELL?" Dandy spit into the grass.

Geoffrey just glared. He'd borrowed heavy gloves from the falconer, but the falcon objected to his help. The bird had a bent toe, and the falconer, who worried like a grandmother, wanted Geoffrey to fix it.

Instead, Geoffrey would be lucky to get out of this with both his eyes.

"Well what? Hold her still, would you, Charlie?"

"She's that anxious."

Geoffrey reflected that the bird was plenty anxious, but so was Geoffrey. He had enough problems right now, and he was vain enough to think that Zelda might not like him so well if he only had half his face.

Dandy just peered at him. "Well, what are you doing?"

"Dandy, do you need something?" The big feathers *whooshed* past Geoffrey's nose. Well, he'd take feathers over claws.

The falconer was still fussing over his charge. "Do you think her beak needs coping?"

Geoffrey squinted. "I can't see it with the hood on, of course."

"Should I take the hood off?" The falconer made to remove it.

"Christ, *no*!"

"I mean," persisted Dandy, "what's your plan? How do you find the servant life? Planning to keep it up forever?"

"I plan to get this toe sorted. Charlie, an animal I can't hold is likely healthy enough. Is she eating?"

"Oh aye, eats like a horse. For a bird."

"Fine. It might be swollen a bit, but it looks well enough. Fetch me if it gets worse, would you?"

"Aye."

Charlie wasn't pleased, but then Geoffrey wasn't pleased either. Not by a falcon trying to gut him, and not by Dandy's questions.

"So?" Dandy said as Charlie disappeared through the back of the stable.

There were more animals to see, and Geoffrey was hungry and wanted another bath. And he was *tired*. He hadn't slept much. Zelda haunted his dreams, not laughing Zelda, but a crushed, unhappy Zelda lying pale in his mother's bed.

Just as she was doing today.

The servants were all a-gossip about the new lady lying in bed. A few thought she was shirking; most just sounded worried. She was pale and languid, they said. She never looked hearty, but today she was pallid.

"Dandy, talk. Or don't. I'm fine either way. I've got work to do."

"Has his lordship offered to pay you?" At Geoffrey's silence, Dandy sucked his teeth and nodded. "So what does that make you? 'Cause that ain't charity."

"What do you want me to do? Steal armor and a battle-ax from the map room and batter down the door? I'd have to be inside to steal the ax!"

"Is it the ax that you want?"

Geoffrey was tired, right down to the core of his bones. Yet he didn't just suspect, he *knew*, that if he were with her now, her head pillowed on his arm, he would have the strength to hold her forever.

She gave him that. And he had nothing to give her.

Except a spot in a straw bed that wouldn't be his once Bernie came back.

"I want a lot of things, Dandy." He didn't; he wanted one. "I suppose I should have thought sooner what my life would be once Vere married. I should have found some trade. Followed Frederick to university."

The book Dr. Burke had sent was *The Anatomy of an Horse* by a Mr. Snape. The engravings were lush with details about things Geoffrey had barely considered about any animal, least of all about the horse. His head was swimming with wondering what to do about Zelda, what he *could* do besides keeping her safe as Vere asked, how she was faring, and the muscles, bones, ligaments, and arteries of horses, oddly enough. They made him want similar drawings of the bird he'd just handled. And more information about the soft organs inside.

Why thoughts of Zelda were all tangled up in his head with thoughts of animals, he wasn't sure. But he did know he should have thought of *all* of this sooner.

"A-hah. Is that the problem with Lord Vere's wedding?"

"Dandy, until or unless you have some woman hiding in that other shed with you, I'll thank you to keep your mouth shut." Geoffrey threw down the heavy gloves. "What do you know about marriage? Or women, for that matter?"

Dandy just scratched the side of his head, watching the rare sight of Geoffrey losing his patience. "I was in love once."

"*Agghh.* Dandy." Geoffrey's shoulders slumped; his very face fell. "I'm sorry. I didn't mean it."

"No, you meant it well enough, and rightly so, too. I haven't said aught about it. Because she died, and I miss her still, and it feels like that's all there is to say. But it isn't, is it?" Dandy nodded to himself, licking one lip as he stared out the stable door. "We were happy. I should talk of her more. A good woman is… love is worth fighting for. Worth anything."

"I believe you."

"Do you?" Dandy's graying eyes focused again, and snapped back to Geoffrey. "What do you know about love?"

"I'm not sure."

"Well," said Dandy, handing Geoffrey the tools for trimming sheep hooves, "let me know when you've riddled it."

He'd spent enough time on animals of the four-footed and winged sort, thought Geoffrey; if he couldn't keep his promise to let Zelda ride the German machine, through no one's fault, he might at least serve her some entertainment. Even a shepherd could do that.

* * *

IT WAS TOO pathetic to jump the way Zelda did when she caught sight of a broad-shouldered form outside the French window of her chamber.

It couldn't be Geoffrey, after all; the stonemasons still worked out there, and likely one of them had wandered up on the portico for some reason. That should be more frightening; that should make her heart pound harder.

But it was no stonemason. It was Geoffrey, and Zelda's heart thumped hard in her chest. She could see the thick, bushy hair under his cap before she saw his big hand come up to place a finger on his lips. *Shh.*

CHAPTER 20

*T*hat wasn't like him.

Mrs. Rawle bustled in from her room. "Griselda, have you had the willow-bark tea? I know it's bitter, child, but you will feel better."

The willow bark didn't help with exhaustion, but her mother didn't listen to that. Still, Zelda had drunk it.

Right now, she didn't want tea or an empty cup. She wanted her mother out of the room.

Geoffrey's form disappeared from the panes of glass.

"Mother, are we out of the wintergreen oil?"

"Not at all, dear. Look. I'll put this by you on the bed."

Her mother lifted the whole cut-crystal tray, then put it down again. "Too heavy. Here, just tell me where it hurts and I will apply it."

Where it hurt was her lack of privacy.

She'd been abed all day, and while she wasn't ready to stroll across Faircombe grounds, she was better.

And that was Geoffrey outside. What if he'd brought the rolling machine?

That was foolish, of course; there was no way to bring

that in here. Though she could try. Zelda measured by eye the distance between the chairs by the fire, her dressing-table, the desk she never used, and the window glass.

She wanted her mother *out.* "Should you check on the supper time?"

"Nonsense. I expect it's as usual, but I don't intend to go without you." Mrs. Rawle shuddered. "All those dreadful men lined up around the table chewing meat like wild boars. It's off-putting, to say the least. I would rather dine with you."

Usually, her mother's company would be preferable; but Zelda wanted to see Geoffrey. Laundry drawings and law dictionaries were lovely, but she'd rather see Geoffrey.

And she was still not best in charity with her mother since she'd returned alone from the village. Her mother had dined silently in the room with Zelda, which was supposed to be a punishment; but since she wouldn't talk about what Zelda wanted to talk about, that seemed perfectly fine.

Certainly Zelda didn't feel bad about one more little lie. "Mr. Paltz wanted to speak with you."

Mrs. Rawle paused in the act of replacing the hot coal pan near Zelda's feet. "Did he?"

He didn't. "He did. While Miss Farsworth was here with her drawings. I've only just remembered."

"Well."

There was something between her mother and Mr. Paltz; Zelda was sure of it now. But what it could be she couldn't guess, especially since her mother didn't leap at the bait. "I'll see him later, I'm sure. You'll sleep, I suspect, very early."

She likely would. But that would mean she'd have to survive the next few minutes without dying of curiosity. And that would be difficult.

Geoffrey's form appeared again outside, just barely visible against the gray spring gloom. Perhaps he could hear what they were saying within, perhaps he could tell she was having no luck ridding herself of her mother. She saw his shoulders shrug.

Slowly, silently, the glass-paned door swung in, and Zelda wondered if Geoffrey really was about to walk right into her chamber. Her heart beat hard at the idea of it, for so many reasons and none at all. The plain and simple thought was: *Geoffrey.*

Instead, he bent down in an odd sort of crouch, and she saw him move slightly; then he withdrew, and the floor-length window swung closed.

What?

In the next moment, Zelda realized what had happened as her black-spotted lamb appeared in the middle of the Aubusson carpet. He spread all four pointed little feet, planting himself among the wool-woven swirls of color.

"Bleeaaahhh!" he said at the top of his little voice.

Mrs. Rawle jumped at least a foot.

"Oh no! Oh dear!" Slumping forward, Zelda laughed, laughed harder than she really could. But it was impossible not to.

"What in heaven's name!? An animal! There's a wild animal in here! Griselda! Stay in the bed!"

Her mother had started to wave the little creature around the room. The lamb, excited by all the new furniture legs and weaving his way through them, led her in circles. "Bleeaahh!" he announced, with the soft fast *thip thip thip* of his feet on the wool carpet—first from under the bed, then under the dressing-table.

He did like to explore under things.

"No no, Mother, it isn't a wild animal. It's a pet lamb of mine, that's all." Zelda slid her feet toward the floor. The chill seized them as soon as they were free in the air, away from the heat under the coverlets; but she couldn't stay still another minute.

"Stay in the bed! What pet? Who knows what it will do? Perhaps it will bite. No! *Griselda!*"

"Mother, I thought we had had an excellent conversation about me doing what I wish to do."

Zelda knelt and looked under the dressing-table. The lamb had all four feet splayed out, ready to run. Or jump straight up.

"Don't do that, silly," she told it. "You'll hit your head. You're not frightened, not really. Come see me."

"Bleeaah!" said the lamb, but trotted out fairly complacently. Zelda sat on her heels, and the lamb butted her in the thigh again. It had a positive craving for that.

"Now be nice," Zelda told it, scratching its head.

"Griselda! *Really*! Willfulness is one thing, but that's a *wild animal in your room*!"

"Yes, terribly wild." Could she keep hold of it with one arm and still rise? She could. Using the coverlets, she managed to pull herself upright.

She wished she had her slippers on, and she wished it had taken longer, but she took it to the door.

"How on earth did it get in?" Mrs. Rawle called from where she was effectively hiding behind one of the heavy chairs by the fire.

"I told you," Zelda called back over her shoulder carelessly, "it's a pet."

"Don't open the door! Just get it out!"

Zelda didn't bother to unravel her mother's inconsistencies.

She opened the door and slid the soft little fuzzy body outside. Gave it a pat.

And looked to her right. There was Geoffrey.

"I thought you'd let it run around for a while, terrorize your mother," he whispered.

She couldn't have stopped her grin for anything. "You're a bad person," she whispered back.

"At the worst times." His Viking features grew soft. "Are you well?"

"I'm well enough." Her toes were freezing against the edge of the stone, but it felt like losing a few would be better than leaving him. "I'm sorry to have missed our engagement."

"For what? Trying the new machine?" Geoffrey scoffed and waved at the gray sky. "A poor day for it. Feel better first."

"And you're well, too?"

"I'm always well, Miss Rawle."

No, Zelda thought to herself as she closed the door before she ran into his arms, *you're not*.

But she could trust him to be there tomorrow. Of that, she felt sure.

Even though he was here again, luring her out of bed with livestock.

She supposed that was better than luring her *into* bed with livestock.

Maybe.

"Get back in the bed! Oh my heavens. What a horrible disease you will catch."

The idea of catching diseases did make Zelda's smile fade. The complicated side of attraction still seemed overwhelming. And very, very dangerous.

But she loved new things, and Geoffrey had just set loose a lamb in her chambers, and that was impossible to resist.

Bewitched by lamb, woman suffers terrible fate.

All too likely.

* * *

"WHAT ARE YOU DOING?" Charlotte, as abrupt as always, crossed her path with Geoffrey's on the green; she must have seen him coming from the general direction of the portico. Their mother's portico, as Charlotte knew very well.

Geoffrey suppressed his grin at the thought of Zelda's delight, and let the lamb go. It trotted to its mother, who had brought friends; a little pack of sheep now grazed between the pink Portland stone and the garden. "Stop asking." Even to say that much felt like a whole new level of assertion for Geoffrey. "What are *you* doing?"

"Leaving."

The word hit Geoffrey like shot from a shotgun. "No. Charlotte."

"Don't look so glum! I'm happy." And she looked it, which was proof this was real and, Geoffrey supposed, good. He felt gutted, but she nearly glowed. "Delina and I are going farther north. We have wanted to do this for a while, just waited for the right moment."

"And now is the right moment?"

The frustrated noise she made was reminiscent of her horses. "He treats Delina like a servant. I won't have it."

"He treats everyone like a servant." For what else were his demands that Vere behave as he said? "Everyone except you."

Had anyone asked Geoffrey, he would have said that Charlotte must enjoy being the favored only daughter of the Marquess.

But she just shook her head, her loose curls bouncing across her shoulder to the extent her riding bonnet would allow. "He's not easy with anyone, and he was only pleased that I decided not to marry for as long as he thought it meant I would keep house for him here. But there's nothing he can do about my inheritance, and as I *won't* marry, it stays with me." She bit at her fingernail, and didn't meet his eyes. "You needn't stay here, you know. You could come too."

The tenderness her speech evoked in him shocked him. Thorny, spoiled little Charlotte had truly grown into a sister, to think of him at a time like this.

But she had clearly asked because she thought she ought, not because she wanted him, not entirely. If she and Delina had been hatching these plans for a while, they wouldn't want a ham-footed brotherly type traipsing all over their hand-stitched carpets, or whatever they planned to have.

"Thank you." He meant it. "I'm not leaving Faircombe. But thank you."

"Not ever? Doesn't it—I mean, haven't you found that Faircombe feels quite small?"

"Just because I am large?" That reminded him. "There's a cottage on the grounds up to the north, in the woods there, Charlotte—did you know about that?"

"No." She didn't look interested, either, but that was Charlotte: always far too interested, or not interested at all. "I don't know whom you could ask, either."

"Augie suggested I ask old Mrs. Hull in the village." Feeling himself stepping on some of those awkward eggshells that went with being the grown brother of a supposedly ladylike sister, he added, "You do know who Augie is, don't you?"

"Yes, and I've met him. Has the London fiction that all young ladies are brainless cage-raised mice infected your brain, Geoffrey?"

"I subscribe to the notion that women are people, Charlotte, as you know perfectly well." If he hadn't before, these last few days with Zelda would have changed him. In fact, they already had.

He was courting more strife with his father every time he entered the house, but he had to see more of that delighted look on her face.

In fact, he had another idea. He was having ideas more and more frequently now, and he liked them.

* * *

WHEN ZELDA WOKE AGAIN, night had fallen. That meant nothing; the spring sun was weak and gave up early. But she knew she'd been asleep a long while.

A tray stood nearby, holding an orange and tempting bites of buttered toast, but Zelda didn't feel hungry. Shrugging into her quilted coat, she slid her feet into stockings, didn't bother to roll them up, then added her walking shoes.

When she pulled back the yellow damask curtains to see what she could see, she clapped both hands to her mouth to stifle her indrawn breath.

The entire world was carpeted in white, flawless snow.

It lay against the silken tent and the garden bench, coated the marble portico, made it soft and mysteriously shadowed. It reminded Zelda of Delina's laundry drawings, and the mysteries of temporary things.

Beyond, the green of the grass was lost beneath a landscape of white, white that heaved up to cascade over the shapes of hedges in the garden beyond, the ragged edges of dark underneath the white only emphasizing the stark bright smoothness of the landscape.

How long had she slept? What time could it be?

The whole scene made Zelda feel as though she had slept for a hundred years. Perhaps she had been trapped in a fairy realm, where no one ever escaped.

Well, she was used to escaping what couldn't be escaped.

The yielding *crunch* of the snowflakes under her shoes only thrilled her with the ridiculousness of the thing she was doing. *Zelda sculpts snow.* She wished she could make beautiful things the way Lady Charlotte and Delina made music and art. She also wished to throw a snowball.

As long as no one was around, no one could stop her. The benefits of being alone!

Cautiously, she stepped to the edge of the portico, where it raised over the ground to give a better view. Before she thought twice, she scooped snow up into her hands and crushed the fragile stuff into a wet ball.

And threw it at the stonework.

* * *

GEOFFREY COULDN'T REALLY HIDE how he was hovering around Zelda's door.

As soon as the snow had started, Guinevere, low with her lambs, had marched straight into his shed and stayed there. But Nemesis, as he'd decided to call the goose, was following him about.

Nemesis gave everyone and everything grief, in fact, except for Guinevere. It pecked at the pigs, trying to start fights; it honked at the cattlemen; and it ate its weight in insects, as far as Geoffrey could tell from its constant company.

And now the goose was following Geoffrey in restless wandering about the estate.

Geoffrey ought to be in bed. But the way the deep clouds trapped all the light and sound down on the earth below called to him, as did the wide expanse of unbroken snow.

He liked making bootprints in it. Faircombe might never remember one penniless third son; but for a moment, he could make a mark.

And Nemesis could too. The triangles left by the goose's feet were funny.

Zelda would like them.

Geoffrey had ventured north to check on the burnt cottage in the quiet night. Surely the snow would keep away lovers. It was somehow less menacing in the gray night. Its burnt stones were smothered in comforting snow, and the floors were still clean; its doors and shutters were snug.

He must make his inquiries about the thing.

And he came back along the edge of the estate to make sure none of the sheep had lambed alone. That was what he would tell anyone who asked.

He walked for so long even Nemesis became bored, and waddled off.

It was luck that he saw a ball of snow fly over the parapet of pink stone near the garden portico. It gave him the excuse he needed to go there without worrying about waking her.

The soaring sensation in his chest when he caught sight of her, dark hair streaming down her back, silk mittens determinedly crushing snow into another ball, ought to have given him pause. He was a man who believed in family. He took it seriously.

Yet when he looked at her, all he saw was *her*. His feet started toward her of their own accord. And all he wanted was *now*.

"You should be in bed."

He must have startled her; the snowball rolled off her suddenly limp mitten.

But she barely showed it, brushing back her hair so that the snowflakes still on her mitten showed white in the dark strands. "I've been abed all day."

"Do you feel better?"

"Well enough," said Zelda with that secret smile of hers, keeping her eyes down. She scooped up more snow, patted it into shape.

"Well enough to be out here?" Her stockings were unfastened; he saw them under the hem of her gown when she moved. God, he shouldn't get hard from the sight of stockings gathering round her ankles. But he did.

She gave him that slow look from the corner of one eye. "Well enough for anything I please," she told him, and then *whap*, hit him square in the chest with the snowball.

With grave dignity, he wiped away the splash of snow on his chin.

"Then I guess you truly feel well enough for anything," he said, advancing on her slowly.

"That's what I said! Wait. What do *you* mean by *anything*?" Warily, she backed up and backed up till her legs met the low stone fence around the portico's edge meant to keep people from falling off. She put her hands behind her atop the fence to keep her balance.

He was enjoying himself too much to answer. He ought to bundle her inside; but she had color in her cheeks, she looked well enough, and it was fun, it was just plain fun, to watch her watching him that way.

"What do you think I mean?" He was leaning so close he could see the tip of each tantalizing eyelash.

"Like… a kiss?"

Her lips as well as her cheeks were flushed now. She was breathing more heavily than one might from simply backing across a few yards of marble. And her eyes were locked on his.

"A kiss? Only brigands and pirates steal kisses in the middle of the night. Who do you think I am?" He wanted to be the man who stole kisses from Zelda in the dark. He truly did. Perhaps he even was that man. Perhaps she would tell him.

The look that came over her face then was a wash of puzzlement, pity, and a bit of distance, where the moment before, he had practically felt the touch of her eyes. "I'm not sure I know."

"Well," he had to admit, "I'm not sure I know either."

And he swooped her up in his arms, much the way she had scooped up the snow.

She had the most perfect curves, fitting against him in ways no one could plan. It had simply happened. The taste of her lips, warm and sweet with little crystals of snow, made him forget everything: who he was, where he was, and what he ought to do with her.

He only knew what he *wanted* to do with her.

The instant they finally parted he wanted to draw her back against him. To sink back and let her sprawl all over him. To never leave her kiss.

Her eyes, those sleepy warm eyes, were looking at him as if her imagination had beaten him to the idea.

"I think," she said slowly, "that you are here to seduce me with livestock again."

Breathing deep, he backed up a step. He could hardly devour her—he could hardly *ravish* her outside in the snow. He'd lost his mind.

Instead of hauling her in by the fire and showing her how much he wanted to seduce her, he pretended to remember an idea, and snapped his bare fingers. "I am."

Just as he'd known she would, Zelda looked intrigued, and tickled, and desperately curious all at once. "Then where is the livestock? Have you a bird in your pocket?" She bit her lower lip, then grinned. "I didn't feel one."

She would kill him.

He made a show of examining her feet, bending low for a good look. "Have you good shoes on? Very well, come with me."

Like an innocent child, she put her hand in his and followed him down the steps—he watched her balance carefully—and across the unbroken swathe of snow to the edge of the garden and beyond.

The ghostly shapes of the snow-covered topiaries and decorative trees didn't cause her a moment's hesitation. "Where are we going?" she said with the air of a person who was desperate to get there.

"Somewhere close, but special."

When he rounded the far end of the path, he turned her to look back over the garden through which they'd just walked. Zelda looked even more puzzled.

"You must stay warm." His breath ruffled her hair, he leaned so close.

Zelda jumped a little as he slid off his sheepskin coat.

He pulled it snug it around her, wrapping her in it like a blanket. It reached her knees.

"Don't chill your legs," he told her sternly, then crouched down on his haunches.

"Won't you be cold? Geoffrey, be careful!"

Miss Zelda Rawle worrying about him was almost as warming as her kiss.

"I'm quite warm now," and he smiled to give her a hint that she was the reason. "Lie on your stomach, keep your hands out of the snow. That's it."

When she'd gotten into position, he used his other hand to push the lowest hedge branches out of the way.

"Can you see?"

When he raised the edge of the green hedge like a skirt, Zelda could see a fluffy ball of fur curled up underneath its shadows. "Oh! A rabbit!"

"It's a hare," he said, as somberly and gently as he said almost everything. "The rabbits are all underground and snug in their beds. Hares are quite hearty and for them, this will do. Can you see?" he asked again.

The faint edges of her fur blended into the dark. Geoffrey had not disturbed the animal's sleep.

Zelda had no headlines for this. This was real, and right here, and as extraordinary as any adventure tale. Zelda could just barely see the creature's fur move with the rise and fall of its breath. It was almost too real to bear.

The hare shifted a little, and under its chest Zelda just glimpsed a tiny gray something. A foot? No…

"Is it a baby hare?"

"Yes! Don't touch."

"I wasn't about to try. But they won't freeze?"

"It's quite warm out, isn't it? Here you are, very naughty, without even your stockings on properly." He didn't look at her again, but she suspected if he did, those eyes would be bright and hot. He knew how her stockings were.

Zelda felt herself flush.

"Because the mother keeps it warm?"

"Them. There are two little ones; I saw them a few days ago. I'm glad the snow isn't bothering them."

Zelda turned to see his profile, an oak tree of a man, all hard muscle and bone, worrying over baby hares in the snow.

"The world is full of such cruel people," she said before she thought. "And yet here you are, not afraid to have such a gentle touch." As she heard her own words, she thought he must think her very forward. But it was only the truth. He could lift mountains with those arms, and his fingertips held the fragile branches so gently that they were barely disturbed.

"Who could be afraid to be gentle?" He let the branches go, and with a soft rustle they settled back just as he'd found them, dropping a few beads of snow. "It's the opposite that should make one worry."

"But men aren't. Gentle."

Geoffrey braced his forearms on his knees. The snow dripped from his hand, melting in the heat from his body. Zelda knew how it felt.

"Perhaps it's only the biggest men who can afford to be gentle. Perhaps life is a forest full of wolves." He said it as though it were a quote from something; did he have headlines of his own running through his head?

Zelda's head had gone silent. She was no longer waiting for something important to happen. It was happening, right here, right now, in the snow next to a rabbit hole. No, a hare's nest.

"Then you must be the gentlest man in the world." In the shadows, the mother hare shifted, but Zelda couldn't tear her eyes away from the man beside her.

"I am nothing that special," muttered Geoffrey.

"And here I thought you were wise. There are no men in New York like you, Geoffrey, and I'd wager none in London, either."

"Perhaps we grow best out here in the country." His mouth had a wry twist. "Any man in the village would do as much." The twist put mischief into his eyes. "You said you thought I was out to seduce you with livestock."

"Aren't you? Some men bring diamonds or pearls; you bring lambs and hares."

His smile faded. "Wouldn't you rather have diamonds?"

"I *have* those."

The space between them grew smaller and smaller, even though neither of them moved. The quiet of the night, which had seemed empty a second before, was suddenly as close and intimate as a closet with a closed door.

"You should stand," Zelda whispered. "Don't get wet just because of me."

Even as she said it, she put out her mittened hand and

pushed at his knee. It was like pushing at the corner of a house.

But he took it with his free fingers, and bent low enough to bring it to his lips. "I am quite well," his voice spread through the little space under the snowy hedge like warm honey. And she could feel the warmth of his kiss through the mittens.

It seemed more intimate than anything else they had done, lying in the silent, snowy world staring at the miracle of a little family surviving all the world had to throw at it.

Suddenly, Zelda thought she must move, or she would cry.

As soon as she shifted, Geoffrey jumped up, helping her quickly to her feet. His hands brushed the lower part of her skirt, which was the only part that had become dusted with rapidly melting snow.

"Take your coat," she urged.

"You should have it for now."

"Geoffrey." Zelda couldn't think what to say. He'd given her the coat off his back. "You're not—you're *not* trying to seduce me with livestock, are you?"

Instead of meeting her eyes, he drew her closer to him. Slowly, she moved too, till she found herself nestled quite naturally against the broad, muscular beam of his chest. It was warm there, and safe and quiet.

His cheek stroked her hair a little. She could feel the stubble of his beard. "I'm not exactly trying to do it, no."

"You're not a bad man at all, are you?"

"Well, I've leaped to a wrong conclusion or two."

"This only makes it all worse."

"Makes what worse?" His voice was too steady and soft to have an edge to it, but it also forced her to answer.

"You're not bad at all, and I *am*, Geoffrey. I *do* wish to marry just for my dowry money and sail away forever and leave Lord Vere sitting here alone with no heirs for the Faircombe line. But I also don't wish it, all at the same time. So I'm confused as well as bad. And I wish you were the sort of person to be in this quandary with me, I really do. I hate being in this alone."

"Perhaps I am bad enough to keep you company in a quandary," his voice settled her inside, like a cozy quilt over her heart.

"You're not bad, Geoffrey. Don't let anyone tell you that you are."

"Well, I'm a little bad." His neck bent, and that always-upthrust chin lowered into her hair. "Because I want to be here with you too, Zelda."

Zelda couldn't smother her sigh of contentment, burrowing into his arms. His coat smelled of him, and snow, and grass, all at the same time; of early spring, but better. "I wish this were all I wanted. I wish I was as serenely confident as that mother hare, with her babies snuggled up under her and never wishing for anything more."

"Hares don't need much," Geoffrey agreed. "They don't go far from where they're born."

The warmth of his cheek against her head made Zelda feel surrounded in a most wonderful way.

"Hares don't have maps," she said against Geoffrey's rough jacket. "I suppose the mother and father hare dance attendance on their… bunny lambs and they all never leave one another."

"Bunny… lambs?" Geoffrey sounded wondering, and Zelda knew he was laughing, even if it was only on the inside.

"Lamb-bunnies? You know what I mean."

"The father hares do almost nothing," he said, suddenly sobering. "Even the mother hares do little. They leave their young alone almost all the time."

"That sounds lonely." The bunny-lambs would grow up alone.

And Geoffrey would never do that to a bunny-lamb of his, Zelda was sure of that. Just as she was sure that he wanted bunny-lambs of his own. Ones with his name, whatever last name he had. Ones he could teach how to mend sheep and birds and little children who fell under the ice and lonely young women who sorely needed a hug.

"You might not have untoward aims," Zelda murmured into his jacket, "but you are extremely good at this."

CHAPTER 21

*H*is answer was to tighten his arms around her. Which was deliciously warm and reassuring.

The sound of his heartbeat, gentle under her ear, could have lulled Zelda back to sleep standing right there in the snow.

"Zelda," he said in a whisper like winter trees, "I'm sorry for the liberties I took the other night. There was no excuse. No apologies can convey my regret. It must have been a great shock. It ought not to have—*I* ought not to have come upon you like that, so suspicious and so wrong."

"It was a shock, but not an unsurvivable one. I forgave you long since, you know."

"But you still don't trust me." Rooted to the ground as he was, Zelda thought that he could be moved at this moment by the slightest touch of her little finger. He was waiting, listening to her. For her.

What a feeling of power.

"Trust is a complicated thing." She only wished he would not move. "You don't entirely trust me, either, do you?"

"Of course I do."

"Do you?" She'd just explained why he shouldn't. He could see a great deal, but he wasn't terribly good at listening. "Do you know something very peculiar?"

"No," and she thought she felt him smile, "but I suspect you do."

"These last few days since I met you have been the first time I've wondered if the world could just stop."

That surprised him. She felt the solid, warm muscles roped around his arms flex and pull her closer, tighter.

Zelda added, "If I put out my finger while a globe is spinning, I can make it just stop. I never realized what a phenomenal power that was. Imagine if I could make the whole world stop just at the perfect moment, and time would never bother us again."

Had she imagined his arms holding her more tightly when she had said *us*?

"There must have been many who have wanted a power like that," and now his voice was warm summer against her skin, even in the depths of an unseasonably wintry night.

"It's not the only power I want. Sometimes when we are close like this, I feel that if I simply held on, if I didn't let you go, you would be mine, all mine, and I would have you, have you to myself, just as if I had picked you up and stuffed you in my pocket. Like the compass. Like a jewel I found on the ground that had been forgotten, but was easily mine once I picked it up."

"Really?" Had his voice grown a little hoarse? "Because I remember every time we are close like this that you are a jewel who has been claimed, and that trying to pick you up and put you in my pocket would be nothing but wrong."

"It could be a little right."

"How? When you are betrothed, and I am a shepherd with barely a few coins to my name?"

Hadn't she cried out that she couldn't marry him, the

night she'd thought he'd compromised her? Well, he *had*. But it was all so much more complicated than that. And she *couldn't* marry him, for so many reasons she couldn't remember at all.

"It's just right because it is," Zelda said simply, burrowing even more tightly against him. He was strong and hard, and it thrilled her that he bent slightly just to encompass her.

A heady power indeed.

"Zelda. Taking what isn't yours is never right."

"Yes, it is. If it asks to be taken."

She felt, heard his heartbeat race faster. "You don't even know what that means."

That made her angry. "I do. I saw the horses. I know what it means."

"Not in the slightest."

"Then explain it to me."

"Never."

The word had an awful finality. Zelda wanted to kick him. And she wanted to put him in her pocket, too. She wanted him to tell her whatever he held back, and she wanted to tell him things, too. She wanted all the awful parts of the world to melt away and leave them alone with sleeping hares in the snow, with the promise of exciting rolling machines, and a flying carpet that would take them all around the world and then bring them back again so she could help him collect his own first cow, and they could share this hug, forever this.

"Doesn't it mean something, that we fit together this way?"

He pulled slightly away. Confusion drew his brows together, bunching up his great bushy eyebrows. "It means I'm unlucky. But I already knew that."

* * *

It was heavenly, holding her in his arms like this, and yet it was a heaven that cut. Because even if she gave up her plan to marry his brother, she had not given up her plan of sailing on.

Britain, and the Faircombe estate, were simply way-stops in a life of grand scope. It wasn't just in the things she said; it was in the way her eyes were always watching the horizon.

He'd got her to look down around her feet, and the immediate simplicity of the life around her astonished her.

But that would never be enough for Zelda.

So he had no luck at all.

His answer upset her. He'd never seen her frown before. "Geoffrey, it is only bad luck that you were born as you were."

Tall? Wide? Worrisome as a mother hen? How did she think he'd been born?

It was the first time Geoffrey had looked at himself the way others must see him. Delina's mirror hadn't done it; but in Zelda's eyes, he could see himself the way he must seem to the world.

He had always been able to see complications in others, but he himself was very simple.

He loved Faircombe, and his family. He loved the village, and the ponds in the trees where he'd played as a little boy. He loved the wild animals and the tame ones, and everything that roamed or swam or flew across this estate.

He hadn't been avoiding children all this time, he realized; he desperately wanted those children. With someone who would share them and see them grow.

He had dreams too. And they could not be more different from Zelda's.

"There's a grand world in your eyes, Miss Zelda Rawle. So much grander than anything I can imagine." He closed his eyes and swallowed and said what he did not want to admit. "Far grander than one simple man could ever make."

"You're not less than anyone else, Geoffrey."

Nothing was as warming as her conviction when she said that. "No, I'm considerably more," he tried to joke, but failed to be funny.

And suddenly the cap loosened, rattled, on everything bottled up inside him, the rage and the fear from his mother's death. His father's indifference, his fractured family, even piglets that had almost died. Why was all this on his shoulders? Just because they were broad?

Nobody had ever asked what he was doing till the last few days. Why hadn't he asked himself, and found his path? Why was he still *here*?

It was his own fault that now he knew what he was doing, what he wanted, and it wasn't anything he could have.

He stood there, searching for the right words to explain to Zelda why he couldn't have this, why they couldn't do this, when Dandy came puffing up to them through the snow.

"Sorry," said the old man as they parted, not because she pulled away, but because Geoffrey did. "Guinevere's 'avin those lambs."

Not now. Not tonight. This wasn't the night to lose one more thing.

"Geoffrey, what is it?"

She must have seen it in his face; Geoffrey wiped his expression. "Just a ewe. We've been waiting for her to lamb for a while."

"Just a ewe!" Dandy gaped at him. "You've damn near hand-fed that ewe through ten lambings! Begging yer pardon, mum."

"My pardon is yours," Zelda made it sound expansive, to cover anything. "Is she ill? You need Geoffrey to come?"

"He's been hangin' round that ewe for the last two weeks,

so worried 'bout her he practically rocks her to sleep at night. I knew he'd want to know."

"Geoffrey! We must go."

"*You* aren't going anywhere, except back into bed. Is there a fire still in your chambers?" If he couldn't go into the house, he could steal through the kitchen and find someone to build it up.

"No, I'm going with you." Zelda settled herself in his coat, still partly crusted with snow, her loose stockings and walking dress and quilted wrap underneath. "We're coming right now," she told Dandy. "Excuse me. We haven't met."

"You're not coming."

Zelda reached out to prod Dandy's elbow with one mitten. "You should introduce yourself when a lady is present."

Dandy, eyes wide as plates, blinked, and blinked again. "I'm very sorry, miss. Never did that before. I'm Andrew Coggins."

"You are?" Geoffrey had never heard his whole name. "I thought it was Dandy."

Zelda half-curtseyed, not letting her stockings dip into the snow. "Geoffrey. Introduce me."

Geoffrey rolled his eyes. Zelda Rawle never stopped surprising. "Dandy, this is Miss Griselda Rawle. Just stay here a minute; I'm putting her back in her room."

"Geoffrey." She stepped away, her hand dropping from his arm. "I will not be *put* into my room."

That twisted his gut and his exasperation at the same time. What an exciting ball of trouble she could be. "Miss Rawle, I think we're done talking. You should be abed, and I must see to this ewe."

"Geoffrey," she said in exactly the same haughty way, making Geoffrey realize how he sounded, "I will accompany you to this ewe. And *Dandy* may refer to me as Zelda."

When neither man moved, Zelda simply started following Dandy's footsteps in the snow.

"Son," said Dandy, watching her retreating back wrapped in Geoffrey's sheepskin coat, "you've got a problem."

"We're in it together now." He ought to blame Guinevere for the timing, but he blamed Dandy. "Don't even try to run away."

* * *

"I wouldn'ta come found you if it were going well."

The lambing pen had a roof, and clean hay on its floor, but it was still cold. Geoffrey was fairly burning inside with desperation to get Zelda back where it was warm. That fear, the deep fear he'd felt carrying her back into his mother's room, was lurking there, ready to let go; and he'd endured enough emotional turmoil for one night.

Now they were too far from Faircombe Hall for Zelda to walk back alone. And though Guinevere knew what she was doing, it was clear that Dandy was right. Something was wrong.

"Zelda, I am *begging* you. Please let Dandy see you back to your rooms."

"You're truly worried, I can tell."

"Yes. About you."

"No. About her." Bending down, Zelda patted Guinevere's head. It was a sign the ewe was already tired that she barely shifted an ear in acknowledgement.

"How long has she been pushing? Get Miss Rawle a bucket to sit on."

Dandy did just that, turning the thing over and brushing off the straw; it made a low perch but Zelda took it without question.

"Almost an hour, and nothin'. Honest, I wouldnt'a bothered you else."

"I know. It's fine." Poor Guinevere here pushing all this time, and no lambs? Geoffrey felt a little guilty.

Then he put that aside. There were dozens if not hundreds of animals all around Faircombe, and he couldn't be there for every one. He did the best he could.

But he *had* been waiting for this birth, and he was worried.

"What are you thinking, Geoffrey?" Nestled in his great coat, arms clasped around her middle, Zelda seemed warm enough; but she clearly wanted to know what was going on.

He sighed.

If it had been improper to mention to Delina Farsworth that Guinevere carried three lambs, he was about to go much farther with the last woman in the world he should.

She was here now; there was nothing he could do about that, and if he were honest with himself, it just made him feel better. Whether Guinevere or her lambs survived or not, he wouldn't be going through this alone.

"She's got three lambs in her. They're all ready to be born and jockeying for position. Someone's packed up against someone else and they aren't making it out."

Zelda's dark eyes were so wide open they looked round and luminous in the lantern-light. "Oh *my*."

She doubtless had many, many questions, but the one she asked proved that Miss Rawle was no fool.

"What can you do for her?"

"Little." Damn it all to hell, Bernie was supposed to be back by now. Geoffrey mourned for him, because the fact that he was still gone didn't speak well for the state of his mother. Geoffrey hoped she'd survived. But they kept the boy on partly because his little hand served them well in the lambing season. "Sheep can be a bit delicate, and my hands are too big to help her much. Dandy's the same. We have a lad who helps with lambing, but he's away."

Zelda, still wide-eyed, stared first at Geoffrey's massive hands, then Dandy's wide gnarled ones, then back at Geoffrey's.

She clearly put together the reason that very large or rough hands simply wouldn't do. "She's not that small," she said with her usual lack of preciousness, as Guinevere was lying there quite obviously just as she was and ready to deliver, as open as a sheep ready to deliver got, "so I assume the problem is… within?"

"Bloody h—" Dandy suddenly seemed struck by the peculiarities of this situation, but Geoffrey just quieted him with a look.

"Yes," he told Zelda, trying to stay calm. He'd had to slaughter ewes that couldn't deliver their lambs, and it was horrible. He wasn't ready for that tonight.

But then, that was the life of livestock. It wasn't when you were ready; it was when they were ready.

"But then what can be done? What skill does it require?"

Perched on her bucket, Zelda was looking up at him as if he knew everything there was to know in the universe. It wasn't true, but it steadied him.

"Bernie would sort out what part comes out with what. The lambs are like this—" He remembered it from when he was littler, helping Dandy with the sheep even then. Geoffrey flattened both hands and laid one beside the other. "They're supposed to come out with two front hooves and a nose. Picture your little black-spotted friend and another just like him. If their legs get tangled—"

"Yes, I quite see." And he could tell she did. Her dark eyes darted all around, seeing everything, as she always did, and putting it together into a whole new picture.

"Well," she said, standing, "I suppose I should get to it."

"What? What're you doing?" Dandy, clearly rattled by his first late evening with Miss Rawle—Geoffrey felt some sympathy—spread both his hands out the way he did herding sheep. Presumably to catch her if she tried to dart past him.

"I'm the one here with small hands. I must try, mustn't I?"

"Zelda. I don't think you should. You'll have to lie on the ground. And we ought to get you somewhere warm."

"I'm quite well." Her nod was serious, perhaps the first time he had seen her do any such thing. "I'm recovered for now, and rested. And while I'm not warm, the quicker we do this, the quicker I will be."

"You're not tired out from the walk?" She was tougher than people knew, Geoffrey knew that. And not easily frightened. But she was talking about putting her *hand* in a *sheep.*

Zelda looked back over the snow, where their footprints led up to the far side of the house with its tumble of new pink blocks of stone. "You know, I'm not?" And her smile wasn't secretive at all; it was openly pleased.

Still, he felt she shouldn't try this. He knew how badly this could go for Guinevere; but how badly could it go for Zelda? "Zelda, you don't have to do this. It will take some strength to move the lambs, and you've been exercising your legs, not your arms."

"Well. Time for your racehorse to work some new limbs." Zelda stood and stripped off his coat. "Should I lie on this?"

His fear for her crawled along his skin. He'd lie beside her to keep her warm, and Dandy be damned. "Yes."

"I've some sacking, hold on…" Realizing they really were going to do this, Dandy shook himself into motion, bringing some sackcloth, a bucket with water in it, and a wooden bowl, then going to sit at the ewe's head just as he would if Bernie were here.

Just as she had in the snow, Zelda went ahead and lay down, but this time staring into a sheep.

"This is extremely odd," she said, turning her head as Geoffrey lay down next to her, tucking her against his side to keep her warm.

But there was a sparkle in her eyes that told Geoffrey she wasn't alarmed; she was excited.

"You really do like *anything* new, don't you?" he murmured into her upper arm, kissing her there before he realized he was doing it.

"I've never done this," said Zelda, closing her eyes and summoning her courage.

"All right, stop. Take a breath."

Her breath *whooshed* out; she'd been holding it.

"Now just imagine those lambs. You'll have heads. Chins, jaws, forelegs." He scooped some goose grease from the bowl into his own hand, rubbed hers. "Hopefully, none of the lambs will be turned fully around, but they might. Be careful of the mouths; they might bite."

"Bite me when I'm helping them be born? How rude!"

Geoffrey had to agree with her there. "Very." He wiped his hands on the sackcloth and settled back beside her. "Feel gently along; you don't want to poke one in the eye, either. And it might be the lamb's rear end! Can you feel the lamb and picture what part it must be?"

"Oh yes." She sounded utterly confident. "I'm very good with peculiar shapes. You should see me with maps."

Well, that would have to do. "All right. Guinevere won't kick, I won't let her. Be gentle. Don't yank. There is no need to rush."

There was, but it wouldn't do to let Zelda feel that. Geoffrey desperately wanted this ewe, who had worked so hard for him, to live through this. He wanted her lambs, too.

But he wanted Zelda unhurt far, far more.

Her nerves were steady. Closing her eyes, she felt her way along into the ewe slowly, but without the squeamish fits and starts of many a new shepherd. Geoffrey saw her pat Guinevere's haunch. Zelda clearly had empathy for the sheep, and didn't want to draw this out.

Her dark eyes closed and she lay for a moment, hand extended. Geoffrey tried to hold on to his panic. "Are you well?"

"Quite. Give me a moment. There are so many different parts!"

Christ. She was just doing what he said and tracing the lamb parts together. Geoffrey tried to stuff his heart back into his chest.

He never feared for himself, for what could hurt someone so large?

But this woman, she could be hurt by any number of things. And that terrified him.

As gamely as she started, she did tire fast. Geoffrey saw her head droop, saw her wince when the sheep strained; no doubt squeezing her hand against some uncomfortably bony lamb part. "Still well enough?"

"Yes," panted Zelda. "I thought you said there was no rush."

No, except that I might die, thought Geoffrey, blood thundering in his ears.

"I think I can feel a little face," said Zelda, "but the nose is stuck. Is that possible?"

Swear words piled atop each other, dying to come out. "Yes. We would normally want to put a little rope around its jaw, behind its teeth, and help guide the jaw around. Do you think you can do that?"

"How can you do that when I'm already in this ewe?" Tired, she blinked slowly.

She was so brave, and so strong. It had nothing to do with the strength of her muscles and everything to do with her heart. His was falling apart, and might never go back together.

"You would need to take your hand out and take a little rope in. Do you think you can do that, dearest?"

At that, Zelda's eyes popped open, and she looked aghast at him.

Geoffrey just held her close. "Do you?"

"Yes." She was tired, but she hadn't given up. "I can do it."

When he gave her the little loop, he cautioned her again about sharp lamb teeth, and Zelda nodded, grave, all her attention on the task at hand.

* * *

THIS WAS beyond a peculiar thing to do.

Being called *dearest* was even more peculiar than trying to deliver lambs. So peculiar that it was easier to focus on the sheep.

Zelda's mind was just spinning with all the possibilities she had never even considered. Every one of those countries on the maps must have its own sort of animals; she'd never seen a hare in Manhattan. For that matter, she'd never seen a sheep up close.

And *babies*. Babies had seemed to be magical things, or curses, for the young lady caught unawares by a bad man. Now she was quite knowledgeable about them and where they came from and how they were made.

There ought to be books on all this for unmarried women.

But she had to concentrate. She barely knew Guinevere, and this was a very personal thing to do, and she felt awkward about it. Perhaps not as awkward as she would have without her experience of Geoffrey's attentions, but awkward. Still, Guinevere was still pushing, and if Zelda didn't get on with it, she could get squeezed in some very painful ways. There was no time to be timid.

And the little lambs wouldn't last forever, either. There were all sorts of nameless, horrible fluids in there, but lambs needed air, Zelda knew that.

She simply had to get that noose around those teeth. She simply had to.

Holding the loop in her fingers hurt. Gripping it so that she didn't lose it as she moved it gently to where the lambs waited? That hurt till it burned.

She tried to loosen her grip for a moment, but just a tiny bit; she wouldn't risk letting go altogether.

This took strength, but delicacy too. She was proud that Geoffrey trusted her enough to let her try, but worried that it wouldn't work. Not terrified; she knew better than anyone that one couldn't force life or health. If Guinevere or her lambs died, Zelda knew that it wouldn't be her fault.

But she wanted to save them, for Geoffrey. For big sweet gentle Geoffrey. No one ever seemed to do anything for him, and he did things for everybody.

And perhaps it would somehow earn her one more magical night in his arms. She couldn't wish for a day.

She was stronger than she thought she would be, but the pain meant she had to stop more than she wanted. This couldn't take forever. There was only so much time. Time was in such short supply, as she'd just told Geoffrey.

Somewhere in her, she felt everything come together: awareness of the muscles of her legs, her stomach, her back, along her arms where they were already weakening, in her fingers. There were spots of pain everywhere, but she was all part of one whole, the way she'd felt whole in Geoffrey's arms just a little while before.

And he lay right there, keeping her warm, not pushing or pulling her, just trusting her to do what she could.

She could find it in herself to push that rope just a little bit farther, because he believed in her, and she was starting to believe, too.

* * *

When she managed to get the loop just where he told her, she whooped.

"All right, all right," said Dandy, knowing just what to do. He pulled the rope gently while Geoffrey talked Zelda through moving the jaw around.

"The nose is stuck under the bone. Is it a bone? It's as hard as a bone." Zelda was red with effort now, and Geoffrey could see her wilting. She'd winced as the effort to be strong and slow with her hand had hurt her, he suspected hurt her terribly; she'd even cried out once, but she hadn't stopped.

She picked paths and walked them without hesitation. He admired that.

"It is a bone, dearest. Try to push the head away from you; I know it makes no sense, but Dandy will pull and if you push, you may get the head where it is supposed to be. Can you imagine how it goes?"

"Yes," and she set her teeth, forgetting to breathe again, but Geoffrey didn't disturb her. He would breathe for her if he must, but wasn't about to stand in her way.

And in the way of it, the slow gentle push and pull moved the baby lamb where it should be; and Guinevere, tired and drooping, must have felt the hope, because with a push she helped the baby along the way, and then there was a new lamb.

"Zelda delivers lamb," murmured Zelda, staring down at the wet, wriggling, disgusting mess. "It's beautiful."

Geoffrey knew what she meant. It was the way he always felt, too.

Guinevere took over. The second and third lambs had no trouble; they were smaller than the first.

"Smaller and better organized," said Zelda, still breathing hard. She wiggled up till she was kneeling on the coat, hair swinging forward with straw in it; Cleopatra delivering lambs.

"Are you all right?" Geoffrey could see a long, angry red scratch on her arm, where the hoof of one of the little lambs had raked against her in its eagerness to be born. She didn't answer, absorbed in the miracle before her. Geoffrey gently raised her bare arm over fresh straw so he could clean it.

There in the hollows of her elbow he saw the white nicks of scars, and he had to stop.

This beautiful, brave woman. This goddess. Who would have dared to do such things to her?

He had never known before where to keep the anger he was afraid to let loose. Now he knew where he would keep it. It was deep, deep down where the doctors who had done this better hope he never met them on this earth.

"I'm quite tired," she said, as if pointing out a pleasant passage in one of Charlotte's pianoforte pieces.

Geoffrey made a noise of agreement. "You have every right. Guinevere is tired too."

The ewe was an experienced mother; she was cleaning her lambs, nosing at all three of them, trying to get them sorted the way she wanted. Dandy was experienced too, and had helped by wiping their noses clear so they could breathe.

"You are amazing," he whispered in her ear. It wasn't half of everything he wanted to say, but he didn't have the words.

"You are that, miss." Dandy had his hat off to Zelda, his scraggly white cheeks pink. "I never saw a lady do anything like, and as I'm standing here, I'll be slapped if I ever see anything like it again. You're a treasure, miss, a genuine treasure."

"Why thank you, Dandy!" There was nothing sly about Zelda's wide smile. "I've never had such a nice compliment. I'll remember it."

"You do that."

Dandy was so dazzled that Geoffrey half expected him to challenge Geoffrey for the right to take charge of Zelda from here. But he didn't say a word as Geoffrey carried Zelda off into his borrowed room. What else was there to say?

* * *

As it turned out, Zelda had much more to say.

"Dandy pulled out some of Guinevere's milk, just like a cow," she went on as their shoes crunched on snow. "Must you do that every time?"

He steered her gently by the elbow. "It's just in case the lambs are tired."

She paused as she approached his shed door; he thought she might be repulsed by the little building built into the hill.

But it was only Nemesis pacing back and forth in front of her feet.

The goose raised both wings with a warning gray-striped flap, and honked.

"Nemesis!"

"He doesn't want me to go in." Zelda spoke goose.

"He doesn't get a choice."

Gently but firmly, Geoffrey scooped the goose out of the way with one foot while opening his door.

Dandy had done something when he'd gone for the warm water. Or someone had done something. There was a huge half-barrel tub by a cheerfully crackling fire in the shed Geoffrey had borrowed. And next to it, a stack of pristine white linens.

Bless Dandy's grizzled heart.

And someone had gone to the house. There was a cake of the fine milled soap the Eliot family used for bathing, and a folded stack of ladies' linens beside. They looked suspiciously like Zelda's size.

The men might have fetched a bathing tub and hot water, but some woman had brought the rest.

Well, servants knew everything. Geoffrey had known that his entire life; he'd just never had anything to hide before.

Oddly, it made this easier. "You're going to have to bathe."

"Yes, all right," but Zelda sounded distracted. Still thinking of lambs. "And the mother licks them clean?"

"Yes." Fortunately, Geoffrey had seen such ladies' gowns before and puzzled out the buttons and ties. "Zelda."

"Yes, Geoffrey." Her mind was still wherever it had gone. "Very nice of you to take off that dress. Will we have to burn it?"

"Let the laundress try washing it first. Zelda, may I take off the rest?"

"Oh yes, it's fine." Her careless wave of a hand was one she would have given a footman rolling her chair.

"Zelda." Geoffrey felt he had to get her attention, somehow. Lambs *were* absorbing, but he didn't want this to be another shock. And it had to happen; there was no question of taking her back to the great house in this state. "I have to bathe you. You do understand, don't you?"

"Yes, I—" He saw it hit her. "Oh. You don't want to startle me. Again."

This was the time to make a joke about seducing her with livestock.

Geoffrey simply couldn't do it.

"I'm only going to bathe you and get you in bed."

"What bed?"

Geoffrey jerked his chin toward the massive bedstead.

Zelda was fully present now. She looked at the bed for what felt like a long time.

"Time doesn't stop, does it, Geoffrey? If we hadn't delivered those lambs, Guinevere would have died."

He had done *nothing*. "Yes."

"It's funny, how clear things feel now. I've always thought of tomorrow as a grand adventure. But nothing guarantees tomorrow will come, does it?"

Delivering lambs had made Miss Rawle feel her mortality? That was an odd way to react. "You're quite safe. Let's get you bathed and in bed."

"I've already told you, Geoffrey." She looked up at him with those big dark eyes. "I'm not a good person. I all but asked you to take me. You said you wouldn't. But time isn't infinite, here we are, and I'm cold. Please take me to bed."

CHAPTER 22

*I*n a crisis, Geoffrey always did what he could.

He could see now that it was an approach that lacked foresight.

But his approach had saved lives wherever he could. As in the Greek tragedies he'd read at school, his nature led him along an inescapable path, just as Zelda's nature led her along her own path; and there was no avoiding their fates.

The truth was that he would give her anything he had. And all he had was himself.

"You must bathe." Even as his mind was turning over all the possibilities, he slid off her chemise, and then knelt before her to slip off one loose stocking and then the other. The silky surfaces and hidden places of her body filled his vision; he forced himself to stand and help her into the tub.

The *ah* she made as she sank into the warm water almost undid him.

He had no comb; he ran his fingers over and over again through the silky strands of her long dark hair, removing the straw and chaff. When his hands moved up and massaged her scalp, she made a little moan.

He was no saint.

"I want to adore you that way, Zelda," Geoffrey admitted, stroking her hair.

Startled, she turned. The water sloshed.

"Shh, shh." Slowly, her eyes staying on him till the last possible moment, Zelda did as instructed, reclining back into the warm water.

Her hair, her head, her whole body was in his hands now. To be careful of her, he understood now, was only to be careful of himself; because she had his heart.

"Do you know when you last had your courses?" The practiced sentence sounded foolish to his ear now. This was not a woman like the others; and he would *adore* a family with her.

If only he could feed them on the feelings in his heart.

"No," she jerked a little, but stayed still. "And what does it matter?"

The last piece he hadn't explained. "The act does not always result in a child," he said, taking up the thick bar of soap and lathering it in his hands.

She surged forward again to turn and meet his eye, making a little wave slop over the edge of the tub. "It *doesn't?* So we could do *that?*"

How had he not known before what an aphrodisiac enthusiasm was?

He felt himself smiling even as his heart pounded in his chest, his trousers grew tight, and his hands slid her back under the water. He stroked the lather over the scars on the inside of her arms, between each of her fingers, then folded the hands over her breasts where they peeked out of the water.

"What did you think we would do in the bed?"

"I thought you would do what you did before."

"We can do that." Could she *hear* the pounding of his heart?

"No, no! If there's a chance of the other, I want that. I want everything."

Christ. "Zelda, I know you like to take risks—"

"I *don't.* I like to *live.*" She didn't turn around again, but her hands waved in the air as she spoke. He let himself smooth his lathered hands down her back. "I stayed in the same room for years and stared at the same pattern of knots in the ceiling. I can still see it when I close my eyes. And I knew there was a whole world waiting for me if only I could get *out.* All I had to do was turn down every offer of marriage in New York. And I *did.* I climbed a slippery wooden plank onto a ship that smelled of dead sea things in the middle of the night and crossed an ocean with no one to talk to but my mother and Tansy. All the sailors were Italian, you know, and only the captain spoke any English."

His hands stopped.

Zelda didn't look weak as she put a hand on either side of the tub and heaved herself up, turned and faced him. Water sluiced off every curve of her body.

"I don't know what I'm going to do next, because there is something going on in that house I don't understand. Tansy found a legal dictionary, you know, and *indemnification* wasn't even in it."

This was the most peculiar seduction he'd ever been part of.

But Zelda wasn't finished. "But I am not giving up. My body belongs to me. My *life* belongs to me. I don't know how I will keep going, but I *will.* All I *do* know is that I want this. I want you. I don't like *risks,* Geoffrey, I like *my life.* And you make me feel alive the way nothing else does."

He surged to his feet. Wrapped her in a drying linen even as he clutched her to his chest. "So do you."

She didn't know everything he meant with those words, but it was everything.

"Well then." She wiggled in his arms, and he realized her feet weren't touching the floor. "We've already had the livestock part of the seduction, so…"

It was both easy and the hardest thing he'd ever done to lift her from the water, arms sweeping under her, and lay her in his bed.

He dried her feet before tucking them under the quilts.

She looked around as if she didn't care for her situation. "By myself?"

The thought of her lying in his bed pleasuring herself made his body jerk to attention. Well, she'd see what effect her seduction technique had on *him*.

"I thought you liked to see new things."

He tossed his coat to the floor, his sheepskin vest atop it, then pulled the shirt from where it was tucked into his trousers. Her eyes were wide and she watched every little movement he made. If he hadn't already been hard, that would have done it.

He couldn't help but grin as he tossed aside his shirt. He knew how it made his muscles bulge to pull it over his head like that. Zelda's jaw dropped open.

He'd had women look at him speculatively, hungrily. Zelda looked at him like a new continent, or a baby hare. He had a feeling he was about to be discovered.

He also realized that he liked it.

"I am torn," she said, snuggled down in the quilts, "by two thoughts at the same time: that Miss Farsworth should draw you like this, and that I don't want her to see it."

Something tugged in his chest at the idea that Zelda was *jealous* of him. He'd been wanted, but not to *keep*.

Someday she'd stop feeling that way—in Italy, maybe, or on a Pacific island, or sailing up the Amazon River. She'd be far away, somehow, because that was Zelda; and he'd be here, because that was him.

For now, he'd revel in it.

When he slid off his trousers, with his smallclothes, he kept turned away. When he looked back over his shoulder, there was Zelda, reaching out with one of her hands. It looked bare without the big diamond ring on it; very bare, and reaching for him.

"Aren't you going to turn so I can see?"

"You've seen," he teased, but he did as she asked.

And the sight of him made her fall back against the mattress, eyes full of things he couldn't name except for astonishment.

* * *

"Is there a word more than *amaze*?"

Geoffrey was carved of muscle everywhere. *Everywhere*. It was as if an old gnarled oak tree had learned to walk and talk, but he was young, and bursting with life.

No wonder he could save children from drowning in ice and discover baby hares in the snow. His skin practically *glowed* with heat, flushed nearly all over, and the darkest red where he was hardest and pointing proudly straight at *her*.

She hadn't expected the white-gold curls on his broad chest, and she hadn't expected them to narrow and thin down the hard surfaces of his belly till they burst out again as a nest of spun gold for *that*.

Perhaps she ought to feel shy of it, but she didn't. She *had* seen it before, but not from this angle. And not with this type of anticipation.

The suspense was *delicious*.

Bending, he took up the same bar of soap he'd used to wash her with, and rubbed it all over himself. All. The lather it made in his curls, wherever there were curls, was like a veil of clouds over a far horizon; it only made her want to go there more.

When he rinsed himself, standing in the tub, and the water sluiced him clean, he looked completely bare and utterly at ease with himself at the same time. The king of every animal that walked or crawled, for was he not a magnificent beast himself?

He stood, showing off *for her*. The droplets of water chasing each other down his skin might grow cold, but he would stand like that forever if she wanted it of him.

Her shepherd, her giant. A god in disguise.

Hers.

"Please, come here?" She stretched out a hand toward him. All of him. She wanted it all.

"Yes, ma'am," he said in that voice like warm honey, and after quickly drying himself, he finally joined her.

The feeling of his heat enveloping her under the heavy quilts was indescribably luxurious. No velvet did this.

"How does one do this?" she murmured as she rolled against him and felt his heart jump underneath her hand.

"However you like." And he still wasn't shy as he pulled her body against his, and Zelda had wondered if they could possibly fit together more beautifully, and they *could*.

"No, I mean..." Usually he was so good at understanding. "Do I need to hold you up, like that mare? Because I won't be strong enough. But I'm willing to try."

Again, she felt the pound of his heart. Was hers going the same way? It felt like it was, and she felt warm, right down to her toes.

"Zelda dearest, you didn't before, did you? And wasn't that easy?"

It had been wonderfully easy. "It was a bit hard to hold

my legs like that. And if I am to have *all* of you, I don't know if I can stay long whatever way you need."

"What position could we possibly need that I couldn't hold for you?" As if proving his words, he rolled, bringing her up to sprawl across his chest.

She had a vision of him buried between her legs, as he had been on that startling night, but holding her legs up for her, cradling every bit of her in his strength.

It made her blood pool somewhere low down, and grow hotter.

She didn't need him to explain that there were many possible ways to do this. His words implied it, but so did her own mind.

At the same moment, she wanted them all, and saw exactly how little time they had. This night couldn't last forever; morning always came, and after the dreams of majestic discoveries came the moment of waking, and pain.

He couldn't help her out of the trap all those scheming men had laid for her.

But he could show her what she most wanted to know right now.

"So why this position?" she asked with her most curious self, her fingers sprawling through the curls on his chest.

She felt as well as heard the soft growl. "One thing comes to mind..."

She gasped as his enormous hands closed around her, just under her arms, and hauled her up and closer.

And cried out when his mouth closed over the tip of her breast.

Horses didn't do this, Zelda thought a little crazily as the soft, gentle motion caused shockingly large effects. As new things went, it went to the top of the list.

She'd never felt that tiny spot crinkle that way, or grow so hard. His lips, his teeth, his tongue all had different sensations as they stroked her skin and, most astonishingly, teased and even scraped the now-swelling bud and sent the tautness through her skin to spread everywhere inside her.

Just the thought of the pleasure he'd given her with his mouth before tightened everything inside even further, and the sensation went from too much to not enough.

"How long can you do this?"

"As long as you like," he told her, carelessly shifting her weight in his hands so he could reach the other one.

She was going to have to explain before she lost her breath completely.

"That wasn't what I meant—can one die from this?"

His eyes were sleepy, hungry. He looked different. "It's called the little death, *la petite mort*. The peak. You felt it before." His inescapable implication was that she was going to feel it again.

That did not calm things down inside her.

"What if I faint?"

"From this?" He bit her, lightly; she put a hand to her mouth to stifle her cry. He only did it again before he said, "You won't faint. Not from this. But if you do, I'll take care of you."

There were no more seductive words, except possibly *we*. He had carried her to the house when she truly had collapsed. Nothing bad would happen to her here, not with him.

This was dangerous, as he'd said; but he was the one who *told* her that.

"I am trusting you, you know," she said as the pleasure made her shiver, and all that held her up was the strength in his hands.

His eyes came back to hers, and now there was something in them beside the hungry pleasure, something she'd never seen before that made her shiver again. "You can."

"Can I? Because I want... more. The pleasure you gave me before. And you inside me." It was almost impossible, to look into his eyes and say such things, but she did it. "Can you do them both at the same time?"

"Perhaps." And with that, he heaved them again, so that now she was tucked under him. But his massive bulk was balanced on his knees and elbows; with only inches between them, she felt only protected and warm. "Let's find out."

She thought the next feeling would be his thrust, but he only pulled her belly up against him with a hand at the small of her back, nuzzling her throat, the little valley between her breasts, her ear.

Each stroke of his rough cheek only lit more sparks along her skin, only made the pooling fire between her legs hotter.

"Are you going to do it?"

"Don't rush, Zelda. I don't want to startle you again." His hand released her and wandered over her hip to dip between her thighs. She loved it and hated the way it made him lean farther away so he could reach.

Surely the way his fingertips slid inside her, slick and fast, proved that now was the *time* for rushing?

"Geoffrey." She grabbed both his ears and shoved herself upward. "*Go.*"

"I will do whatever you please," he said, utterly serious, and sank inside her.

He was still taking it slow—and now Zelda was glad that he didn't do *everything* she said. She had to stretch to take all of him, and it took a moment.

More than a moment. But eventually, slowly, he was sheathed all the way within, and Zelda gloated over having him so close, all hers, nestled against her body in a way no one else had ever been.

She felt like she'd stolen him after all. She felt like she'd *won*.

He groaned in her ear as he withdrew, slowly again, and she wrapped her arms around his neck. "You're well? It doesn't hurt?"

"It is only difficult not to rush this and collapse over you like that stupid horse you know all too well," he rasped against her neck, and she felt his massive forearms sliding under her, pulling her close as he slid inside again. "I don't wish to hurt *you*."

"I am *very* well indeed. Geoffrey. Faster."

He groaned again before he ever moved, and Zelda didn't know why. But she felt his muscles trembling with effort as he rose above her again and slid inside, then again, and again.

This must indeed be a great deal of work for him, and Zelda was grateful for every herculean effort.

She had never felt closer to anyone. This was awkward and desperately welcome at the same time; wild, and yet closely intimate.

If it only felt that way between two people who were perfectly matched, she must have found her match.

Then his massive body shifted slightly, and, panting a little, Geoffrey asked, "Would it pain you to straighten your knees?"

She had been trying to keep herself as open as possible for him. But yes, that would be lovely. The strain was beginning to hurt her hips; perhaps he knew that.

Or perhaps he knew other things. As his next stroke lit a fire in her that burned so hot it put the previous heat to shame. *This* was the goal. *This* was the conflagration she wanted to burn her down.

Again and again he did it, his heavy breath rasping between them, her gasps becoming cries.

"You must stop, it's too much work," she finally was able to say, even though stopping was the last thing she wanted.

Were those gasps sobs? Laughter? His chest sank against

hers and his hands came up under her shoulders to cradle her head. She was completely caged in his arms, and it felt like soaring in her dreams felt.

"The effort is not to spend until you have had your pleasure," he gritted between his teeth.

"Oh. Could you not simply keep going after you spend?" It seemed logical to her.

"No," he said, and thrust harder.

* * *

Geoffrey had lived his life thinking he knew what *home* meant.

He'd been wrong.

He was a simple fellow and he loved Faircombe and all its animals, his stubborn, foolish family included.

But that wasn't home.

Home was in Zelda's arms.

Her softness, her heat surrounded him. It was her eyes that showed him what he needed to see, and her gasps that told him what he must do.

He must delight her, over and over and over and over...

If he could only do one thing with his body forevermore, it would be this.

He understood now the thrill of the risk, of living life to its farthest edges. This was riskier than anything he'd ever done in his life, but what if he hadn't taken the risk? He could have lived his whole life without ever feeling truly at home.

Selfishly, he wanted her forever here with him, even if it meant sleeping in a borrowed bed. Or no bed at all.

He thought he'd found the right angle when she started to cry out. Her hands clenched on his shoulders; he sat up to make her grip release.

His Zelda mustn't hurt herself in her eagerness for her pleasure.

It was nothing for him to grip her thighs and pull her closer. The sounds she made said that he still pleased her.

"I will hold you, just like this, as long as you like," he managed to say aloud, and something about his words or his body or both must have pleased her, because he felt her find that elusive, rippling, explosive completion. Her head was thrown back, bare throat gasping, but he knew she heard him. She wasn't ignoring *this*.

The incredible grip of her almost pushed him over the edge. But he was greedy. He wanted more. Who knew when this day would ever come again? Or if?

"Shall I stop?" he asked, politely he thought, but Zelda only waved away his words. Or rather he thought that was what she was doing; her mouth was open, but she made no more sounds. But he trusted her to keep breathing, the way she trusted him to keep doing this.

When she exploded again, he felt a deep pull inside from somewhere, he didn't know where, to follow her over the cliff, to empty himself inside her.

But she trusted him.

He pulled himself away from his beautiful goddess, just beginning to sink, pliable and flushed, into the straw tick, recovering from the overwhelming wave of her pleasure; with a quick, desperate motion, he let himself go against her belly instead of deeply inside it as he'd wanted.

He'd stolen nothing. She'd given him everything.

Even if it was nothing he could keep.

Clenching over himself, the last pulses pounding through his hand the way his heartbeat sounded in his ear, he muttered "Zelda" to himself again, because it was all that was in his head.

And when he collapsed next to her, instead of rolling away, she rolled closer.

"You look exhausted," she murmured to him. He just managed to snag one of the drying linens to clean her again.

She looked flushed and rumpled and glorious. He didn't welcome the drowsy wave that threatened to wash away consciousness; he'd rather look at her. "The male animal... sometimes has to fall asleep at times like this." He hoped he'd wake up still wrapped up with her.

"I shouldn't wonder," said the astonishing Miss Rawle, and wrapped herself around him.

He fell asleep in her arms.

CHAPTER 23

*I*t was only a few minutes till Geoffrey roused enough to see that Zelda was comfortable. Which he conveyed, delightfully, by putting his hands nearly everywhere.

"I'm fine," she murmured with a sleepy smile.

It was a peculiarly intimate thing, thought Zelda as she drifted off, sleeping next to another person. Especially one so large and *hot*.

There was only a wool blanket or two over them, but she fell asleep into a summer heat generated solely by the man beside her.

It felt like it had only been minutes, but when she blinked awake, the sun was well up. She could see it around the cracks in the door, and through the lone small pane of glass beside it.

The Faircombe estate was rich indeed, able to buy glass even for a shepherd's hut.

Which this was, she thought, rousing sleepily enough to take in more of the place in the dim light.

Her joints screamed at her as she shifted a little, but no

more than normal. She could hold still for a few moments longer, if it meant Geoffrey would sleep.

Zelda tried to ignore the little various spots of pain, as cataloging them never made anything better. But this morning she had a delightful alternative to distract her: cataloging the various spots of pleasure.

Her breasts were tender till they felt larger than they were, and even crushed against the hardness of his body, they cried *more, more*. It was an understatement to call that new. He had hair on his *legs*, too, which brushed against hers and made the most delicious tickling motions; it was at odds with the solidity of his limbs, which could have been carved of wood had they not been warm, with the softest skin.

He shifted closer to her in his sleep, and Zelda smothered an indrawn breath. That part of him was awake; she almost hoped it would go back to sleep, it was so... *obtrusive*. But then, she'd be happy if it didn't.

There was no part of her that felt that she had done anything wrong. Perhaps she had given up morals altogether; but that hadn't felt like a vice.

It was far more difficult to decide what it *had* felt like, besides *overwhelming*.

Her usual aches and pains were mixed with aches so delicious she wanted them to go on. She was pleasantly sore in places usually not so stretched. And the memory of how the waves of pleasure had washed over her and left her shaken only woke the hot places inside of her again.

In fact, just the idea of staying inside this little shed, with the cooling banked fire and the one tiny smudged window, made the swirling inside of her go faster.

Her eyes popped open. That was thatch above her, straw packed in against itself as if held in a giant's fist.

It wasn't the knotholes of the beams in the ceiling of her

father's house, but it pressed down and down on her till she could not take a deep breath.

Like listening to Lady Charlotte's piano, there was no pleasure so great that it was worth being shut up inside a box.

Suddenly even the weight of Geoffrey's presence beside her was too much, the space she had too little. She scrabbled at the covers, gasping, trying to sit up.

"Whoa, whoa," murmured Geoffrey in his soothing voice, just as if she were a sheep, or a hare in a trap, and Zelda needed to sit up. She needed to be up. And out. Immediately.

Even the slubs of the heavy linen sheets seemed to grab at her as she thrashed free of their wrappings.

"I must wash," she said, panting as if she'd run.

Geoffrey had propped himself up on one elbow to look at her. The little sunlight there was sought out his hair, thick locks of it tousled by sleep, and the curls that spread over his muscled chest. A part of Zelda asked why she was being fool-ish, and prompted her to crawl right back into that bed.

But the rest of her wouldn't allow it. She needed air; she needed to *move*. She already had a betrothed, an appalling potential father-in-law, a faithless father, and a houseful of scheming lawyers and businessmen to worry about. She must be light and fast to reach the Continent and get beyond; she saw that now. She couldn't be weighed down by any attachments to a beautiful, gentle, letter-writing, French-speaking...

"Who sent you that crate?" Ideas were slotting themselves into place inside her head now, thick and fast. They were the first words to tumble out.

"What?" His bushy eyebrows drew together, the ones so like the Marquess'. "What makes *that* the first thing you ask me this morning?"

That machine was valuable. It might not look like a

diamond or a pearl, but Zelda could tell. It was an odd thing to send to a penniless shepherd, even a baseborn son.

But a baseborn son of the manor did not learn French.

Zelda hadn't learned much either before she'd been shut up in her room to be ill. But she learned a little, from a tutor with a genuine French accent of which her mother had been very proud.

And she remembered Geoffrey describing *la petite mort* as if his voice had carved the words in her skin.

That was it. She couldn't stay here another moment, not with one more new problem. She had reached her limit.

She had expected it to be easy to carry out her plan. She knew now how foolish she'd been. And she knew too how strong she was. She could live a big life.

But not in this shed with this... whoever he was.

"I must wash," she said again, her eye falling on the last bucket of clean water next to the sighing, cooling coals in the hearth.

It ought to have felt odd to stand here unclothed as she was in front of his watching eyes, but she was too busy feeling odd about everything else.

There was straw in her hair. How could she get it out? She would never again deliver lambs without a hair-comb.

Geoffrey was no more able to stay in the bed than he would have been to stay away from a lambing sheep. He hovered over everything that needed care, that she knew about him. But it wasn't reassuring. She didn't want to be hovered over because she needed *care*.

"Let me help," he said in that way of his, but this morning, it only wound her agitation tighter. He looked hurt when she managed to toss him a tight smile and an "I'm fine." But she didn't have words to explain. She was cold. She should dress.

Her father had known she wanted out of New York and had laid a trap to keep her at least in Britain. To keep her poor, and to keep her away from her dreams. Why wasn't she allowed to dream?

Why couldn't she have the big brawny shepherd, put him in her pocket, and wander away into the rising sun like the adventurer she wanted to be?

Zelda... does what? Goes where? Accomplishes... was there anything left she *could* accomplish, as tangled as everything was?

A lying shepherd wasn't her biggest problem—well, he was, she acknowledged as she watched him dance around her without touching her and without banging his head—but he was way bigger than a feather, and even a feather could break a camel's back when he was far too heavily loaded.

She had to stop collecting problems and start finding solutions. Fast.

"Zelda. Stop."

"I mustn't." The scrubbing of her hands in the water, against the clean linen, grew frantic. Could she pretend now she was worried for her reputation? "The sun is high. The yard men will see me leave. I don't know how to get back to the house, but I must. Tansy has likely already been to check on me." She shivered into the clean chemise folded on the edge of the tub.

He had shrugged into a billowing shirt and some trousers, looking at her as worriedly as he did at a starving piglet.

"I *am* starving, too," she said before realizing she was letting her thoughts out. It was only true, and another good reason to go back to the house; here among the mud-chinked walls, she could see no food.

"Of course."

He didn't reach out to her, not to fix her hair or anything, which was a blessing, and sorely missed. She *wanted* him to touch her. To touch her everywhere, forever.

But she couldn't have that and stay in this little box and she needed *out, out, out.*

She threw the dress over her head, then realized she had no idea which way was the front. "Can you button those buttons? Thank you. You do have the makings of a clever ladies' maid."

When she heard her own words, Zelda stopped. His eyes had dropped. And he was fastening her gown, just like the servant he wanted her to think he was.

Did he simply do this often?

That last wave of emotion threatened to knock her off her feet. "You cannot accompany me back to the house."

"You cannot walk alone."

"I must."

"The men are about."

"That's why I must."

Before he could stop her, she'd thrown open the shed's little door.

"*Zelda.*"

"Yes?"

She shouldn't have looked back at him. He shone in the morning light like a diamond.

And an avalanche of different emotions crushed his shoulders closer to the ground. She couldn't tell what they were, but they were falling over his face one after the other.

He cleared his throat, but still his voice creaked. "Avoid cake at the breakfast table."

"Cake?" She paused, looking over her shoulder at him. "You think I should prove I can abstain?"

"I have some good advice that it may help. Less wine, and less cake."

She muttered as she turned away, "No wine, no cake—it's a bit late to curb my vices." He must stop looking at her that way. As if he were about to starve to death.

Then she looked back again. He was still there, which made her perversely glad.

She ran back to where he stood and reached up to grab his ears again. And then, just as he had done that other night, she kissed his forehead.

And then, just as he had, she kissed his lips, because the forehead wasn't enough.

"May I still try the rolling machine?"

That obviously disappointed him and started an avalanche of emotions. Shock, surprise, disappointment, hope—

"If you can bring a chaperone. Perhaps to the front lawns, after you dine. Bring two."

"You're still worried for my reputation?"

"More than ever," he said, looming closer, "as I will not let you walk out that door alone."

"I'm not alone, I have..." Whirling, she darted out the door. "Why, Mrs. Truett!"

Zelda didn't play cards, but she could have bet that *those* words would stop Geoffrey where he was. And indeed, he stayed in the shadows of his hut, so she could at least pretend that picking her way over the cattle yard toward Mrs. Truett was exactly what she wanted to do.

When really her heart was bending so far back in Geoffrey's direction that she felt in true danger that it would break.

* * *

Mrs. Truett didn't seem the least surprised to see Zelda in the sheepyard in the early morning, which was the most surprising thing about her, Zelda thought.

Until she spoke.

"Miss Rawle. I'm so delighted to be able to accompany you on this early morning constitutional."

A what now? But the older woman fell into step next to Zelda exactly as if they had walked the length and breadth of the Faircombe acres, and she was just turning with her to go back towards the great stone hulk of the house.

That was the first moment Zelda realized that she was wearing her own linens and gown, and they were clean.

What she'd worn to the lambing must still be in Geoffrey's shed.

But how had the clean clothes, *her* clean clothes, gotten there?

"I'm really very glad for your company," Zelda said with true feeling, her steps falling into rhythm with those of Mrs. Truett.

"I'm glad to hear it," said the housekeeper, her left hand appearing from nowhere to slide a piece of straw out of Zelda's hair and drop it on the ground without mentioning it.

Zelda had not expected this. But she was at her best in the face of the unexpected.

"You must be a woman of great experience, Mrs. Truett, as you have visited London and all." When the housekeeper's sharp profile turned her way, raising an even sharper eyebrow, Zelda added quickly, "Where you saw the gelatine tower."

"You must be a woman of little experience, Miss Rawle. In general." Mrs. Truett kept her eyes on the ground to avoid stepping in anything untoward. When she raised them, it was only to ensure they still walked in the direction of the house.

"I am, that's true." Lying had accomplished little, and for some reason a woman who had made a gelatine tower because of her, and been chastised for it, deserved a little honesty, Zelda felt.

Besides, talking with her kept Zelda from turning around to see if there was a woebegone shepherd staring after her.

"A woman of great experience would know to keep her proclivities secret, whatever they might be, until she had safely married. Then her peculiarities would be taken out only in private and only in front of trusted servants, if anyone at all."

"Unfortunately, my peculiarities are on constant display."

Mrs. Truett's eyes shot her way, then back to her path. "You may have allowed me my first peculiarity, Miss Rawle." When Zelda turned to stare at her, Mrs. Truett added in a stern, arms-length way, "I liked it."

Zelda felt a laugh bubbling inside her at the thought that perhaps all she had accomplished was to get one tightly-wrapped housekeeper to let loose by making a gelatine tower.

But this time, she wasn't helpless to quash the laughter. Mrs. Truett would be so insulted. It was only in Zelda's head that she waved a little flag and thought *Zelda cracks open a cage and lets in some daylight.*

If that were the only accomplishment of her life, she could be proud, she thought.

"It's only Faircombe that is so forbidding to normal human peculiarity, Mrs. Truett."

"That's not so. There's many a house in Britain that frowns on peculiarity. One is supposed to at least keep it *hidden.*"

Zelda didn't know much of the British, but of the little she knew, nothing sounded more British than that.

But she needed more than general insights. "Is that why no one speaks of Lady Faircombe in the house? She had too many peculiarities?"

Mrs. Truett stopped. They had almost reached the new-cut pink stone, Zelda saw. Her steps had eaten up the yards without her noticing. Another triumph.

She'd still rather retrace her steps in the fast-melting snow and see her giant again.

Well, if he kept his promises—and she knew he did—he'd let her ride the rolling machine today.

Mrs. Truett was looking out over the house the way Zelda looked over a map: trying to puzzle out all its detail, even the things she couldn't see.

"Lady Faircombe was gentle, kind, loving, generous, and forgiving to a fault."

"You knew her!"

"Oh yes. I've been here that long. You wouldn't think Lady Faircombe was much of a match for his lordship. But she was, she was." Mrs. Truett had her hands folded tightly together, her brow furrowed with thinking. "She knew when things were wrong, but she just glanced right past them. She made anyone happy if Lord Faircombe made them unhappy. Except herself, I think."

"How did she die?"

"She had a wasting disease, awful to see when she was already so pale, even her hair was—" The housekeeper stopped.

"It was white-gold, wasn't it? Thick waves of white gold." Zelda moved around to see Mrs. Truett's face. "Wasn't it?"

"Yes," the other woman sighed.

"How many sons did she have, Mrs. Truett?"

"She had three, madam."

"*Three!*"

Zelda had been prepared for two, but three was a massive number.

As massive as her giant… "And one of them is Geoffrey, isn't it?" She thought. "It should be *Lord* Geoffrey, should it not? Even if he is the youngest?"

"I can't say a word to his lordship, not a word. And I never do! Do I task him for the way he tracks mud all over the house after hunting, then wants the carpets perfect? No! Do I clean up whatever he spills if he falls drunkenly asleep in his study? I do! With my own two hands." Mrs. Truett seemed obsessed with her hands, and Zelda looked at them too. They were strong, if a bit thin, and less swollen at the joints than Zelda's. Mrs. Truett had done a great deal of work with them on Lord Faircombe's behalf. "But it was just because he was so distraught, he *truly* was, Miss Rawle, when her ladyship died. He was felled like a tree. Lay in his chair for a week drinking himself stupid, with those little boys and Charlotte all tiptoes trying not to make him rage."

Well, *that* didn't paint a picture of a happy household. Zelda's heart ached for the tiny little white-haired boy Geoffrey must have been then. Why hadn't anyone hugged him? Who had cared about *his* distraught?

But Mrs. Truett only shook herself and looked up with a stony set face. "All these years and I never said a cross word to him. I know he took it hard. And the one time, the *one* time I step a little out of the line he set for me, he talks to me the way he did. It's humiliating, you know."

"I can't imagine. Well, I can; my imagination is excellent, but I've never been treated like that. I'm so sorry for that."

"I've known for a long time. I see him encouraging little Grant—Lord Vere to be just like him in all the worst ways. It ought not to be allowed." Her eyes narrowed. "Mind you, I'm not about to let Lord Vere get cuckolded in his own house with his own brother, either."

"Mrs. Truett!"

The housekeeper ignored Zelda's shock, though it was real.

"But I don't think you're going to marry Lord Vere; are you, Miss Rawle?"

The hunting birds at the mews behind her couldn't have more piercing eyes, Zelda thought with an uneasy shifting of her weight from foot to foot. "The simple truth is that I don't know what I'm going to do."

The housekeeper made a tiny dry windy noise that might have been a snort. "You didn't know last night you were going to deliver those lambs before you did it, did you?"

"You knew about that?"

"It's all the men can talk about."

Well, that was simply splendid. Zelda's shoulders slumped. If every man on the place was talking about it…

"Now don't you think for a moment that every servant talking about it means Lord Faircombe will hear. Or Lord Vere, for that matter. Their rules don't allow for any mixing, you know."

"But there are tradesmen, and *lawyers*, staying in the house! Like guests!" Zelda knew Lord Vere didn't think well of them, yet there they were. At every meal.

"And eating us out of house and home!" That didn't answer the question whether they knew about her lambing expertise. "Never you mind. His lordship, Faircombe I mean, sees them in the morning and afternoon and only ever asks if they're done. Otherwise, he leaves them to their own devices. Except if they are willing to go hunting with him."

It was chilling to imagine those men riding over the countryside, killing things together and discussing her fate. "Please, won't you just tell me what it is that has them so tangled up? Why haven't they settled the contracts?"

"I don't know, madam, and that's only the truth." Mrs. Truett looked sufficiently woeful that Zelda believed her. "The maids and I don't really follow what's being talked about most of the time. The only outline I can gather is something to do with shipping, they want to do shipping, and they go quiet when I go in."

"And they put Lord Geoffrey out of the house to do it?!"

"That was all Lord Faircombe. Though I think Lord Vere didn't mind." That had lowered both lords in Mrs. Truett's opinion, obviously, and Zelda thought even better of her for that. "And I'll tell you, I'd finally up and leave if I didn't know Lord Faircombe would give me no character reference now after that whole affair of the gelatine."

"Oh no! Never say so. I would give you a *perfect* reference, Mrs. Truett; you can rely on me."

"Well." Now Mrs. Truett looked like the starched, practical woman she was. "That's going to depend on whether you're the next Lady Vere or the tart tumbling the family cast-off in the sheep sheds, doesn't it?"

"Mrs. *Truett!*" Zelda let the bubbling laughter loose now. "I think you positively enjoy being coarse!"

"Maybe a little," the housekeeper admitted, and the convulsions of her face as she walked again toward the house might have been a smile trying to escape.

As they drew close to the portico, Mrs. Truett added, "I'm going to ask you a serious question, and I expect a serious answer. What *are* you doing?"

And Zelda had no stories to spin for stolid, forthright Mrs. Truett. "I don't know."

"Then you had better do nothing, nothing at all, till you understand what you are doing." Her tone didn't always match her words, but Zelda understood. Mrs. Truett might have run out of patience with Lord Faircombe, but if Zelda *was* a tart tumbling Lord Geoffrey while planning to marry Lord Vere, Mrs. Truett wasn't having it.

"I won't do a thing," Zelda promised, and she meant it. "Well, one *little* thing, but only out in the daylight where everyone can see."

* * *

Her mother never even blinked at the sight of Zelda walking up the courtyard steps in the company of the house-keeper, even in the morning light.

"Out so early? And while the snow is melting, too! Your dress must be dirty. Come, let us put you to rights. I don't want you to exhaust yourself when Lord Vere may return at any time."

She could spend a lifetime sitting inside waiting for Lord Vere, Zelda thought bitterly to herself. Some of which bitterness must have shown on her face, for Mrs. Truett added, "It's laundry day, Miss Rawle, if you have yet more clothes for us to prepare in case his lordship returns."

She was a sly thing, thought Zelda, better suited for a king's court than this cold house of a marquess. She was as good as saying that she would wash the lambing dress and keep Zelda's secrets. Yet she'd conveyed that she didn't expect Zelda to go traipsing back into Geoffrey's arms.

Which was what Zelda wanted to do.

Nonsense, she told herself with an invisible shake. She'd practically just *run* from his arms.

From his warm, caring, *lordly* arms.

She'd left him determined to cut down on her problems, and here were more. Because he was disowned, or something like it, from the family into which she was supposed to marry. And why hadn't he told her?

Though she also felt a bit shamed because she hadn't noticed sooner.

His speech was nothing like that of the other men around the estate; but Zelda must forgive herself for that. They all sounded odd in different ways, to an American.

There was still some part of her that had hoped that Lord Vere would return from London with a lawyer to give her help. That part had been fading with time; and now, after Mrs. Truett's revelations, it was nearly crushed.

Indeed, she'd do well not to kick Lord Vere the moment she saw him. How *dare* he remove Geoffrey from this house?

This house, this *family* he no doubt loved. For here he'd hovered all around it, staying close, when she thought he'd been drawn close because of her.

She was far too confused to face him again, yet she couldn't wait.

CHAPTER 24

Geoffrey couldn't think himself clever any more, watching Zelda walk away across the livestock yard with the housekeeper.

He hadn't felt this alone in…

…in fourteen years.

He'd stopped counting the days. Somewhere in all the uproar of being tossed from the house, and Zelda (actually, the uproar was all Zelda), he'd let go of the grim clock in his head counting up the moments since he'd lost the one person he'd known for certain loved him.

He had been that person for so long. It was a weight he didn't need to keep dragging. He ought to feel new. Young.

Instead, he felt hollow.

Last night Zelda had shown him how to define *strong*, and *home* too, all in the same night. He hadn't missed his own bed, the coffee, or his finer clothes.

And he didn't miss them now, either. He only missed her.

What had he said wrong? What had he *done*? He must have done something wrong to send her spinning out so fast this morning. Had he dreamed of a morning after a night like that, he would have dreamed of soft kisses and long confidences.

She'd run out as if she'd stolen something.

Geoffrey was half-inclined to check and see if she had.

He felt listless, only shoving his feet into boots so he could cross to the lambing pens, shirt flapping in the breeze. As often happened, the snow had warmed the world, and now, like everything that warmed the world, it was melting away.

Guinevere stood in a hay-filled pen, her three little offspring around her. The biggest one was suckling, his tail waving like a pennant in the breeze; the smaller two seemed to be waiting patiently, as was the experienced mother.

It was all not enough for the little lord of the sheep pen, who butted his mother right in the teat.

"Oi," said Geoffrey, gently sliding the lamb's rear-quarters aside, trying to make room for his siblings.

One of them tried to suckle as well; but the biggest lamb was having none of it, head dived in, eyes closed in bliss, and shouldering everyone smaller out of his way.

"I suppose that's what the oldest does," Geoffrey muttered to the little fellow, "but you almost killed the rest with that fat head."

Unheeding, the lamb went right on doing what it was doing.

Well, Geoffrey still thought his father was wrong that the world was a forest full of wolves and men had to make a fist, but nature did often favor the biggest. If only that were always true, Geoffrey would have what he wanted right now.

He'd have Zelda.

"I'm watching you," he said with uncharacteristic cynicism to his voice. "You shut the others out completely and I'll have you on another mother."

Not that it would likely notice. The lamb didn't seem discerning.

He'd gone mad, trying to woo Zelda with hares and lambs.

She didn't want a life in the sheep sheds; she never had. She'd never even hinted she would. She'd wanted big strong Geoffrey, like other women had; and then, once she'd had him, she left him.

He closed his eyes. The damage was done, though, because now whenever he even thought of lying with a woman, it was her soft body under his, her eyes dark with pleasure, her silky hair streaming over his skin that he'd picture.

When he opened his eyes, Bill Pike was standing right in front of him.

"What?" He had used up all his graciousness.

"Nothing. Ya don't look good. You've looked better." The steward looked a bit apologetic. "You need anything?"

Well. They'd used him to catch geese and hold up cows, and perhaps they'd all finally realized he was just as human as they were.

Though luckier, because he *had* slept with a goddess.

Luckier even than the shepherds in the old Greek poems, because there were no more goddesses coming to wreak jealous vengeance after that one. Britain could only hold one goddess like that.

* * *

By the time he'd shuffled back to his shed, Nemesis had come out of nowhere and started following him, and honking.

"I. Am. Not. Interested," said Geoffrey for the half-dozenth time, kicking his boots back off and lying down again in his unmade bed.

It smelled of her.

"I've got a sheep down," said Dandy, following the goose in the open door. Nemesis honked at him, too.

"You can keep your damn goose and your sheep for five minutes, Dandy. I'm in no mood today."

"But—"

"And if you say one word about paying for my bed, I'll—" There wasn't much in reach that was his. He picked up the heavy volume of horse anatomy. "I'll throw this at your head."

"She's *down*, Geoffrey."

"Oh, son of a—" Muttering curses to himself he never said out loud, Geoffrey tucked in his shirt and reached again for his boots. He might be a penniless shepherd, but a shepherd he was. Or something like it.

* * *

ALL THOUGHTS of his own problems fled once he knelt next to the ewe.

She was big, twin lambs, most likely, and it wasn't uncommon for a ewe so big to go down late before birth. The lambs needed so much of whatever she ate, it was as though she couldn't eat enough to satisfy the little bodies inside her.

Geoffrey recognized her; she was a good mother.

Damn.

"It's the twins," Dandy echoed his thoughts. "Too big for her. As cold as this winter has been."

It had been the coldest winter anyone could remember, and it was dragging on. But it had been warm enough yesterday to snow. And before that, the ground had been soggy enough to wet Miss Rawle's skirts when she collapsed.

"But it's not that cold now, Dandy." It helped to talk it over with the old man, more than his personal problems. There wasn't much Dandy hadn't seen happen to sheep.

"It's been long and cold the whole winter."

"We graze them so they always have enough." The paddock fences had indeed been very expensive, just as his father had complained; they meant that the sheep only grazed in one area long enough to crop the grass short and let the rest of the land rest. When the grass had grown long enough, the sheep were moved.

"It's not like the Scots invented sheep, son." Dandy looked a bit sour. He'd never admired the fence method Geoffrey had brought back from his travels in Scotland.

"She hasn't been short of food, Dandy. And not that close to lambing, either." Geoffrey looked around. Half of learning what ailed an animal came from looking closely at it; half from looking closely at where it lived. The grass was struggling, but there was green; and besides, there was hay and grain back in the pen.

Lord Faircombe's sheep herds still ate well, at least.

No, this was something else.

He cast his eye farther afield. There was the mews with the hunting birds, and beyond that, the stables with the horses his father never let him near.

Now why had that thought intruded into his head?

Concentrate. There was something waiting for him to notice it, and it wasn't just that he was the only Faircombe not obsessed with the horse stables. What was it?

He'd avoided looking toward the house, as if Zelda would somehow see and notice. He didn't want her to know how badly he wished she would come back out.

The Portland stone blocks, cut and stacked ready to be

built into the new wing, had been there for more than a year now. The small crew of men his father had hired were painfully building walls with ropes and pulleys and not much else. Geoffrey ought to have done something about them before his father had thrown him out. They were just like him now: outside the house and eating and sleeping wherever they could. In fact, he was better off, as all his meals were provided by the estate.

There was that stupid ewe over there again, with her black-spotted little lamb right beside her. Geoffrey could tell her even at this distance. And she'd led over more sheep.

He'd be chasing sheep away from Zelda's portico at this rate, and she'd accuse him again of trying to seduce her with livestock.

God, if only he could.

Wait. There weren't just two or three sheep, there were a handful—was it four? Five? Grazing around the base of the big pink stone.

"Don't sheep sometimes know what they need, Dandy?"

"Oh aye. They're not dumb."

Well, Geoffrey sometimes thought he could argue with that, but he felt his point was right. Sometimes sheep were struck weak from a shortage of feed, and sudden cold or constant rain didn't help. But this was something else, he was sure of it. Or else why weren't more of his sheep down?

As if hearing his thoughts, Dandy said, "If this is a bad disease, we'll have it through the whole herd next. Ought to slaughter her quiet and out in the woods, away from the herd."

This sheep looked weak. If there was one thing Geoffrey hated, it was butchering a ewe carrying lambs. Dandy would likely do it, with one of the other men. He might escape that chore today.

But if this was a sickness, they'd all be doing it soon, as most of the flock were carrying lambs.

"See if you can get some of the men to help you herd the ewes still carrying lambs over toward those blocks."

"This isn't some trick to get you close to the lady! You ought to leave her well enough alone!"

"What?" His eyes focused back on the grizzled man beside him. "You were her willing subject last night."

"And so I am! She's a fine lady, too fine for Faircombe, there's no doubt in ma head! And what are you doing with her? And *why*? If she marries Lord Vere, she'll never go hungry a day in her life. Do you know what the rest of us would do to say that for a woman we love?"

Geoffrey's hand fell of its own accord on Dandy's shoulder. "I'm sorry for whatever your lady-love went through." He felt Dandy's thin, stringy shoulders slump. "I'm not trying to ruin Miss Rawle's life. I don't know *what* I'm doing. But this *is* about the sheep. See if you can keep them grazing up there for a little bit, can you?"

"The grass ain't long," Dandy grumbled, but he looked that way. "All right. I've seen everything to do with sheep, but you've a knack. I'll see what we can do."

"And I'll take care of this one."

"Never mind it, lad, I know it turns your stomach."

Geoffrey laid his hand on the sheep's bent neck. "Never mind it; she's gone." And her lambs. He sighed. The brightness of the day had already had no effect on him; now the light seemed even dimmer. "Let's get the rest up by those stoneworks. Either it's something they'll all get, and I will have killed them pushing them together, or that wandering ewe will have the last laugh."

* * *

HE DIDN'T NEED to watch the men do the herding; he didn't want to go that close to the house, either. There seemed to be that unspoken current of understanding between him and many of the livestock men now, because no one asked him to go, either.

Kicking off his boots one more time, he fell back on his bed. And bumped his head.

The big heavy volume of horse anatomy was still right there.

Geoffrey's head was too thick for sense to be knocked into it by a mere book. Yet as he sat up and stared at the thing, rubbing the back of his head, he had a glimmer of an idea.

He was a third son and Faircombe was Vere's, not his. Even Charlotte had chosen her own life and would soon be gone. Frederick must have found some way to build a life on his own; he'd never come back.

Geoffrey hadn't followed him to university, because he'd had his fill of Greek poets and French in school.

But what if there were another way to make a life that hadn't occurred to him then, because he hadn't been looking?

He grunted, craning his body upwards again. He wasn't the only Faircombe son to ever have to find his own way. He'd been arrogant, and foolish, not to look for a path more like the village men walked. Why shouldn't he be more like them than the residents of Faircombe? They liked him better.

There was at least one person in the village who could advise him on making his own way in the world.

Plus, he'd been so busy showing Zelda baby hares that he hadn't asked old Mrs. Hull about that burned cottage to the north, either.

* * *

"Tansy, can we find my riding habit? I'm going out later today to ride a rolling machine."

"I beg your pardon, *what?*" called her mother from beside the fire.

"I need my riding habit." Zelda couldn't get through this day or all the ones after it if she constantly had to juggle her mother's peculiarities.

She didn't agree with Mrs. Truett that peculiarities in general ought to stay hidden. She just didn't want to deal with those.

"I thought you said you needed your riding habit for a rolling machine." Mrs. Rawle bustled in.

"So I did. What do you think, Tansy? Riding boots? Or should I wear low shoes?"

"You would know better than I, Miss Rawle," said Tansy, sailing out and staying far away from flustered Mrs. Rawle.

Mrs. Truett's words had made their impression. Hurtling pell-mell from one thing to another had only heaped up Zelda's problems till she'd lost count of them. She needed to slow down and sort herself out.

But she was going to ride that rolling machine.

"What do you mean, it rolls? What sort of machine? Gracious, Zelda, what does it do to you?"

"Mother." Zelda gripped her mother's arms. "Nothing bad. It is so that I can breathe fresh air, and grow stronger. And for *fun.*"

"A little fun isn't worth—"

"Yes, it is." Zelda didn't even let her finish the sentence. "It absolutely is. Who knows where we may be or who we may be tomorrow? Life is short, Mother. If we don't enjoy it, what is it *for?*"

"For the things that make up a life! For a roof over one's head, for a home, for *children*—" She cut herself short.

Zelda bent a little to look right into her mother's worried eyes.

"And you did all those things. You married a man with money to be safe and have a home with children, and how has it been, Mother?" She loosened her hands, then pulled her mother into a hug. "Have you had any fun?"

Slowly her mother's arms came round Zelda's back. "A little," she admitted.

"You have sacrificed so much for me, and I *thank* you for it. I do. I am not repudiating the gift you gave me, all those years, all this life. I just want to try the rolling machine." Zelda tried to smile a watery little smile and blinked fast so she wouldn't show tears. "It's not dangerous. Perhaps you should try it as well."

"Zelda." Mrs. Rawle pulled away and dropped gracelessly into the armchair by the fire, just staring at her daughter. Finally, she waved to the other chair. "Come here."

Zelda sat.

"I checked on you last night to see how you fared after one of your bad days," her mother simply stated.

"Did you?" Zelda's mind raced. She had no plausible excuses not to be in bed in the middle of the night. There were no bees in here.

"Don't bother, I've no taste for stories today."

Zelda curled in on herself a little.

"I would just like to know what *you* want. Not the physicians, not your father, and not the Marquess. Not even Lord Vere. You."

Every breath seemed to catch. Zelda didn't want to cry. "I don't *know*. But thank you, Mother, for asking."

Her mother sat in the chair, her slightly rounded figure settling into its cushions as she waited for an answer.

She wasn't moving, Zelda realized, till she had one.

It was easier to give back a true answer to a true state-ment, Zelda found, when accompanied by genuine regard.

"I promised myself many things. I made promises to Tansy, too—" that startled Mrs. Rawle—"and to Lord Vere." She could play word games and say she'd never made those promises; she hadn't, not out loud or in writing, not to him. But she'd made promises all the same. "I've lost track of all my promises."

Had she promised Geoffrey anything? No, not with words. But some sort of promise had been exchanged last night, and she wasn't sure what it was, much less if she could keep it.

Her mother let her sit silently for several moments, thinking, before she said, "I haven't made the best choices, and I regret some. I won't say you shouldn't think perhaps more broadly than I did. But have a care for your safety, Zelda, dear. I have only one daughter. A dear one."

Her mother's use of her shortened name did not go unno-ticed, though the *dear* pinged in Zelda's bones. "Thank you," Zelda said, with one of her rare open smiles.

"All right then, if you're going to do mad things, keep doing them out in the open where no one can spread nasty stories about you," her mother said, her brisk tone restored to normal. "And I'll come see you ride this… rolling machine, you called it? Like a wagon?"

"A little like a wagon, but small and two-wheeled. It will take balance."

"Two-wheeled? Where do you sit?"

"Astride a little saddle slung in between."

Mrs. Rawle looked overcome, sinking back into the cush-ions. Zelda almost ran for the wintergreen oil.

"Never mind, never mind. If you can do it, I can watch. Just—just let me bring my basket."

CHAPTER 25

Zelda would have been a fool to ignore the advice of both Mrs. Truett *and* Mrs. Rawle.

Zelda was no fool.

"Is the light good enough for reading, Mrs. Rawle?" she called.

The footmen had brought piece after piece of oilcloth, stacked them on the cold wet ground, and placed rugs atop. Mrs. Rawle was comfortably ensconced in the sun, her epistolary adventure novel tucked carefully into her hands.

"Quite," her mother called back, clearly nervous to take her eyes off Zelda but yearning too to read the page.

Next to her on a similarly situated chair, Tansy sat flipping through the law dictionary.

A brace of footmen stood off to one side, awaiting any lady's request… and watching.

"You don't make things easy, do you?" Geoffrey couldn't help whatever was on his face as he looked down at the top of Zelda's head. She wore a snug bonnet with only three peacock feathers waving from it, and a rare set of coral beads flashing bright at the neck of her practical, dark gray riding habit.

"Of course I do." Zelda wasn't even looking at him, she was so busy examining every part of the rolling machine again. "If we keep our voices down, we have perfect privacy and no one the wiser. And stop looking at me the way you are."

How she knew Geoffrey didn't know. But she did. He tried to look more sober.

"To start, I think it will be best if you—"

Zelda flung her leg up over the saddle.

Thankfully, the voluminous skirts of the riding habit did not flash her stockings to the world again.

Unfortunately, she was now astride the thing. If she stood, she had an awkward large machine between her legs, which did not appear to contribute to her calm. If she sat, it wobbled.

"Zelda," Geoffrey hissed. "Try balancing a little first while standing still."

"How will I set my direction? I must be able to move this," said Zelda peevishly, trying to sway the rudder bar from side to side while Geoffrey still held it in one beefy hand.

"You'll move it when I say you may."

"Oh, *don't* try me for determination today."

Their eyes met, and they gave each other nearly identical flat stares for a long, long minute.

Then dropped their eyes at the same time.

"Is this how it must be?" Zelda pretended to arrange her petticoat ruffles over one ankle as she spoke, bending low where the footmen couldn't even see her lips move. "Are we no longer friends?"

No, Geoffrey wanted to shout, but that wasn't true either. They *were* friends. They had shared confidences, and all that didn't go away in a moment.

Especially once they'd slept in each other's arms.

"Have you no more faith in me, Miss Rawle?"

"Of course I have. You told me I could grow stronger, and I believe you." Her dark eyes under the edge of the riding bonnet were steady. "I have always believed you."

Right. Very well. He could not fault her for not feeling the way he felt, as if all his sun and stars had departed with her. "Then believe this. If you lose your balance and are too far for me to catch, you will take a tumble."

"And I would return to you that a tumble is not the worst possible fate."

She really did want to kill him. Couldn't she hear how that sounded? Geoffrey hoped his cap hid the way the tops of his ears were turning red.

"I think I grasp the operation of the thing," Zelda went on to say, as if she hadn't just been utterly inappropriate. "If I have no speed, I will fall over. You'll see."

Well, if she could visualize lambs inside a ewe, she likely had a better grasp of shapes and their interchanges than he did. "And if you rip your gown?"

"I'll buy another," said Zelda, and pushed the thing forward with both feet.

There was nothing about Miss Rawle to suggest that she had ever been short of funds, or ever would be.

There was nothing about Miss Rawle to suggest that she would be happy living with him in a sheep shed.

* * *

It wasn't difficult to look calm while standing next to her own sweet-hearted giant in the sunshine, in full view of her mother and Tansy and a gaggle of footmen.

It was impossible.

Surely they must see. What she'd done. What they'd done.

Zelda couldn't keep track of her own feet, she was so turned around, wondering what showed on her face.

She couldn't look right at Geoffrey. He'd shaved. His cheeks were pink and smooth, which was ridiculous since they were also broad and muscled like every other part of him, and it was simply impossible not to run into his arms.

Zelda hadn't left behind the sensation of being overwhelmed when she'd run out of Geoffrey's shed. She had only left behind the sensation of being smothered.

Out here? She wanted to do very inappropriate things to him indeed.

She'd simply have to roll on wheels instead.

"Does it hurt?" he asked in that solicitous way he had for everyone, not just her.

He must mean the wooden plank of a saddle between her legs.

"It's not wildly comfortable, but it isn't painful," she assured him, trying not to look up and see him. She would blush, she knew she would. It *ought* to be painful, perhaps, given the fresh new activities she had taken up in that area just the night before.

But it wasn't, and she was grateful; she just couldn't stop blushing.

Oh, never mind. The footmen would take it for what it was: embarrassment over riding this thing.

She pushed again.

The machine wobbled, too, between her legs. She planted her shoes, scudding her heels in the packed earth of the Faircombe drive. She thought one ankle might turn, but no. And she was still upright.

Geoffrey jog-trotted after her. "You're quite well?"

"Perfectly well." She tried to turn the thing around to go back the way she'd come; the rudder bar barely moved. "It is not very flexible."

"Flexibility isn't needed." Geoffrey put one hand under the saddle behind her and the other under the framing bar in front of her, and picked up the entire affair with her in it.

As her world turned round one hundred and eighty degrees, Zelda mused that he excelled at that.

Before Geoffrey could say or do anything else, she pushed off again.

It was fun, the rolling, but it stopped after a few feet, and then she had to catch herself again. As the machine wobbled, Geoffrey once again steadied it.

"You must be running very fast," she observed, twisting round to see his pink face.

"It's not exercise, it's terror," he said flatly and for only her ears.

Balanced again, she looked up.

Had anyone ever looked at her that way, as if the sun rose and set right over her head?

"I'm quite well, just… trying to understand everything," she told him, hoping he knew she meant far more than the rolling machine.

"So am I."

That unbalanced Zelda more than the machine, for Geoffrey always seemed to know everything about… that. What did *he* have to be confused about?

But before she could ask a suitable question, he had let go, letting her hold the machine up.

"Try one foot after the other, the way you would run. I think your balance will hold. But Zelda," he said, grabbing the back wheel before she took off, "don't rush. If you roll off the drive, you could end up careening over the green, or even into the pond. Don't rush."

Don't rush. Wasn't that always his approach? Well, except when seducing her with livestock.

Her cheeks, Zelda knew, were *very* pink. "I'll be slow."

And just like that, she was off.

He was right; it worked better one leg after the other. As she gathered a little speed, she thought she heard her mother call behind her; and someone let out a little whoop. Had that been a footman? Or Tansy?

She'd dreamed of flying. And now she was.

The saddle board bumped uncomfortably into her at every divot and rock, and she could barely make the thing turn by swaying the rudder bar. But it worked. It worked!

The energy of her push kept the wheels rolling forward, forward, and she was rolling much faster than she could have walked or run.

"Miss Rawle! Stop!"

That was the sound of a giant pounding after her.

Zelda realized what Geoffrey must have already grasped: there was no apparent means of stopping.

Well. She could figure this out, or she could crash.

No ship moved forward without wind in its sails, nor carriages without pulling horses. If the propelling force stopped, she should stop.

Confident, she settled on to the saddle and pulled up both feet.

It would not have worked had she been rolling downhill, she saw, and made a note of it in her mind. But the ground here was level. She rolled to a stop.

Quickly putting her feet down before she or the machine fell over, she felt herself steady just as Geoffrey grabbed the rear wheel again.

Quick as a flash, she jumped off and stood next to it, pointing a shaking finger at the thing.

"That," she said, knowing her voice was shaking as well, "*that*... is possibly the most fun anyone on earth has *ever* had."

Shocked, arm half-extended to reassure her, Geoffrey stopped, mouth open, and stared at her.

And then he laughed. He laughed the way *she* laughed, unable to stop it, the laughter rocking him from his feet to his head. The rolling machine wobbled in his fist.

"Don't—people can see!" She hissed it at him, one eye toward the footmen and her mother, standing now, looking toward them with obvious worry.

"Yes," he finally said, his massive shoulders shaking uncontrollably as he wiped tears from his eyes with his free hand. "They see me laughing. You never stop amazing me, never."

Zelda amazes giant. That was quite a headline. Funny she hadn't thought of *Zelda flies over the earth on a rolling machine* first.

"Who built this thing? Why has he built it? What is it *supposed* to do? Did I do it correctly, do you think?"

None of those questions had occurred to her before she'd come off the thing, knees wobbling, heart pounding. Now they were all she could think of. Along with doing that again.

And how much she wished she could kiss Geoffrey.

The shortcomings of her clever plan of doing this in full view were now obvious and discomfiting.

But she wasn't ready. She couldn't talk alone with him till she could understand that choking, pressed feeling she'd had this morning, much less how she was going to get what she wanted. Or even what she still wanted.

Half of her simply wanted to wait till Lord Vere came home and decide then. It would be so much simpler when faced with his boring ears.

"Truly, who built it?"

"A German fellow," was all Geoffrey would say, and Zelda remembered that he didn't know she knew who he was. He was still trying to keep secrets.

Poor man. And he was so terrible at it, too. She knew a bad liar when she saw one.

"I'm going to do that again. Oh, wait! Am I building up my racehorse muscles doing this?"

Geoffrey sobered a little. "Well, in full view of the firing brigade there, I can hardly examine your muscles. But you had to push to propel yourself, didn't you? You made an effort?"

"Oh yes! But it was easier than simply walking. Or at least it was different."

"I'd say that's what you want, then."

The cool, raw breeze smelled of melting snow and possibility.

Zelda had come to Faircombe to be unrestrained. And she had achieved that. She would puzzle out what to do next soon. She could feel it.

Because she had a giant on her side, and a rolling machine. And an unrestrained imagination.

* * *

AT NIGHT, she slept more easily than perhaps she had ever done. Sometimes she opened the drawer at her dressing table and looked inside at the knife she'd collected there, and the compass, and the blue-stone ring.

Stealing things didn't make them hers. She didn't know what did.

And even if she could find a way off this estate without marrying Lord Vere, she couldn't try to tear Geoffrey out of everything he had ever known just because she wanted him.

Which she did. Oh, she did. Her body remembered him and ached for him, not in the joints, but in secret places.

She tried to touch herself the way he had, just to ease the ache, but it made her fingers hurt far too much to move that way for that long, and she had to stop.

It left her lying in that bed staring at the trees painted on the wall, wondering if the baby hares had ventured out yet, and if she had only been strong enough to save that lamb because Geoffrey had lay next to her, holding her.

* * *

Geoffrey had thought himself able-bodied, but every afternoon, an hour of chasing Zelda up and down the drive on that damnable rolling machine wore him out.

More importantly, it wore *her* out. And since that was the goal of receiving the thing in the first place, he would be satisfied with that.

He wasn't satisfied, of course, and he wouldn't be until he could sweep her up in his arms again and show her all the things he was feeling. But since that might be never, he would have to settle for this.

She looked so *triumphant* when she marched back to her mother and her maid, a little sweat showing under the brim of her fine feathered bonnet. She had mastered that machine as she mastered everything, fearlessly questioning until she had it right.

Maybe he could trust that the same would pertain to whatever was between them. She wasn't toying with him; that had been his hurt feelings. She wasn't Joan. She simply didn't know what to do yet.

He scolded her for rushing, but he had been rushing her from the moment they met.

This would take a little more time if it was to work, like waiting for the delivery of a fully grown lamb. No one was served by rushing that process.

Besides, he had to tend to something else he'd avoided for far too long.

* * *

ZELDA BEHAVED JUST as her mother wanted day after day, living for the moments in the drive, practicing on the rolling machine and trying not to touch Geoffrey.

It was becoming easier to behave a little, but she wouldn't have bothered if she hadn't wanted time to breathe. She no longer wanted Lord Vere to come home at all, she admitted to herself late at night. He'd never interested her from the start. A fraught exchange of flowers and then nothing. That was the sum total of their relationship.

The problem was what their relationship represented.

Mr. Paltz had taken to walking the grounds, sometimes staring at her while she rolled. Whether he was impeding the contract proceedings by not staying in conference with the other men of law, she didn't know. But Mr. Highland never appeared, nor the stick-like Mr. Wapping. And the business-men, clock-watching Mr. Wallinson and slovenly Mr. Lyndon, only appeared at dinner.

There was a footman or two who seemed to hover over her at meals, making sure she took the tenderest meat; they did not serve her sweets or wine. Zelda wondered if Geof-frey was paying them. But she doubted it; his pennilessness seemed real.

She spent her dinners watching Lord Faircombe as best she could without staring. Without Lord Vere on one side or Lady Charlotte on the other—for Lady Charlotte and her companion seldom dined with them—he only looked like a sad, deflated old man.

But Zelda didn't drop her guard for a minute. Not around Lord Faircombe.

* * *

IT TOOK A FEW DAYS' waiting for his heart rate to settle before Geoffrey walked to the village.

Or rather, he told himself it was worry for Zelda, but he knew it was something in himself.

He knew where the smithy was; everyone did. The thick smoke would have marked it on a map even without the knowledge.

"Augie," he called as he entered, silencing the echoing ringing of steel upon steel.

The heat in the place was smothering, but Augie didn't seem to mind it at all as he leaned up from his forge. Sweat traced rivulets through the soot on his bare arms. The sleeves were gone from his shirt, no doubt so as not to catch fire.

"A minute," he said, and Geoffrey understood that hot metal wasn't something you just put aside.

There was time for him to look around the shop and wonder why he hadn't been in before. He knew why, of course; but he had to ask himself anyway. It was time to ask the hard questions about himself and his life.

When Augie finally came towards him, linen cloth rubbing away the sweat and soot stains on his arms and neck, Geoffrey made his proposition before he could lose his nerve.

"I'm going to ask old Mrs. Hull about that cottage at the north of the estate."

"Oh yeah?" Augie's black hair flicked backwards with a bead of sweat, just missing his eyes. "Reckoned you'd already done that."

"I thought you might want to go with me."

"Yeah?" Augie said again. Geoffrey had to remember that Augie's schooling had stopped at the level of learning to read. He likely knew enough math to run this shop, and that was more than most people in the village. He was no worse than Geoffrey, just because he'd been raised to work with his hands.

Or because his mother wasn't the granddaughter of a duke.

"Whatever it is, pertains to the family," Geoffrey offered by way of explanation. Days spent working up his courage for this, and he hadn't found better words?

"Likely." Augie wasn't ever a big talker, and he wasn't helping now.

But he knew what Geoffrey meant, and his eyes challenged Geoffrey to say it.

"*Our* family," Geoffrey said as plainly as he could.

The little smile on Augie's wide cheekbones, so like his own, was real. Augie had never been a bitter person, even while Geoffrey lived at Faircombe and never acknowledged the truth.

"Not my family," he said easily, tossing the linen aside, "but thanks."

"Our father—"

"No more than a bull to a cow in the pasture," Augie said swiftly, swinging his head up and shaking it a little. There was no shame in his eyes, but no softness, either. Not, presumably, for Lord Faircombe. "Not a church match, nor a love match. My mum reckons she made a poor decision." He leaned his shoulder against the wall, a quirk turning up one edge of his mouth. "You must have made a poor decision once or twice."

"At the very least." Geoffrey couldn't decide if this was harder or easier than he'd imagined it to be. Truth was, he'd never imagined it. Not till he had been tossed out of the house himself, and realized what a thin line it really was between some of his father's sons… and others.

"So. No need to trouble my mum. I don't. Don't you either."

"I wasn't planning to trouble her. I thought perhaps you'd want to know whatever old Mrs. Hull knows. It must be something about the Eliot family, something about their history."

"Not mine," Augie said again, just as easily. "Last name's not Eliot."

"Augie, damn it all." Geoffrey had wondered, and had yet to ask. "What's your name?"

"Name? Augie."

"What were you christened, Augie?"

A flash of a whole broad smile. "Augustus Townsend Blakeman. It's a bit grand for a blacksmith."

"Lord Geoffrey Augustus Townsend Eliot, at your service, sir." And Geoffrey put out his hand.

After a bare second's hesitation, Augie took it.

He'd known, somehow, when he was still young. Even without knowing Augie's name. It was in the air, in a small village.

And he knew his mother must have known.

But it wasn't her fault. And despite the feelings he'd had as an angry young boy, it wasn't Augie's fault either. Or, likely, his mother's.

No, he felt entirely comfortable now blaming Lord Faircombe. With a little distance, away from the crashes and thundering reports, it was easier to remember the Marquess was just a man.

"What's the Augustus Townsend about, then?" Augie said it with the broad carelessness of a young man who secretly cared a great deal. How long must he have wondered? And who would have ever told him had Geoffrey not pulled together the courage to do this?

"My—our great-grandfather. He died young. Twenty-two years old, perhaps twenty-three. Remembering him, I suppose." They had things between them, even if they never spoke. But Geoffrey didn't want them to never speak. "Come with me to Mrs. Hull's. She might know something about that cottage. And even if I don't have any family to share it with, I could… use a friend."

"Yeah, all right," said Augie, tossing out the words as he'd tossed away the linen, but Geoffrey knew this was something big.

* * *

ON A LONDON STREET stood an implacable building more than a century old and convinced of its importance. It conveyed this through its heavy stone front, its closed doors, and its silence.

At least it was silent at nine o'clock in the morning, when Vere woke, slumped against its steps.

Immediately, he put his hand to his head to keep it attached. What had he drunk last night? And where? How much had he lost? And what was he wearing?

He had no idea why the harlots these days were so obsessed with his clothes. But he'd lost a coat again last night, that he knew, because he wasn't wearing one.

He looked past the stained gray steps. There were servants stirring on the pavements, no one of note, and yet Vere felt that they silently remarked upon him.

Or perhaps they were only glad that he hadn't frozen to death, slumped drunken and coatless in the street.

Not that a club this venerable would allow a peer of the realm to freeze to death on their doorstep.

But they must have put him out for some reason Vere was glad he couldn't remember.

The smell of the stone made Vere think that generations of venerable peers had pissed on it, too, down over the generations.

It was a situation that made him think that perhaps he had played around long enough.

He was in London on an errand for his soon-to-be wife. If she didn't motivate him, perhaps thoughts of his brothers —his brother—would. Because Geoffrey was still at Faircombe, and this morning, with the piercing clarity that came from waking up on stinking cold stone in a very historic place, Vere realized that if he didn't want Geoffrey taking his things, perhaps he should go home and look after them.

Plus, he'd run out of coats.

CHAPTER 26

"You are a clock."

"You are a pigeon." When Delina looked confused, Zelda turned in her chair. "No? Then how do you play this game?" Before Delina could answer, Zelda made a half-disgusted face. "This isn't charades, is it? I have mixed feelings about charades."

Delina blinked and lowered her drawing hand. "No, I didn't mean it to be a game. It is simply how you move during the day. Shall I describe it?"

"Please!" Delina, Zelda thought, seemed to be the one person in the house who understood that conversation did not have to be literal to be entertaining.

Delina went on drawing the flowers before her, but she wasn't speaking of flowers. "In the morning, after you take breakfast, you take a constitutional with your maid past the mews and the vegetable gardens. After dinner, you sit in the sun in the blue parlor, off the courtyard, and your maid reads to you from a law dictionary. Which seems a bit odd."

"I've heard worse. Continue."

"Then you hover about the receiving parlor in your riding

habit until it is time for you to go out to the drive and ride that bizarre machine."

"I prefer to think of it as astonishing."

"After which you retire to your room and look out over the gardens, where *someone* is letting the sheep graze. They're nibbling the topiary. The gardener complained of it to Lord Faircombe this morning."

That dampened Zelda's mood. "Disgraceful sheep."

"Were anyone to notice, they might see a distinct pattern where you start your day to the north of the house, progress around to the east and south and wind up on the west." Delina drew a small circle in the lower corner of her paper. "It's odd, but I would swear it mirrors the way the shepherd travels about the house each day." Delina's eyes flicked from the flowers to Zelda. "You've met the shepherd, haven't you?"

"And have you seen me even speak to him, except when we are riding the *deux-volant?*"

"*Deux-volant?*"

"I am trying to invent a name for the thing. I like the sound of French. Your *shepherd* says that the word isn't bad, but that I ought to use German as that country produced the thing. He's very educated." Zelda's smiles had all trickled away. "Honestly, Delina, no one could accuse me of doing anything inappropriate with the shepherd, who is not a shepherd and everyone knows it."

Delina traced the circle with a fingertip. "Yet you follow him like a flower follows the sun, all around the circumference of the grounds. Or is he following you?"

This conversation wasn't entertaining, it was unsettling. Possibly painful.

Zelda was behaving utterly appropriately. It only made her feel better to sometimes see him, her giant, wrestling with a pig or *tsk*-ing the sheep.

And feel worse, because he looked her way, too. He had a longing in his eyes that wanted answers she didn't have.

Perhaps ceilings were the problem. They should live in a house with no ceilings at all, only a column of air straight up into the stars and she would never feel trapped.

The practicalities would be difficult, but she was nearly ready to try.

"Have you ever been in love?" she asked Delina.

Who put down her pencil. "That is a more difficult question than you might think, given the circumstances of my life."

"Out here alone with Lady Charlotte, I suppose, who does not care for city life, your social options are curtailed," Zelda mused, reclining again in her chair.

The smaller woman's face dropped a bit toward the paper, hiding her expression. For some reason, she pretended to use her rubber to take away a mark. "I have had a few options and made my choices."

"Really? Well, I wish you would tell me all about it, because I've had none and made none."

"Haven't you?"

"No, I haven't. Love seems to me an unruly thing; if one could put it in a box, one would lock it. What good does it do for a person who can barely walk up stairs to fall in love with someone who hasn't got any? No, that doesn't sound right; that would be the best possible option." Zelda couldn't explain this to herself. How could she explain it to someone else? "I want many things. I have spent years dreaming of seeing the wider world." An understatement; she could practically draw the road she would take over the Alpine mountains from her own imagination. There were flightless birds that only swam, living off the coast of Peru. The blue-patterned plates from which they ate purported to show Chinese houses whose roofs turned up at the edges, like the brims of jaunty hats. Was that real? How would she know if she never went to see? "The long and the short of it is that I must learn not to be ruled by my feelings. Even if I cannot do everything I've always longed to do, I cannot stay forever locked up in a house, either."

"No one who loves you would lock you in," Delina said with a delicate stroke of her pencil.

"No one who loves me can take care of me alone." And there was a problem Zelda hadn't wanted to put into words, or to face. "I take work. Sometimes I must lie in bed. Sometimes I must be pushed around in a chair. I cannot launder or cook; I cannot even draw. My hands ache just from brushing my own hair."

As she had tried doing more lately, thinking perhaps her hands could be strengthened as her legs had been, by exercise. Lady Grantley had inspired her; she had seemed so *effective.*

But the pain hadn't stopped just because she moved more, and though she was stronger, the heavy brush usually won their tests of will.

She might well be a clock. She knew exactly where Geoffrey was, every moment of the day. She tried not to follow him about the estate, but it was as if a magnet in her chest kept pulling her toward him, as if she were the compass and he was her true north.

The last time she'd opened the drawer in her dressing table, she'd looked more closely at the ring. She was sure now that it was one carved slab of sapphire. And that it was not too big to fit the hand of the servant she thought had stolen it.

Sometimes she tasted the kitchen knife, which no longer bore traces of butter.

Sometimes she twisted the compass violently, wishing its needle would, for once, do something new.

But it didn't; it always settled in the same attitude. Leading Zelda nowhere at all.

Lord Vere surely would be home soon, and Zelda could no more imagine marrying him than she could imagine marrying a garden bush.

But her giant, her Geoffrey, was a disowned son clinging to the edge of his home and spending his days working among the sheep.

She'd like to have the kind of strength it would take to hold Lord Faircombe down for a while and give him a few thoughts he ought to hear. She'd like to be able to compel him to recognize his son, and do something to make things right with him. It might be allowable under the law to treat his son this way, but it was disgraceful.

The only consolation she had regarding those urges was that Geoffrey actually seemed to *like* being among the sheep.

And that wasn't much consolation for a woman who couldn't live in a sheep shed even if she wanted to, and who was terribly afraid that she saw no way to marry the man she might well love.

* * *

"Thank you for coming with me." Geoffrey was finally on the stones leading up to the widow Hull's door, and Augie was beside him.

"Said I would," though as always Augie didn't seem much interested in affairs Faircombe. "Said I would days ago. You do move slow."

Well, he generally did, except when his head was spun round by a goddess full of surprises.

Mrs. Hull didn't look the least surprised when she opened the door. "Oh, do come in! I've just taken some bread out of the oven. Boys like you are always hungry." She waved them toward the hearth of the little cottage, and two stools that looked like they *might* bear their weight.

Geoffrey was no more delighted with his diet as a shepherd now than he had been at first; his stomach rumbled.

Mrs. Hull only laughed. "Did you follow the smell?"

The world outside had grown greener and warmer, even in only a week. The passage of time was so much easier to see when Geoffrey lived in it day by day.

He could almost feel the world spinning under his feet like Zelda's toy globe. He wished she would learn how to make it stop.

But if he had to do something with his time other than be with her, it wasn't bad, sitting at Mrs. Hull's little table faced with a cooling loaf of fresh bread and a bowl of butter.

"You are too kind," he said before he began stuffing his face. He didn't get quite enough to eat, not as much as he'd like; he'd lost some weight, though he was too big for anyone to notice.

"A visitor is always a pleasure! Even visitors who don't talk." She smiled kindly at Augie, whose easy-going smile back didn't need words.

Augie looked excited about the bread, though, too.

Mrs. Hull clapped her hands. "You didn't come for any leaf teas? You both look wonderfully full of health. In fact, I might have you lift something heavy for me before you go."

"We're quite well, thank you, Mrs. Hull." And then, when he'd swallowed the next bite of bread, "Thank you for the willow bark tea you've sent to the house. And to the Wilson boy."

"I get paid for my efforts, but thanks are always welcome."

And as the two men sat eating wonderful bread and the woman watched them with evident pleasure, all happy not to talk, Geoffrey realized that perhaps conversation in London was so lively, especially about the topics of who planned to marry whom, because there was nothing else to do.

Or perhaps, he thought as Augie nodded his thanks again, and Mrs. Hull cut him more bread, this was what it felt like to be the *older* brother.

No wonder Vere was so bad at it.

"We wanted to ask you about the stone cottage back in the woods north of Faircombe Hall," Geoffrey finally stopped chewing long enough to say.

Mrs. Hull's eyes snapped. "Now why would *you* two boys come here to ask me that, eh? What makes you want to know now?"

"I don't," Augie said between bites, pointing a definite finger at Geoffrey. "*He* does."

"Mm-hmm. And you, Lord Geoffrey—" She spoke right over Geoffrey's attempt to interrupt her, "*Lord* Geoffrey, you've had your whole life to come and ask me questions about that house. Why now?"

"I just learned of it!"

"Did you now." She looked more closely at him, with something like pity. "And how can such a wise young man not see what's just past the end of his nose all these years?"

Well, there was a question that contained multitudes.

"Not that wise," Geoffrey muttered, trying not to sound sullen. "Thinking of other things."

"And I wonder what you're thinking about now. Never mind, that wasn't a question. I get curious, living alone out here only talking to the trees. Well, what do you want to know?"

"Whose is it?"

"Faircombe's," she shrugged.

That must have been obvious, of course; otherwise, someone would be living in it, Geoffrey supposed.

"Has anyone *ever* lived in it?"

"After a fashion."

What *after a fashion?* Geoffrey must have spent too much time with Zelda; he imagined people who perched only on the windowsills, or walked on the ceiling.

"Mrs. Hull, you're teasing me. *Who* lived in it?"

"The only people I saw live in it were your grandfather's mistress and his other children."

Too astonished to say anything at all, Geoffrey's mouth just gaped open. Augie helped himself to more butter, shaking his head with a sad *tsk tsk* sound as if he had never heard of such goings-on.

"His what? When? What now? And when was that?" Geoffrey finally found his voice. "Why didn't Dandy *tell* me?"

"Oh, Dandy wasn't here then, nor Mrs. Truett. You were too little to recall? When your grandfather died, his lady up and left, took her children with her. I always assumed she'd got some money somehow. Don't know where she went, but she went there. The house was empty after that."

"She left safely, you're sure? She didn't burn?" All he could imagine more horrific than this revelation was that the family had somehow died in that fire.

"Oh no. The fire was years later. No one had been living there for quite some time."

"If no one was living there, how was there a fire?"

"I don't know." She had the sway in her eyelids of an older woman, but her face was fresh and plump; Geoffrey didn't know why the villagers called her *old Mrs. Hull.* But there were depths of time in her eyes as she said, gently, so as not to startle him, "The fire was years later. Right around the time your mother died."

Geoffrey's near-constant appetite was gone.

He knew country folks well enough to know that when they said *right around the time,* they meant, most likely, the same night. "My mother didn't die in a fire. She was at home. I know she was. I saw her die."

"Did you?"

Even Augie looked up at that.

"She was in her own room. She talked to me—" *look after them, Geoffrey,* but he swallowed those words, "—and then she seemed too weak to talk more. And a little while after that, she was gone."

"I'm sorry, son." Mrs. Hull laid a small, work-worn hand over his big one. "What a heavy day that must have been for a little boy."

Yes, it had been. He'd rather have anything, do anything, than see death like that again.

It kept happening, of course, often; such was the nature of life among the animals, whether they were wild or tame.

Illnesses and age ended, in their time, in their place. He hadn't ever been frightened of death.

Only of being left alone.

He wanted Augie to see the place, though why, he wasn't even sure. Augie was more interested in this bread. He wasn't a complex fellow, Geoffrey thought.

But then, at heart, neither was Geoffrey. He'd loved Faircombe and his family as hard as he could, even when they still surprised him. Perhaps because they still surprised him.

Perhaps he was built to love things that were constantly surprising.

"You could have come and talked to me any time," Mrs. Hull admonished as she fetched both of the men some water. "Or anyone my age. Those Heaton folks could have told you. You're not a big one for asking for help, are you? Don't want to pay for it? Well, I'll tell you what my help cost today."

"Absolutely. If you need anything moved, or a tree uprooted—"

Augie nodded vigorously.

"What I'll ask is that you help this one find a wife."

"Wha—?" Augie froze mid-chew.

"Haven't done it on your own yet, have you?"

"I'll see what I can do, Mrs. Hull," Geoffrey assured her as soberly as he could, "but amongst my kin, *not* being married seems to be our greatest strength."

Augie just nodded, bringing down the chunk of bread in his hand as if banging a final gavel.

THE BREEZY SOUNDS of spring morning were rattled apart by Vere's approaching carriage.

He hadn't been gone long, he mused as he glanced out the little glazed window. Yet the grass had grown more lush, a deeper color of green.

As his carriage rolled past the front pond to Faircombe's grand, sweeping reception stairs, a goose honked at him, most viciously.

Rude.

At least his traveling companion had proved good company. Once Vere had made up his mind, it wasn't difficult to find referrals to the gentleman he wanted. Those dandies in clubs could be very devils at night, but they weren't so bad by morning, not really. At least, not unless he owed them money.

Vere was a bit uncomfortable about the amount of money he owed now; his debts had rather mounted during his journey. Bad luck at the card tables, plus he'd had to have a coat made up in a hurry; he'd made it two to be safe.

He wanted to impress his guest with the front staircase, forgetting it meant he must climb it himself. He was a bit winded when he reached the top, but the view was stunning.

The fellow beside him blew and puffed as he swept off his

stovepipe hat, but he recognized its greatness. "As if the world all spread away from here."

"Quite."

Mr. Croft opened the door as promptly as anyone could want, and he always looked as if he'd had a foot crushed under a pig. But where was everyone else? "Is my father about, Mr. Croft?"

"His Lordship is riding, I believe, sir."

"And Lady Charlotte?"

Croft's weeping-puppy eyes only fixed on Vere's right lapel, for some reason. "She is caring for the horses in the stable."

Vere almost asked about Geoffrey before he remembered.

"Well," he said to his guest, "is there any reason to linger? Shall we walk on through? Or should we dine first?"

"I'd prefer a quick meeting to begin," said his colleague, shrugging off his coat and handing it to Mr. Croft. "But then, as you say, dinner, by all means."

CHAPTER 27

"It's a demon." Zelda leaned back, hands braced against the billiards table, so she could squint at the cap of the plaster column, high up against the eaves.

"I think it's a fish." Mr. Paltz was far more absorbed in his cup of tea than in plaster carvings.

"A fish? With that mouth? Look how wide! It could swallow a chair!"

"I don't know what makes you think it a demon."

"The chair-swallowing mouth. And the eyes. And the way it hangs there silently, I suppose."

Subtlety was not Zelda's great strength, but she had to try something with Mr. Paltz. The man was constantly watching her out of windows, yet said nothing. A direct approach wouldn't do to extract his thoughts, and she'd rather lost her taste for lies.

Fortunately, metaphors were not lost on lawyers. "Don't take silence for evil, Miss Rawle."

"I never would. Is that tea quite sweet enough for your taste?"

"Quite. I thought you wished to play billiards?"

"Did I give you that impression? I've no idea how to play. Perhaps you will teach me some evening. Perhaps my mother would also like to learn."

Mr. Paltz chuckled into his saucer at the thought of Mrs. Rawle playing billiards.

Zelda thought she might fish for news. "She seems to think well of you, sir."

"It is a hazard of the profession that those who consult us often may appear to be friends."

"So she is consulting you? As a lawyer? And what affairs could she have back in the States?" Zelda's voice lowered. "Except my father. She does wish to divorce him, then. She does not wish to go home."

Mr. Paltz's soft features sagged as if only just now affected by weight. "The law is not a forgiving language, Miss Rawle, as I suspect you know very well. A married woman has little recourse."

How well Zelda knew that, *now*. "Yet she's here. And he's there."

"Your father's instructions to myself and Mr. Highland pertained to his business affairs, nothing personal."

"You've not met my father, sir. Marriage is nothing personal to him."

Mr. Paltz' pained grimace showed that at least he knew how much importance Mr. Rawle placed on his own marriage when compared to business. "Unfortunate."

"Unfortunate?" Zelda could pretend that the small hurricane of feelings was contained, in no danger of breaking loose; but the effort left her voice hard. "Are you married, Mr. Paltz?"

"I am."

"And whatever business affair my father intends to trade in exchange for me. Is it a fair exchange, do you think? Fair to include the rest of my mother's life, as well?" For there was no going backward for Mrs. Rawle, whether or not she accompanied Zelda on any further travel.

Mr. Paltz set his cup down swiftly.

"That is the very question," he said, with overt agitation now. "What price is a life?"

"Have you and Mr. Wapping agreed upon a number?"

The round little man launched himself from the table so quickly he almost overturned it.

When he stood staring at Zelda again, the same way he stared out the windows, Zelda finally placed the look. It was the look she'd seen on an imprisoned bear, carted along by a menagerie that had stopped in Manhattan and charged a penny for its sights.

The bear had looked hopeless. So did Mr. Paltz.

"Numbers are not absolute," he mumbled to the glass. "A coin in Bristol is not the same as St. Croix, or—" She could barely hear what he said to himself. "So a life in London is not the same as one in Boston or Virginia, and cannot be exchanged at the same rate, even if carried there by ship."

He did not turn or say anything else.

"Sir," Zelda finally said, "you don't wish to tell me the nature of your business. Very well. But if it does not sit well with you, why do you do it?"

"Pride, I suppose." His clasped hands gripped one another behind his back; he turned to look out over the billiard tables. "It was an elevated position, joining Mr. Highland to help smooth pathways for trade where there are none. I came for one affair and wound up confined here by the war; I could not go home. I was lucky to find a place that would take a man like me."

Zelda felt she could explain to him the possibilities of illicit Italian ships, but did not want to digress. "A man like you?" Did the law discriminate by height?

"There are no Jewish solicitors or barristers in Britain,

Miss Rawle." Again, his mouth twisted with a suppressed bitterness. "Mr. Wapping takes such affront at my very existence that I suspect it is his single-handed mission to keep it that way."

Zelda had so long focused on the idea of leaving that she had not considered the feelings of a person who wished to go home, but couldn't.

He and Geoffrey had much in common, then.

If he wouldn't tell her about the business or how he had consulted with her mother, perhaps he would answer the only question she had for herself.

"Mr. Paltz." She should have a more delicate way of putting this, but she didn't. "You'll admit I have a legitimate interest in my own dowry."

"I suppose."

"I imagine it says that the money will be bestowed once I marry Lord Faircombe's son." She must look calm, even as the hurricane in her chest picked up speed. "Does it specify *which* son?"

"Oh, Miss Rawle." He came back to his seat, flipping the tails of his coat out behind and perching next to his tea with a sad shake of his head. "Men of the law do not take up this work to discover ways to defraud the intentions of others."

"And my father, sir. His intentions are entirely honorable, are they?"

He could not answer her there.

"Miss Rawle." A footman interrupted the silence. "Lord Vere is returned, and wishes to see you."

The footman's words plopped into the thick emotion in the room, *plop plop plop,* like stones in water.

Zelda felt herself grow calm, even chilly. She didn't wish to marry Vere, but he'd gone to London at her request. Perhaps he had brought help.

She must find a way to accept that help and tell him that,

although she had crossed an ocean to marry him, she didn't wish to do it. All in the next few minutes.

Standing, Zelda patted her skirts into place. For the first time in days, she wished she had a glass of her whiskey. Not for her joints. "I'll see him in—" Surely she'd learned not to entertain gentlemen in her room. "The study next to my room. Yes, I'll be right there."

The footman bowed. "Of course. There's a gentleman with him; they'll await your pleasure, Miss Rawle."

A gentleman? Vere *hadn't* ignored her request! She ought to have had more faith. Hadn't he dashed away as soon as she'd asked?

Had he invited guests to the engagement party as well?

Much restored, Zelda rose in her slow, deliberate way from her chair, but set out for her chambers as fast as she could. She hadn't used her cane in days, but she didn't chance a fall when perhaps a man of the law, who would actually help her, might be waiting.

* * *

"No more dead ewes."

No, and Geoffrey couldn't say exactly why his speculation had proven right. But he was grateful for it.

"I think that first girl ate the grass and felt better. And she got the rest to follow her." He'd have to change his opinion of that ewe. She wasn't stupid at all.

"But what for? Why this feed?" Dandy kicked a tuft of grass with his toe.

"I can't say." It pained him not to know. Geoffrey had been studying the horse anatomy text in his spare moments. Its sweeping display of the innards of horses had sparked ideas he'd never had before about the interdependence of life, of the way animals were made. Just look at how many diseases could be helped by care and clean water alone.

Right here in this spot, between the quarried stone and the garden, was a cure for whatever had killed that poor ewe; he just didn't have the tools to find it.

The grass sloped away from the house to the edge of the garden. It was green as an emerald right here, greener than the rest of the lawns. "There's no clover here."

"At's right," Dandy agreed, "don't want clover for breedin' ewes."

"But they're all in lamb already. Clover's rich eating. And why by these stones?" Geoffrey eyed the slabs of pink Portland stone as if they were a book, too. "One ewe has even been nibbling at the rock. You can see the marks of teeth there."

"Wonderful," muttered Dandy. "Those stonemasons will have another bellyache about that."

Whatever the mystery was, no more of the sheep had gone down, and three more had lambed.

He'd gambled, and he'd won.

It was a peculiar feeling for a man who'd fallen from a height determined by birth. He'd believed himself fallen low, and he knew it now, because it felt odd to soar this high. He'd done this, or if at least the sheep had done it, he'd helped.

Perhaps no one would ever see the difference, because all that showed was a lack of dead sheep. But he knew. And Dandy knew.

Why had he let himself be convinced about what made a man worthwhile? Worthy, in fact? Of respect, or money, or even love?

What was he going to do with himself now that he saw things differently?

* * *

ZELDA SWEPT INTO HER APARTMENTS, braced to accept Lord Vere's help, and then reject him. Her hair was tied up at the nape of her neck, the soft sandy color of her day dress was a perfect high-necked frame for the emerald pendant she wore; none of it was inappropriate.

She knew he preferred that.

"My lord," she said as she glided into the room, nodding to Lord Vere and to his guest.

She'd forgotten that Lord Vere truly was an attractive man; he was only pallid in comparison to Geoffrey. He swept up out of the chair, seemingly eager to greet her, and she warmed for him a little, and worried that he might have genuine feelings about what she was about to say.

He might not understand that she still wished to consult the lawyer, even though she had no intention of marrying him.

It was too much to imagine that she might somehow, some way, find a way she and Geoffrey could be together; but she also grasped that her impossible dreams, if realized, would make for awkward family gatherings.

"Miss Rawle." He allowed himself half a smile. Did he look relieved? "I'm glad to see you looking so well. I have brought you Mr. Fallow for consultation."

"Did you?" Mr. Fallow had eyes set like bricks in his head, and the sort of nose that didn't approve of upward motion. His forehead traveled much of the way backwards to his neck, and his chin had stopped growing before its time.

"Miss Rawle. I do hope I may be of assistance."

"I hope so too. I have a few questions for you of a delicate nature, but if you please, I'd like some privacy first to speak with Lord Vere for a moment."

"It's an inappropriate request; but then that's the nature of the problem, isn't it, Miss Rawle?" He turned over his shoulder and opened a small wooden chest resting on one of the chairs; he must have brought it with him.

From it he took a leather pouch and unrolled it upon a nearby table.

The roaring in Zelda's ears was such that she almost couldn't hear what he said.

"Release of blood cools the organs, of course, including the brain, and should give you some rest. Lord Vere has described a very clear case of internal agitation, my dear, but we should soon have you feeling much better."

His perfectly ordinary fingers took up one of the blood sticks, and the fleam with its tiny glinting blade.

"You only need more rest," he said, and took a step toward her.

Zelda's vision went white.

She saw and heard nothing. Only the threat, knowing that he was near, coming toward her; that was all she knew, and it wiped away everything else she'd ever known.

"Geoffrey!"

No terrified animal's scream was ever more piercing.

Stumbling back toward her chamber, Zelda almost tripped on the hem of her gown. The physician might have said something; Zelda couldn't hear.

"Geoffrey! Geoffrey!"

She couldn't explain. She had no other words. Only the ability to move. She had to *move.*

They followed her in. Vere was saying something—had he raised a hand to silence her? To stop her? The physician only kept walking toward her with those things in his hand.

"Who are you? Get out! Get *out* of here!" Mrs. Rawle, never too far away, had rushed in so fast she'd overturned a chair; but the physician was paying her no heed. Tansy looked frozen in horror, just inside the door behind her.

Zelda backed against her dressing table. There was no

thought to the way she whirled and ripped open the drawer, or how her hand found the kitchen knife. Only knowing it was there and she needed something, anything, to hold them off until he could come.

And to scream with every ounce of strength in her.

"Geoffrey!!"

* * *

THE COOL SPRING air seemed split by the sound of a woman's screams. *"Geoffrey!"*

Over and over she called, and it made time slow like congealing ice, made it seem as though it took hours, days for Geoffrey to race around the stone and the portico and up to the lady's portico.

In fact, it took moments; but moments in which she'd already screamed four times, each time nearly stopping his heart.

One kick, and in that instant his boot splintered the locks, the latches, the frames, and much of the glass of his mother's French windows.

There was Zelda, shaking, looking ready to scream again until her bones rattled with it. She had her stolen kitchen knife clutched in her hand. A few yards away stood his oldest brother and a man holding bleeding equipment.

He understood immediately the scene, even as Zelda ran for him, her hand growing nerveless and dropping the knife, and he caught her against him just as it seemed she might fall. "Geoffrey!" she cried into his rough sheepskin coat, her arms thrown around his neck, all her strength and bravery shattered like the glass in the door.

"I have you, *shh, shh,* I have you." How well he knew how well they fit. He pulled her so tight against him that her feet left the floor, all of her sheltered and rocked in his arms, his bulk surrounding her. "I have you, Zelda. I have you."

From the corner of his eye, he saw the rippling effects of her piercing scream. Lord Faircombe opened the door, took in the shattered windows, the curtains rippling in the spring breeze, Lord Vere and his guest standing on one side while Geoffrey cradled Zelda in his arms in the middle of the room for all to see.

Behind Lord Faircombe there were a few of the footmen, jostling to see while trying to remain dignified.

In a crisis, Geoffrey acted.

"Listen, dearest," he whispered into her ear, desperate to keep her here in his arms for the rest of his life but unable to do one more thing until she was safe. "You run to the north. Keep the sheep pens on your right and go straight into the woods. When you cross a footpath, a faint one, turn left on it and go where it leads. Shut yourself in tight. Can you do it?"

She was shaking too hard to sob. Geoffrey feared she could not catch her breath. Every tremble through her body ran through him, too, and he knew it would be that way even when he let her go.

But it was still his brave, strong Zelda. "I can do it," she breathed faintly back to him.

"Good. Take Tansy and your mother with you. Don't let them out of your sight. Go on, now. I'll be right behind you. Can you do it?" She could, she said she could. He just didn't want to believe it, didn't want to let her go. She was going to rip his heart in two and take the pieces with her.

But he had to finish this now, because this must never happen again, no matter what happened to him.

"Mrs. Rawle. Go outside. Take Zelda for a breath of air." He yanked the little woman forward and fastened Zelda's hand in hers; she took it and went. He jerked his head and Tansy followed.

With every step they took toward the swinging, broken door and outside, Geoffrey felt himself growing, not more calm, but more enraged.

Once they had gone, and he heard their shoes on the steps toward the garden, he turned.

With three slow, steady steps like Zelda's, he was nose to nose with the doctor, his whole vision filled with the man's startled face.

"Run," he said.

Whatever the man of lancets had expected from this engagement, it wasn't the view that suddenly became his whole horizon: a bright-haired wall of a man with hands the size of ham hocks ready to dismember him and looking fully committed to doing it.

He ran.

Geoffrey didn't even wait for him to disappear from view before he turned to face his father and his brother.

Planting himself in place, arms half-spread, he looked like a tree that could be felled by nothing.

"How *dare* you."

"Only some idiot idea of your brother's, Geoffrey," Lord Faircombe managed to be appeasing and disdainful at the same time.

"I thought it would help!"

"Because you think she is frail. Weak."

"Better that than declare her mad!"

"Vere, silence."

"I will not be silent." Keeping his distance from Geoffrey, Vere nonetheless turned on his father. "You were preparing to put her in an *asylum*. You wanted me to marry her, then hide her away. What kind of life is that for either of us? What made you think I would settle for that?"

"You always settle for what you get," Lord Faircombe sneered, but his eyes flicked back and forth between his sons.

"If she isn't well, I thought a physician would *help*."

"As you can see, the lady does not care for them." Geoffrey felt the urge to crush something receding, but he did not put down his hands.

"Yes, thank you, I noticed that," snapped Vere, also without taking his eyes off his father.

"The pain of treatment is part of the healing. She's earned it." Lord Faircombe's words were clipped short.

"You think she's earned *that?*" Geoffrey took a step towards his father.

"She deserves it. That's what comes of the way she thinks, the way she acts, the things she does. She *is* sick." Lord Faircombe measured Geoffrey's step closer, and the way his shoulders had seemed to swell. "Don't menace me, boy. We both know you don't want to do any more damage to your mother's room."

Geoffrey's eyes grew wide too, and he backed up a step, making his father relax and his sneer return.

Then Geoffrey slowly bent down and picked up the knife.

Still facing his father, he backed up again, and cut through the tasseled ropes holding back his mother's beloved yellow curtains.

Gathering them on either side in both hands, Geoffrey *pulled*.

Like Samson, he brought the window dressings crashing down all around him.

"I will pull this *house* down with my bare hands if I must, to keep her safe."

Dragging a curtain in one hand and the knife in the other, Geoffrey advanced again.

"If you do anything, *anything*, to cause Miss Rawle the tiniest instant of pain, to her person or her mind, I will cut this curtain apart to make a rope to hang you with, and that would be a final purpose for it which I'm certain *my mother* would approve."

Silence.

Finally Lord Faircombe shifted, just an inch. "Well, I think that's fairly clear."

"Geoffrey, no one here will harm Miss Rawle. I swear it to you."

Vere's words startled Lord Faircombe as if he'd forgotten that he had another son. "See here, Vere—"

And then *Vere* advanced on his father, and his Faircombe shoulders grew wider, too. "The very way you turn and turn again proves your words are faithless. Your appetite for inflicting pain is endless, you have no soul, and it never has once occurred to you that I loved my mother, too."

This astonished everyone more than Geoffrey half-destroying the room.

"*Vere.*"

"You wanted me to develop a fist, your lordship." Vere's sneer had more acid to it than his father's version. He turned to the gaggle of footmen still jostling each other, gaping, behind his father. "You all understand, don't you? His lordship's word no longer means anything in this house. To anyone." At their fierce nods, Vere muttered, "I don't care if anyone even passes him the salt when he wants it."

"Vere, you can't do this! You don't know what's at stake!"

"Yes, our grandfather's vision, wah, wah, wah, wah," Vere mocked his father's droning.

"I've got a few things to tell you about our grandfather, too," Geoffrey put in grimly.

Vere rolled his eyes. "Wonderful."

"It's not your grandfather's vision! It's this house! Today! You think that stone outside lays itself? Where do you think your food comes from, boy? Your horses? Your damn coats?

We don't just need the girl's money to build; we need it to survive!"

Lord Faircombe's impassioned outburst rocked his sons backward more effectively than any blow.

Vere turned to look at his brother. No accusations, just reaching out for the truth.

"It could be true," Geoffrey admitted. "Those stonemasons are seldom paid. About to slit my throat."

"We don't get paid neither," one of the footmen put in from the back, only to be shushed by his friends. "Not now, Albert. Always sharp as a pound of butter."

"No, I want to know." Vere looked more his age than he ever had, worried and wondering what to do about it all at the same moment.

"Why? There's nothing you can do about it," his father spat out, as disgusted by his sons as ever.

But this time, they were both disgusted with him.

Vere drew closer to Geoffrey. "The horses haven't paid their way for a while, I don't think."

"And Charlotte is leaving."

"Is she?" That made Vere look older and sadder too, the Roman-emperor curves of his face falling. "What of the sheep?"

"Money, but not enough if it's as empty a pocket as he says. What's he done with the rents?" For many of the villagers paid for their land to the Faircombe estate.

"No idea." Vere looked back over his shoulder at his father, who looked as if he still didn't believe his reckoning had come. "So what do we do?"

"No idea," Geoffrey said back. Unable to restrain himself any further, he stepped out through the shattered door to check on Zelda's progress. He ought to have gone with her. The horrible need to be in two places at one time.

Just past the portico, all the livestock men were standing

about among the sheep. The men were trying to look nonchalant. So were the sheep.

"Everything all right there, Geoffrey?" asked the fellow who had shown him the stone cottage.

"You heard the screams?"

"Everyone heard those screams," said another man, the master of the hawks. "Housekeeper woman came and met Miss Rawle and her folks round the end, by the kitchen, and she and Mr. Pike went with them all over the greens."

"Well done Mr. Pike, then." Geoffrey had a hard time believing Mrs. Truett would be soothing in such a situation, but her accompaniment was better than none. "There's no fight brewing, lads. Except…"

He crooked a finger their way and beckoned them to follow him up through the door.

Once they were all arranged in ragged ranks behind him, he spoke loud enough for them to hear. He drowned out whatever fountain of bitterness Lord Faircombe seemed to be spewing in Vere's direction.

"Lord Faircombe has had a terrible bout of illness," Geoffrey said loud enough to carry to the gathered footmen behind the inner door as well.

"Has he?" Albert the footman sounded surprised.

"He has." Geoffrey stayed somber. "Apoplexy, I think. Sadly, there are no doctors anywhere nearby. There had better not be," he added as a grim aside. "Lord Faircombe should have a few men with him when he wants to go riding. We can't let him wander too far afield; he may injure himself."

"Oh, sure," said one of the men behind him, and there were general choruses of agreement all round.

This was the first thing that raised Lord Faircombe's ire. "You'll not keep me imprisoned in my own home."

"Of course not. *Prison* is a cold cell in an asylum far off in the country where no one can hear you scream," Vere reminded him with bitterness.

For the first time in many, many years, Geoffrey felt he could leave a problem up to his older brother.

"I must see to Miss Rawle," he said, and his father sneered again.

"You've ruined everything just as I knew you would, but even I never expected you'd tumble that cracked American b—"

In the mad scramble, a vast mountain of Geoffrey cut off the last word, pressing his father's collar tightly and back up against the wall.

"I don't know what our grandfather taught you, and I don't think I want to know," said Geoffrey, clearly trying to breathe evenly though his forehead was furrowed like a charging bull's. "But you will, by God, finally learn to speak of her with a civil tongue."

"Or what? You'll rip it out?" his father choked.

Slowly, Geoffrey let him lower to the floor.

"I am simply taking the reins. Showing who is in control. You know where we all learned that."

And with a nod to his brother, Geoffrey left through his mother's destroyed French windows.

CHAPTER 28

The shock kept Zelda's mind wiped clean while the part of her that reveled in maps noted the sheep pens and the way north, even without her compass.

She could have grabbed that heavy brass compass and threatened the doctor with it just the same. It hadn't been thought. Just the action of the moment.

She wished Geoffrey were here now. She wanted his arms back around her. She was cold, but it was more. She was hollow without him.

Mrs. Truett had come running out the kitchen wing nearly as soon as the three women passed it.

"You're not hurt? You're all right?"

Zelda was far from all right, but she just shook her head tightly *no*, and kept walking.

It was easy, walking all this way. Her legs, strengthened by the afternoons pushing the rolling machine—thanks to Geoffrey—made short work of the steps across the greens and towards the buildings all around where the livestock lived.

Heavy steps thudded behind her on the grass; Zelda whirled.

And her tiny mother shoved in front of her.

"Ma'am," said a narrow-shouldered man whose shirt front flapped in front of him as he ran. "Bill Pike's my name. I'm the steward. Just walking with you to make sure you're all right. Geoffrey would like it."

Would he? Why wasn't he here? But then he couldn't be, could he? His brother was home and her honorable Geoffrey wouldn't marry her, even if he could, because of his brother; or because he had no money with which to keep her. Zelda had her pick.

Either way, this wasn't a problem. This was the end.

It had never been a question of whether to follow her dreams or stay with Geoffrey. It had always been a question of how to fit her dreams into a new world built all around him.

Zelda read maps. She didn't make them. And she didn't know how to puzzle through this.

The path was just where he'd said; she'd have missed it had she not been looking. And at the end of it, the stone cottage appeared out of the trees like one of her majestic dreams. It wasn't huge, but was so solid, it looked like it had grown from the earth itself.

The burnt end was clearly a wound that remained unhealed, but the door and the shutters were whole.

"Should we go in?" Tansy did not look thrilled by the prospect.

But Zelda was clear. "Geoffrey said to go in, and lock it up tight."

After the little group stood around in the darkened inside for a few moments, Mr. Pike reached for the door.

"*Don't!*" Zelda felt cowardly, but her insides still shook.

"Just getting some wood, ma'am. I think this room calls

for a fire. And you could use the heat," he said without judgment as he let himself out.

It gave him something to do, carrying in loose wood and trying to build a fire, muttering about the wet weather.

"Let me get some—"

"I'll help you pick kindling, Mr. Pike; I have a knack," Mrs. Truett put in, and followed him out the door.

Zelda's mind was racing even faster than her heart.

She had to solve her problems, and they were many. Money, marriage, two men, and her mother. And Tansy's promise, which she had not forgotten. "Mother, you and Tansy must discuss your escape. Neither of you wishes to go back to America, and I have no way of engaging you a place on a ship without Lord Faircombe's money. Your only hope is that Mr. Paltz may help you, and he has my father's credit. Unless you can make friends with Mr. Lyndon or Wallinson, and neither seems appealing."

"Friends? Why?" Mrs Rawle clearly preferred to skip over the part where Zelda explained that she'd gathered her mother's desire not to go home.

"The business they wish to establish with Father's money. It has to do with shipping, and wherever there is shipping, you can sail."

"Sail where?"

"Sadly, not Europe!" Almost shaking her hands with despair, Zelda forced her eyes shut, though why that should help a person remember sounds, she had no idea. "Everything Mr. Paltz said had to do with shipping, I'm sure of it. A life here or in London, Virginia or Boston are not equal, but coins can change value between Bristol, St. Croix, I'm sure he said St. Croix, and… wye-dah? Weh-dah?"

Tansy's head snapped around. "Ouidah."

"Do you know it? Why don't *I* know it?" grumbled Zelda, staring at Tansy now.

"A tendency to overlook Africa," Tansy said in clipped words. "Ouidah is on the coast, in Dahomey. The west coast."

"Oh. I do like the east. I'm very fond of the name of Madagascar."

"Bristol and St. Croix and Ouidah form a slave trade route." Tansy's steadiness now had gone stony.

Zelda wasn't stupid enough to ask if she was sure. "I didn't know."

Tansy was kind enough not to say she'd expected as much.

Zelda's eyes went to her mother. "He wouldn't do *that*."

Mrs. Rawle had gone pale. She'd come out without her hat; her face was bare to the world, and her shame. "He would," she whispered.

"That's why they didn't write down the nature of the business. They didn't want it written. They're ashamed—"

"They're not ashamed." Cool, collected Tansy was reddening, clearly in high anger. "The slave trade is illegal in Britain. Illegal for British ships."

"But not for American ships. And when the war between the two is over—"

Zelda felt she was going to be sick.

She wanted nothing more than for some carriage to somehow make its way through these trees, and take her away, to Roseford, to London, anywhere. If Geoffrey were driving that carriage, she would go, go, go.

But this problem was the last stone in a vast, vast wall.

Geoffrey didn't *want* to travel around the world, of that she was certain. She faced a future of learning how to wash his shirts with her painful hands, or living without him. She was afraid she couldn't live without him. But wasn't he the one always convinced of what she could do?

And she couldn't simply walk away from this and leave

Lord Faircombe to his own devices. Not to do that. Her father was out of her reach; Lord Faircombe wasn't.

And she must know if Lord Vere had been a part of this plan.

Geoffrey deserved to know, too.

Restlessly, she paced, even if elegantly, rubbing her arms with her hands and wishing Geoffrey would find his way to her side.

* * *

"Geoffrey, wait."

Just as he had the night of the dining-room incident, Vere came running after his younger brother.

This time Geoffrey stopped, though every part of him demanded he keep going till he was back by Zelda's side.

Vere puffed a little as he stumbled to a stop. He bent over to catch his breath. "Geoffrey. There's no way to say this but to say it. You aren't planning to… to make a kept woman of Miss Rawle, are you?"

"Don't."

Vere raised both his hands. "I said nothing to defame the lady! I asked that you not defame her, either."

What was his brother on about? He'd heard Zelda calling for him. He'd seen the way Geoffrey held her. "Miss Rawle and I—"

"Don't—tell me something I cannot un-hear." Vere put his hands down with a squeamish expression. "I have no wish to know if you have taken a liberty or two with a young woman who may not be insane, but who is definitely forward."

A liberty or two? Well, if you could call it that... But Geoffrey didn't have the stomach to reveal true confidences, not about that, not to Vere.

"I'm only asking you not to compromise the young lady further."

"What *are* you talking about?"

"I still want to marry her, Geoffrey. I need to marry her."

"You're joking." Here he'd thought he'd met a brand-new Vere, and this one was just as much of an ass as the old one.

No, this one was more lucid, and far more dangerous.

"Geoffrey, think. The woman came here to marry me. The marriage exchanges are under way. Give me some time to understand the contracts; I must talk to the solicitors. That Mr. Wapping makes me want to vomit. It's going to take me a little time, but I did invite people here for an engagement party for her, just as I said I would."

"You *did.*" Geoffrey's mind didn't know which way to spin.

"Look, I'm no fool. I know you want the girl. But be serious. What can you offer her? A sheep shed?" Vere at least had the sense to look a bit chagrined. "I ought to settle some money on you, and I will. But legally, I have no control over our father's money. I have no idea what it will take to convince him to be fair. It could be years. And meanwhile, what have you got on which to marry?"

A dreadful hollow opened up just inside Geoffrey's chest.

"I know you like her. But I'm offering her a life of comfort. As Lady Vere. And she isn't just any woman. She *needs* a life of comfort, Geoffrey, sufficient servants at the very least. For her pain, and, well," here Vere just shrugged, "she isn't very practical."

Geoffrey just stared. Vere couldn't honestly be asking this of him. Vere had discovered his spine, but he was no different. He still thought one woman was pretty much like another. And that Zelda would think the same of men.

"You've never grasped that the question isn't what I want.

Or you. It's what the lady wants. Have you ever thought to ask her?"

"Really?" Vere looked as surprised as if Geoffrey had suggested sheep could talk. He looked like an owl when he got that way, Geoffrey thought. "We could ask her, certainly."

"And abide by her wishes."

"I suppose."

One of the stonemasons caught up with them. "All's well, is it?"

"Yes, it's fine," Vere swatted a hand in his direction as if averting the approach of a fly. Then, "One moment. Take a message back to your men, would you? If you'd like some new work, I could use help keeping track of Lord Faircombe. He's had an attack of apoplexy," he added, glancing at Geoffrey.

The stonemason didn't ask how a woman's horrified screams signified that the lord of the manor had suffered apoplexy. "Might be done," he said slowly, "if you can pay us a bit more often than the building work?"

"Yes, all right."

Geoffrey waited till the man had gone and kept his voice down; there was nothing to block his voice till he reached the trees he was desperate to reach. "And how will you pay them?"

There was that older look in Vere's eyes. "I've *got* to marry her, Geoffrey. I don't have a choice. I gathered bills in London just now, clothing and lodging and… and gambling." At Geoffrey's disgusted noise, Vere just shrugged. "Till this hour, I thought I was heir to a fortune. Now I find there's no money even to pay the people in Faircombe's employ. I was supposed to build this estate into a legacy that would last forever. Now I won't even have anything to give my sons if I don't find money somewhere, and soon."

Before Geoffrey could answer, they both saw Charlotte

striding across the lawns toward them. Hatless, her caramel-colored curls flew everywhere, and her arms pumped as she came. Her hands were fists.

"If you two plan to kill each other, have done with it. What did you do to Mother's room?"

"Charlotte—"

"Miss Farsworth is locked in her chamber. I thought you were out here murdering people. I heard a scream likc a woman had been gutted, and some fellow ran in to the stable crying out for a carriage. He's well gone, by the way."

"I hope he pays for the carriage," said Vere. "It was hired."

"*What* are you two *doing?* Wait." There was no blood or hacked limbs, and Charlotte took a deeper breath. "Are you two doing something? Together?"

"Yes," said Vere.

"No," said Geoffrey. "He still thinks he will marry Miss Rawle."

"Miss Rawle? I assumed that was her scream I heard. I could be wrong, but wasn't she screaming for Geoffrey?" Charlotte folded her arms and glared at both of her brothers.

"Yes," said Geoffrey, unashamed.

"Perhaps," said Vere.

"Gentlemen, you make me glad our mother experienced the joy of having one sensible child: a girl. Neither of you can make Miss Rawle marry anyone. That *is* the law, you know."

"Yes, thank you," Vere was exasperated now, "we had just come to that conclusion between us."

"Vere, what ails you? The woman isn't running around screaming *your* name."

"Charlotte, I think you mean *cutting*, not *sensible*." Vere had to settle his coat across his shoulders to calm himself. Then he looked down at the fine wool where he clutched his own lapel, and winced. Gently, he released it and smoothed it down. "Lord Faircombe has not been paying the staff. Not the stonemasons, not the footmen. I doubt he's paying anyone. He has debts, possibly… larger than he knows."

"Definitely larger than he knows," muttered Geoffrey.

"Yes! I know that! You think I am working in the stables all day solely to keep the horses company?"

"You knew?"

"You didn't say?"

Both brothers looked surprised at this news.

"Yes, in London before Christmas, he asked me to stop buying so many gowns."

"Did he?" Vere winced again.

Geoffrey never swung his arms around thoughtlessly, but he seemed to be working to hold himself still. "Why didn't he mention it to Vere, at least?"

"Because Vere's an idiot. No offense," Charlotte added.

"Offense very much taken! Come, Char, you can't always make fun of me to feel better. Was that why you couldn't find a husband when you were in town last winter?"

"No," and then Charlotte's face softened. She had a smile that started small and turned inward, as if what really pleased her was known only to herself. "No, my story played out rather differently than that." But then her smile faded. "I came back to help as long as I could, but now I won't stay, I can't stay, if Father insists on treating Miss Farsworth like a servant."

"To be fair, he treats everyone like a servant," Vere pointed out.

"*Sir*," Geoffrey waved a massive hand in Vere's face.

"Yes, some more than others," his brother huffed.

"See here, I can't actually make our father do anything." Vere's face fell again. "I can keep him from leaving the estate, but that's likely all. And what will that do? His is the money and the title. I ought to *let* him go."

"You could let him go and we could try to rebuild this family," Geoffrey pointed out.

"Delina is fairly set to leave." Charlotte bit her fingernail, clearly thinking.

"What does it matter what Delina wants compared to the family?" Vere recoiled when Charlotte gave him a glare that could slice steel. "All right, all right."

"I don't know. I will consider it. Discuss it with Delina. But this family has never been much of a family." With no compunction about how much space she occupied, Charlotte's arm swung wide, perhaps encompassing the estate. "If all we are is the Faircombe title, I must say, I've lost interest. And if it's about our father, shouldn't we include the boys in the village?"

"Boys? What boys?" Vere's head snapped towards her.

"*Boys?*" Geoffrey said over him.

"Augie and the younger one. I never knew his name. I know he's younger than me. He used to come to the edge of the woods and watch me ride. The nurse said I shouldn't play with him, but I wasn't about to. He always looked angry."

"What in *hell*, Charlotte!"

Geoffrey couldn't tell if Vere was angry that Charlotte knew, that she had told, or that there had been someone else even after Augie.

"I feel bad for him, for all of you boys. Not much to have in common, a rotten father."

"And you too, Charlotte. This family is the worst." Geoffrey offered one arm, as if to give Charlotte a hug.

But this was Charlotte, and she didn't want hugs. "Possibly," she said thoughtfully, biting her fingernail again. "I think that depends on the two of you."

Vere, in his London fashions, diamond winking on his hand, turned to his younger brother, dressed in rough undyed wool. "Give me a chance," he pleaded. "The whole family depends on that woman's dowry."

Geoffrey did not appreciate the low blow of appealing to Geoffrey's love of family. "I don't care about the dowry. I care about the *woman*."

"Well, you had better find out what she cares about, since you are both at her mercy," Charlotte said as bluntly as ever. "I wouldn't be surprised if she wanted a carriage away from here. I'm going back to the house."

CHAPTER 29

"Geoffrey!" Zelda felt lighter the moment she saw him shoulder his way into the dim room. She started for him so fast that she stumbled the next instant, when Lord Vere followed him inside.

"Oh, no. What..." Zelda didn't even have a way to put Geoffrey between them. There he stood, next to his brother, looking so serious.

Zelda shrank back against the wall.

"You have to go. You aren't welcome." Mrs. Rawle spread her arms out in front of her daughter, and the very action restored some of Zelda's heart.

"No," she said, recovering and stepping forward, "you are not."

"Please, let me speak."

"No! Why should I?"

Lord Vere blinked. There was that owl look again. "Because we're betrothed?"

All she wanted was to run to Geoffrey and throw herself again into his arms. He was standing right there, arms folded over his chest, feet planted as if he wouldn't be moved by a herd of elephants.

Why couldn't this dratted Vere go away and leave them in peace?

And take her mother and Tansy and Mrs. Truett and Bill Pike with him.

The cottage room wasn't crowded, but it was full, and even the tiniest whisper between them would be heard.

Zelda tried not to look at Geoffrey; she'd already broken down with unforgivably extreme emotion, and if there was one thing that hadn't been welcome from her at Faircombe—well, nothing about her was welcome at Faircombe, but definitely not emotion.

Surely Lord Vere could tell from her face that she was only extending him the barest courtesy. "Then speak."

He stepped forward, drawing her attention away from his brother, his eyes wide and sincere, his brow furrowed with concern. She couldn't take if it was real or counterfeit. "Miss Rawle. I deeply apologize for bringing the physician. I truly only wished for your good health. Please," he went on as she was about to interrupt, "my father had mentioned the idea of an asylum for you, and I thought him extreme. I thought a good physician a better choice."

Zelda wasn't going to show him her scars. She wasn't going to tell him anything. She didn't trust him an inch, and she would tell him so in no uncertain terms, but there was Geoffrey standing right next to him. Had they reconciled? Was Geoffrey about to be rejoined with his house, his family? She wanted that for him so badly that it hurt, deep inside, where none of her burning pains ever reached.

"It was not," was all she said, shortly.

"I apologize." He spread his fingers as if cornering an angry bird. "I understand."

Zelda doubted that, but she didn't know what to say.

He only astonished her further when he said, "Please give me another chance to make a good impression."

"*What?*"

"I was misguided. Misled. The impulse came from good intentions. I wish you no ill—I intend to *marry* you, Miss Rawle. I couldn't bear the idea of a wife of mine locked away."

That Zelda believed; the first thought in Vere's head would be the inconvenience to himself. Still, she gave credit where it was due for telling the truth, even if she didn't always do it herself.

Beside her, Mrs. Rawle had gone from spreading her wings to wringing her hands with worry. But Zelda wouldn't get caught up in discussing any of her particular concerns. Time had given her some perspective on her pile of problems. She had to solve what she could when she could before progressing to the rest.

"To be very clear, Lord Vere, I have no intention of marrying *you*."

"Quite. Quite." He kept pressing the air between them, as if flattening any objections she had before she could say them. "I completely understand your position. I only ask that we return to Faircombe Hall and attempt to… rebuild our connection. We have a great deal to discuss." And he dropped his voice into a quieter register, a smoother tone that sounded all too disturbingly like Geoffrey. "I assure you, I have been utterly serious in my activity regarding our wedding. The physician was the wrong impulse; I know that now and I won't repeat it. But I have also tried to please you. I've invited guests, and a house party to begin in just three days. Just as you wanted."

She had wanted those things a lifetime ago.

She turned to the still, silent man planted immovably in the middle of the floor. "Geoffrey?"

"I ask only what you want."

It weakened her knees, just having him near, and not for want of strength. She had grown accustomed to his support, his constant presence. It made everything easier, even wanting him.

She didn't answer his question, because it was impossible to say aloud in front of all these people, until she had settled far more she did not know and could not discuss. She needed a quieter way to find out if Lord Vere had been involved in his father's business plans as well as marriage plans; and he had so shocked her twice already that she did not feel steady about judging him rightly.

There was so much at stake, and they claimed their only interest was in her. That was so new she had no idea what to do with it.

She should return to the house to talk to Mr. Paltz at the very least, but the idea of going there when Lord Faircombe still roamed freely gave her shivers.

She looked Geoffrey in the eye. "You would let me return to Faircombe Hall?"

"No."

The relief she felt almost made her stagger. It had truly felt for a moment as if he no longer cared about her, he looked so distant and cold.

"I thought you were supposed to let her decide things!" put in Vere.

Geoffrey just went on. "You should stay here. I'll make it as comfortable as possible for you and your mother. And your maid if she likes," he said with a nod toward Tansy.

"Here?" Vere objected with his tone, his eyes, the disbelieving wave of his hand, everything.

"Here." Geoffrey was implacable. "The doors and shutters are solid. It can be made warm."

That sounded so stark. Zelda didn't know if she could live

in a place that had only those qualities. *Solid doors and shutters. It can be made warm.*

But she also wouldn't sleep at all if she tried to return to Faircombe Hall.

And she couldn't go sleep in the sheep shed with Geoffrey.

"I agree with you both." How many times had she heard her father agree with two sides of an argument, not realizing till she was much older that he was only postponing the inevitable for one of them?

Surely Geoffrey realized that she loved him, that she could never be happy without him?

She wasn't going to say it here, not now. She had to trust that he knew at least something of how she felt.

"I will stay here. I accept your offer, sir, to make this cottage as comfortable as you can."

Slowly closing her eyes and taking a deep breath without letting it show, she then turned toward Lord Vere. And opened them. "I accept your offer as well. It is kind of you to arrange a party, and I accept your invitation. Of course, as the contracts are not signed nor the banns read, it perhaps anticipates our actual marriage too much."

"But we do intend to be married," Vere jumped upon the idea, "so we needn't fear public humiliation where we do not intend to deserve it."

If he thought Zelda worried about public humiliation, he truly had no idea who he was dealing with.

"It's kind," was all Zelda could say, though he was clearly hoping she would voice more agreement.

"Are you sure?" Geoffrey didn't call her Zelda, or Miss Rawle, or anything. He only looked at her with his deep, knowing eyes that right now looked hollow and lost.

These words Zelda had to choose carefully. But she didn't go closer. She couldn't say this if she were any closer.

"I'm sure you understand how thoughtfully I must weigh a choice that affects my entire life." She willed him to understand. If he only trusted her now. "I have not one decision before me, but several. It isn't possible for me to convey in words all the subtleties of the world of trade and finance, not when I know it is outside your experience. But I must discuss them with Lord Vere." Geoffrey seemed so far away. "I hope you understand how heavily this decision weighs upon me, as it must. I am a stranger in this country, with few supports on whom I can rely, serving as the whole family of my mother, and protector of our staff."

Did he understand? His body was here, but his soul seemed somewhere else. And he said nothing.

She turned back to Vere. "You see three women before you trusting to your gentility, sir. And your word."

"You will never regret it, madam." Vere actually rubbed his hands together.

She already regretted it.

She couldn't think of a different solution, but she hated what she'd said and done.

"We'll bring in some beds and tables, miss, that'll do fine," said the steward after he cleared his throat in the deafening silence.

"Fine. Please. I am going to need to sleep."

"Good luck." Geoffrey couldn't be moved against his will, but he simply dropped his arms and bowed his head. "Madam."

And with that, he went out.

Zelda couldn't bear to see him go. She would run after him. She should.

Public humiliation didn't bother her, but private humiliation, here, among these people who knew her and had practically begged for her restraint, was more than she could bear right now.

"Good day, Lord Vere," she said weakly. There was not even a chair. Where would she sit? Sleep? Exist?

When would he come back?

"We should discuss—"

"Good day."

Vere was forced to withdraw as well, leaving Zelda more trapped than she had been when he entered.

* * *

Bill Pike didn't say anything as he walked with both the Eliot brothers back out of the woods and toward the great house.

"Take the bed out of my shed and put it in the cottage," said Geoffrey. "Take Dandy's too."

"That's what I thought of," said the steward. "That's where they came from, you know."

Geoffrey just shrugged it off. What was another revelation right now? Though it explained the source of those massive well-made beds.

Alone again with Vere, he didn't bother to look him in the eye. "You know I'm trusting you with everything I hold dear. You know if you let any harm come to her, the fact that we're brothers won't matter at all."

Vere really didn't seem to grasp what affected Geoffrey so. But he did hear. "I won't let any harm come to her! She is too important."

"To you. For money." Geoffrey wouldn't look him in the eye. He didn't want to see how empty his brother was. "No one has loved me since our mother died. I think she might have loved me, if you had given her the chance." He'd never forgive Vere, but he had no stomach for vengeance. Perhaps his father was right that he was the weak one.

He certainly couldn't match the bitterness in Vere's voice

when Vere said, "You're the lucky one. No one ever loved me."

He didn't need to add *and neither will Miss Rawle*. No one was pretending that their marriage would be about anything but money.

"I'll pity you when I can," Geoffrey reassured his brother, and then turned again towards the woods, not in the direction of the cottage, but towards the stables. The road started there, and he would use it.

He would walk.

* * *

SHE KNEW THAT BED.

Bill Pike took her silence for distaste. "It's a fresh straw tick, and thick sheets. You'll be floating like on a cloud, I can promise you that."

He directed the men carrying the thing to maneuver it closer to the wall but at the head, so one could climb out on either side.

"I suppose we will share," her mother said, less than enthusiastically, but for entirely different reasons.

"I suppose we must."

"We've another we can bring, ma'am," Mr. Pike assured her, red from helping to haul the solid wood frame through the trees.

They needed other things. Chairs, and a lamp; it was likely still sunny outside, but no one would know in here, with the shutters drawn and all the trees around. "It's fine, Mr. Pike, thank you." Zelda could feel the life in her draining away, and no whiskey would make her limbs lighter. She would soon have to sleep.

And she'd rather sleep in that bed than anywhere else, but not alone, and not with her mother.

Mrs. Rawle could see Zelda fading, and took over direction. "Thank you," she said, following Mr. Pike out.

Tansy tiptoed closer. "Shall I loosen your stays? I have no wrap to put you in, no nightrail."

What did it matter? She was trapped in this wooden box in the middle of nowhere, and something about Geoffrey's empty eyes made her fear he hadn't understood at all. And she didn't have the strength to follow him to explain. "We'll take them off."

Once she was down to her chemise, rolling in the bedding that the men had carefully brought through the woods, keeping it clean, then simply dropped upon the ticking, she murmured, "You needn't stay here, you know, Tansy. You can find your way back to the house, can't you?"

"I'll sleep in the woods before I sleep in that house." Tansy surveyed the wide old bed. "Perhaps there is room in here for three."

"It would help us keep warm," but Zelda was already drifting away, the fire in the room building up the heat so she was in less pain than she might have been.

They were all so kind, and it was all so meaningless, she thought as she fell off the cliff of her exhaustion into sleep.

* * *

THE WEATHER WAS FINE; the road was dry. Its occasional tuft of grass reminded Geoffrey that he'd left behind the sheep.

But no, this was the time to decide that sitting at Faircombe caring for sheep could not be the total of his life.

Zelda must have reasons for wanting to stay and play a part in Vere's charade. Her reasons weren't always apparent, but she had reasons.

The reasons didn't matter. If she were willing to stay anywhere near Faircombe after the fright that she'd had, for some consideration only Vere could serve, then Zelda had never understood what Geoffrey had wanted to make clear.

In his mind, they should face problems together.

She still hadn't seen him as Vere's equal, as *her* equal. Simply putting on his old clothes, Geoffrey thought, wouldn't do it.

As the afternoon wore on, his stomach reminded him how little he'd eaten. He ignored it. He couldn't eat grass like the sheep, and there was nothing else.

The feel of his footsteps on the packed earth pounded more clarity into him every moment. Just as when he'd left the house, and the waves of anger brought on by encountering his father had faded, so with every step farther from Faircombe, his purpose became more clear.

He had seldom had ideas before, but since he'd met Zelda, they just kept coming.

Fortunately, he knew the road to Roseford, whether walking or driving. And just as fortunately, he was able to walk the ten miles.

When the Roseford butler opened the door, to say he was astonished to find Geoffrey standing there in a workman's jacket and dusty boots would be an understatement.

"I own a cow," he told the Grantleys' butler. "And I am about to ask for a number of favors that I cannot repay. So let me repay this first one. The cow in exchange for a ride to London."

CHAPTER 30

Zelda dozed fitfully for the rest of the day and into the next one.

In a period of wakefulness, she was deeply chagrined to find that Mrs. Truett had walked all the way out to the cottage, more than half a mile, carrying a tureen of soup.

"It isn't heavy," the housekeeper insisted as she set the silver pot on the table that had appeared from somewhere, and pulled napkins from her apron pocket.

Indeed, the kitchen maids she brought with her were making the affair a picnic party. It was a romp for them to pretend the little table was the same as the big one in the dining cavern with its murderous chandelier. They laid out the dishes of food they'd brought in the same French square they would have used on the massive dining table, with little casks of olives and raisins framing the bread and beef.

"Adorable," one of them pronounced it, lighting the lone candle from the fire in the hearth.

"Thank you, thank you so much," Mrs. Rawle tried to sweep them out still in their good humor. "Thank you, Mrs. Truett."

"We'll call back in an hour or two," said Mrs. Truett, as if there weren't a footman stationed outside that the ladies in the cottage could send running at a moment's notice.

The soup was full of barley, and likely as nourishing as anything else Mrs. Davies could have sent. Food for strong people, and people who wished to be strong.

Zelda felt like neither.

"He hasn't been outside? You're sure of it? He might not come to the door."

"I am sure we will see him soon," said Mrs. Rawle in that false cheery tone she used when she was lying.

Zelda hoped her mother hadn't picked up the habit from her.

"There isn't a letter?"

"There is not a letter, no." The cup her mother handed her was full of the rich hot soup.

"Mother." Zelda's dry, rasping voice finally arrested her mother's bustling activity. "What have I done?"

"My darling," Mrs. Rawle said, as gentle and firm as ever, "the best you could." Her mother never squeezed her hands, not since she'd grown. It hurt too much. But she patted them. "I may not be the best example, but at least with age I've decided that the people meant to be part of your life know not to make big troubles out of little ones."

Zelda subsided into the pillows from Geoffrey's mother's room, sipping the barley soup. It was a sound philosophy, as far as it went.

The more her faculties returned, the more she realized she was foolish to wonder how Geoffrey could have misunderstood her intention. She had slept in his arms and then dashed out without telling him of her sudden panic, or what the night had meant to her. She had kept her distance to please propriety and behaved as though there was nothing between them. She hadn't told him of her attempts to draw out Mr. Paltz, or her decision not to marry Lord Vere.

What if *she* had made their little troubles into a big one?

She closed her eyes. "Please come home," she whispered to her teacup.

* * *

It was late morning before the three men on horses reached the outskirts of London.

"You needn't have come with me," Geoffrey told his companions for the dozenth time.

Anthony had given up answering him long ago, preferring to settle into his long cloak and be still. Geoffrey suspected he'd mastered the ability to sleep while riding. They had left Roseford late, slept by the fire at an inn to make the shortest possible trip, and Anthony didn't seem to like doing things in a hurry.

David, as sunny as the weather, was simply able to stay awake. Or perhaps it was the talking that did it. "We've traveled this road many times. It's an easy journey, but not one to make by yourself."

"I only regret that you did not allow Sir Michael to send his carriage," issued forth from the folds of Anthony's cloak, proving that he was awake.

"He wouldn't take my cow. You didn't need to come," Geoffrey said, as capable of firmly planting himself in an argument as on the ground.

Sir Michael had finally offered the use of a horse to pay for Geoffrey saving the litter of pigs, as they had all survived. And that Geoffrey accepted.

Geoffrey thought it a fair bargain, but it clearly rubbed Anthony in a sore spot.

Perhaps literally, given the hours in the saddle.

"You have set out to test some interesting questions," said Anthony's hood. "I won't pretend to know Miss Rawle's motivations, but after all this, I dare say you will."

David only snorted. His shaggy mount seemed to do as she pleased and wove from side to side of the road. "Don't be fooled. He is fascinated. Let me tell you another thing about my aunt's butchering business," he added as thicker clusters of houses appeared along the road.

"London family? You must see them. Don't let me keep you from them."

"Not everyone adores their family as you do, Lord Geoffrey," another bitter pronouncement from deep inside the cloak.

"But I do." David swayed easily with the rocking motion of the creature he rode; Geoffrey considered taking a closer look at it. It might not even be a horse. "You'd like my aunt, but you won't have time to meet that side of the family, not if you're going as quick as you said."

The little man's heartwarming assumption that everyone in the world wanted to meet his aunt, and she to meet them in return, knocked away some of Geoffrey's worry. This was the boldest idea he'd ever had, and being bold did not accord well with his habit of trying not to tip things over. Were Zelda undertaking this errand, she would succeed spectacularly, he was sure of that. For himself, not so much.

"Absurdly quick," he acknowledged to David, "and all for naught unless Miss Cullen can help us. Do you call her Miss Cullen?"

"I call her Cass," said David with the cheerful blatancy of a person to whom social rules did not apply.

"That lady is not your only hope, I assure you." Anthony's dour expression didn't get sweeter when it emerged into the sun. "I have some colleagues who will do just what you like, I think. You must remember you are not only asking them for a favor, you are offering them an opportunity. The world is full of people who love to see new things."

"I hope so." Geoffrey did not have enough cows to give around.

* * *

Zelda always moved carefully, to avoid the pain of jarring her bones; but this was different, picking her way through glass.

The spring breeze played as it pleased with the remnants of dangling wood, while the yellow damask curtains lay crumpled on the carpet amongst the shards of windows and windowpanes.

No one had touched the place since it had witnessed the previous day's catastrophe. She wondered if she waited a hundred years, if the remnants would still be here, aging in silence.

She had just picked up the silvery kitchen knife when she heard a footfall, muffled by the carpet.

"Please, Miss Rawle," said Lord Vere as he raised his hands to ward off her gesture. She realized she'd pointed the knife right at him.

"I won't apologize," though her hand dropped to conceal the knife in the flow of her skirts.

"No need." He looked less carefree, though heedless of the rubble. "You won't sit?"

Zelda looked at the armchairs by the dead hearth. She remembered Geoffrey picking her up in one of those armchairs and moving her, chair and all. "No."

"I fully understand your hesitation," said Vere, seating himself and crossing one knee over the other. The smooth fawn-colored trousers stretched over his thighs.

"I doubt it, unless you've been threatened with a knife."

"Yes, I just have." He waved carelessly to where her hand stayed hidden. "You don't believe me, and I suppose we have little reason for mutual trust. But I've only told you the truth."

It wasn't a matter of wanting to believe him. Zelda simply had to start unraveling her problems somewhere, and this might be a fortuitous moment to start.

She hadn't examined everything, but it appeared that her clothes, her brushes, everything was just as she'd left it. He'd only sent wintergreen oil out to the cottage, and a bottle of whiskey.

She braced herself for any response. "You seem to want me comfortable, but if I tell you what you should know, I think you will be anything but comfortable." Where could she sit except one of the armchairs? She was *not* sitting on the edge of the bed.

It was too odd to see Vere in here, where she and Geoffrey had spent their first secret hours alone.

"I am deeply uncomfortable already, Miss Rawle. My father will not speak to me, nor will his solicitor. They are up there right now, plotting something." He pointed an elegant finger at the ceiling. "So despite the loyalty of the servants, I have only a temporary upper hand. One that will disappear as soon as those same servants realize I haven't the money to pay them. I also may end up sleeping with the sheep."

He dropped the crossed leg, suddenly. Zelda jumped. He ignored it.

"We need to marry, Miss Rawle." His face was drawn, hungry. She had never seen him care about anything before. "I need money to right the affairs of this place, and my family is melting away before my eyes. I'm not prepared to fight my father alone. I need an ally. I need you."

"Do you really think of me as an ally?" Zelda felt the suspicion that tightened her shoulders ease.

"Of course. Your father could extend you a letter of credit as well as a dowry. You are exactly the ally I need."

She revised her opinion of him. His greatest fault wasn't having boring ears. "Lord Vere, I've been accused in my life of being selfish. I have to say I sometimes have been. And I might feel badly, except that I have met you. For comparison, you eclipse me. You are the most breathtakingly selfish person I have ever met."

"What is there in life but one's aims? One's duty?"

"The usual. Dreams. Love. *Other people*, Lord Vere."

His eyes were darker than Geoffrey's, but they had the same square shape, not so deeply set. It unsettled her to see eyes like that so tightly trained on her. "I don't think I'm convincing you, Miss Rawle."

That made bumps rise on her arms and the back of her neck, an animal reaction to danger.

"My maid is only in the next room, as well as a footman. They will hear me if I so much as squeak."

"You have nothing to fear from me, madam. I've just explained why I need you; I am nearly powerless in this house." He shifted a little in his chair and glanced toward the open door. "I am as uneasy as anyone knowing my father still roams the halls freely."

"I hate to bring you more bad news, but marrying me won't fix a thing."

* * *

By the time she was finished explaining, Vere had slumped down to lean on his own knees, another gesture so like Geoffrey's that it pulled at Zelda's heart.

But his eyes were far more shadowed than Zelda ever hoped Geoffrey's could be.

"I feel as though our conversation consists of my

protesting my innocence," he finally said in a ragged voice, "but I assure you, I did not know."

"No?"

"No." It was a heavy sigh, final. "And there's nothing I can do about it."

"Sir!"

"No no, I mean, I see what you mean. We cannot marry if such a contract is attached to the bargain." He sat back heavily, too. "I must ask him to sever the connection between us, of course."

"You must *tell* him that no such trade arrangements will be made! What if he seeks other ways to fund his plan?"

"That Wapping has arranged this. I'd wager my last coat on it. He must have money in the deal, and has brought my father and yours together for this unholy bargain. But if they arrange it in a way that is legal, what can we do?"

"What can we *do? Stop* it! Your countrymen fought and argued for years for the cessation of the slave trade. How can you not support them?"

"And yours for the continuation."

"There are *many* Americans fighting this same fight right now," Zelda said hotly.

"And many British content to let the trade happen. I'm only one person. I have no money, and soon," he spread his arms, "no house and no wife. I hope you haven't pinned your hopes on me."

"What I hope is you will be the brother that Geoffrey deserves." With that, Zelda slowly stood. She still gripped the kitchen knife in one hand. She picked her way over the glass and splintered wood and put the knife on the table to open the drawer. She took out the compass and the ring. "A question," she said, turning back to him. "Is this ring yours?"

"No, that belongs to Geoffrey," another careless wave of the hand. Lord Vere didn't concern himself with much. "It was our grandfather's from our mother's side. Geoffrey never met him."

"I thought so," said Zelda, slipping a thumb through the ring, then stuffing the compass in her pocket, heedless of its weight. She picked up the knife again. She felt better holding it.

The tiny jeweled globe her father had given her so many years ago lay on the floor; she left it there.

* * *

THE THIRD DAY, Zelda toyed with the idea of giving up hope.

Geoffrey had simply walked away. From her, from Faircombe. Even from the village. Zelda would never have believed it had anyone said it was possible, but there it was. It had happened.

Zelda didn't believe for one moment that she'd never see him again. She could feel the pull of his heart somewhere out there, tugging on hers. She might face that direction and wait for him to come. She was a clock.

But it was hard waiting, and hard wondering what he was thinking, if he'd understood why she did what she did. And there was always the pounding worry of how to make things right with him.

According to Vere, who looked more and more agitated as the hours wore on, the guests he'd invited from London would arrive soon. It wasn't a large party, some gentlemen and a few ladies, but it would be a flood of guests as far as this big, empty house was concerned.

Charlotte and Delina still intended to move north, but they had agreed to stay for the party, which steadied Zelda a bit. They were nothing like having a giant at your side, but they were steadying. Even Lady Charlotte, a little, as long as Zelda didn't expect her to stay for an entire conversation.

There was the haunting problem of what to do with Lord Faircombe.

Quite literally, as no one saw him, but the remnants of his presence were felt everywhere. They clung to the papers on the walls.

Zelda blamed the flocking.

"I've asked him not to attend." A real conundrum was undoing Vere; he looked less and less perfect every time Zelda saw him. Today his hair was even out of place. "He says he doesn't wish to attend. So there is no problem."

It would surely be a problem. Zelda was starting to develop a sense for problems *before* they hit. Not that it was doing her any good.

She had woken that morning in the straw-tick bed with Tansy wedged against one side and her mother on the other. Her mother, who launched into the same litany she had delivered in the grand house.

"Don't let the air reach your feet, Griselda; it's really quite cold." Apparently, her given name was etched into these speeches in her mother's mind. "Let me fetch someone to build up the fire. It is amazing how easy it is to tie one's own stays. I am half-glad Delphine refused to set foot in here." She seemed to enjoy bustling around and then out the door.

The stonemasons had eagerly become forest rangers with only one prey: Lord Faircombe. At least one mason would be out there, stalking the woods. Mrs. Rawle's only problem with their lurking about was that they refused to be sent on errands.

She might be a while trying to persuade them.

Tansy shifted to her back, staring at the ceiling like Zelda. It was warm in the huge bed with the three of them; but they all had to wake together.

"I will find a way for you to keep going, Tansy," Zelda took the quiet moment to tell her.

"I will find some way for myself, Zelda," Tansy said, and it made Zelda feel better that Tansy didn't pretend to distance when they lay side by side. "Look how far I've come already."

"Lord Vere says the entire Continent will be open to the British soon, and his friends—if such they are—often speak of seeing it. There may be someone coming to this affair who wishes to travel."

"Whether or not we go together, remember what we agreed at the start. We can wish to see the world, and we needn't provide a reason to anyone, for we have as much right to live in it as anyone. No one can question our right to want."

It was so far away, that Bowling Green house where they'd first met. And here Zelda was again, staring at a wooden-plank ceiling.

"I don't question what I want," Zelda murmured back. "I only wish to understand it. I have had this pressing, panicked feeling several times since we came, staring up at a ceiling just like this. A terrible need to escape. And now, nothing."

"Were you happy then?"

Zelda knew that she had been, but could not bear to say it.

Tansy nodded. "I think unhappiness can be a habit. You love to try new things, but a habit of sadness can make you fear losing what you've found. I've seen you sadder here than aboard ship, but I've seen you far happier, too. Don't make it a habit, when you are happiest, of worrying about what you might lose."

"My goodness." One keen-eyed friend could tell her more about herself than a thousand headlines. Zelda wouldn't blame herself for not knowing that; she'd never had a friend before. "Is such advice a feature of our new bed-sharing relationship?"

"Perhaps, but don't expect it to continue. *I* am going to Europe."

Now, waiting for her mother to come and dine with the Eliot children in the ship-bowed dining room, Zelda questioned whether it felt sadder to imagine Tansy going on without her, or sadder to imagine climbing back aboard ship herself and sailing away.

* * *

SHE'D LEARNED the moment she set foot in Faircombe Hall that the new was often more of the old. Wealthy British people's lives were not so different from their American counterparts, at least not when it came to carpets, cold, or paintings of fat angels.

Entering the house again, she preferred its people. Some of them. Even now, even if she must dine without the Eliot she liked best.

It wasn't so bad, except for the omnipresent sense of doom.

Sitting down to dine with the remaining Eliot children felt like sitting with family, like facing some problem together. They were all trapped in the nightmare of their fathers' making.

It made her glad she'd insisted her mother stay behind.

She wanted to tell Charlotte about their fathers' business plans, which meant, by extension, telling Delina. But Lord Vere insisted he should tell her in his own time. Zelda felt she could give him that.

She didn't want to give him anything, but in Geoffrey's absence, Vere was at least occasionally humane.

"Miss Rawle." Mr. Croft spoke at her elbow. "You have a guest."

"From London, Mr. Croft?" Vere raised his napkin. Those he was expecting.

"No. A young lady from the village for Miss Rawle, sir. I told her you were not accepting callers, but she insisted, madam."

The declaration startled Zelda into standing. "Perhaps it is news about piglets. Please, do finish. I'll return as soon as I can."

"I enjoy wondering what she means," Delina said as she spooned her soup.

Both Lord Vere and Lady Charlotte spoke together.

"You can't be serious."

"There's no reason to be purposefully odd."

"If it weren't for Geoffrey, I would think you Eliots had no soul at all," said Delina.

$\mathcal{M}$r. Croft had put their guest in the receiving hall. Zelda found her there, wrapped in a woolen shawl.

She spun around as Zelda entered. She looked furtive, though Zelda doubted she'd stolen anything.

Perhaps Zelda should explain the delights of stealing.

"Thank you for seeing me, Miss Rawle, when we don't know each other. I'm Joan."

"No, you're not." Zelda hadn't entirely given up saying the first thing that came to mind.

The woman's pretty face drew down easily into a frown, showing how often she made one. "I assure you that my name is Joan."

There seemed little point in explaining that the only Joan Zelda had met since coming to Britain was a cow. Surely the woman knew her own name. "My mistake. I was thinking of someone with darker coloring. More spots."

She waved her guest to a place on the couch and settled slowly into her spot at the other end.

The frown didn't smooth away entirely, but the woman did sit.

"I'm not sure how to begin. There are stories—" She stopped.

"I am entirely a person who enjoys the short form of thoughts," Zelda reassured her. "There is no need to take the long way with me."

"Right. Well, there are stories in the village that you are choosing between Ge— Between Lord Vere and... Lord Geoffrey."

"That is an interesting interpretation of the facts. Do go on."

Taking heart from Zelda's indulgence, the woman shook back her hair, which fell in long golden locks across her shoulders. "What I mean to say is, I think you and me are much alike."

That also was an interesting interpretation of the facts, but Zelda wouldn't have stopped this woman for the world. "Are we?"

"Yes." Animated now, Joan clasped her hands, her whole person reaching out for Zelda in inspired confidence. "A girl has to keep her eye out for chances, doesn't she? And I know just what you're thinking. There's the older one with a wallet, and a younger one with everything that keeps a girl warm. Those are tough choices."

"Quite." Zelda was becoming less amused by her visitor's version of reality.

"So I just wanted to say—a girl can't lose if she doesn't make the bet, right?—I came to say that you should pick Lord Vere and leave Lord Geoffrey be."

"Really." Zelda was measuring the woman now and wondering how much strength it would take to heave her down those ostentatious front steps.

"For certain. You like a nice house, nice things—I can see that, right? I wouldn't mind a toy like that." Joan pointed at the square, sparkling diamond on Zelda's finger. "You've really already made your choice. I can tell looking at you that Lord Vere's the right man for you. Lord Geoffrey hasn't come round, has he? And I can tell you for sure that he won't."

"Come round?"

"I know you've been, you know, trying to convince him." Joan dropped a very large wink. "I saw you flashing your stockings at him in the yard at the inn. A bit obvious. He's not that type, and I know you must know that by now. He doesn't give a girl the time of day, normally. Not without a whole wagonload of worry you wouldn't like."

"No?" Zelda leaned back into the cushions and laid one hand atop the other, with the diamond on top. "Tell me about the worry."

"Just what you must know. How a girl spends her nights. Does she like other fellows? Is she sure she's not caught? More chatter than a henhouse, and that's all before he'll give you so much as a kiss."

This sounded disturbingly accurate. "You've experienced this?"

"Not more than five minutes. I was all startled, like, and I should have been slower. But I heard later from a girl I met at Roseford market that *she* knew a singer who saw him in London. And *she* said that was exactly what he was like." Joan plopped her hands in her lap. "I should have just let him rattle on. I was just knocked back a bit, because I'd never had a man ask me things so forward."

Joan was clearly not accustomed to people who were accustomed to lying. She utterly accepted the face value of Zelda's sad shake of the head. "*Tsk.* Such a lot of trouble. I wonder you have any interest in him yourself."

"You mustn't think me a chancer. No, I've had a lot of time to think."

About his shoulders, Zelda thought acidly to herself, but for once did not say it aloud.

"I think I can be exactly what he needs. He ought to be *comfortable*, you know what I mean? And I like cooking and such. I would *like* to look after him, and he'd be happy."

Zelda felt her heart soften. Joan only wanted exactly what Zelda wanted. And she was right, she was much better positioned to give it. She could probably cook all Geoffrey's meals and wash his clothes and chase around his babies besides.

The last thought made her feel sick.

But then Joan added, "And I'd have just what *I* like. I like a man who's big, if you know what I mean."

Well, there went any sympathetic feeling for this Joan.

She hadn't stopped talking, though, clearly taking Zelda's near silence as an enthusiastic half of this conversation. "So it's a bargain, right? You ought to take Lord Vere; he's much better suited. And just so you know, once I marry Geoffrey, there won't be time for any flashing of stockings at the inn or anywhere else. If you know what I mean. I think that's fair. Agreed?"

"Not for a second," and Zelda pushed herself to her feet. "Thank you for your visit, Joan; it has been fascinating. Is that your wrap? No hat? I can take you to the door myself. You needn't stand on ceremony."

All the while she ushered Joan up and back, the young woman flustered and turned around by the sudden motion, right up till the moment Zelda opened the wide front door herself.

"I must say!" Joan gathered her shawl more tightly. "I thought you were being reasonable!"

"I never wish to be reasonable when I might be entertained, but I do like to be a good host. And I am trying to curb my worst impulses and grow my better ones. So for instance, I might appear inhospitable, but at least I am not shoving you down the stairs! Good day!"

And Zelda slammed the door shut.

* * *

"Mr. Paltz. You've got to change the dowry."

"Miss Rawle!" The round gentleman stood as she rushed into the library, nearly overturning his cup of tea.

She waved him down. "You've got to change the dowry, at least. It's got to say *an* heir, not *the* heir. You've got to do it."

"Madam, I don't commit fraud." He looked more affronted this time than sad.

"Only criminal acts? You've simply got to do as I need, and I've got to find a way to make you."

"Didn't I see your maid reading you Giles' law dictionary? Have you not made it through to *extortion?*" He seated himself back in front of his teacup with a righteous flounce of his coat-tails.

"Oh, Mr. Paltz." She had to release her clasped hands; they hurt her, and it would hurt more to hurl herself to her knees to beg. She still considered it. "Everyone has the power to choose to do good things or bad with the gifts that they're given, and I believe you have a decent heart. You *want* to find a way to help me. You just don't want to encroach upon your ethics. But the sad part is, they're already damaged beyond repair."

His round cheeks sank, wiping away any last traces of smugness. "You are not wrong, Miss Rawle. And at least I am comforted that you and your mother wish the same things. She was in here not an hour since, instructing me to stop searching for grounds for divorcement as long as you might have your money no matter who you marry."

Zelda put her hand atop the chair opposite him. Her mother must have just left it. Zelda sank into her place. "Oh, Mr. Paltz."

"Far be it from me to take her place in explaining things to her daughter. But I can tell you, you needn't look so grave. Things are different at our age, your mother's and mine. She wanted her freedom, but has few ideas what to do with it. She'd rather you be happy." He took up his teacup and sipped. "She thinks that might be marriage, children, but that all seems a bit pedestrian to me. I don't know you well, but I don't know if it would suit you. Regardless, it's what you want that matters most to her." He kept his eyes on his tea. "It's a difficult business, law. It's never everybody happy. It's always everybody *un*happy. I think I might hate it."

"I *am* sorry. And here you are, juggling all these different tasks. She was so kind, too kind, to take one away from you."

"Well? What are you going to do about it?"

Zelda had always wondered if her mother would want to travel the world with her; now she realized she didn't particularly want to travel the world with her mother.

She imagine more appealing alternatives. Her mother had given her every chance she'd ever had in her life; this was one more. She wouldn't waste it.

"I'm going to do just what I said. You're going to change that dowry, or I will expose you."

"Oh, *pheh*." He clattered down his teacup. "This really doesn't suit you, Miss Rawle, a life of crime."

"No? I think it surprisingly comfortable, myself."

* * *

A PAIR of hands slid over Delina's eyes from nowhere. A woman's hands, but nicked and scarred.

"Oh!" She squirmed and whirled away. "Lucinda! Whatever are you doing here? Charlotte will lose her mind."

"I won't go near her. Just wanted to see how you fared." The young lady had strong shoulders, thick curls and an unrepentant grin. "I followed the smell of paint. You haven't changed your mind since London? We still intend to go abroad, and when women travel, traveling in numbers is safer."

"I'm using a pencil." Delina had no intention of reminiscing. "Vere invited you? Never say so."

"Not exactly." Her little shrug reminded Delina that Lucinda Merriweather went where she pleased. "While we await the spring and open passage east, I thought I'd come see if any of the rumors about the Eliot brothers were true. Don't fret! I will only enliven the party, I promise. Lord Vere's friends are a dull lot."

"Well..." Not that Delina could change it, it was done. "Do stay out of Charlotte's way. I think you'll like Miss Rawle, but she isn't herself. She has a great deal on her mind."

* * *

MRS. TRUETT MARCHED between the china room, the linen room, and the kitchen with the zeal of an army brigade commander.

Zelda hadn't passed by the courtyard, but apparently carriages had come and gone, discharging their passengers, and Mrs. Truett was nearly beaming with her starch-encased version of glee.

"I've put the ladies in the north wing on the second floor, just under the maids, and the gentlemen in the south wing," she reported as if Zelda were already the lady of the house. "You must take some tea with them this afternoon."

"What? No! Can't Lady Charlotte do it?"

"Lady Charlotte? Among London gentry? You do like to see things flap, don't you?"

"Really, Mrs. Truett, they must entertain themselves. They are Lord Vere's circle, are they not? He'll simply have to amuse them. I am much too busy."

"You are? Too busy to meet new people?"

Zelda paused. Her last guest had been quite enough for anyone's day; still, Mrs. Truett knew what Zelda would find tempting.

But she didn't want anyone or anything new, not half as much as she wanted Geoffrey.

It was amazing how her problems fell away once her dreams became this much more clear.

Zelda gets Geoffrey.

That was the only thing Zelda really wanted. She wanted everything Joan wanted, and more. Things Joan would never know. His clever mind, his generous heart. His future. Zelda wanted those things for her own somehow.

She'd steal them if she had to.

She looked back at the waiting housekeeper. "You have permission to use all my wine and most of my whiskey. I think I need a carriage, Mrs. Truett."

Mrs. Truett's thin nose trembled with emotion at the very suggestion. "Well, think again. The stables are mad with newcomers. There's nowhere to put the carriages, and the horses will eat us to starvation. No one has time to saddle you a horse, much less drive you anywhere."

No, it was pointless; she didn't know where he'd gone.

She was a clock but time did stop when the sunshine went away.

He'd be back. He knew something of how she felt, surely.

She had that, the way they'd held each other in the snow-light, both wrapped in a sense of magic. He couldn't mistake her entirely. He was far too wise for that.

Mrs. Truett's nod had snap. "Now you strap up and be sensible. Lord Vere's nobody's charmer, but he has gone to this effort, and you'll attend."

Why did everyone think she was seriously entertaining thoughts of Vere? "All right. All right." This waiting was killing her.

She'd get through this, then go find him.

She'd arranged for Tansy to dress her, in the upper apartments that overlooked the queen's garden, where Lord Faircombe had wanted her to be. That man was nowhere about; he seemed to have ceded the house to his offspring. For now.

With the house full of Vere's guests, it felt a bit safer.

At the end of the corridor, she paused in the stairway. The one where she and Geoffrey had crossed paths. She could see him, all puzzled gruffness and wool, with his belongings—*his*—slung over his back.

She was different now. Stronger in many ways.

This time she looked up the stairs, and instead of thinking *someday,* she thought *now.*

It was practically easy, climbing stair after stair.

* * *

"THIS ISN'T GOING TO WORK." Night had fallen, and as their carriage rolled up the drive, Geoffrey saw that candles blazed in half of Faircombe's diamond-paned windows.

"I am no expert in matters of love, Lord Geoffrey, but I believe you need to screw your courage to the sticking-place." Anthony was much better company in the comfort of a carriage.

Across from them, the friends Geoffrey knew as Cass

Cullen and her husband Dr. Burke both peered out the window. "More pleasant than Moreland," said the doctor, whose company Geoffrey accepted because he knew the gentleman's heart.

"Everything is more pleasant than Moreland," quipped his wife. She turned back towards Geoffrey; she conversed with great attention, as she often couldn't hear and needed to be able to see a person's mouth as they spoke. "I for one am eager to have a reason to wear something elegant again. He only shrinks from it because he thinks no one will notice he's an earl if they can't see him."

"So we are calling him Lord Rawleigh tonight?" Anthony seemed to find this idea appealing.

"Might as well," groused the doctor. "Lady Rawleigh," he said a little more loudly to his wife.

"*Ugh*," she pressed a hand to her throat. "That does give one the shivers."

Geoffrey, trying hard not to squash little David Castle who was stuffed between him and Anthony, was glad they enjoyed the prospect of this party. Personally, he couldn't. "This is too much. What if she doesn't like it? I'll have bothered all these people for nothing."

"Yes, Miss Rawle hates a grand gesture," Anthony drawled.

David's hands freed themselves from his squashed position and started to wave in the air; Lady Rawleigh spoke the same way in return.

"What?" Geoffrey wanted them, anything, to distract him.

"Mr. Castle says you are as sticky and sweet as a candy made of marsh-mallow, and hopes that's the sort of fellow Miss Rawle likes. My wife says marsh-mallow is soothing, and all ladies like men like Lord Geoffrey, and I must say I'd like to know what she means by that." Dr. Burke—Lord Rawleigh—looked disgruntled.

Since Lord Rawleigh was better described as *beautiful* instead of *handsome*, Geoffrey thought his disgruntlement was feigned. Hopefully.

"Plus the cost of this carriage." Geoffrey sensed he was fretting. "You hired it for days. I won't be able to return the debt."

"Help, stop, don't," Anthony yawned.

"All right." David patted Geoffrey's broad elbow. "Don't mind him. Brace up. Just go to your room, the way you planned, and I'll tell your housekeeper to send you stuff to bathe."

Geoffrey's hair had been cut in London by a barber who'd muttered about leaving some parts long, "So his head didn't look like a boulder." His old clothes were in his room; he didn't know how much difference they would make. How much difference any of this would make.

Zelda couldn't have agreed to marry Vere while he was gone. Could she?

What was he saying? Zelda had *already* agreed to marry Vere. Ages ago, before she boarded a ship. Geoffrey's task tonight was to convince her to break her betrothal to a future marquess.

No, that wasn't it either. Zelda wasn't going to marry Vere. Geoffrey knew that. Knew it in his bones.

He wished he were as sure that he could convince Zelda to marry him.

CHAPTER 32

"*M*iss Griselda Rawle."

Zelda swept into the ballroom, trying not to crush her silk fan, searching every face she saw.

There were the groups of glittering people from London, all wearing similar versions of the same fashions. They were no competition for Mrs. Truett's transformation of what she had called a *small but serviceable ballroom*.

She'd told Zelda what she planned to do, but even Zelda's imagination hadn't pictured this.

Vases had been gathered from all over the house. Mrs. Truett had filled most with cut branches of blackthorn, its feathery white flowers standing out against black stems. Shimmering leaves of aspen stood tied in bundles on tables brought from all over the house to give them some height, and they were studded with so many peacock feathers Zelda wondered if all the poor birds were now bare.

Along with apparently every last candle Faircombe owned, the effect of a fairy grove was complete.

There in the middle was someone in a formal coat, broad dark wool and taller than the rest.

It was only Vere.

Zelda smiled at the faces around the room, nodded. Mrs. Truett's tea plan had proved excellent; at least Zelda knew these people's names and faces, and wasn't meeting them for the first time.

Whether or not they had fun was their business; Zelda had other things to worry about.

When she reached Vere's side she wanted to hit him with her fan and point with it toward another hulking Faircombe shape across the room. She didn't do either one, only yanked on his elbow. "I thought you told your father not to come."

"I did." Then he turned fully round and caught sight of her.

The space that opened in his mouth when his jaw dropped did not make him more attractive.

"Oh, stop. You've seen me before. Your father's here. Over there. By the punchbowl."

"Probably drinking; he does love a good punch. Miss Rawle, I have seen you before, but tonight you are a revelation. Congratulations to you."

"For this?" Zelda didn't bother to spread her arms. The dress had been created for occasions where she must blend in with the young women of London society. Tonight she should blend in; she wore the dress.

Lord Vere clearly approved of it, but Zelda thought it boring. It was white, simple white, with a long flowing line down to her toes, of a sufficiently delicate silk to flow over her hips like water.

But she was not being presented at court, nor was she a fresh virgin seeking a husband. Zelda wore her own jewels.

The full *parure* set of yellow sapphires was foiled to shine as soft as starlight. She wore one sapphire buckle in the curls of her hair, pulled back atop her head and flowing over one shoulder; the other was pinned at her waist. The necklace shimmered round the base of her throat, making it look even more long and slender, and just to be excessive she had worn both bracelets that matched.

Vere looked warmly appreciative and she suspected it was of the jewels. "Have you considered—"

"If you ask me to marry you again, I will scream. Go get your father out of here. Hurry."

He left, but then came Lady Charlotte, like a column of gold, standing with Delina Farsworth, whose pink lace gown was surprisingly un-demure. But Zelda couldn't even face them. She didn't *want* this party. She'd met the people from London and they were dull, dull, dull. She could barely tell the difference between them.

"I can't find him," Vere said, appearing again at her elbow, "but in a moment I'll—"

"The right honorable the Earl of Rawleigh, and the Countess of Rawleigh."

Murmurs didn't just travel through the little crowd, they roared. Vere's head snapped around.

Zelda didn't know the names. "Are they important? Didn't you invite them?"

"They haven't been in society at all. There are rumors—"

Whatever the rumors were, there was the Earl and his Countess. His carved-marble features looked grim, but she was a beautifully tall gray-eyed woman on his arm, and they came straight toward Zelda and Vere. The groups around them parted.

"Miss Rawle. Such a pleasure. We've heard so much about you," said the Earl.

But there was no time to look puzzled.

"Mr. Anthony Hastings. Mr. David Castle."

Zelda's mother bustled up, resplendent in her dark purple with ruffles. "Aren't those the two young men who helped me by the Roseford stables?"

But there was no time to follow those two as they melted into the watchers.

"Baron Andrei Andropov."

This fellow did approach, an older man with a suspicious glare and many, many buttons.

He marched straight up to Zelda as if he had been looking for her.

"Miss Rawle." Zelda thought his accent delightful; it rolled around in his mouth, even with her short name. "I am pleased to bring you greetings from Russia, which I understand has long interested you."

"Indeed it has, sir." She curtsied, and he nodded gravely, as if she had done as she ought.

"I am most grateful to be invited to your home," he said, his eyes still traveling over all the silent watching Londoners, the decorations, even the floorboards. "Allow me to give a small gift in token of my gratitude."

He snapped his fingers, and a young man hurried forth carrying a small wooden box.

The young fellow opened the box and presented it to Zelda.

Inside, nestled on green felt, was a tear-drop pendant like nothing she had ever seen before, like a dollop of captured sun set in gold.

"Oh sir! What a gracious gift. It is not necessary, but I do thank you."

"It's not even your house," Vere muttered somewhere behind her, but someone—perhaps her mother—stepped on his toes and he went silent.

"They are remarkable jewels, quite common in my country," said the Russian, heedless of his own contradictions. "They are the tears of ancient trees, so ancient that their living essence has turned to stone."

"Oh, thank you," breathed Zelda, touching it with a

reverent fingertip. She needed to learn much, much more, but even this much had her mind racing.

The Baron, his stomach carefully balanced in front of him, seemed to be waiting.

"Oh—Please do enjoy yourself, Baron Andropov. Enjoy yourself." Zelda ought to have more colorful language, but this had come as a wild surprise. The Russian gentleman seemed to be new to everyone there, though he immediately struck up a conversation with some of Vere's gaming friends.

No one was really conversing, apart from the young men talking to the Russian baron about perhaps rolling dice; they could all see Mr. Croft conferring with the next guest at the door.

"Haci Mahomet Esad Effendi," Mr. Croft announced next, not without effort.

This was a stocky man with a beard and *moustache*, something quite out of fashion in London society, whose long, loose coat nearly covered the equally flowing tunic he wore beneath. Balloon-bottomed trousers just showed above his soft boots, and his hat was like the wrapped half of a hot, open egg, turned upside-down.

His English had no more accent than any of the London group.

"Miss Rawle." He too came straight for her, through the aisle the guests now made.

Even under all the hair on his face she could see his smile, and he made a little bow as he presented her with a black-lacquered box.

She opened it, and the scents of spring and sugar leaped out. Everyone around her sighed.

"I so appreciate your invitation," said the gentleman. "I understand that your families have agreed to join. This is a happy occasion, and one that should be marked by sweetness. *Loukum* should be enjoyed, and my family has a very excellent prescription for it. We are celebrating too, fifteen years in England since the treaty, and I have made *loukum* here since we came." He spoke as if he and Zelda personally had arranged the treaty.

"Thank you, sir," said Zelda, reaching in for one of the white-frosted bites.

It was a most peculiar sensation on her tongue; it tasted of flowers, which was odd, with a sour bite cutting through the pure sugar. It was chewy.

Zelda *loved* it.

"I have brought enough to share among your guests," the gentleman said, then quietly, "and to still save a few for you, madam."

"Thank you," Zelda breathed. As new things went, it was *exquisite*.

The gift she really wanted had not appeared. But this parade of alternatives was extremely, extremely enticing.

Mr. Croft, the butler, seemed to be conferring for quite a long time before the entry of the next gentleman.

"*Senhor* Gaspar Mendez de Loronha."

"I don't think that's how that should sound," Zelda whispered to her mother, but curtsied. The man's hair was so black he made everyone else look imitation, colorless; and he approached her with a twinkle in his eye.

"*Senhorita* Rawle. I see you from your description." His tousled curls blocked out the rest of the world as he bent low over her hand. "I have been moved to bring you a gift."

"Really?" Zelda was still Zelda. The idea of yet another surprise brought her to her toes with anticipation.

Geoffrey must have done this. She'd rather have him than any of these; but if he had arranged gifts, wouldn't refusing them be rude?

Zelda was nearly bouncing on her toes when the man drew a kerchief from his pocket.

He unwrapped its blue-striped folds.

Everyone leaned in to see.

In his palm nestled a perfect little brown-gold carving of a hare, curled round on its side like a full moon.

"Oh." Zelda felt her eyes fill with tears, and she reached to touch it.

The gentleman turned it, and Zelda saw the first hare was only half. On the other side, another hare fit perfectly into the first one's hollows, the two lean little bodies wrapped together to form one whole.

"*Senhorita.*" He offered it to her, standing close enough to see the tears rolling, unheeded, down her face. "This is very old," he told her as she stroked the carving with one finger, in a room so quiet everyone could hear. "Many hundreds of years ago, a young woman came to my country against her will, sold as a slave. She cried for so many nights that she used up a lifetime of tears, but she never saw home again. She did not forget her home, it is called Giapan, and she gave this to her children along with many stories. It was so long ago, most of the stories have been forgot." He turned the little carving in his hand. "I wish they had been remembered. I am her descendant, and I wish we remembered."

"*Senhor*—is it Mendez? You are too generous. This is too much. This is like giving me the blood out of your body."

He shrugged a tiny shrug. "A little. But if her stories are lost, we should still share the story *of* her, if you understand me."

Zelda rested her hand over the little intertwined hares. "Only to borrow, perhaps. We will see each other again, and I will return it."

That made the black-haired gentleman grin. "A perfect idea! Yes. For now, madam." And his hand turned to leave the hares in her palm.

Hundreds of years old. As Zelda looked more closely, she

could see each groove left by a carving knife, and carried by a young woman to a land whose contours Zelda knew well. Thousands of miles. What a long, horrible journey that must have been, not made by choice, terrified, alone.

Zelda had the chance to make her own choices. That was real luxury.

Across the room, Mr. Croft very loudly cleared his throat.

"Lord Geoffrey Augustus Townsend Eliot," he announced, and everyone turned.

There walking toward her was the perfect figure of a fashionable man in a cut black coat obviously tailored to fit his massive frame. His bright hair had been coaxed into thick waves, his smooth face only a little more weathered than those of the London men.

His chin went up as he approached, though he already looked down at everyone around him. Then he bowed, a sweeping bow that took up every inch of room.

"Miss Rawle," and she hadn't even realized she'd offered her hand, but when he bent over it, he did not merely make the gesture; he kissed her there, so softly.

"Lord Geoffrey." Her eyes couldn't be wide enough to take in all his magnificence at once. He looked so like himself, and yet he looked so different, too.

"I hope you forgive my taking the liberty of sending you gifts I thought you might like." His gentle eyes smiled right into her heart.

"It is very kind of you." Did she sound breathless? She *was* breathless.

"I know you had some business affairs to conclude when last we met."

"They are concluded." *Please take me up in your arms and never put me down,* she wanted to say.

"And am I correct, that you are not currently betrothed?"

"I am not." Another wave of murmurs through the people;

Zelda ignored them. Contracts didn't matter. She and Vere had settled things between them.

"Then, Miss Rawle," said her very own giant, "allow me to ask if you will do me the favor of marrying me."

More tears, and Zelda let them run their courses. He had brought the world to *her*. "Lord Geoffrey, I would be delighted to marry you."

She would have said that and much more for the reward that she got. Because he finally came closer, and right in front of all his family and London society, kissed her completely.

* * *

THE INTOXICATION of Zelda in his arms again almost made Geoffrey forget where he was. And who he was; he still felt awkward, in a fine coat and boots cut to fit.

If Zelda wanted this version of him, she would have it.

As he set her back down on the ground, he murmured in her ear, "Can you stand?"

"Wasn't I standing?" she whispered, with her slow, sly smile.

"And will you keep your promises?"

"To you? Always."

But her smile faded a little, and Geoffrey remembered his beloved Zelda had filled her time with reading a law dictionary.

He thought back over her last few words and decided it was time for action. "Shall we dance, Miss Rawle?"

"We haven't music, Lord Geoffrey."

"Yes, we have."

Zelda looked over her shoulder, expecting, perhaps, to see Lady Charlotte at the pianoforte. But instead there was a group of musicians twanging strings of all sorts, crowding into a corner of the ballroom and preparing to play.

"I came quite prepared," he said as he led her to the middle of the floor.

He made a little wave of his hand, and the music started to play. A promenade Zelda ought to know; New York was not so very far away.

She did.

As he led her to the beginning of the line, he had time to speak again into her ear. "Everyone just saw you kiss me."

The look she turned to him was yearning. "I want *so* much more."

Christ. He'd forgotten what Zelda could do to him with a few words.

"Look around the room." Every head was turning to glance their way. "The story of our startling engagement will make the rounds of London next week."

"As many versions as there are heads," Zelda agreed, but her smile was for him and only for him.

She spun lightly away, and then back to face him; their dance progressed.

"Then tell me why you didn't simply say *yes*."

"Because I *would* be delighted to marry you. But I must be sure you want to marry *me*. Just me, with an abandoned mother and not much strength to help you."

"Only you."

"But if I—"

"Only you, Zelda." He took her in his arms and spun her, slowly, gently, surrounding her as he did.

It was not part of the dance.

"Only you. Only you."

Deliberately, full of care for her as always, he placed her back in the dance.

"Then we still have some problems to solve. But we could do it together."

"That," said Geoffrey, promenading to show off the goddess that he had persuaded to marry him, "is exactly the way I would have it."

"Oh, me too," sighed Zelda, and it was all Geoffrey could do not to sweep her up and out of the room. That sigh was dangerous.

But a public kiss was as shocking a declaration of passion as he thought London could bear; and for the moment—for the moment—he was content to leave it at that.

* * *

VERE FINALLY CORNERED his father in the room full of armor and maps that no one had ever explained to Vere. How did these things manage to be both dull and blood-stained? "Why is this room even here?"

"You bloody fool," said his father, cutting the tip off a cigar with a silver knife.

"*I* a fool? Sir, I may be a fool, but I am not a criminal. Do you expect me to swear out a complaint that you merely plot to break the law, or do you expect me to wait till you do?" Vere folded his arms across his chest and leaned against a wall.

He'd made an idol of this man. His father had always been so certain what to do and how to do it.

Vere would take chaos over that kind of certainty.

"We don't have the money to invest in ships if we don't have that girl's dowry. Hell, we don't have the money for this party."

"I know." The sick, hollow feeling in Vere's stomach this time was knowing that he'd only dug the Faircombe financial hole deeper.

But this party had been his last hope. Especially after all those coats.

And damn Geoffrey had transformed the whole thing into a proposal suitable for the theater.

For a king.

Well, Vere had come to a conclusion. He could not control what Geoffrey did. Nor could he control Miss Rawle.

"I gave her this party because I wanted to do it." Admitting it felt good. Vere was oddly glad he'd done it; he'd genuinely tried to win Miss Rawle, not grasping how her affections were truly fixed elsewhere.

Not grasping, perhaps, what affection *was*.

"You selfish, stupid brat."

Words Vere had heard before.

He felt that crumpling inside him, the confusion he so often felt around his father. But though Miss Rawle hadn't given him money, she'd given him evidence that his father was no model of what was right.

Had he ever imagined such a freeing feeling, he'd have thought it would take months to come, years. Instead, in mere hours, his image of his father had tattered till the familiar words had lost their power to sting.

"I'm not going to sit by and let you find a way to make that agreement," said Vere, pushing upright. "I think the name of Faircombe means more to me than the house." He turned to go, then looked back at where the wisps of tobacco smoke showed where his father sat in the dark. "It certainly means more to me than you do."

And he left him there.

* * *

Harry Rowe was long past caring about stiff-nosed gentry and their problems.

The rest of the stonecutters might be fooled, but Harry was not an idiot. They weren't going to get paid for this new business of following His Lordship around, any more than they'd been paid for honest work.

It was a fun game and all, but Harry only stayed in it for the meals, which now meant suppers too.

The carriages and horses had brought more people than the polished ones who went inside. A better party sprang up over by the garden where the stonecutting used to be.

Harry drifted its way.

Harry didn't give a brass farthing for old Faircombe, nor any of the young ones, either. They were all the same to him. Every pompous tall-hat was exactly the same: nothing. Their word meant all exactly the same: nothing. He reckoned that as much as he was owed, he had no reason to do a thing else, even if he'd agreed to do it.

That was why no one saw Lord Faircombe walk out of the house and into the shadows.

CHAPTER 33

After the requisite three dances, Geoffrey leaned down to Zelda's ear. "I have an impulse."

"Really?" Would that seductive smile ever be old? "I believe in giving in to impulses."

"They have seen enough of our society clothes. Would you like to take a walk with me?"

"To the ends of the earth," she immediately said, and tucked one hand in the crook of his elbow.

They walked out together in full view of everyone.

Zelda took a shawl from a footman as they passed without removing her hand from Geoffrey's arm. "Was all this just to show me how much I wanted only you? I would have chased you to the ends of the earth, you know. I still could. Try running. You won't find it that easy to hide. A man so large is easy quarry, and I could vividly describe you. Right down to your shoes. In fact, if it came to proving who you were, your sheep shed must hold boots that would fit no one but you."

They'd seldom walked this way, thought Geoffrey as he led her down the courtyard steps. It took them a few moments to adjust their strides, his longer legs matching the length of her step, and her stretching a little.

"What I mean is, all this wasn't necessary," Zelda finally said.

"Zelda, you told me twice, or was it three times? That I didn't understand difficult affairs of business. Well, I don't read law libraries for pleasure, but I don't think you ever saw me like this. Like the man I was right up till the moment that you walked in our door."

"The moment? Truly?" Zelda squeezed his arm a little. "You weren't put out of the house because of *me?*"

"I most definitely was." He tried to make it sound dire.

"I am *so* sorry. Geoffrey! How unfair."

"It's not as if I *blame* you," he said, relenting from his teasing, "it was my father's action. It was only precipitated by your arrival."

"No wonder you disliked me from the start!"

He ought to have brought her a true coat, but the night was warm, and selfishly, he liked keeping her close. There were some benefits to selfishness. "I didn't."

"You did! So short with me under the stairs."

"It's not a place for long conversations." He steered them closer to a stand of trees marking the edge of the lawn. Early honeysuckle had sprung up there; he broke off a stem.

And instead of giving it to her, tucked it in the lapel of his coat.

"My first reaction to you was not dislike," he said, pulling her closer to lay her head on his chest, enveloping her in warmth and its sweet smell.

She burrowed into his arms, her slow *mmm* noise almost more than he could bear.

"You gave me the flower? Why didn't I guess? I couldn't have, I suppose. But how much trouble you caused!"

"Really? How can that possibly be so?"

Zelda was slow in answering, so slow Geoffrey wondered if she'd grown tired. He could always carry her to wherever she wanted to sleep.

Finally, she answered, "I might have been too eager to be swayed by gifts."

It satisfied something deep down inside him that her first gift at Faircombe had been from him, and that it had affected her. "Obviously, I hope you still are."

"Geoffrey, you made me miss you so! I think I could have seen you for who you are. I think I *did*." She rubbed her cheek against his crisp shirt. "Not that you are not very handsome in these clothes."

"Well, call me a coward, then. If you'd really chosen Vere—"

"You must have known my heart is yours."

"Is it?"

She looked up at him, her face aglow with reflected moonlight. "I can have a carving made of my heart and give it to you, but it would look just like yours. Wrapped together, like the little hares in the *Senhor's* gift. My heart belongs to you, Geoffrey, and I think it always has. I was waiting for you. I sailed across an ocean to find you, you know."

"You weren't looking for me. You were looking for a way to go anywhere."

"And wasn't that what you gave me tonight?"

He should have known from their first kiss that it would always be like this. A little sweet, a little hungry; pulled from so deep inside them that it felt like their whole being was wrapped in the kiss. It had frightened him a little, how perfectly that carving showed the world the way they were, two souls forming one perfectly-shaped whole.

He hadn't known that things made by hands could do that.

He had told *Senhor* Mendez that it was too much to offer

as a gift, just as Zelda had. But he couldn't turn down his offer either, because it was too perfect.

For such a large place, the world had surprisingly few perfect things in it.

"So you don't intend to sail off and leave me here?"

"No." Zelda hugged him tighter.

He stroked a hand lightly down her back, mindful of keeping her warm. "Because marrying me won't get you your dowry?"

She stepped back at that, taking his big hand in hers. "What if I could?"

"How, my dearest?"

That earned him a startled look. He liked the way she looked, startled. Normally so mysterious, her eyes flew open so wide.

He liked having that effect on her.

"Mr. Paltz," she said. "I have him in what the businessmen call an untenable position. He will have to add just a few strokes to the documents, Geoffrey. Not even real letters. I should get the money if I marry *an* heir to the Faircombe title, not *the* heir."

She looked so hopeful.

He didn't want to squash hopes, hers or his own, so he tried to make his answer gentle. "I don't think you will really be happy, winning your dowry money with a trick like that."

"I could *try.*"

His dearest eager criminal. "I have another idea. I spent half an hour with the head of the Veterinary College near London. It is a whole course of study for the medicine of animals, Zelda."

"Never say so!" She kissed his hand in her hands, and her mind raced off. "Well, they ought to be so glad to get *you*! They can't possibly have other men with your talent. They must know chemistry and cattle feed and things you would *love* to know! That sounds like something marvelous for you, truly magnificent. I assume he tried to persuade you to join them."

She made it sound as if he ought to be giving lectures. "What they care about? Is horses."

She dropped his hand and pulled away, in genuine affront on his behalf. "Horses."

"Horses almost exclusively. They live and die for horses. I've never spent time on the horses here because they are waited on, mane and hoof, by a whole phalanx of men who love nothing on this earth more than horses."

"Well, that's just foolish. Who helps deliver the sheep?"

"That's just it. No one, I'm afraid."

Zelda looked appalled. "Bollocks," she said.

Geoffrey laughed. "Did I ever tell you how much I love to laugh with you? How much I love just sitting and talking to you?"

"No," Zelda answered promptly, as if it were a game. "Did I ever tell you I love you?"

"I know I didn't tell you I love you, because I was dying to be back with you to say it," Geoffrey said against her hair, for somehow she was back in his arms.

"So many words. Who's been reading law now?"

"I do love you," he said, and kissed her again.

When he stopped, she had fallen back, letting him hold her up and ravish her with his lips as much as he liked.

"*Ah*. Don't stop," she told him, reaching for his ears, but he set her on her feet.

"Zelda, if you can wait a few years, I can finish that course of study."

"Bollocks to that."

"Where did you learn that word?"

"And how will you pay for your studies? Or to live at the college?"

Geoffrey hoped he didn't look sheepish. "If I earn enough caring for the village animals for a year or two, I think I can pay my way…"

Zelda pulled back, mouth agape.

"And what am I supposed to be doing all this time? Waiting? And you in the village? You have no idea what goes through other women's heads; I am *not* having that. We must be married, and soon."

"There's no rush—"

"Yes, there is. I am with child. I'm sure of it. The way you kissed me just now? Goodness."

"Zelda."

"No! I won't wait that long! Do you know me at all? I can't wait till a singer is done with a song to applaud! I certainly can't wait for this. No. Geoffrey."

And then the elegant Zelda Rawle shoved her hand down the front of her dress and began the most fascinating wiggle.

Geoffrey just folded his arms and watched. He'd be interested to see how this played out.

"Stop looking at me like that! Or at least *help*. No, don't, that won't be shorter. Wait. As we are speaking of things that fit only you. Here's a ribbon…" She groped around to the side. He remembered the dark beauty mark there. Standing still grew more difficult. "Where has the thing gone?"

"I can help if you like."

"Too late. Sometimes you must leap, sir. Here it is." She took out the sapphire ring, trailing a thin ribbon. "I wanted to keep it safe, but didn't wish to wear it where it might show in case you wouldn't like it. Geoffrey. I have taken care of this ring since the moment I found it, thinking only that it *might* belong to you. I want to care for you the best I can. If I must learn to cook and clean, so be it. Our life together is what I want. I won't wait."

"I can't wait any better than you, you know." And Geoffrey let his fingers intertwine with hers while he untied the ribbon and pocketed it.

She unwound one of his fingers to slide on the ring as if sealing a bargain with him. "My, it has a regal look. Your grandfather must have—"

Her wide eyes opened even wider. "Geoffrey."

"What?"

"Geoffrey. *The ring.* How much is it worth?"

"How would I know? It belonged to a Roman emperor. And my grandfather. I never thought of selling it."

"Is it worth enough to keep us housed while you study?"

Geoffrey stared at the blue stone in the silvery night. Why had he never thought of that?

Because he thought *home* was the things and the place and the people he'd been born with. How it had limited his point of view.

Zelda took his silence for reluctance. "Or, never mind your ring! What about *mine?*" She held up her right hand so the big Brazilian diamond cut faint sparkles in the night.

She was amazing. "I thought you loved that ring."

"I love *you.* Take it. Take this necklace, too. And the bracelets." She dropped a fortune in his hand, even pulling the buckle from her hair. "Geoffrey, there's my amethysts! And my coral beads. I have a diamond neck ribbon as well, and some marvelous blue beads from home—I believe them to be *turquoise* but they are a purer color."

Geoffrey felt a weight he hadn't known kept him down roll off his back. "Perhaps you should keep some of that for the museum collection you intend to begin."

"Museum? Really?" She stopped in the middle of shoving jewels into his cupped open hands. "That is an excellent idea, isn't it? Though how to provide funds for it, that's the question. The college first. The museum must pay for itself. I dare say that will take me some time. Even beginning with a very special Japanese carving of two hares. It is hares, not rabbits?"

"I believe so." His hands full of sapphires, Geoffrey urged them back to her. "Put them on. I don't want them scratched."

He didn't want her to have to give up all her jewels. She did enjoy them so, and he would never be able to afford to buy more.

But Zelda simply squinted at the sapphire buckle, looking secretly very pleased. "Oh, this is a marvelous idea, Geoffrey, one of our best."

She was so determined, so eager. Her hunger for the far reaches of the world would never go away, but what she wanted *now* was a life with him. He'd best capture her before she sailed away. Because he had no doubt Zelda wasn't finished with her journeys.

And he had to be with her.

The last empty piece inside him turned and fitted into place. He had done what his mother asked; he'd done all he could. Now he could look after Zelda. And she would look after him. They could chart a path together.

He looked back toward the house as Zelda fastened her jewels.

Faint laughter drifted across the greens; Dandy would be celebrating with the other servants, and there was louder music out beyond the queen's garden. It sounded like that man from the Stony Barrel with the tin whistle.

The sound from the musicians in the ballroom didn't travel this far. He was on the wrong side of the great house to see their candles, the fires in the kitchen, or any other lights bobbing from hand to hand inside.

But he could hear the party outside. And it was likely better.

The world was bigger than Faircombe, and tonight he felt at peace with his past, but more eager for his future.

He was a third son. Perhaps he should never have loved Faircombe so. But perhaps it had taught him to love what he shouldn't.

He was glad to have it back, glad enough to let it go.

* * *

Both their steps turned toward the stone cottage in the wood.

"Are we going there to sleep?" Zelda asked. "Because it will startle my mother and Tansy."

"I'm just going there because my feet know you sleep there at night," Geoffrey admitted.

"The three of us are in your bed! Where will you sleep?"

"I might make a terrible sacrifice and sleep again in the nice *wool* bed I enjoyed before my father threw me out. Vere doesn't have much confidence he can bring the man to heel, but I think at least I can sleep in my bed."

"So far away."

"Or," said Geoffrey, slipping his hand around her waist and loving again the way they fit, "I might just lean against a tree under your window and fall asleep."

"Awful! Won't you be eaten by bears?"

The stone house would be around the next bend. "There are no bears here, Zelda."

"What if that honking goose—"

Their steps stopped together, too.

"You smell that?"

"Has the party lit a bonfire?"

"No, we just left it; I saw no bonfire."

It was only the smell that gave it away, till they rounded the bend.

Before them, the trees dripped fire.

Many were spring wood; they scorched but refused to burn, billowing choking smoke across the path and into the woods. Already the moon looked hazy.

In between, the old dead branches of winter, with stubborn leaves, blazed merrily in the trees and on the ground where they fell.

Or where perhaps the flames had started.

The haze thickened so fast that Geoffrey lost sight of the gray bulk of the cottage. Not that it mattered; it had half-burned once, it might succumb this time. He wouldn't trust it with their protection.

"We need to go back," he called, already the sound of crackling growing so loud it might drown out his voice.

Coughing, Zelda only nodded.

It should have been easy to turn and retrace their steps. They had come through a long stretch of woods, but it had all been clear.

Now it wasn't.

The fire had moved around them, as slickly vicious as any murderer and so much larger even than Geoffrey.

Geoffrey felt the first real pang of fear when he realized their path had two dry trees pressing closely on either side, just yards away, and both were smoking. No, they were aflame.

The orange crackling moved as if with malicious intention.

"If we strike out through the woods, we could be lost." In a crisis, Geoffrey did the best he could, but this one could take his everything. It was a struggle to stay calm and find the way out.

"No, we won't," Zelda told him. "I've walked through it several times. I know where we are."

There was no time to doubt her, and he didn't. "Pick a way that isn't burning."

"Toward what?" For once, Zelda was thinking before she leaped. "If we cannot reach open ground, is there another place to go? The cottage?"

"No. We need water. Is there a pond?"

The ponds scattered through the forest to the east had been his favorite places to play. He knew them well. Did they spread this far?

He opened his mouth to prompt her when she answered. "Yes. Which way is the cottage?"

He didn't answer; the acrid smoke burned his throat. He grabbed her and pointed her in that direction, himself alongside.

"And the house?"

He turned them, knowing she would picture the curve of the path as it led through the woods to where they stood.

She surveyed the trees tattered with fire before them, took his hand. She pointed, and watched his face.

He nodded.

For a moment, he thought they'd gambled together and lost. The space between the trees that was not burning grew smaller and smaller. Zelda stumbled, her eyes nearly closed, and Geoffrey caught her. His throat burned as if afire too.

Then he saw it. A black space. Emptiness had never been so welcome.

And realized what he was about to do.

Urgent, he drew them both to a stop at the water's edge. "It will be cold. Can you bear it?"

She only nodded.

Was she right? Cold made her pain worse, and Geoffrey knew well how it could force one's breath to stop.

He would have to trust to Zelda's tough will, and his ability to keep her safe.

It was warmer than it had been the night of the ice. Geoffrey supposed he should be grateful. There wasn't time; he ripped off his coat and sloshed it in the water.

It was difficult to make dense wool wet, but it was also difficult to make wet wool burn.

"Here we go, dearest." Christ, his whole life was in his arms as he hauled her against him and charged into the black water.

He felt her gasp. "Keep breathing." A burning branch fell into the pond a yard away; Geoffrey drew his soaked coat over both their heads.

It made a little tent of utter darkness. Zelda clutched her arms around his neck. He could stand on the bottom here and hold her, even if her feet did not reach the earth.

But it was cold, mercilessly cold, and Zelda was barely breathing.

"Keep breathing," he told her. The air between their heads was warm. If only he could extend that space all around them. "Breathe, Zelda. Breathe."

She nodded tightly against his neck.

"I don't think we can stay here as long as it will take for the fire to burn out." Her very skin was cold against his lips. He recalled the little boy's chilled blue body in his arms and knew again how lucky he'd been to revive the child. Zelda's head was not under water, she was in no danger of drowning; but there was so much he did not know about saving such a precious life.

And so much he was in danger of losing.

Zelda only nodded. He could feel her shivering against him. Her clothes were thinner than his. And her body felt so fragile, and so small.

Geoffrey shifted to hold her in his arms, ready to carry her, as he had done before. She groaned as her body moved through the water. He knew how the cutting cold felt; one was warmer until one moved.

He had lost all sense of time. Had they been in the water for seconds, or hours? He couldn't know. He had to peek.

Were the flames in the trees dying down? It was almost impossible to see. The thick, choking smoke drifted like the fur of a live thing threatening to weigh them down.

Staying still could cost him every dream he'd just learned to dream.

"We are leaving, dearest," just as if they ought to stroll out of a ballroom party, and Zelda made a noise of assent. He hoped that didn't mean nodding was no longer possible.

Had the fire's heat dried his coat?

"We are going to duck into the water and wet my coat. Can you hold it?" Shaking, her hands crept up and clenched the fabric. He wanted as little smoke to get under it as possible, but he doubted himself when he saw her slender fingers clench. They must be quick for so many reasons. "You must hold your breath. Zelda? Can you hear me?"

Her teeth chattered when she answered, "Breathe, now don't breathe. Stop changing your mind."

Zelda was still with him.

"Here we go, on the third count. One, two,…" On *three* he pushed up and then bent his knees so they were both underwater.

Both of them pulled down on the wool, and the slight *pop* when Geoffrey felt air escape from its bubble was horrifying. But then when he pushed up, careful to keep it close around them, there was still only a little smoke, and they were good and wet through, as was the coat.

Now he only had to be strong enough to carry them out through these burning woods to safety.

He could do a lot more if it would save Zelda's life.

He didn't bother to warn her. They were going together, after all.

Even her shivers had slowed, and in pitch darkness, he had the sense that her eyes were closed.

It took powerful pushes to raise his body and hers out of the water. He felt rivulets sluice away and wanted them back. Every drop would help protect them through the fire, even though they were leaching away Zelda's life.

A terror that was all too familiar threatened to choke him more surely than the fire. He knew all too well that some lives he could save, and some he could not. The thought that he might lose the only living person he knew for certain loved him threatened to take his breath as surely as the icy water.

But just as he'd told Zelda a lifetime ago, it was impossible to save creatures who gave up.

Another step, and another, and he was at the edge of the burning trees, and he didn't stop to think about the heat and the smoke, just kept his feet moving.

"Which way, dearest?" His rasping voice was painful. But it was more painful to see Zelda stir, but say nothing. She only turned her head.

Her vagueness caused his heart to clench again, in yet a more painful way, and he held her tightly and followed her direction.

He might be imagining it, since the world seemed to have stopped, but he felt like there were fewer burning leaves around his feet.

Two more steps, three, and he decided to take the risk.

He fell to his knees and was nearly smothered in the coat. Zelda still had tight hold of it.

He fought his way free. The trees in front of him were not on fire.

Gently, he loosened Zelda's grip. She cried out with the

pain, but did not open her eyes.

She had brought them halfway home. Surely he could take them the rest of the way.

Hefting her up into his arms again, Geoffrey launched himself forward. His legs seemed heavier, his steps slower. Perhaps even his strength had limits. Perhaps he would reach them.

But he would not give up.

Zelda was not a tiny woman but she felt so small, curled up in his arms. She hadn't gone limp. But when he called her name, "Zelda, dearest," she didn't answer, either.

Big men did not often run.

But Geoffrey did.

It was more lurching than running, catching himself with his feet as he staggered forward over and over with Zelda in his arms. He desperately hoped it was not his imagination that the trees were thinning. He needed it to be true.

Soft grass. Something must be wrong with his eyes; Faircombe still seemed too far away, and so hazy. The soaring pink stone parapets filled him only with the hope that Zelda would soon be warm.

There was a soft fluffy shape near to him, and growing nearer. He thought he recognized Guinevere, surrounded by three frolicking lambs.

But his heaving chest was not cooperating with him, either. Somehow, he didn't have enough air, even though they were free of the water and the smoke. Sharp, convulsive coughing shook him more with each step, as if his body needed what it did not have, and would hold him ransom to get it.

The grass was smooth here. Those were the sheep sheds on his right, the paddocks to his left. He would be nearly home, except that home was in his arms.

When he fell, he twisted his body to cushion her fall.

CHAPTER 34

Zelda woke in the music room and decided she must be dreaming. She'd slept here before.

But she hadn't dreamed this big, luxurious bed.

Or a strange man slapping her wrist. Though he stopped once her eyes opened. "Good. You're awake."

She didn't recognize him, but something about the way he sat at the bedside reminded her of physicians.

Heart pounding, she tried to lunge from the bed.

"Stop, stop. Don't hurt yourself. You should stay in the bed where it's warm. Breathe slowly, please," he also demanded, when her exertions made her cough.

He wanted to dictate where she was and how she breathed. He was definitely a physician.

But as she sank back into the shifting mattress, she felt a big warm hand groping her way. It settled over the thin linen that covered her belly, and there was a quiet noise of contentment from deep in the pillows.

Geoffrey.

"He'll wake in a moment. He doesn't stay still unless you're still." The physician—she *did* know him; it was that earl, the Earl of Rawleigh—straightened on the stool beside the bed. "*Are* you awake, Lord Geoffrey?"

"Mnggh," grunted the big warm lump beside her, and Zelda didn't care who saw, she dove down to snuggle again beside him.

"There's water here; you both need to drink. And a pot under the bed for the necessary."

"My lord, one question: are we in a music room?"

The doctor snorted. "I challenge you to carry Lord Geoffrey up the stairs. This bed was standing in a room that had been demolished; I had them bring it, and him, in here."

"Are you well?" she asked Geoffrey, digging through the pillows to cradle his big head in her hands. He didn't answer. "Is he asleep?" When he made only another wordless noise, she looked back at the doctor. "Is he *drunk*?"

The doctor's smile faded. "No, he's not drunk. He's breathed as much smoke as I've seen men do on the battle-field. I think he's just had enough."

Her memory felt as hazy as the smoke they'd both fled. Her hair still smelled of that smoke. "What happened?"

"I don't know much, but you fled the fire through an ice-cold pond, which likely saved your life; neither of you has a burn on you. His lordship managed to bring you to the edge of the lawns, but collapsed. When the men went to see about the fire, they found a flock of sheep nosing at something in the grass, and some goose honking himself silly. They inves-tigated and found you." He leaned back now that both his patients were somewhat conscious. "Dandy, the shepherd, says the animals have a vested interest in his lordship's survival."

"Why doesn't Geoffrey talk?"

"I can talk," but his voice was as hoarse as hoar-frost. And talking made him cough.

Once the wracking coughs had lessened, Zelda kept a hand on his chest, and looked to the physician.

"An interesting lesson for your lordship who wishes to study medicine. Two cases of illness strike simultaneously, and yet they are different. You, madam, suffered from the cold, but little else. His lordship inhaled smoke, and forced himself to exertion without enough good air. I think it will take a little longer for him to recover."

"And we're here. Together. *You* did this?" She couldn't imagine the terror she'd have felt if she had woken alone after all that, and Geoffrey would have felt the same, or worse.

"You were chilled to the bone, madam, and there is one efficient way to warm such a patient. And I believe it was sufficiently proven last night that you two are betrothed." He rose, tugging his coat into place. "And I have little time for preciousness when it comes to the practice of medicine."

"Thank you, sir. Thank you. Oh! Is there a footman about? Albert? Matthew?"

Matthew stuck in his head; Zelda could just recognize him across the broad polished floor. "Madam?"

"Have Mrs. Truett make up more of that barley soup. Ask her to make up some ice cream, too, please. And some soft white bread, no crust, with butter."

The noise Geoffrey made at that seemed one of approval.

"Oh, and I must see Miss Farsworth when she has a moment."

"Madam," said Matthew, and withdrew.

"Well, I'll leave his care in your capable hands, then," said the Earl.

"Thank you, Lord Rawleigh. Thank you. You must know that you have done far more for us than whatever moved you to visit a country party."

He turned to give her a small smile. He had extraordinary

eyes, the color of her *turquoise* stones. "I would prefer to be remembered as Dr. Burke." He bowed and left.

* * *

"I DON'T WISH to stay in bed."

"Stop fussing! If you feel better, I'll have a bath drawn and we can wash the smell of smoke from your hair."

"Then I can go see what's become of my sheep."

"Your sheep have been counted, your geese are all home. If you don't sit still, they'll be comfortably eating the grass from your grave."

"I'm nowhere near death."

"You're mistaken, because I'm going to kill you." For the dozenth time, Zelda tucked the quilts around Geoffrey's big body. He looked a bit gray, though the soup and bread had restored a little of his color.

She could wait to wash the smell of smoke from his hair, if it meant ten more minutes of rest.

Geoffrey's bushy eyebrows pulled down into a frown. "It hurts," he rasped, "and I need distraction, diversion. A visit to the sheep pen won't hurt me."

"Did you not hear what the doctor said about your exertion? You need to rest and heal, like any hurt thing."

"It feels as though staying in bed is causing my weakness."

"Geoffrey, honestly, you are a terrible patient! How far could I have come if I behaved this way when I was ill?"

Caught between sulking and startlement, Geoffrey shrugged.

"Now. If you feel utterly well, let us bathe and dress you and you can dine with your family… as long as we roll you in the wheeled chair."

"I feel I should thank you," Geoffrey grumped, "but I also don't wish to."

"Well," and here Zelda wiggled up to sit in his lap and lean her head upon his shoulder, "pain makes a person ill-tempered, so that makes perfect sense."

His arms came up to surround her. It was bliss, no matter the aches in his chest and arms and legs. As long as he had breath in his body, if he could hold her, all would be well.

"I think you are prickly because you thought it would always be you taking care of me. Would it make you feel better if I tell you I'm glad that when you need it, I can be of some help?"

"You can. You are." He felt better with some of the barley soup, and the buttered bread had tasted like heaven, even though it felt like it grew three sizes when he tried to swallow it.

Zelda had also requested a tankard full of honey-water. She reached over him now to fetch it, her soft curves pressing him down.

If he must be ill, he had the best nurse.

"Sleep some more," Zelda urged, "and we'll see your family. I promise."

His family. He let her put the tankard back, reveling in the feel of her. Geoffrey had no idea what his family would make of him sleeping in the music room with his new betrothed.

His.

His life had taken some excellent turns.

Sighing silently, he slid down into the sheets and pulled her down along with him.

* * *

IN THE MID-MORNING SUN, Delina Farsworth watched Londoners carefully climb down the courtyard steps, then up into the polished carriages that would carry them home.

It had been absurdly short for a house party, but then it had been well-packed with excitement.

Lord Vere, his hands stuffed in his trouser pockets, swayed from side to side as he followed his guests down the steps, more loose-boned than Delina had ever seen him.

"Are you sorry to see them go?" She usually steered wide of Vere, but he looked different today.

"I wish I were going with them."

Her head tilted like a bird as she looked with one eye.

"Failure doesn't taste delicious, you know," he told her with a small quirked expression that had some resemblance to a smile. "I was instructed to marry and bring in a suitable dowry, and now that I've well and truly failed, I've no idea what to do next."

"Well, you can keep trying, or find something else to do with your life. Freedom is a horrible thing. Speaking of which, please excuse me."

And she left him to run lightly across the broad staircase.

"Miss Merriweather."

The young woman's halo of loose curls waved in the breeze as she turned to see who called. Of course, she wore no bonnet, but she did wear a wide smile. "Miss Farsworth! What a pleasure this is!"

Delina just shook her head in quick admonishment. "No, it isn't. But thank you for staying out of Charlotte's path. You're not staying?"

"Do you want me to, or not? I could spend quite some time examining those Portland rock faces." The young woman pushed her thick braid back over her shoulder.

"Behave. And no, I don't, not long, anyhow. Are you still hoping to reach Bessarabia when you can travel on the continent again? To see the salt mines?"

"Absolutely."

Delina nodded. "Do walk in with me, won't you?"

Tansy was packing the remainder of Miss Rawle's belongings. The glass and fragments had been swept from the room, but she still checked her steps carefully while folding things into the big trunks.

She nodded to Delina. "Miss Farsworth." She dropped the small silver-and-jewel globe in Delina's hand. "I wish you would safeguard this; if Miss Rawle doesn't care to own it anymore, she may wish to sell it."

"An excellent plan. Tansy, Miss Rawle asked me if I knew of anyone traveling further east. Miss Merriweather is a great traveler, and intends to travel as far as she can, as soon as she can."

Tansy curtseyed, and murmured "Miss Merriweather," in the style of maids, but the guest just strode forward and offered a hand. Confused, Tansy grasped it.

"Lucinda Merriweather. Delighted to make your acquaintance."

"I am, ah, Tansy Tate."

"The Merriweathers are Quakers," Delina said to explain the surprising hand-clasp. "Regardless. If your interests coincide, you should have a conversation."

She leaned toward Miss Merriweather again before she went out. "And behave."

"I'm the very picture of discretion!"

"I hope so," Delina heard Tansy say as she left them to it, "for a reputation is valuable when far from home."

She wasn't sure if their meeting was the best idea, but she suspected that Tansy, like Zelda, didn't mind the occasional risk.

* * *

Lord Vere's message requested Lord Geoffrey and Miss Rawle join the rest of the family for dinner. They both found the phrasing heartening.

Matthew and Fred both had to push Miss Rawle's rolling chair once Geoffrey was in it.

Geoffrey insisted Zelda use her cane, and Zelda indulged him as she wanted to have it handy in the event she felt like poking someone with it.

But the dining room was hushed, under a pall. It reminded her of that first night. The drafts that brushed the chandelier now made it look, not frightening, but fragile. Though Zelda could still hear the footsteps of others, only Charlotte, Delina, and Vere stood nearby.

Vere now looked utterly destroyed. His collar was askew, his trousers smudged with black; only the thought that he must have ventured into the woods kept Zelda from a tart remark regarding the suitability of his clothing.

"I half-formed the idea…" His voice broke. He cleared his throat. "I had half-formed the idea that I might swear out a complaint against Lord Faircombe. I am mindful that it would take the agreement of the House of Lords to declare him guilty, and I have no influence with those gentlemen at present." His voice faded through the last words into silence.

Delina took Charlotte's hand; Charlotte just frowned at her eldest brother.

"However, even the faintest hope for justice of that sort is usurped by a greater action. The men have—I asked the men to take stock of the fire, its extent, and they wished to fully account for the damage. There was some livestock, not ours, a bullock and perhaps a horse, I will have to make amends to those families somehow."

This time the crack in his voice ended on a wail, and tears washed down both sides of his face.

"As there seems little doubt that our father—"

Geoffrey leaned forward, engulfed his brother's hand in his. Vere's look was both grateful and anguished.

"Our father set the fire, and has died in it. He is quite beyond other justice."

Horrified, Zelda's palm pressed to her lips.

Geoffrey's painful, hoarse voice seemed both mourning and explanation. "You are sure?"

"Quite sure."

No one wanted to make him explain his certainty, not now.

Geoffrey's hand just stayed, steady and quiet.

"I don't know how, Geoffrey, I don't know how to do this, do any of it, and what I learned was from him! How can I trust myself to—"

"All right. Shh. You're the man you should be. I've never felt it more."

Painfully pushing himself out of the chair, Geoffrey went to the head of the dining room table and pulled out the chair.

"Come on. Come. Let's eat."

"I can't." Vere's tears streaked a sleeve when he wiped at his face. "Not now. Not like this."

"Would you feel better dining with an empty chair?" Geoffrey's big hands wrapped around the gilt-framed leather. "This is how it works. The title lives on; and we are here with you. I don't know why. Perhaps you will tell me, someday."

Charlotte's sob echoed against the glass, and she clung to Delina, her face buried in the smaller woman's shoulder.

Zelda felt both that this moment was not for her, and that she was here for Geoffrey, and for that she was glad.

"Why don't you sit, Vere—" she sensed he was not ready to be called Lord Faircombe, "—there is some good barley soup. You should eat something. We should all eat a little."

And she pulled back the chair to his right and beckoned Geoffrey to sit beside his brother.

Delina was whispering something to Charlotte, but Charlotte only murmured, "I'm all right, I'm all right." She took Delina's hand along with her and pulled out the chair on Vere's left for herself.

For years afterward, Zelda remembered the scene, and she never remembered what they said or ate, only that they were all there together.

* * *

"I DON'T KNOW what to do." Zelda sipped her whiskey. Tonight was a night for it.

The sun had gone down and the remaining guests had organized themselves into quiet games of dominoes in the game room. It astonished Zelda to see it used.

She wondered if it ever would be again.

Geoffrey had said, before he'd drifted off to sleep, that it was a heavy load for Vere, and Zelda felt she understood far better than Geoffrey. The finances of Faircombe were precarious, and there was no way to help.

"That's the nature of such things. There is no way to help." Delina drank her wine and watched the players. She had gray circles underneath her eyes.

"There's my father, beyond the reach of Britain's law, and now so is Lord Faircombe. And Vere left with the pieces, and problems beyond anything of his own making."

"That's the nature of it, too." Tiny little Delina's look hardened. "Men have those opportunities we do not, to escape the evil things they do."

"Never say so. I don't think you think that way. Look at *Senhor* Mendez, keeping his ancestor's memory alive." The little hare carving had never been in danger, as the gentleman had kept it with him all during Zelda's and Geoffrey's dances; he still insisted he would leave it with her.

At Zelda's approach, one of the footmen moved a chair for her. She sat by the man from Portugal, who was discovering the pleasures of small dotted tiles.

"*Senhor* Mendez. I hope you will stay for a while," Zelda offered, hoping she didn't overreach. She was not yet married into the family, though circumstances were, to say the least, both peculiar and in that regard certain. "We would like to hear some of your stories."

"Ah, good! People have fought this fight for hundreds of years. Even if it is hundreds more, if we keep alive the memory of people torn from their homes for profit. I hope the victory one day will be—" He searched for the word. "Decisive."

"Never say so," said the young lady who sat opposite. "What is the point of such sad tales? I would rather enjoy myself. Life is short, you know."

"The point is not to live one's life at the expense of others," said another player, a man with a bristling tangle of sun-kissed dark curls. "Or if you must, at least admit it."

"Excuse me," said the young woman, gathering up her skirts with a remonstrative flounce, and departing with speed.

Zelda's sad frown swept across them all. "My apologies."

"If anyone upset the lady, it was I," said the other domino-player. "I've no time for ignorance. Some of us are spending our lives on this effort, and it is not a foolish one."

"Is that what you are doing in Britain, sir?" For his accent sounded of her home.

"Yes," he said shortly. "When I can. Not enough. The political work may kill me, and there is never enough money. If *Senhor* Mendez had not funded the *Halia*'s last voyage, we would not have—suffice it to say we all do what we can."

"I don't believe we've met," Delina put in, prompting Zelda to remember manners.

"Do forgive me! Miss Farsworth, this is Captain Joshua Brice. I met you as one of our London guests, Captain, but didn't know you knew *Senhor* Mendez."

"We are old friends. Enemies? No, always friends," chuckled the gentlemen, teasing the Captain's short smile.

"Then do forgive me, Captain, for presuming on short acquaintance," Zelda went on, "but if an American were plotting to conduct some horrific business, particularly, let us imagine, breaking the law against British citizens conducting slave trading across the sea, would you, could you do something about it?"

The man's startled eyes snapped up toward Zelda's.

She only nodded and left it to him to answer.

"You are asking if the law is enforced, and I would say it is, equal to the proof that can be brought."

Zelda knew enough of the law now to know that would be slow and difficult.

But worth it. Always worth it.

"Do stay with us a few more days, won't you? Faircombe would love to have you," she impetuously offered.

"I ought to have thought before so many guests departed. But you should ask the rest to stay," said Delina. "You might like a few guests at your wedding."

"A wedding?" Zelda had almost forgotten that the end of interminable contracts and betrothal was supposed to be a wedding. "Yes! I'd forgotten it, but it must be a delightful thing to have. Albert," she said, leaning back towards the footman, "ask Mr. Paltz to join us here, would you? We have a few things to discuss."

She nodded again at Captain Brice as she turned back to the table. "A scrupulous man of high ethical standards. You'll want to meet him, Captain."

"I will," said the fellow, and his air of determination suited Zelda's hopes.

"And Miss Farsworth is right, do stay! If you enjoy a wedding."

The Captain's mobile face went through a series of remarkable contortions. "In a fashion. I have attended my sisters'."

"Oh! Then you must tell me what to do. I've never been to a wedding at all."

* * *

It was peculiar, how un-peculiar it was to climb into bed next to Geoffrey.

Some might have thought it was peculiar because she was sleeping in a music room. But no, that wasn't it.

"Hello, dearest," she murmured as she slid between the sheets.

He shifted and rolled towards her. "You must want sleep."

Indeed, she was drooping with fatigue. It made her angry, the moments it stole. She wanted to lie awake with her beloved and count the stars in his eyes all night. There would never be time to waste staring at the ceiling.

"This is not what you wanted, when you imagined returning home," she told him, soft and low, as she slid under the coverlets.

"This is exactly what I wanted," he whispered, saving his voice, and pulling her closer as soon as she was within reach.

"It will be so much simpler to plan a wedding now that I have no dowry."

"Fine."

"And no illegal affairs of business attached to the contracts." She nestled closer. "Does it not feel odd? Everyone knows we are in here together."

"And yet such will be every day of our married life."

She gave him one of her slow, sly smiles. "So this is how a lord of the manor is indulged? I think this is what Mrs. Truett meant when she said I should hide my peculiarities until safely married. And yet I'm not."

"Won't be long."

His certainty thrilled her. She had never expected that.

She could be certain and still tease him. "I think I should have asked many more questions before I agreed to our betrothal. For instance, I heard some disturbing rumors about you. I believe I should have asked if you have vices."

"I do," Geoffrey managed in a quiet version of his more usual voice. "Come closer, and I'll show you."

"Drinking, I suppose. And opium? I suppose you even gamble."

She could see him fighting down a grin, even if his pain and exhaustion made it a small one.

"I cannot say I have been restrained in my life," he murmured into the little space between them, "because I had no great urges to be *un*restrained. Not until I met you."

"You did *wonderful* things."

"I mended a goose."

"Geoffrey. You take lives—and people's livelihoods—into your hands, every day. You needn't seek thrills. You are an incredible adventurer. You go places no one else goes, and do things no one else can do. I am in awe of you, sir."

She thought she saw the tips of his ears redden a little.

"You've made me so much more than I ever was before," he whispered, pulling her close enough to kiss her forehead.

"No," Zelda told him, reaching up to smooth his eyes closed, "I didn't. You fascinated me the moment I saw you. You have always been *you*."

"I think you invent things when you discover them. Don't

give up the idea of seeing the world, Zelda. I would carry you across continents if I could."

"I know you would." She nestled into his arms. "One can't enjoy everything there is to enjoy all at once. We'll start with London. Then perhaps Scotland. Isn't Scotland an excellent country for sheep?"

Once his breathing had slowed and deepened, Zelda lay listening to it as long as she could. Falling in love, she could see, would be a kind of balancing trick for the rest of her life. He was something endlessly new; she could enjoy constantly discovering him, as long as she didn't make a habit of being afraid to be happy.

She could do it. He'd shown her how to strengthen her body; he'd help her practice joy. Perhaps she'd try rolling around in contentment.

She would be just as careful of him as he was of her. He had no idea what a treasure he was, or how many people loved him.

It would be interesting, devising new ways to show him.

* * *

"LORD RAWLEIGH OFFERED to pay for the party."

The two brothers picked their way through the ashen rubble. Stubs of burnt trees and the ashen underbrush made the whole ground look burnt and black.

Geoffrey stepped carefully and tried not to breathe deep. He'd progressed well, the doctor had said, but ought to be gentle with himself for a while.

He might not get much chance; Zelda devoted herself to being gentle on his behalf. "Did you let him?"

Vere—Geoffrey could not think of him as Faircombe— still looked as drawn as he had the afternoon they'd learned of their father's death.

"I don't know. Everything our father taught me is suspect. *Does* an honorable man let another pay such a bill? Does a host?"

"Perhaps if he is a friend? You're among them now; you must accept them accepting you."

Vere made a noise of disparaging disbelief. "London barely knows Lord Rawleigh exists. He prefers it that way. And the people who know me, know me only as a spendthrift oldest son." Vere's hands rose and fell, going nowhere. "That is my reputation. All I have is that, some property, and a growing stack of debts."

"You will not be the first peer to be poor."

"True, but I don't know how."

Rain had improved the air in the woods. They could see the stone cottage, stolid and sure, long before they reached it.

Geoffrey knew he would be wracked with coughing if he bent over; he scuffed at a burrow with his toe. Vole? Rabbit? "Whatever was in this must have died." He knew his face betrayed his grief. Death happened, but not this senseless way, not unless someone wished to destroy.

"How do you bear it?"

"What?"

"This constant sympathy for everyone, everything. How do you know what to care about, Geoffrey? We grew up in the same house, and I have no idea, none."

"It's not such a difficult answer." He squeezed Vere's shoulder, trying to make him look less lost. "What do you love?"

The saplings thrusting up around the burnt end of the cottage were still there.

"The fire didn't touch these." Geoffrey pushed them from side to side, testing their roots. "Not this time."

"And you say this burned the night our mother died?"

Geoffrey wasn't sure how to answer. The weight on Vere

was heavy, and he was more slender than his brother; he might snap.

But Vere just jerked his chin at the marks of the past fire. "A person who uses fire as a weapon once will do it twice. It must have been Lord Faircombe. Otherwise, he'd have found the miscreant and had them hanged."

"But what for? Why take out his anger, if anger it was, on this old house?"

His brother stood staring at the scorch marks for so long that Geoffrey wondered about shaking him awake.

But finally Vere said, "All the wrong things I know, I learned from my father. I imagine so did he. If our grandfather taught him that the proper way to be a marquess was to bear an heir and keep a mistress, I don't think our father had it in him to find a way beyond that lesson. He knew how he'd hurt our mother, and likely the first and last time he wished to make amends was the night she left him forever. How he must have hated the old man."

The word *hate* shook Geoffrey. "You needn't be like him."

"As he so often said, I am not."

Geoffrey's unease made him more restless than the ache in his chest. "Will you be well? When we are gone? What will you do with Faircombe? Or this?"

"No idea." Vere said it more easily than he ever had before, and Geoffrey wondered if he felt it too, the calm that came with distance. He wouldn't have wished for the distance to come this way, but their father had chosen his own road, and it didn't mean his sons couldn't have peace. "Would your betrothed like this for a museum?"

"You're joking."

"No idea," Vere said again. "Our father loved convoluted contracts as well as having sons, apparently. I cannot make heads or tails of what I've inherited. It may not even be entailed. Were you not going to London, I would ask you to look after the place. Charlotte is still set on leaving."

This felt delicate, as Vere had not mentioned Frederick either, but Geoffrey must try. "I don't suppose you'd ask Augie…"

"You know, I would. I have. He laughed in my face." Vere chuckled, a dry chuckle at his own expense. "I think I like him."

"We intend to go to Scotland later in the year. I will send back more aspen trees, if I can. Perhaps a few sheep."

Vere laughed.

That lightened Geoffrey's heart. Vere would be well. "Wherever we are, as my lady wills and as we can, we will never *leave* you, Vere. Wherever we are, you won't be alone."

"Thank you."

It felt awkward and then it didn't, to gather Vere close in a hug. It was as if they were little boys again in the nursery; whichever was taller, their bond was still there.

EPILOGUE

The bride and the groom rode to the church together. No one even suggested separating them.

Mrs. Rawle rode with them too, her basket of treatments at the ready.

After Geoffrey handed down his bride, Mrs. Rawle adjusted the silvery bridal train. "There, you look perfect."

As Geoffrey led Zelda toward the church, Zelda whispered to him. "Will it rain?"

Their trunks, packed for Scotland, because Zelda had changed her mind about the order of the trip, were already strapped atop the carriage. Faircombe would have some sort of breakfast afterwards, but Zelda couldn't wait a moment longer.

"The weather will be fine, the trunks will be fine, and so will we." Geoffrey's eye fell to the lawn beside the village church. Some of the sheep cropping the grass there looked familiar.

One lamb darted forward and butted Zelda right in the leg.

Geoffrey scooped him up with one hand and just questioned the shepherd with a look.

It was unfortunate that the only word for Dandy's expression was sheepish.

"Rascals saw the carriages rolling, and just took off. I couldn't keep 'em back. We need another shepherd; that Bernie is never coming home." Dandy made a face. "Or better fences. They oughta be at the summer pasture by now anyhow."

"I'm sure Bernie's just where he needs to be. Never mind it, as long as you didn't bring the goose."

"I didn't *bring* the sheep."

Geoffrey leaned close, sweeping off his tall silk hat. "Did I turn out to be the kind of man you thought I would be?"

"I won't lie, you did better," the grizzled old man clapped his shoulder, and turned away quick, trying to keep Geoffrey from seeing the suspicious sheen in his eyes.

Dandy poked his head into the church to see all was set. Lord Vere—Lord Faircombe stood in the family pew; his brow was always a bit furrowed now, but he stood tall. Lady Charlotte stood beside him, with Miss Delina Farsworth at her side, and then wedged into the pew, of all things, was a desk.

In a different village, people might have muttered about it, or pointed out that the young Lord Faircombe's title had aged him. They might have even muttered about the bride being a touch too knowing, with that smile of hers, and how that wasn't right, not during a ceremony like this.

But no one dared insult the home or family of Lord Geoffrey Augustus Townsend Eliot, as he took both more seriously than anyone. And while strangers, from near and far, might have wished not to anger such a big man, friends, from near and far, just wished the gentle fellow to be happy.

Zelda had prepared for the wedding with many questions

no one could answer. Why was she supposed to carry flowers? What did it matter if her dress was nice? Since the banns
were read, why must she and Geoffrey bother to come to the
church one more time?

But if she got no real answers, she was satisfied to have
questions, and had passed the time waiting for the event
listening to stories from *Senhor* Mendez and consulting with
Miss Merriweather about precious stones found in the
ground.

She was grateful the Merriweathers had decided to delay
their departure, for it meant that Tansy could also be there.
The new Lord Faircombe had made her a gift of the law
dictionary, which was perhaps over-confident of him at the
time he needed it most; but as he'd engaged Mr. Paltz to help
unravel his father's affairs, perhaps that timing was perfect.

As Dandy rejoined the happy couple waiting together for
the ceremony to start, a gray goose came flapping down the
road. He leapt in long hops, flapping his wings, and honking.
Always honking. Still honking, as he settled among the
sheep.

"Dammit," muttered Dandy, trying to catch Nemesis. "He
comes back and back like a bad penny."

"He's a good example," Geoffrey reached for Zelda's hand,
slipped it into the crook of his arm.

"Really?" She peered at the twisting head of the goose. "Of
what?"

"The power of persistence."

She was always wrapped in sunlight and starlight to him,
but today everyone else could see it, too. The oak leaves on
her gown, etched in sparkling beads, made her look like a
particularly British goddess; but she could wear the robes of
another country tomorrow—in fact she probably would—
and she'd still be Zelda, his dearest love, and his home.

As they took their places before the altar, Miss Farsworth

took up a pencil and began to sketch the bride and the groom together.

"I saw you eyeing the incense boat," Geoffrey said, too quietly for anyone else to hear.

She shifted uneasily, then reached up to straighten the sprig of honeysuckle he wore in the lapel of his coat. She carried them, too, along with delicate ferns and primroses. "Isn't it there to be seen?" Her hand hurt; she handed him the flowers.

"No," he said as he took them. "And that gown surely doesn't have pockets, either, so don't try anything."

"I think of the two of us, you ought to admit my superior expertise. *If* one of us wished to steal something."

"No," said Geoffrey, leading Zelda on the first steps of the longest possible journey, the rest of their lives. "I won't concede that at all."

* * *

Geoffrey's and Zelda's is a forever story that could never fit in one book;
Subscribe to the Judith Lynne newsletter and get your free bonus honeymoon chapter!

SPECIAL OFFER *for readers of* He Stole the Lady:

10% off Judith Lynne books when purchased straight from the author
using code **bigman**

Visit judithlynne.com to pick your next favorite book from your preferred bookseller.

. . .

Turn the page for a sneak peek at what's next…

NEXT IN LORDS AND
UNDEFEATED LADIES

*A **sneak peek** from*
  No Titled Lady...

Jesper had rushed to London vaguely picturing someone practical. Someone to manage the manor and help keep order in the village. Someone who *didn't* throw buns across the Easter table.

That idea was sliding away. The emptiness inside him was appeased by the idea of someone *fun*.

Someone sparkling and gay. Like Lady Hortense.

Would it be crass for him to ask how many siblings she had? Large families tended to produce large families. It felt a bit like bringing up cattle breeding. But ladies' skirts, with billowing sides and covered with bows, made it impossible to tell how wide Lady Hortense's hips were. She could have been built like a barn under there for all he could see.

"Have you any brothers and sisters?" he asked her, hoping she wouldn't understand why.

"A few," she grinned, "would you like some?" Yes, she was incredibly forward. Pretty and pert.

"Have you many suitors this season?" He was a terrible at flirting. Doing his best. With any luck, he was already nearly done.

"I don't think that's a question that you can properly ask me," she said and he wondered if her father had perhaps studied law.

"It's *not* a question he can ask you, Lady Hortense."

The young woman who appeared at her friend's side had eyes like slammed doors. She was much taller, and graceful where Hortense was lush. In every way the opposite of Lady Hortense.

And he'd already met her. "Your hair is on straight."

He recalled those lips very well. They curled to one side with disdain. "How do you come to be so brash, sir?"

"Living a long time," he told her, with half a bow.

He ought to thank her. Meeting her had revised his goals. From that moment, he'd wanted someone entirely different.

He hoped his brusqueness would make her leave.

It didn't. "You may be old, but you do not understand how to treat a lady. Lady Hortense, I do believe that Lord Overburg would love to have the next dance with you."

"Would he?" Did Lady Hortense look torn? She knew, just as her friend did, as Jesper did, that their conversation had already passed the bounds of propriety and ought to be cut short. She fluttered her fan, and her eyelashes, for Jesper's benefit. "Unless you were planning to drive to Gretna Green..."

Her friend gasped, but Lady Hortense looked half hopeful. He suspected that, had he proposed they leap into a carriage and start for Scotland, she would have come with him.

He wasn't *that* ready to be done with his search for a wife.

When Jesper hesitated just a second too long, "Of course,"

Lady Hortense said to her friend, "I would be delighted to dance with Lord Overburg."

Jesper expected them both to leave, but instead the sober young woman merely nodded and let Lady Hortense trail away, sparkling laugh and sparkling slippers disappearing with her.

Then the lady's friend turned on Jesper. Unlike Hortense, she had her head-toppings perfectly under control, and the delicate lace edging her sleeves never shivered as she sliced her fan down through the air like a government minister's gavel.

"Lady Hortense is very sweet," she pronounced her judgment. "She does not deserve trifling."

"I was not trifling with her, I assure you." Nor was being scolded the least bit amusing. "I have a very legitimate wish to marry. And Lady Hortense, I suspect, doesn't hate the idea."

"Lady Hortense likes everyone she meets. If you have any regard for her, you will pay her proper court and get to know her before making any improper suggestions. Or better yet, don't make any improper suggestions at all."

"I hate to disillusion an innocent young woman," Jesper said, watching how she gripped her fan like a club, "but I didn't begin the improper suggestions."

Her jaw snapped shut, and the ice in her eyes snapped with sparks.

"Be a man," she finally exclaimed, skirt swaying as she leaned away. "Pox and perdition! How hard can it be to ask politely for what you want? It's not as though her father is intimidating. He's quite pleasant. Things between you could be perfectly delightful if you'd only get over your self-infatuation, pull your head out of your armpit, and speak as if you had a brain between your ears instead of wet moldy straw from the countryside!"

"Whoa. Madam." She looked like she might literally breathe smoke. This steaming young miss couldn't be Lady Hortense's chaperone, not with a neckline cut like that. "Are you her chaperone?"

"You can consider me her chaperone until you learn how to behave," the young lady said, with a snap of her fan that could have broken a small animal's neck, finally following her friend into the crowd. It wasn't until her slender figure disappeared that Jesper realized he still didn't know her name.

* * *

Keep reading No Titled Lady!

AFTERWORD

I always like to say about the history in my books that I have pulled no rabbits from hats. I stay as close to history as I can with every detail I can find. In this case, I had the problem of writing a book that is close to me, as I have a pain problem that is not rheumatoid arthritis, which Zelda has, but which does require exercise to keep it under control. I know that one needs to find exercise that one likes, and it seemed clear to me that Zelda badly needed a bicycle.

Thus a fascinating adventure in research followed. Because a simple online search will tell you that the bicycle, as we know it, was invented in 1817. And as my faithful readers know, here we are in early 1814.

And I don't like to fudge dates. But...

When faced with such a puzzle I always like to ask: well, what happened *before* that? Because no brilliant invention simply appears fully-formed on the market. As in *The Caped Countess*, where I knew people had to have some portable way to make fire even before the invention of the friction match, and stumbled on the fascinating story of the Chancel match that lit through chemical combustion (and many other side adventures into chemistry, which has added a character, and a book, to that series), I asked myself where Baron von Drais got the idea for his *draisine*.

After much backing-and-forthing online, I found I had to go to a book to get the answer. Yes, an actual book.

Tony Hadlund's and Hans-Erhard Lessing's book *Bicycle Design: an Illustrated History* (2016, from MIT Press) lays out the progression. Baron von Drais did indeed apply for a license to sell, a "privilege" from the Napoleonic government, in 1813, for two four-wheeled foot-powered vehicles; it was denied. Those foot-powered *Fahrmaschinen* wouldn't have looked surprising to anyone who's ever seen a paddle-boat. By 1817, he had a two-wheeled device instead, so I imagine that there were variations in-between. In my story, there were likely few avid correspondents interested in helping people's mobility as much as our Cass Cullen Burke Howiston etc., from *The Countess Invention*; so I am assuming that once mail opened up between the Continent and Britain, just in time for our snowy spring, the Baron would have sent a sample device to his devoted correspondent to see if it might sell in Britain.

The dashing *draisine* invention was reported, but likely not in "headlines", because the word "headlines" was not originally associated with newspapers. They were the running tags at the top of pages of novels, which usually chronicled the adventures of excitingly inappropriate young ladies. Zelda longs to be in one of those novels, and I am half-sorry that I did not accommodate her.

The history of enslavement of Japanese people is well-documented; it is not as well known as it should be, perhaps, that one of the reasons Japan closed its borders to Europe was to stop the enslavement of its people, which had gone on for decades despite its Emperor's repeated protests. That is the type of research that is broadly known, well documented in print and online, and available for anyone to find. The beautiful carvings of *netsuke* are often collected across the world, and our appreciation ought to come with richer knowledge of their owners' complex and interconnected history.

And there's just too much to say about hares.

Our snowy spring and the constant presence of bread and butter in this story are due to my obsession with *Ladies' Own Bakery*, my Regency romance serial, whose readers sadly had to wait for the end of season 1 so that I could get this book out to you. Though I can no longer eat bread very often, as it contributes to the aforementioned pain problem, I baked it weekly for many years, and my obsession with it is only renewed through the research I did for that series, and my beloved Misses Bickering. Rest assured, my LOBsters, not only will we soon finish season 1, but there will be a season 2. And it will foreground that winter between 1813 and 1814, London's coldest for a long, long time.

I have a personal pet peeve with characters whose physical challenges are somehow all better at the end of the book. People don't have to be perfect to be loved, and if this series is about anything, it's about that. So Miss Rawle has the exact same rheumatoid arthritis at the end of the book that she does at the beginning, and that's by design. I've tried to represent her illness fairly, and for any shortcomings, I do apologize, and feel free to send me feedback. I always want to do better.

Her illness did send me down a rabbit hole (see what I did there?) of researching rheumatic fever, rheumatoid arthritis, and their links to heart disease, which were so interesting that they will appear in a different book. (*No Titled Lady.*)

This will not be the last *Lords and Undefeated Ladies* novel. In fact, there are several more in the works, along with some stories of the London characters who wander between these books and my *Cloaks and Countesses* series. Because that is how I roll.

Other history notes will already be familiar to readers who follow me on social media. Come chat with me, I'd love to hear from you. That carved-sapphire ring is real; you can do an online search for "2000 year old sapphire ring" and see it yourself. I hated to give Geoffrey a ring that belonged to a terrible emperor, but such is the nature of aristocracy, I suppose.

And I used the famous Witley Court as a (very loose) model for Faircombe Hall. As the British aristocracy emerged from these twenty years of war and more with the rest of the world, they had plenty of people among them who wanted more justice, more democracy, and more freedom. Those are the characters I write. Some British aristocrats went the route of expanding colonialism and capitalism and funneling more and more money back to themselves to build bigger and bigger houses, full of incredible opulence, that lead to what we picture as the Victorian era. Right around the time our book is set, there were plenty of British families who did just that. I wanted to write about a family that went the other way. The previous Marquess' plans for Faircombe Hall are going to have to rot in that drawer, because whatever happens, they will not have enough money to build the palace that he imagined. But I think whatever they decide to do with Faircombe will be far more interesting. I like Vere's idea of making it a museum. The idea is not so far from what happened with many of Britain's great buildings, though more often after World War I.

On a final note, my social media followers will also know that I read the James Herriot books about being a country veterinarian in the Yorkshire dales over and over again as a child, and my vision for Geoffrey owes a great deal to him. Dr. James Alfred Wight, the author of those books, understood germ theory and had sulfa drugs; but along with my best attempts at research, he gave me an interesting model for a country vet and I feel like I could have made this book twice as long just writing some of Geoffrey's adventures in animal doctoring.

I liked the idea of transforming Geoffrey into my particular version of Cinderella, with an angry goose and a pregnant sheep for friends instead of mice who can sew. Less practical, you may say, but more suitable to my books. And I was particularly proud of Geoffrey that he deduced that there was more than met the eye to the limestone, which the famous Portland stone actually is, to help his sheep out of the long winter. I hope he and his Princess Charming stay with you; they do with me, and I thank you for reading this, and coming on this journey along with me.

ACKNOWLEDGMENTS

It's a particular delight when a reader wants more of a character, even (or especially) when the reader is an old friend. Since I also adore Geoffrey, writing him his love story was no hardship. Well, it was only a small hardship. (It's hard to write a fellow so *good*!) Holly, I hope you loved your book.

Beyond that old friend and Geoffrey-fan, this book is for every reader of the first four books who asked, "But will there be more?" Yes. And hopefully soon, still more.

Deepest thanks to my friend Anne, a great storyteller in her own right with a trustworthy eye for a tale, who kindly reads my work even as it is taking shape; and thanks to the spouse who is the stars and the sunrise for me, as he is an excellent story *reader* as well as the person who most believes in me.

Chief among fans, another old friend, J.D. who has been a steadfast reader of every one of my books. J.D., you are sharp-eyed and generous with your praise always, and for that I am deeply grateful.

ABOUT THE AUTHOR

Judith Lynne writes rule-breaking romances with love around every corner. Her characters tend to have deep convictions, electric pleasures, and, sometimes, weaponry.

She loves to write stories where characters are shaken by life, shaken down to their core, put out their hand…and love is there.

A history nerd with too many degrees, Judith Lynne lives in that other paradise, Ohio, with a truly adorable spouse, an apartment-sized domestic jungle, and a misgendered turtle. A past writer of SF and screenplays, she pens Regency romances of love you can believe in, with a rich sense of place and time.

If you enjoyed He Stole the Lady, *help keep these books coming - share a review at your favorite bookstore, Bookbub, or Goodreads!*

Sign up for the author's newsletter, including exclusive book news and sneak peeks,
at judithlynne.com.

ALSO BY JUDITH LYNNE

Lords and Undefeated Ladies

Not Like a Lady

The Countess Invention

What a Duchess Does

Crown of Hearts

He Stole the Lady

No Titled Lady *Series prequel*

Maids Done Waiting

The Lord Trap

The Lady Escape *Forthcoming*

Cloaks and Countesses

The Caped Countess

The Clandestine Countess

The Castaway Countess *Forthcoming*

Ladies' Own Bakery

Ladies' Own Bakery Season One: The Collected Episodes

Ladies' Own Bakery Season Two: The Collected Episodes

www.ingramcontent.com/pod-product-compliance
Lightning Source LLC
Chambersburg PA
CBHW061534190726
48289CB00004B/1040